"You're not engaged to anyone, are you?"

Chloe shook her head at his question. "No, I'm not. Why, Dominic?"

"In that case, will you consider becoming engaged to me?" he went on.

The color drained from her face. "Are you telling me that you love me, Dominic?"

She saw his expression change. His eyes looked wary. "Is love of such paramount importance? I respect and trust you. You see," he explained, "I've got a most urgent reason for asking you to be engaged to me for a while."

"But we—"

"I know it's a lot to ask of you," he continued. "But afterward of course, you'll be perfectly free. Would it be so terrible, Chloe?" he demanded with a flash of charming warmth she could never resist.

It would be all I'd ask of life, she told herself—*if he loved me, if it were real....*

Great love stories never grow old...

And we at Harlequin are proud to welcome you, our readers, to HARLEQUIN CLASSIC LIBRARY—a prime selection of time-tested, enduring favorites from the early lists of Harlequin's best-selling Romances.

Harlequin Romances have been read throughout the world for many years. Why? There are as many reasons as there are people. But longtime readers tell us that our books combine the enjoyment of travel, the intrigue of good plots, warm and interesting characters and the thrill of love. Each novel possesses an emotional appeal that sweeps you right into the wonderful world of romance!

As publishers of **Harlequin Romances**, we take a great deal of pride in our books. Since 1949 Harlequin has built its reputation on the solid base of quality and originality. And now our widely popular paperback romance novels have been translated into eighteen languages and are sold in more than eighty countries.

So...if you relish a classic love story, one whose appeal has lost nothing over the years, read the timeless Harlequin Romances in the HARLEQUIN CLASSIC LIBRARY. We hope you enjoy this story and all the others in our special selection of beautiful love stories from years past.

For a free catalogue of the books available, write to:
HARLEQUIN READER SERVICE
(In the U.S.) M.P.O. Box 707, Niagara Falls, N.Y. 14302
(In Canada) Stratford, Ontario, Canada   N5A 6W2

Summer Lightning

JILL TAHOURDIN

Originally published as Harlequin Romance #615

HARLEQUIN
CLASSIC LIBRARY

TORONTO • LONDON • LOS ANGELES • AMSTERDAM
SYDNEY • HAMBURG • PARIS • STOCKHOLM • ATHENS • TOKYO

Original hardcover edition published by
Mills & Boon Limited 1960
ISBN 0-373-80009-6

Harlequin edition first published September 1961
Golden Harlequin Library edition, Volume XLI, published September 1973
Harlequin Classic Library edition published March 1980
Second printing January 1981

Printed in Canada

CHAPTER ONE

CHLOE'S NEIGHBOR GLANCED UP, eyebrows quirked, from the learned-looking papers he had been immersed in since he had taken his seat, seeing her half rise in her seat, clutching its arms, as she felt the plane become airborne.

"Your first trip by plane?"

The question fell into the sudden quiet after the revving of the four engines and the roaring rush down the runway. One or two heads turned to look at Chloe incredulously, or with the calm superiority of the seasoned air traveler.

She turned on her friendly, disarmingly candid smile.

"No, of course I've flown before. But I still hate the moment when we leave the ground."

Her snapshot assessment of him had noted a well-shaped dark head, a lean, rather long, heavily tanned face, an imperious nose and fine gray eyes whose casual survey of her was half-tolerant, half-impatient.

"Well, take it easy," their owner recommended. "What goes up has to come down, you'll find."

It was cold comfort to offer. Her eyes remained apprehensive behind their thick fringe of lashes. The fluttering in her stomach could still be felt.

Her neighbor was already deep in his reading again. Evidently his conversational limit had been reached. . . .

She concentrated on watching, through the window on her right, while the crazily tilted landscape below righted itself, then retreated till it had the look of a school contour map done in colored clay and stuck with toy houses, trees, roads, railroad tracks. As they soared steadily upward it gave place first to a rash of small, fluffy clouds, then to a solid, cotton-wool layer that hid the earth entirely.

Above this the plane rose with such stately dignity that

she relaxed and leaned back in her seat with a sigh of near pleasure.

So here I am, on my way to Malta, she thought with a kind of astonishment—for until a week ago, no place had been further from her thoughts. It had been the purest chance, her bumping into Ronnie Fairfax, whom she hadn't seen for months, in Fleet Street after a visit to her agents in Ludgate Circus.

They had practically collided as they waded, shoulders hunched against the sleety February wind, through the abominable gray brown slush that was yesterday's virgin snow.

Ronnie had let out a whoop of mingled agony and delight, grabbing her by an elbow to steady her.

"I think I'm concussed, but no matter. Well met, Chloe, my sweet. You don't know it, but you're an answer to prayer. Look, let's come in out of this foul wind for a minute." Drawing her into the shelter of a convenient office building, he had given her an intense look, full of harassment, excitement, appeal.

When she laughed at him he said urgently, "No, listen, girl, this is serious."

"I'm listening."

"Look, a few months ago I took a three-month assignment in Malta, starting next week. But meantime I've somehow got engaged to Rosemary...."

"Lucky you. She's a darling."

"Thanks. But the thing now is...."

"You no longer want to go to Malta?"

"Absolutely not. I mean, three months...."

"Unthinkable."

"So how about you going in my place, Chloe, pet? The work is right up your street, and I can fix it by sending a telegram to this archaeologist—he knows me, I've done stuff for him before, you know, at Salamis in Cyprus."

"Oh, but...."

"Come on, Chloe. Have a heart."

"But mightn't he...?"

"It'll be spring in the Mediterranean," Ronnie reminded

her in the dulcet tones of the tempter. "Could you bear to miss it?"

Chloe glanced at the gloomy weather outside. Could she?

"I'd have to know a good deal more about the job first," she temporized. But she was only putting up a token resistance. Already her mind's eye was seeing asphodel and almond blossom, purple blue seas sequined with sunlight, skies so blindingly azure one needed sunglasses....

When Ronnie had finished explaining she said with sudden gaiety, "Well, why not?"

She was always eager for change, new places, new faces.

And what was the use of being a free lance, answerable to no one but the most tolerant and uncensorious of godmothers, if she couldn't make these snap decisions?

It would take a few days to disengage herself from current work and dates, and get suitable clothes for a kindlier climate. And then....

"All right. If you can fix it for me I'll go," she promised, without any further weighing of pros and cons.

"Angel! I'll fix it."

Wringing her hand till she winced, Ronnie slipped adroitly into the moving crowd on the pavement before she could change her mind.

Have I been led up the garden path, she wondered as he vanished. Then she had laughed aloud. Her volatile spirits had soared as she stepped out again into the driving sleet.

THE COPILOT'S VOICE came over the loudspeaker, informing the passengers of the plane's height, speed and position. Chloe listened and gasped—so high and so far, in so short a time!

She would have given voice to her astonishment—for this was, in fact, her first flight in a plane of this size and power—if her neighbor's attention hadn't been so completely taken up with his maps or blueprints or whatever.

The plane chose this moment, however, to plunge abruptly earthward like a lunatic elevator. Before she could stop herself she had half risen in her seat again.

Her neighbor came out of his trance to lay a firm brown

hand—whose excellent shape she noticed even in her state of alarm—on her arm.

"Just a little air pocket," he told her, using the soothing tones of one reassuring a nervous horse. "There she's steadying again. We're climbing back. You can relax."

"I'm trying to," Chloe said rather shortly. Her reactions to flying always mortified her, for she was a seasoned traveler by road and rail and sea.

"All right. All right."

His good-humored tolerance annoyed her, so did his immediate return to his studies.

But after she weathered a few more abrupt plunges with increasing nonchalance, he spoke again.

"She *is* bumping rather, isn't she? But I see you're getting the idea. Perhaps you'd like to talk a bit? Takes the mind off the motion. How far are you going?"

He had returned his papers to a briefcase, which he locked. Now he slewed around a little in his seat, as if to get a better look at her.

As their eyes met he smiled—a swift, warm, wholly charming smile that lit and transformed the dark, serious face.

It was her instant undoing. It happens like that, once or twice in a blue moon, when a girl meets a man for the first time. A spark—something electrifying—seemed to flash from him to her. It felt like a thousand watts. Suddenly she was deeply, excitingly aware of him.

Not that she knew what had happened to her. All she knew was that her heart had seemed to turn right over....

With an effort she pulled herself together and summoned the poise on which as a rule she prided herself.

"I'm going to Malta," she said.

The words brought to her mind how her godmother had remarked with a twinkle, on hearing of her plans, "They used to call them 'The Fishing Fleet' in my day—gals who went out to Malta in the season, looking for husbands in the Navy."

Lady Stanton, whose Kensington flat had been Chloe's home since her mother had remarried and sailed for Nassau, was a vice-admiral's widow.

"Of course, there's something in the very air of Malta—as no doubt you'll discover—that seems to *breed* romance."

"But I'm going there to work, godmother. I expect the dig will be miles from anywhere social."

"I do hope not. Naval occasions can be such fun in Malta—waltzing on the quarterdeck—the uniforms and colored lights—the ship's band.... You're very devoted to that career of yours, aren't you, dearest?"

"I suppose I am. But not to the exclusion forever of love and, well marriage, if that's why you're shaking your head and sighing."

"I'm relieved to hear it."

"It's just that I want to have something of my own to do, that I'll never get tired of. Then when I marry—if I do—I won't find myself with nothing to live for, as poor mummy did, except thinking about whether her husband stays home or goes away, keeps on being in love with me or doesn't...."

"So wise of you, Chloe, dear. I so agree."

Certainly it had been with no ideas about getting herself a man that she had taken on this assignment and still less of feeling this way about one she had only just met, whose name she didn't yet know, who might already be married, a family man....

He had been opening a pack of cigarettes. Now he offered her one and flicked a lighter.

"I'm going to Malta, too," he said. "You're on a visit, I suppose?"

"Not exactly a visit."

"Then...?"

Such was the impact of his personality that she found herself launching at once into explanations, though she was usually reticent with strangers. In any case, she had nothing to hide, so she could speak freely.

"I'm going out to work. Actually I'm taking someone else's place. Only for three months, but it was altogether too good a chance to miss."

She saw he was watching her from under black brows that had suddenly come together in a frown.

"Go on," he ordered, so curtly that she threw him a quick uncertain glance and hesitated, her mouth half-open.

"Well?"

"I'm a press photographer. I rather specialize in architectural subjects. Stone fascinates me. I love its textures and colors."

"Hardly a woman's line, I should have thought."

"Oh? Why not? Well, the person I'm going to work for is an eminent archaeologist, an Englishman whose mother belongs to the noble Maltese family. I never knew till now that Malta has its own nobility, did you?"

"I did. Go on."

"It seems this man has made another important Stone Age find on the island and wants detailed photographic records in color. Well, that happens to be my line. I think it's going to be madly interesting work."

"The devil you do!"

There was no mistaking, now, the note of sharp anger in the man's voice. Chloe's eyes opened wide in surprise and shock. They were a clear golden brown and set a little aslant, giving a piquancy to the charming oval of her face. He met them with implacable gray ones. *What can I have said,* she asked herself nervously.

"Is your name by any chance C. Linden?"

At his tone her chin lifted.

"I'm Chloe Linden, yes. How did you know that?"

"You evidently aren't aware that I am the archaeologist for whom you propose to work?"

She gave a little gasp. She was completely taken by surprise. She hardly knew what she had expected her employer to be like—elderly, scholarly, perhaps bearded and rather scruffy....

Certainly the vague mind picture she had formed couldn't have been less like this man, with his comparative youth—thirty-four or five, she judged—his strong masculinity, the vitality, overlaid with an air of confident authority that made him somehow formidable.

"You mean to say *you* are Professor Vining?" she exclaimed incredulously.

"I am Dominic Vining. And let me tell you at once that if I'd had the slightest idea that the C. Linden mentioned in Fairfax's telegram was a girl...."

He stopped short, with a gesture of barely suppressed irritation.

Waiting for him to go on, she fancied she saw a glint of humor in his eyes. But when he spoke again it was with quelling decision.

"Naturally I'd have declined the offer of her services."

Chloe felt her color rise.

"Why naturally?" she demanded with asperity.

When he shrugged his shoulders and didn't at once reply she went on more calmly, "I can assure you, Professor Vining, that I'm perfectly qualified and—and competent to do the work you require. Otherwise Ronnie Fairfax would hardly have asked me to take his place."

He gave her that implacable look again. It affected her so unpleasantly that she wondered how in the world she could have felt about him as she had, when he smiled at her with such warmth and charm only a few minutes before.

"That doesn't happen to be the point."

"Then tell me what it is."

"The point is that I will not have a woman—let alone a young and...attractive one—on a dig."

So I'm attractive, am I? Thanks very much, Chloe thought derisively. She felt on the brink of hysterical laughter but held back, being well aware that hysteria wouldn't get her anywhere with this man. Calmness, coolness to match his—that was the line to take.

So she waited, her eyes wide, interrogative.

"Women always cause trouble on a dig, sooner or later," he stated didactically.

"Trouble?"

He frowned impatiently. "Emotional trouble. Rivalry, jealousy, sex if you like—surely I don't need to particularize, Miss Linden."

"I don't understand. I would be there to do my work—as efficiently, I hope, as a man would. There'd be no need to bring emotion into it, would there?"

"No need. But that's how it goes. Women *are* emotion

mongers, as I know from painful experience. And that sort of emotion can disrupt a team of men who'd normally work together happily for months on end."

She wanted to shout, "You can't say women do this, women do that, as if we were all as alike as peas in a pod. You can't generalize about women. It's illogical. It's absurd."

Instead she said quietly, "So you think I would make trouble, Professor Vining?"

"Perhaps. At any rate I prefer not to take the risk."

"If you think . . . ." she tried again, and fell silent, biting her lip.

How could she assure him, witheringly, that she had no emotional interest whatsoever in any male member of his precious dig, when only a short while ago she had been thrown into a tumult of emotion, simply because *he* had smiled at her?

"I—I think you're utterly unfair," she said lamely.

"Possibly. Nevertheless. . . ." His tone was final.

With a gesture of frustration she ran her fingers through the shining chestnut hair that curled softly around her head. Professor Vining flicked a brief glance at it, his face expressionless. She dropped her hands into her lap.

"May I know what you intend to do, then?"

"I'm sorry, Miss Linden. I must send you back to London."

Back to the cold February wind, the sleet and slushy snow.

"Oh, no, *please*."

She bit the words off—they had escaped before she could stop them. As his eyes met her bright, troubled ones his expression became less hostile.

"Not right away, of course. Having made the journey you'll want to see something of the island. It's charming now, in spring—quite the best time of the year. And I promise you the architecture and antiquities will amply repay you for any inconvenience you may feel you've been put to."

"I hope you're right."

"Of course, your expenses during your stay will be my responsibility."

Her chin lifted again.

"Thank you, that won't be necessary."

He looked at her with that infuriating gleam of humor.

"I happen to think it will."

The stewardess walking down the aisle with an armful of glossy magazines, saved Chloe from having to reply. She chose one at random and leafed through it unseeingly.

"Back again from your jaunt to London?" the girl said archly.

"I only went over for an evening lecture—hardly a jaunt, Miss O'Malley," he answered pleasantly. The girl laughed as if she didn't believe him.

"Want a magazine?" she offered.

"No, thanks. I've got some work to do."

The work lasted him a good hour and a half, during which he made notes absorbedly and ignored Chloe's existence. She sat looking out of the window at the endless expanse of cloud and simmered with indignation. Her pleasure in the flight was ruined; she could hardly wait for it to be over and done with.

She tried to read. She tried to doze. But she was far too vividly aware, in every nerve, of her irritating neighbor to do either.

I *detest* him, she told herself. But just then the stewardess brought them their meals on plastic trays. Professor Vining abandoned his work, and laid himself out to be agreeable. He explained in detail what she must see and do in Malta. He was attentive, courteous, companionable. She found herself capitulating without a struggle.

AT LONG LAST the warning "Fasten Your Safety Belts" flashed in red at the end of the plane.

"If your ears hurt as we go down, clench your teeth and swallow hard," Dominic Vining advised Chloe.

She surprised him by a little spurt of laughter. His black brows shot up.

"Even though you're going to send me back, I'm excited," she explained. "New places, new people, things happening always excite me. A sort of champagne feeling."

Had she been looking at him then, she might have detected a flash of something not unlike regret in his eyes.

Guided by its winking red light they came down at Luqa airport, in Malta, sometime after midnight.

In the darkness it was much like any other airport, except that not far off there was an enormous baroque church outlined in lights, above which fireworks exploded in golden geysers and fountains and stars, and gave off formidable bangs.

"It's a religious *festa*," Professor Vining explained. "You'll soon discover that in Malta religion is the butter on the dry bread of everyday life. Nearly every date in the calendar is its patron saint's day for some Maltese village. Which means a *festa* with street decorations, processions of priests with parasols and holy images, flower heads strewn underfoot, music and above all, fireworks and petards."

A rocket exploded loudly into a white puffball overhead as he spoke, making her jump nervously.

"They fire them from the rooftops to scare away the devil," her mentor told her with a grin. "After a bit you won't even notice them."

Very likely, since I won't be here, she thought wryly. A pang that really hurt told her how desperately she wanted to stay.

They separated for the customs formalities. When the officials were through with her, she found that he had vanished.

He reappeared almost at once.

"Ah, here you are. All clear?"

"I think so."

"We'd better book you in at the Felicia for what's left of the night. I'll drive you there and fix it. I live out at Medina, in the center of the island. I'd intended to take Fairfax out there for the night, and on to the dig, which is over in the southwest of the island, tomorrow. He would have lived in camp with the others, of course. As it is. . . ." He broke off with a shrug of his shoulders.

The color flamed in her cheeks again, but she swallowed her resentment and said coolly enough, "Thank you. I'll go and tell them about my luggage."

He nodded, and watched the slim figure in its neat gray

suit, and the long beautiful legs, with involuntary approval as she moved away from him.

Pretty girl, he was thinking. *Walks well. Got poise and plenty of spirit. I like a woman with spirit. But she's much too much of a woman to let loose on the dig. A nuisance having to send her back. It means delay—but better that than trouble later on.*

Outside, weary passengers were piling into a big bus. A small, plump, dark-skinned man whom Chloe took to be a Maltese was stowing her suitcase into the trunk of a powerful-looking car.

"Please get in." Professor Vining opened the door for her. When she was settled he tucked a blanket around her knees.

"Although it's spring, the nights are still at bit chilly. Warm enough?"

"Yes, thanks." Her chin was snuggled down into the collar of her big camel's-hair traveling coat. She felt relaxed and comfortable.

But when he got in beside her she found herself thrilling again to his nearness. In a panic she tried to laugh herself out of it. This—love at first sight—was teenage stuff. Something she didn't believe in when she read about it in romantic novels.

Somehow, though, she didn't feel like laughing. It was as if something—it had happened in a flash, like summer lightning—had taken possession of her, creating a strange, exciting confusion of feelings....

Oh, nonsense. All this on account of a handsome stranger who can't wait to send me back to where I came from, she thought with sudden impatience as they roared off into the night, which was moonless, starry and dark in a velvety sort of way.

She could see little but occasional flat-topped dwellings and odd trees, caught in the tunnel of the headlights. There were really very few trees; it seemed a featureless landscape of flat fields roughly divided by stone walls.

Now they had reached a village or small town. They were moving down a long, dark street between high cream buildings. It was shrouded in silence, sleeping, mysterious seeming, with only a few mongrels and gaunt skittering cats astir.

Soon she caught a glimpse of water and the outlines of ships, anchored in a sort of creek that ran inland between quays lined with more tall buildings. They swooped down to a wide stone archway, soared up a rise and passed an area of geometric flowerbeds.

Now they were skirting the cavernous entrance to a walled city. Valetta, Chloe guessed. In a moment they pulled up beneath the portico of a deluxe hotel.

"Behold the Felicia, the pride of Malta," said Dominic Vining, breaking a long silence.

Chloe put the blanket aside and got out of the car. He said brusquely, "Go on in," and held the door open for her.

The ornate foyer hummed with people off the plane and uniformed bellhops. A harrassed reception clerk was allotting rooms and keys. The bellhops ran around briskly with baggage and ushered people into the elevators.

Evidently Professor Vining was well-known here. He took charge and achieved quick results for Chloe. Within minutes she was going up with him in an elevator. At the door of her room he handed her its key, and waited till a bellhop brought her cases.

"Better try to get some sleep now," he advised. "I'll come tomorrow to discuss arrangements with you."

"Thank you."

"You'll need to fix your return flight right away, or you may find yourself held up. Reservations aren't all that easy to get. Will ten o'clock suit you?"

"Of course."

She spoke casually, as if it didn't matter one way or the other. But it did matter. She felt sick with disappointment.

He held out his hand, and she took it. His clasp was warm and very firm. He was looking down at her with what seemed like approval—thankful, she supposed wryly, that she wasn't making a scene.

She watched his tall figure till it disappeared between the doors of the elevator. She didn't want to be in love with him. . . .

Summer lightning, she told herself firmly. A flash, a moment of high tension—and then nothing. It was too instantaneous to be real, lasting. And too one-sided....

She was more tired than she had realized.

Her last waking thoughts were that tomorrow morning she would be seeing him again; that he couldn't really mean to send her packing without a trial; he couldn't be so unfair, so stupidly prejudiced, so uncivilized.

"I simply won't believe it," she said aloud into the warm darkness of her room. As if the sound of the words reassured her, she drifted at once into sleep.

CHAPTER TWO

NOT TILL THE CHAMBERMAID knocked and brought in her early tea, and pulled back the curtains to reveal scintillating sunlight and cool, crïsp air, did Chloe stir.

"Oh, thank you. What time is it?"

"Seven o'clock, madam."

"What is your name?"

"Mariucha, madam."

Black hair, black eyes, pomegranate red cheeks, wide smile showing perfect teeth. Nice. Much nicer than her godmother's old Hester with her morning complaint about the weather and her bunions, thought Chloe sleepily. Mariucha smiled again and left her.

Patting back a yawn, Chloe poured out a cup of tea and sipped it enjoyably. She pulled a thin dressing gown around her and stepped out onto her own little balcony.

"O-oooh," she murmured on a sigh of delight.

There below her lay the fabled Grand Harbor of Malta, its winding, many-inleted surface smooth and pearly in the morning light. Lion-colored rocks surmounted by lion-colored fortifications of towers and bastions, some castellated, some picturesquely crumbling, rose steeply around its shores.

Units of the fleet rested in it, and trim launches laid foaming tracks between them and the quays. A cruiser backed with infinite care out of a creek.

Up the main fairway crept a liner, shrinking a little amid all this naval grandeur. It was pursued by an avid pack of painted *djaisas*—the water taxis of Malta—propelled by standing oarsmen like gondoliers.

As Chloe watched, a little breeze sprang up. Small waves made bold to slap the warships and the sun struck sparks off the ruffled water. It was an enchanting scene.

Reluctantly, vexed that her time to enjoy it was to be cut short by a man's tyrannical whim, she turned and went indoors to bathe and dress.

After breakfast she wandered out into the sparkling sunshine to explore the hotel's flowery gardens.

There was color and rich greenness all around her. The sky was flawless blue, birds twittered in the trees, a boxer dog came to greet her with a quiver of his stumpy tail and turned to pace sedately beside her.

She ought to have felt happy; instead she was strangely ill at ease. She longed for the meeting at ten o'clock with Dominic Vining, but dreaded it even more.

When he came, what line should she take? Should she protest again, argue, even forget pride and dignity and plead to be allowed to stay? Or should she be wise and go tamely back to London before her heart became more deeply involved?

She couldn't make up her mind. She could only wait and let events take their course—and hope.

At five minutes to ten she stood waiting in the foyer, outwardly cool and poised, but with butterflies fluttering inside her.

When ten had struck, he hadn't arrived. Instead, the doors opened to admit a rough-haired, clever-looking young man with thick-lensed spectacles and an agreeable expression.

After a glance around the foyer he came straight over to her.

"Miss Linden?"

"Yes."

"Good morning. I hope they made you comfortable?"

"Very, thanks."

"Good. I'm Mark Tenby, one of Vining's team. His personal secretary, actually. He was delayed by a telephone call from Valetta, and sent me on ahead to make his apologies. He shouldn't be long."

He was eyeing her with candid admiration, thinking how fresh and charming she looked in her trim suit and crisp, coral pink blouse. He liked her bright hair, her slim grace, her voice.

"I say, isn't it just too bad that Dominic has this thing about not having women on a dig?" he burst out irrepressibly.

She couldn't help laughing.

"It's perfectly absurd. It's medieval. I'm furious about it really," she declared. "But there isn't much to be done, is there, except retire gracefully?"

He nodded rueful agreement. "Not," he qualified loyally, "that he hasn't had good reason to feel as he does."

She waited, dissembling her eager curiosity, for him to explain.

Instead he said, "Excuse me a minute. I've just seen somebody. It's my younger brother. And good heavens, *Louise!*"

He had left her and was greeting a good-looking young naval lieutenant and a tallish, auburn-haired woman whose age Chloe put at thirty-two or three. She was very thin, and in her exquisite pale shantung dress and spike-heeled shoes, had the bizarre, improbable elegance of a fashion drawing.

"Mark, my dear!" Her voice was a vibrant contralto. She made play with a pair of large, sparkling eyes, the color of seawater. Her heart-shaped face, with blunt nose and curly mouth, had a mobile brilliance. *She's no beauty,* Chloe thought, *but she's devastating all the same. Devastating—and probably dangerous.*

She heard Mark Tenby say, "What on earth are you doing in Malta, Louise?"

Louise's laugh was as deep as her voice.

"My pet, can't you guess? I've come to visit my elusive cousin by marriage. Also to cast a proprietorial eye on Santa Clara."

When he looked puzzled she went on vivaciously, "Surely you remember their grandfather left the place equally to Dominic and Dick, the sons of his two elder daughters, after both of his own sons died in the 1942 siege?"

"Yes, of course—I'd forgotten."

"I could never get Dick to bring me out here. He doesn't fancy Malta. Too many pompous naval types lording it around, he says—sorry, Robert, my lamb. He hates the climate, too. Sirocco, sun and sweat, didn't somebody say? But I pine for sun—and ladies don't sweat! So I thought I'd see for myself. And here I am."

For a moment Mark seemed at a loss. "Does Dominic know?" he asked at length.

The sea green eyes glinted wickedly. "Of course. I telephoned him this morning, as soon as I came ashore from my ship. He'll be here any minute now to collect me."

Mark stared, but swallowed whatever he had been going to say. Turning to Chloe, he pulled her gently forward.

"Then let me introduce Miss Linden, she's waiting for Dominic, too. Miss Linden, this is Mrs. Carlyon."

The sparkling glance changed direction. It raked Chloe swiftly from head to foot. Was it her imagination that it held an instant, veiled hostility?

The deep voice said dismissingly, "Oh—how d'you do?"

Chloe murmured politely.

"And my brother Robert, playing hooky from his aircraft carrier, I don't mind betting."

"Then you lose, I have the day off. Welcome to Malta, Miss Linden. We must see you enjoy your stay here."

Chloe smiled her thanks. It was impossible not to like Robert at sight. She guessed him to be a little older than herself. He was a charmer, the type older women love to spoil. He had startlingly blue eyes, full of laughter and fun, which he used to give point to his tritest remarks.

Before she could say anything Louise broke in. "Simply marvelous to find you two here. I've always heard it's no good expecting a good time in Malta unless you're well in with the Navy. So you must rally around Robert, my sweet."

Robert promised to do his best, though his ship, he said with candid regret, would be off on NATO exercises soon.

"Then we'll make the most of it while you're here. And what are *you* doing, Mark?"

"Working for Dominic," he told her cheerfully. "I took my diploma in archaeology last year, and he kindly invited me to come in on this dig as his assistant."

"Dominic and his digs," Louise exclaimed derisively. "Tell me, Mark, is he just as antisocial as ever?"

"Better ask him," Mark said shortly. "Here he comes."

Chloe's heart skipped a beat as Dominic Vining came in, bareheaded, through the revolving doors. His handsome face looked a trifle moody. He stood still for a moment, looking around; then he saw them.

Louise put out both her hands in an enthusiastically loving gesture and glided to meet him as swiftly and smoothly as if she had skates on her feet, or wings.

"Dominic, my *dear*," she cried thrillingly, and leaned forward for him to kiss her smooth cheek.

Chloe saw Mark's eyebrows go up in a sardonic quirk. She saw Dominic's face darken with some emotion that might, she suspected, be annoyance. She heard him say formally, "How are you, Louise?"

"Thrilled, darling, to see you again after all these years."

Dominic muttered something. Freeing his hands, he turned to Chloe.

"Good morning, Miss Linden. Let me introduce you to my cousin, Mrs. Carlyon."

Louise spoke impatiently from just behind him. "Darling, we've all met already. Could you perhaps finish your business with Miss Linden, whatever it is, while I'm having my hair washed and set? And then may we go out right away to Santa Clara? I'm longing to see it. I tried to make Dick take me out, but he never would—and now, poor darling, I don't suppose he ever will."

"What news of Dick, Louise? Anything fresh?"

"Not a word, darling. They're beginning to say on the radio that any hope of the party's survival must soon be abandoned. That's one reason why I came out. I felt I *had* to get away, cheer myself up...."

"I'm sorry, Louise," Dominic said in a low voice.

Chloe thought that the sadness of her answering smile and shrug were more perfunctory than genuine. She was sure of it when Mark caught her eye and gave her a swift, indecorous wink.

"You *are* going to be free to give me lunch, aren't you, darling?" Louise persisted.

And that, Chloe thought wryly, *disposes of me.*

She could hardly hide her astonishment when Dominic said crisply, "Of course. We'll all have lunch in Valetta. Miss Linden has come out here to do some specialized photographic work for me, Louise, and will be staying at Santa Clara with us. I'm afraid, though, we're all going to be very busy. The work at the dig has reached the exciting stage, and we shall be spending a lot of time out there."

Chloe listened in a daze. Between indignation at his high-handedness, wry amusement at Louise's air of chagrin and plain, heartfelt relief, she didn't know what to say or think. Mark, she could see, was just as taken aback by Dominic's abrupt change of front as she was herself.

Louise, however disconcerted, was quick to recover herself. "You must take me along with you," she said sweetly. "After all, it won't be the first time I've joined you on a dig—remember?"

Mark smothered an exclamation. Dominic's face darkened again—this time certainly with annoyance.

"I'm afraid there won't be quite so much—scope for you this time," he said rather grimly.

His cousin by marriage threw him a mocking glance.

"Just try me, darling."

Mark appeared to be feeling some alarm as to what she might say next. Evidently he knew what all this was about. Robert looked bored and vague, as if *he* at any rate didn't. When he caught Chloe's eye he quirked an eyebrow and shook his head despairingly. *I wanted to have a talk with you,* his look said, *but not a hope.*

After a moment Dominic took the situation in hand.

"If you'll excuse us, Louise, I'll take Miss Linden off— we have things to discuss. Then Mark and I have an appointment in Valetta that may take some time—things often do in Malta. I suggest we meet for lunch at one- fifteen. How about you, Robert? Can you join us?"

Robert brightened.

"Delighted, sir."

"At the club, then. It'll be less crowded than here. I'll call for you and Miss Linden here at about one o'clock, Louise."

"But I.... Oh, very well," she agreed sulkily.

"Ready, Miss Linden?"

Docilely Chloe followed him down a corridor lined with showcases full of dolls in Maltese costume, exotic underwear, cosmetics and bottles of scent. He turned into a big lounge—empty at the moment—furnished with comfortable armchairs, settees, tables.

Waving a hand at one of the settees, he said pleasantly, "Please sit down."

She was glad to do so; her legs felt suddenly weak.

She took a cigarette from his proffered case, and let him light it. Drawing on it, she waited, obstinately silent, for his explanations.

He remained silent, too, studying her, his expression inscrutable. She felt her color begin to rise.

"I suppose you're very angry with me, Miss Linden," he said at last.

"Bewildered, rather, Professor Vining."

He grinned—rather endearingly. "It *was* rather a volte-face, I admit. And it still goes against the grain, I'm afraid."

Seeing her stiffen, he went on quickly, "This sudden invasion has altered the whole situation, you see."

"I'm not sure I do see."

"I gather my cousin proposes—intends to make a long stay at Santa Clara. It was willed jointly to Dick, her husband, and me, though my mother occupies it for her lifetime. So Louise can, in point of fact, stay as long as she chooses."

"But...."

"It would be doing me a great favor—little as you probably feel I deserve it—if you would stay on to do the work you came out for and—well, help me out by coming to live with us at Santa Clara."

"I—really, I..." Chloe stammered.

He paid no attention. "My mother, I should explain, is an invalid, and seldom leaves her room. It would be a great help in every way," he finished with emphasis, "if you could bring yourself to do as I ask."

Though she considered he deserved a snub, she knew she

wasn't going to administer it. She went so far as to demand
with spirit, "You're prepared to risk my baneful influence
on your team at the dig?"

His eyes twinkled. "No option."

She couldn't help laughing.

She had meant to carry off this scene with immense
dignity. She hadn't intended to agree till he had properly
humbled himself. But it was no use—she simply didn't
want to fight him.

She still wasn't clear why Mrs. Carlyon's arrival had
caused him to change his mind so promptly, but she didn't
much care. The thing that mattered was that she was to remain in Malta.

"All right, then, I'll stay," she said. "I would have been
very sorry to go back without having a chance to justify
Ronnie Fairfax's sending me in his place. And besides, I do
want time to see Malta, now I'm here."

"So you shall. Do you drive a car?"

"Yes."

"Then Mark will fix you up with a local license."

"I have my International."

"Have you indeed? That makes it simple. One of the
cars at Santa Clara will be for your use when you want it."

"Thank you. You're very kind."

His eyes twinkled again. "Am I? I wonder."

Standing up, he held out his hand to pull her from the
low settee.

"Can you amuse yourself till lunchtime?"

"Of course. You forget it's all new to me."

"And exciting?"

"Wildly."

He smiled and left her, and she watched him go,
thoughtfully, before stubbing out her cigarette.

Firmly, she cautioned herself against feeling too elated.
Still more firmly, against weaving romantic dreams around
a man who had shown her plainly enough that she was only
to stay on sufferance, because it happened to suit his
schedule.

But her heart refused to be cautioned. It sang and
wouldn't be bidden.

She knew perfectly well what had happened to her. She had fallen head over heels in love with Dominic Vining. At first sight, like the heroine of a magazine story. Unasked. And most unreasonably—for what did she really know about him?

Well, she was going to live at Santa Clara, work with him, share his daily life. What more could a girl newly in love ask?

Except, of course, to have her love returned. Unlikely as that seemed at present, she glowed at the possibility. And there was no law against a girl trying to make her employer fall in love with her, was there? But it looked like being as tough an assignment as she had ever handled. . . .

Strolling out in the open, she found a courtyard with flowers in tubs and chairs and tables set under gay umbrellas. People in summery clothes and sunglasses sat under the umbrellas reading, or chatting with Mediterranean zest.

Chloe found a vacant table and sat down. By now the sun had a crystal brilliance, and its heat was that of a real summer day at home.

She sat blissfully absorbing it, and sipping the long, cold lime drink she ordered.

At another table a beautiful Latin young man in pearl gray and sideburns tried persistently, with a wolf's single-mindedness, to hold her glance. But it passed over him dreamily, unseeingly. Crossly he asked himself how these English women could be at once so maddeningly desirable and so cool. . . .

CHAPTER THREE

THE CLUB WHERE THEY MET for lunch was in Valetta. Its cavernous entrance, a long tunnel piercing the tall massive battlements, Chloe had glimpsed last night.

Dominic parked the car down in the square in Kingsway, the strident main street. It teemed with humanity and echoed with voices and raucous radio music.

"On our left the Royal Library, on our right the Grand Palace. That's where the Grand Masters of the Knight of St. John held court during the two centuries when the Order found sanctuary in Malta," Dominic told them. "It's Government House now."

"But what a lovely city," Chloe exclaimed as she looked around her. Tall cream houses with ornamental stone balconies, stately palaces—she hadn't dreamed of such elegance, such architectural splendor.

"'A city built by gentlemen for gentlemen, where every house is a mansion, and every mansion a palace,'" Dominic quoted. "Wait till you've seen some of the interiors—the Cathedral of St. John, the Palace armory and tapestry chamber and so on. They're amazing."

Louise broke in impatiently, "*Must* you be so guidebook, darling? I die for a really cold dry martini."

"Very well, Louise. I expect the club barman can manage one for you."

"Then let's go—if Miss Linden can tear herself away."

There was a distinct edge to her voice. Was Mrs. Carlyon *not* going to be friendly? How awkward that could be, with both of them staying at Santa Clara.

In the club a pleasant-looking, animated group of people were enjoying prelunch drinks and the day's gossip.

The men were mostly in naval uniform. Though there was a sprinkling of soldiers and civilians, the general atmosphere was distinctly nautical. There was even a tubby little rear admiral with a monumental wife and a ravishing young daughter.

Dominic led them to a comfortable corner and ordered martinis for Louise and Mark who, with Robert, had met them in the foyer, a pink gin for Robert and dry sherry for Chloe and himself.

As she watched him lighting a cigarette for Louise, Chloe had a sudden sense of danger—of the runaway possibilities of a situation involving Dominic and his cousin's wife. She had an intuitive certainty that there had been something between the two of them in the past, and that Mrs. Carlyon was determined to rekindle it.

During lunch, however, Chloe got the impression that Louise wasn't quite as sure of her welcome as she pretended. She talked and laughed too much, on the extreme edge of gaiety. She drank the wine Dominic offered her too fast, too carelessly.

A good many heads turned, from time to time, to look at her. Some faces—male, mostly—expressed interest, speculation; more had faintly raised eyebrows, a hint of disapproval.

All in all, it wasn't a very enjoyable meal for Chloe. She sat silent, listening, for Louise monopolized the talk as well as ignoring her as far as possible.

Robert Tenby, however, took the first opportunity to speak a line he had generally found effective as an opening gambit. "I say, we must see more of each other, Miss Linden."

"Must we?"

He looked a little crestfallen, though she hadn't meant to be snubbing. "Well, *I'd* like it. And I'd hoped you might, too," he said engagingly.

Chloe smiled. "I'm afraid I'm going to be very busy. I've come to Malta to work, you know," she said with a glance at Professor Vining.

"But even wage slaves like you and me must play some time—mmm? You're going to work for Vining on the dig?"

"Yes."

"Then that'll be all right," Robert said easily. "We'll enlist my brother's help."

He went into action when the talk—steered there determinedly by Louise—turned to naval festivities.

"There's a match for a cup at the Marsa polo ground on Saturday. It should be quite good. I'd be delighted if you'd bring Mrs. Carlyon along sir, and have tea with me afterward," he told Dominic.

Louise blew him a kiss. "Of course we'll come, my pet."

Glancing at their host, Chloe again had an impression of that barely concealed irritation. However, he said pleasantly, "Thank you, Robert. If we can spare the time from work."

"Of course you're invited, too, Miss Linden." Robert's look was guilelessness itself.

"Oh, thank you. I'd love to come." The words were out before she stopped to think.

The swift color rose in her cheeks as gray eyes met her own across the table.

"I think we must arrange our working program before you make any social engagements, Miss Linden."

His manner was courteous enough; his voice so chilly that she felt gooseflesh rise along her arms.

Wow! I asked for that, she thought vexedly.

As she murmured an apologetic, "Of course, Professor Vining," she noticed Louise. Louise was watching her discomfiture without a trace of woman-to-woman sympathy or friendliness. Her eyes held derision, cool appraisal, and even, Chloe realized with surprise, *malice.*

She resents me, Chloe thought. *But why? What have I done?*

Robert gave her a comical, rueful grimace.

"I know how it feels. Like when my captain has me up on the mat," he murmured. She smiled, her spirits restored.

They finished their coffee, lit cigarettes.

"Sorry to hustle," Dominic said, "but it's high time we got along to Mdina, and work."

As they stood up, Louise tucked her arm possessively through his.

"Work! Phooey to that. You mustn't be pompous and dreary, my pet, now Louise is here at last." The words, in her deep, carrying voice, caused heads to turn.

Without replying Dominic called their waiter, signed the bill, and led the way out. Robert, maneuvering himself next to Chloe, touched her hand and whispered, "May I telephone? You're at Santa Clara? I must see you again soon."

"Remember, I'm a working girl."

"As Louise would say, phooey to that. So long."

Louise had slid into the front seat with Dominic, chatting vivaciously. Chloe got in behind with Mark and looked around, alert and interested, as they left Valetta and the long, crowded main street behind them and drove into more open country.

She saw with delight that it was full springtime—the magical Mediterranean spring that almost overnight throws a brilliant, flowery patchwork over the winter-scarred, stony earth.

She had met it before—in Corsica, in Majorca, in Greece.

"Isn't it heaven?" she said to Mark; but Mark had overeaten and was too somnolent to do more than nod vaguely.

She feasted her eyes on massed poppies, marigolds, pink asphodel, blue iris and crimson clover. She could smell the wild thyme that carpeted the verges.

They passed through another tall, apricot cream village and skirted the bosky gardens of the palace of San Anton. A little distance ahead was a hilly ridge. Green terraced slopes of tender young vines and fig trees led up it toward high, massive ramparts. Behind these she glimpsed a storybook citadel, with rounded domes and tall towers.

"That is Mdina," Dominic said, half turning his head to include her. "They call it 'the silent city.' I'm afraid you're going to find it far too dull and quiet for your taste, Louise."

"Don't worry, we'll soon wake it up," she assured him blithely, taking off her bizarre sunglasses to get a better look. "My *dear*, it looks terribly phony, doesn't it?"

"Phony?"

"Untrue. Like a backdrop. Or like something thought up by a Hollywood mogul."

Dominic said nothing, eloquently, and Chloe saw Mark grin.

They were climbing a steep length of road that turned sharply to the right into an open garden square. Here red buses stood like panting dragons, crowds milled around food stalls, radios played full blast, horns tooted, donkeys brayed and fireworks exploded shatteringly overhead.

"Did you say silent, darling?"

"This is Rabat—and today happens to be one of their *festas*," Dominic said testily. "Mdina is inside the ramparts."

They crossed a bridge over a wide moat, dry now, very wide and deep. Ahead of them was a high stone archway with heraldic carvings.

They passed under it into a dreamlike city of stately apricot cream palaces, churches, convents, divided from each other by meandering paved alleys, only just wide enough for a car to pass. In an open square a vast cathedral raised its towers and domes. A friar walked softly, reading his breviary. A line of young men was entering the gates of what might be a college for priests.

It certainly was silent. Only the whisper of their tires broke a silence that could almost be felt.

Louise stared around her with candid disbelief.

"My goodness, it *is* a movie set after all," she exclaimed. "I bet it's hollow behind."

Chloe saw with amusement that Professor Vining was having considerable difficulty in controlling his temper.

Luckily they seemed to have arrived. They turned right into an alley where massive gates, set in a high blank wall, opened from within at the discreet toot of their horn.

Passing between these, they pulled up in a shady, flowery courtyard. A fountain played tinkling music in a stone basin. In one corner a curtain of bougainvillea glowed purplish crimson.

Louise clasped her hands and gazed around her at the massive walls, broken by tiers of long windows with outcurving wrought-iron guards.

"Our palazzo in Malta, yours and mine, Dominic. I can't tell you how thrilled I am," she said intensely.

Chloe saw Mark grin again. He seemed to be finding Louise as good as a play.

An Amazonian woman, swarthy-faced and wearing the black garments of the island peasantry, had arrived from the house to help the porter with the luggage. The pair of them hauled out Louise's expensively matched set of pigskin with gold initials, and Chloe's two light bags.

Dominic went over and spoke a few rapid words in Maltese, and the woman nodded impassively, glancing at Chloe.

"That is Lotta, our housekeeper," he said, returning. "She will show you to your rooms."

"Oh, but you must take me on a tour of the place first, Dominic dear," Louise insisted gaily.

"Mark will take you."

"No, darling, *you*."

He shrugged.

"Very well. Then perhaps Miss Linden would like to go upstairs with Lotta."

It was an order. Obediently Chloe followed Lotta up a curving marble staircase, and skidded in her wake along miles of black and white marble squares like a chessboard. She glimpsed—and marked down for further consideration—the handsome portraits, very dark and Old-Masterish, that brooded on either side, and the splendid suits of armor standing beneath the long windows and looking as if at any moment they might step forward and engage each other in battle.

As they passed a half-open bedroom door Chloe stopped, startled by a noise like the rapping of a stick on the floor. Lotta stopped, too. A harsh, imperious voice called out, "Lotta, is it you? Who is that with you?"

Lotta swung around and pushed the door wide open with her knee.

"*Contessa*, it is the new young lady."

"A young lady? What do you mean? Bring her in here at once."

Lotta beckoned Chloe inside the room. It was vast and

gloomy, with a painted ceiling, massive dark furniture, a deep-piled carpet, heavily draped curtains of thick silk damask drawn across the windows and a monstrous four-poster bed.

In the bed, propped against a mound of pillows, lay a handsome old woman. Her snow-white hair contrasted oddly with her dark olive complexion. Her fine, dark eyes were full of a restless brillance.

His mother, Chloe thought. *I can see a resemblance. It's easy to see where he got his looks—and temperament.*

"Who are you?"

"I'm Chloe Linden."

"English?"

"Yes. I've come out here to do some photography for Professor Vining."

She smiled as she spoke and the old lady's hand, splashed with the brown stains of age and heavy with rings, stretched out to take hers in a surprisingly strong grip. The brilliant eyes studied her for an embarrassingly long time.

Suddenly the old lady began to laugh, with a sort of relish. "Well, well. So you are going to work with my son, are you? An English girl—and a pretty one. Excellent. Welcome to Santa Clara, my dear. Tell me, where is your home?"

"I live in London, *contessa.*"

"With your parents?"

"No. With my godmother, Lady Stanton."

The white head nodded approvingly. "The wife of the vice admiral? Ah, of course. I knew her when they were here on the island. A long time ago. I hope she and Sir Amyatt are well?"

"He died two years ago."

"Ah. A great loss. And so she is your godmother? And your parents? Are they still alive?"

"Only my mother. She has married again and left England."

"For where?"

"For Nassau. Her husband has an estate there."

"I visited there once. It was even hotter than Malta. And your father—was he in the Navy, too?"

"No—in the Colonial Administration."

"So."

Chloe had the feeling that she had been weighed up, placed and found acceptable.

"You poor child," the *contessa* went on kindly. "Santa Clara must be your home while you are in Malta. I'm very glad indeed you have come, though Dominic didn't tell me. So, we shall see...."

The searching, penetrating scrutiny was hard to bear, but Chloe forced herself to endure it smilingly.

"Tell me, has *she* arrived?"

"She?"

"My nephew Richard's wife. Or his widow, perhaps—who knows? I mean Louise Carlyon."

"Yes, she's here. I left her downstairs in the hall, with Professor Vining."

"Doing what?" Dominic's mother snapped.

"She wanted him to show her over the—the palace."

"*Did* she? The effrontery of her! Forcing herself on us—a telephone call this morning was all the warning we had—no doubt hoping to upset my poor Dominic again, as if she hadn't done enough, spoiling his life, turning a normal young man against women, against marriage.... You've seen her—what do you think of her?"

"I only met her this morning—it's a little early to say, contessa. She's very attractive."

"Attractive! A siren, no doubt. And as heartless. There should have been sons by now to carry on the Valmontez name. Instead it looks as if the family must die out. Louise has driven Richard away, he's gone, lost, poor boy, probably dead...."

She broke off, coughing violently between gasps. Chloe ran to fill a glass from a water jug and brought it to her. With an arm under the frail shoulders, she supported her while she took a few sips. The *contessa* rested for a moment against her, trying, it seemed, to regain her composure.

"I think I can guess why she came here now," she said at length. "That is one reason I am so glad you have come, too. Perhaps you and I, between us, can manage to spoil her plans, my dear."

Puzzled, Chloe said nothing.

"You'll help me? Promise. You must promise."

"Of course," Chloe murmured, anxious to soothe the old lady, and not stopping to ask what she was promising. As she watched her apprehensively, the contessa fell back on her pillows.

"So tired...rest a little now...keep *her* away," she muttered, and was instantly asleep.

Chloe stayed on for some time, watching her compassionately and thinking over what had been said.

The *contessa* had confirmed her suspicion that there had been something in the past between Dominic and Louise.

Surely a love affair that had gone wrong? And that Louise would like to resuscitate? All the signs pointed to that....

When she slipped away at last from the *contessa*'s room, Chloe felt oddly dispirited; she was almost ready to wish she had never accepted this assignment in Malta.

CHAPTER FOUR

LOTTA WAS WAITING, with impassive patience, in the marble-paved corridor. Now she threw open the door of a room across the hall from the contessa's, and a little farther along.

Chloe got an instant impression of space and light.

Investigating, she found that the windows of her room were flush with the ramparts; the palace must actually have been built into their massive thickness on this side. When she opened the sash, she found she was looking down a sheer drop to the terraced vines and fig trees below.

It was as if, she thought delightedly, she were standing in a high tower, with all the island spread flatly around her. Overhead, a jet plane scraped chalk marks on the blue arch of the sky. The distant sea bordered the coastline in misty azure.

"What a wonderful view," she exclaimed. "And this room is quite lovely, Lotta."

Lotta's face remained impassive. "Yes, *signorina*. You would like the bags unpacked now?"

"I'll do them myself, thank you."

"As the *signorina* pleases."

She opened a door leading out of the bedroom.

"The bathroom is here. It is for the *signorina* and *signora* to share."

It looked sumptuous, with sea-green tiles and modern chrome taps. Evidently Santa Clara had had its plumbing modernized, however medieval the rest of it might be.

A glass door led from the bathroom to a tiny circular balcony, with a low, beautifully patterned wrought-iron balustrade.

Mrs. Carlyon's room, then, must be on the other side of the bathroom.

I'll have to ask her about times, Chloe thought. *She looks like the type who would indulge in prolonged scented soaks, at all hours.*

Shutting out of her mind the disturbing speculations roused by her talk with the contessa, she deftly unpacked her light cases, disposed her new wardrobe of light, summery clothes in a closet like a mausoleum and laid out her toilet things, nightgown, robe and slippers. *Now I'm installed,* she thought with satisfaction.

A glance in the antique gilt-framed mirror satisfied her that there was no need to fix her makeup. Nobody had told her where or when she was to report. Professor Vining had been headed off by Louise. But he had, she remembered, said, "Time to go back to Mdina, and *work*."

She hesitated for a moment, standing at the window, gazing at the wide, shimmering prospect. Should she go downstairs now? Her mind made up, she walked sedately along the chessboard corridor and down the marble staircase. The palazzo seemed enormous. She had no idea which way she should turn at the bottom of the stairs.

She chose left for luck. As she walked tentatively past a line of closed doors, one of them opened and Mark Tenby came out. She heard Mrs. Carlyon's deep contralto before he closed the door on it.

"Whew!" she heard him exclaim to himself. Then, seeing Chloe, he said, "Ah, Miss L. Doing all right?"

Behind the owlish glasses his blunt face broke into an engaging grin. Plain or not, he had oodles of charm, she thought.

"I rather think I'm lost," she confessed.

"And no wonder. These big Maltese houses are like the Minotaur's maze. The thing is to use a pocket compass till you've got your bearings. Library south by east, dining room due north, salon sou'west and so forth. Very helpful. I'll have to lend you mine."

"Thanks. Or I might unwind a ball of string as I go, like Ariadne."

"You'd make a fine cat's cradle of it if you did." He laughed.

"I don't even know where I'm supposed to report."

"Oh, the library, I should think. That's where we work. When Dominic manages to shake off Louise, that's where he'll want us. I'll take you there now, if you like."

"Please."

They turned and walked side by side. On a sudden impulse she said, "I don't want you to think I'm unduly inquisitive, Mr. Tenby, but. . . ."

"Better call me Mark, everybody does," he suggested.

"All right. Look, Mark, I do wish you'd brief me a bit about things here at Santa Clara. I'm all at sea. I've just had the oddest conversation with the *contessa*."

"Contessa? Oh, you mean Mrs. Vining."

"Lotta addressed her as *contessa*."

"Yes, of course, all the servants do. Her father had the Maltese title of count—very old, these titles are. Dominic doesn't use his. His mother uses hers when she mixes in Maltese society."

"I see. So I can call her either *contessa* or Mrs. Vining?"

"Yes. I suppose she wasted no time in bringing up her pet topic?"

"You mean. . . ?"

"The carrying on of the Valmontez line. Her nephew's wife's failure to produce an heir. Her son's failure to marry and ditto. It's an obsession with her, poor dear. Although she married an Englishman—as did also her sister, Dick's mother—she's passionately Maltese, devotedly Valmontez."

Chloe was remembering her promise, so rashly and unthinkingly given, to help the *contessa*. Help her to do what? Heaven's above, what had she let herself in for?

"Anything wrong, Miss L.?"

"No, no, it's all right. Go on, please."

"I expect you noticed that Dominic wasn't exactly overjoyed at Louise's unsolicited arrival?"

"It did occur to me."

"You wouldn't know about him and Louise?"

"Only guesswork, from observation and what the contessa said. I had never heard of her till we met this morning. Ought I to know about it? Shouldn't you tell me, Mark?"

He opened a massive, carved door and waved her into a book-lined room of impressive size.

"This is the library. And yes, I do think I'd better put you wise. I know the story because the Vinings and my family come from the same bit of Sussex. Near Midhurst—know it?"

"Very well. I was born in Amberley."

"Good Lord! And I never met you."

At the candid regret in his voice and expression she burst out laughing.

"Please—go on about the Vinings."

"Of course Dominic's a lot older than me. Old enough to have been in the last years of the war, actually. He went through some special sort of training, mixed Commando and cloak-and-dagger stuff, you know, and then was parachuted two or three times into enemy-occupied territory. Sooner him than me," concluded Mark with a laugh.

"Did he know Mrs. Carlyon then?"

"No. Met her after the war. His family—the Vining side—wanted him to go into the diplomatic service. But he wasn't having any. He wanted no part in postwar politics. Archaeology was his great love. When he proposed to Louise he told her the sort of life he meant to live—off to the Middle East on digs a lot, tents, discomfort, what have you."

"And she didn't mind?"

"I imagine she was furious—she probably fancied herself as an ambassadress."

"Then why...?" It was a form of torture, hearing about Dominic's early love, but she had to know.

"She probably got engaged to him with her mind made up to give him no peace till he fell into line. He was due to go off to Cyprus right away—a party going there had invited him to join up, and I don't suppose it occurred to him not to accept."

"And then...?"

"Imagine his embarrassment when Louise turned up there, uninvited. A chap who was there told me she created havoc in the team."

Chloe felt she was beginning to understand. She had

thought Dominic utterly unfair, prejudiced, unreasonable.
Perhaps he had had some reason to be, after all.

"She caused unholy chaos in the team. There was a
young couple, newly married, and she started on the husband. When the wife heard what was going on she threatened to start divorce proceedings. Finally Dominic told
Louise plainly to get out, take herself off to Nicosia or
Kyrenia, out of harm's way."

"And she went?"

"And how! She went with his cousin Dick, who *was* in
the diplomatic service and had flown out for a holiday and
to look at the dig. Within a week they were married."

"Oh." So that was how it was.

"Dominic took it badly. I suppose he simply hadn't
believed she could resent his absorption in his work—
especially as he'd warned her. And he was thoroughly
disillusioned, too."

So now he prejudges all women because of Louise,
Chloe thought flatly.

"His mother has never stopped trying, since then, to get
him to marry. He's very eligible—plenty of money on both
English and Maltese sides. And women seem attracted in
spite of his indifference. I expect it acts as a sort of
challenge," Mark explained sagely.

"You don't think he's still in love with Louise?"

Mark shrugged. "Could be, I suppose."

"Where is her husband?"

"In the Antarctic. *He* chucked the diplomatic service to
go exploring, too. Must be in the blood. He hasn't been
lucky. His expedition's been out of touch for about two
years. You heard her say they've more or less been given
up for lost."

"Oh, how terrible. Poor Mrs. Carlyon!"

Mark looked skeptical.

"Some of their friends say he went to the Antarctic to
get as far from her as he could. She's madly extravagant—
and a bit promiscuous, too. I can't help thinking she
doesn't mourn much for his absence. And her turning up
here is mighty odd, don't you think?"

"Mrs. Vining seems very displeased about it."

"She is. She resents Louise on account of Dominic. I'm afraid there'll be trouble sooner or later. All the same, I can't help rather relishing the piquancy of the situation."

Mark spoke with the cheerful gusto that seemed to underlie his attitude to life. Behind the thick lenses his eyes gleamed amusedly. "Anyway, not to worry. And it's had the good effect of making Dominic change his mind about keeping you here. Perhaps he felt he needed a chaperone."

Chloe nodded ruefully. Mark was probably right. If not a chaperone, a sort of buffer. There was nothing in that for her comfort....

Mark began showing her the library.

"Behind there—" pointing to a massive screen placed across an alcove "—are my desk, telephone, typewriter and so on, all for your use if you should need them. And behind that, in the paneling, is quite an efficient little darkroom for you."

He was showing her how the paneling swung open if a certain knot in the carving was pressed when Dominic Vining came in.

Chloe felt her heart swerve. She told herself she'd better get over him. There was no future in loving him....

"I see Mark is showing you the ropes. Is your room all right, Miss Linden?"

"It's quite delightful, thank you. Such a view!"

"Good!" She thought he wore a look of strain she hadn't noticed before. Perhaps he hadn't quite recovered from the shock Louise's arrival must have been to him.

"We'll talk over plans here, this evening. Then tomorrow we'll take you around the dig. Will the darkroom do for you?"

"Perfectly, thanks."

He smiled at her.

"That's good. We'll have tea up on the terrace today— it's warm enough. In a quarter of an hour, Mark will bring you up there." He was thinking, as he talked, what a nice sensible girl Miss Linden seemed to be. She hadn't made a fuss over his high-handed treatment of her. She was quiet, controlled and unprovocative.

Unlike Louise. Louise aimed herself shamelessly at the

male in a man. In his own case she seemed set on waking up desires long since forgotten.

At the thought of her installed at Santa Clara for heaven knew how long, the dark shadow crossed his face again. He turned away and walked quickly out of the library. Chloe watched him go, with love and longing.

Mark took her up to the terrace a few minutes later.

"Here's my pocket compass," he said. "Now steer a course north-fifty-nine east and up four flights. Hope your wind's good."

Chloe's laughter—a sound as spontaneous and pretty as the splash of the fountain in the courtyard—reached Dominic as he followed with Louise.

"Your Miss Linden is a fast worker, Dominic, my dear," Louise commented, acid sweet. "First Robert— now Mark. Better be on your guard, my lamb."

"You never did care much for your own sex, did you?" Dominic observed mildly, and she laughed and shrugged.

She was too shrewd to insist. But she meant to have this girl out of Santa Clara, by hook or by crook, by fair means or foul, before many days had passed. It didn't suit her at all to have her there; though the girl was no fool, it should be easy enough to drive her away. Meantime, better make some sort of a show of amiability; no point in letting Dominic realize what she wanted—yet.

On the terrace, now flooded with hot afternoon sunlight, Lotta had set the tea table beneath a pergola curtained in purple red bougainvillea. Massive silver, delicate china, a rich fruit cake and piles of melting pastries, filled with a creamy cheese mixture.

"They're a Maltese specialty, and really scrumptious," Mark said greedily.

"Please pour out for us, Louise," Dominic said.

"Of course, my pet. Sugar and lots of milk—you didn't suppose I'd forgotten?"

Chloe wondered how she dared. *You don't look very happy, my love,* she thought, looking at Dominic. She suppressed with something like panic the idea that he was fool enough to love Louise still, and might feel it was worth being unhappy to have her there.

Conversation during tea was patchy. Dominic seemed preoccupied. Chloe was struggling with the strange tongue-tied state her electric awareness of him induced in her. Mark was frankly gorging, like a schoolboy at a party. Only Louise, poised and very much at home, chatted with undiminished vivacity.

"My first evening here—what shall we do, darling?" she asked. "Shall we go out somewhere?" Her eyes danced at him over the flame of the lighter he was holding to her cigarette.

He gave her a cool, level look. "Sorry, Louise. For me—and Miss Linden and Mark—the program this evening is work. Miss Linden will only be here for three months. There's a mass of detail to discuss and arrange if she's to get through all I want her to do in that time."

Louise's eyes narrowed. "But it can't be all that important, can it? If it's only to do with this old temple or graveyard or whatever that you've found? I mean, surely your hobby can wait?"

He threw her a look of exasperation.

"I'm afraid it can't."

"Oh, but I insist," Louise said easily. "Actually, I promised the Hallorans we'd join them for dinner. They traveled out with me, perfect pets they are. I simply won't take no for an answer. They'll want to go dancing afterward. And Monty knows of a naughty nightclub in Floriana."

Dominic's eyes were cold. "I should have thought, under the circumstances, Louise...."

She flared up at once.

"You mean Dick, I suppose?"

"I do mean Dick."

"Then let me tell you once and for all that I refuse, absolutely *refuse*, to behave like a mourning widow. Dick chose to leave me and join this idiotic expedition—if he's dead he's only got himself to thank. He was determined to enjoy himself in his own way—he didn't consider me. So now I intend to go on enjoying myself in mine."

"Even so, I'm afraid I must ask you to excuse me this evening." There was ice in both look and voice now.

Louise sprang to her feet. Her eyes flashed dangerously. "Then you won't mind if I make my own plans?"

"No. By all means, go ahead."

His blandness infuriated her. She rose and made as sweeping an exit as her sheath dress and spindle heels allowed.

Chloe avoided meeting anyone's eyes. She put her crumbly cheesecake down on her plate with a feeling that if she tried to eat it she would choke. She hated scenes. They made her feel hot and cold and horribly embarrassed.

There was quite a pause before anyone spoke. Then Dominic asked for a second cup of tea.

"If you'll both come down to the library in half an hour, we can begin planning and get something done before dinner." His voice was taut; as soon as he had emptied his cup he set it down and with a word of apology left the terrace.

"First round to Dominic," Mark said. "But he's shaken. I wish I knew why she's come here. She's dangerous."

"A femme fatale?" Chloe asked skeptically. Was that how Louise saw herself? Or was she merely a spoiled, vain, heartless woman, angry at a man who had once loved her and didn't any longer? Or did he? Passionately Chloe wished she knew.

Dominic was waiting for them in the library, and drew up a chair for Chloe. He had a lot of plans and drawings spread out on the big table.

"I don't know how much Fairfax told you."

"Only a general outline."

"Very well. This is a plan of the dig, as far as we've gone. You see, we've partly uncovered a Stone Age temple or sanctuary, probably the most perfect of a number that have already been opened up on the island. Here, you see...."

He talked brilliantly. He was keen and enthusiastic and completely master of his subject. His voice seemed to lay a spell on Chloe. Time stood still....

IT WAS NEARLY TWO HOURS later when she went upstairs to bathe and change for dinner. The sense of tension and excitement Dominic had roused in her was still tingling in her veins.

When she looked at herself in the mirror she saw that her eyes were very bright, her color high. She gave an uncertain laugh, surprised at herself, not altogether pleased. She promised herself to keep her emotions, in future, under better control.

When she went down to the dining room, she found Mark and Louise already there—Louise in a swirl of billowing, jewel red skirts, with a mink cape swinging from her arm. It looked as if she planned to go out.

"A martini, Mark, my dear. I die for one."

Taking his arm, she drew him away to the table on which glasses and bottles and ice were set out.

Dominic came in a few minutes later and went over to the fireplace where Nibblu, the manservant, was putting on fresh logs. He gave Chloe a smile when she looked up from a miniature she had picked up from a table.

"My English grandmother," he said.

His eyes took in the quiet elegance of her full-skirted, dark silk dress. They lingered for a moment on her shining hair and the long, smooth throat, unadorned with jewelry.

Chloe gently laid the miniature down. "She must have been a lovely girl."

"She was a reigning beauty of her day. Her portrait hangs in the hall."

She longed to hear more about the slender beauty whose gray eyes were so like his own, but he had already left the subject.

"Let me bring you a glass of sherry."

"Please."

He had no sooner brought it than Louise joined them. As usual she took charge of the conversation.

She seemed quite to have forgotten her annoyance with him. At dinner she talked with her usual vivacity, nonstop. She was amusing, malicious, even scandalous about people she and Mark knew, but Chloe had never heard of. Dominic listened politely. Once Mark caught Chloe's eye and gave her his indecorous wink.

When they had had their coffee Louise rose, her skirts swirling alluringly. "How long do you mean to go on toiling, my poor pet?"

"Impossible to say." It was Dominic's voice that had an edge to it now. Chloe saw how Louise's eyes narrowed, how her lips twitched as if with some secret resolve. Her look was wickedly feline. But she waved a careless hand. "Enjoy your homework, my dears," she said mockingly, and left them.

Dominic left the salon after her, to pay his usual after-dinner visit to his mother. He found her in a difficult mood.

"Where is Louise?"

"Off to the Felicia, I fancy, to meet some friends she made on the voyage out."

"A good riddance. And the other girl, Chloe Linden? Do you like her, Dominic?" Searchingly the restless, brilliant eyes studied his face for the answer.

"I think she's going to be very useful, mother."

"Useful! What do I care if she's useful or not? She's young, charming, unusually pretty. Well-bred, too—I made sure about that. Have you got water in your veins? Can't you think of her as a woman?"

"My dear mother, she's come out here to take photographs in the sanctuary," Dominic said patiently. "She's a professional photographer. That's how I prefer—and intend—to think of her."

"Bah! You make me angry. Are you blind? Don't you see why Louise has come here? Can't you understand that now they are on the point of assuming Dick's death, she means to have *you*?"

"She broke off our engagement before. Why should you think she wants me now?"

"Because I'm not a fool. You are famous now as well as rich. I can see just how her mind has worked. She won't rest till she's got you under her spell again. But don't you see? If you were to marry—shall we say this other girl who has so conveniently turned up here, this Chloe Linden—you would be safe forever from Louise."

Whatever effect this suggestion had on him, Dominic's face showed nothing. His mother went on persuasively, "Luckily we Valmontez are not Catholic, so there would be no difficulty there."

"I promise you, dearest, Louise won't stay long," he said gently. "When she sees I've no intention of leaving my work for her, or letting Mark off, either, she'll grow bored with Santa Clara and go away. This isn't her kind of place at all. She'll soon be tired of it. Now, lie down and rest. Good night, mother. Sleep well."

The white head fell back on the pillow. Soon her breathing told him she had fallen into one of her facile catnaps. He watched her for a while, with pity and love and extreme exasperation. Then he quietly left the room.

He was thinking he must try to keep Miss Linden away from her. It would be too awkward for her—and for himself, too—if she found out how his mother's thoughts were running. It might give her ideas, romantic ones, of saving him from the consequences of a past folly.

He didn't want saving—at least not in that way. He wanted no more emotional adventures. He preferred the physical exertions and adventures of the intellect that archaeology provided. He wanted no women in his life.

The shadow darkened his face again as bitter memories swept over him. After the peculiar rigors of his war experience, of time spent living among the enemy in constant fear of discovery or betrayal, he had been ripe, when he met Louise, to let a woman make a fool of him. Only to think of the episode with her humiliated him now. Whereas she seemed determined not to let him forget it. It was going to be unbearable, having her here, deliberately working on him....

He would have to do something to get her to leave Santa Clara. He thought of his mother's suggestion. Fantastic though it was, he didn't altogether reject it. He found himself wondering just how far he could bring himself to go, to get rid of Louise....

CHAPTER FIVE

BEFORE UNDRESSING, CHLOE WENT UP to the terrace again. Though there was no moon, the myriad stars seemed bright and near enough for her to see by, once her eyes were adjusted to their diamond light.

Leaning at the stone balustrade, she looked out over the island. She could see the distant lights of Valetta and the harbors, the landing lights of Luqa and other fainter lights that marked the position of the villages—*casals*, Professor Vining had called them—dotted sparsely over the plain.

She breathed in the warm southern air with delight. How silent and mysterious this place seemed. The clamor of the cathedral bells, harshly announcing the hour of eleven, quite startled her.

She listened till the echoes had died away. Then she strolled across the terrace. It was really a roof garden, with a central balustrade surrounding an open well reaching to ground level—to the courtyard, in fact. It had greenery, pergolas draped in vines and bougainvillea, and many angles and oddly shaped corners.

In one corner she found a kind of lookout. It was a small, high stone platform, railed around with wrought iron and reached by a little curving stone stairway.

When she climbed up to it she found that she could look right over the romantically shaped rooftops, domes and towers of Mdina to Rabat, the big *casal* beyond the ramparts.

There the streets still glittered with lights strung along and across them. A procession of men, chanting and carrying life-size statues, had just emerged into the packed square. Above Mdina's silence she could hear the distant roar of voices and the brassy din of bands. An occasional rocket still sprayed the sky with fire.

"I told you Malta loved its religious festivals, didn't I?" a voice asked beside her. Her heart leaped. For something to say she asked if he ever took part in them. He shook his head.

"Unlike most Maltese families, we Valmontez are Protestant." Dominic moved beside her and went on, "So you've discovered my favorite thinking place?"

She turned her head to find him smiling down at her, melting the resistance she was trying to build up against him.

"I hope it isn't private," she said with a touch of diffidence.

"If it was, I hereby make you free of it."

"Thank you." She stole a glance at him, unseen.

He began pointing out the various *casals* whose lights they could see, and telling her about them.

"They're unlike any village you've ever seen," he said. "They're more like forts, with tall, thick-walled buildings. It's the easiest thing in the world to lose yourself in them. They're a maze of narrow twisting alleys and cul-de-sacs. I recommend you to get Mark or myself to go with you the first time you try to navigate any of them. We wouldn't want you to disappear without a trace."

She laughed and gathered her stole about her shoulders, thinking he probably wanted his aerie to himself.

He thought how young and lovely she looked in the starlight. She didn't, he assured himself, arouse any emotion in him other than pleasure and admiration—but still, he was glad he hadn't sent her back to London."

"Going down? I expect you're very tired."

"A little. The excitement and novelty of everything, perhaps."

As she looked up at him she caught again that flash of warmth and charm that evoked an immediate emotional response from her, in spite of herself.

"Don't let excitement keep you awake," he warned. "We've quite a day before us tomorrow."

"I won't. Good night, Professor Vining."

"Good night."

As she picked her way across the terrace, a sudden blare of car horns shattered the quiet.

Startled, she swung around. She heard Dominic mutter, "Good God, what is it?" Then she saw him move quickly to the balustrade surrounding the well that gave on to the courtyard below.

She went to look, too, frankly curious. She heard loud knocking, shouts of, "Nibblu! Open the gates!"

Nibblu came out a minute or two later, struggling into his coat and yawning, a look of astonishment on his dark round face. When he swung open the big gates, three cars drove in. They decanted a hilarious party of men and women in evening dress.

Louise was among them, in her swirling, jewel red gown.

"Welcome to Santa Clara," her deep voice called. "Open the doors, Nibblu. And in you go to the dining room my pets. Oh, and put out the drinks, Nibblu, and glasses and plenty of ice. And ask Lotta or one of the girls to rustle up some snacks. We're starving."

"*Si, signora.*"

Nibblu sounded unwilling and doubtful, though polite enough.

"We'll turn the stereo on—roll up the carpet and dance when we've had a drinkie or two," Louise went on gaily. "Time this old morgue was wakened up."

There was a lot of loud laughter and noisy ragging. Someone tried to carry Louise across the threshold.

Then suddenly the courtyard was empty. The visitors poured in a mass into the house and the doors clanged shut.

Chloe heard Dominic let out a long breath, as though he had been holding it.

"That's just a taste of what we may expect to happen so long as Louise is with us," he said grimly.

"Will your mother...?"

"Luckily her room is far enough away in the other wing. She wouldn't be likely to hear anything. Your room, too. If you like, I'll show you a way there, so you'll be in no danger of running into any of that mob."

Taking it for granted she didn't want to meet any of

them, he led the way through a small door at the other end of the terrace. They went along several corridors and down short flights of steps. She realized again how enormous Santa Clara must be. She had completely lost all sense of direction by the time he brought her to her own door.

"Will you go down and see them?" she asked curiously.

She saw his jaw tighten. "Not for the world." He looked so horrified at the suggestion that suddenly she found herself laughing helplessly.

He eyed her with disapproval. Then he began to laugh, too—unwillingly, but irresistibly. For a moment or two the pair of them rocked with laughter.

"Nibblu's face," Chloe gasped.

"And mine, I expect."

"Yes, yours, too."

When they had sobered she saw that the tension had gone out of his face.

"Bless you, Chloe," he said. "I'd very nearly lost my sense of humor over that little invasion, I'm afraid. I can see you're going to be good for me. Now, in you go. Good night."

"Good night."

"Sleep well."

He was still smiling as he closed the door on her. As she undressed she said to herself. *It's no use, I adore him, I can't help myself. It's absurd. He's ten years older than me. He isn't my type at all. He isn't even attracted by me. So why?*

But the heart, she knew, has its reasons that reason knows nothing of.

She lay listening for a while. But no sound of whatever bright fun was going on downstairs reached her. Soon she was fast asleep.

WHEN LOTTA CAME IN with the early tea next morning Chloe saw that she was bursting with talk.

"I hope the *signorina* wasn't disturbed," she began excitedly. "The *signora* brought a big party of guests here, late."

"Yes, I know. I was up on the terrace. I saw them arrive."

"And heard them? *Dio mio*, what a noise! Car horns, shouts. Nibblu must get up and dress to open the gates. I must get up to prepare food. Nibblu must fetch drinks, ice cubes. They turned the dining room into a dance hall. They rolled up the carpet, and there are rings, *signorina*, on the beautiful polish of the furniture, where they put down their glasses and spilled the drinks. When I tell the contessa, what will she say? I'm afraid to tell her."

She was rattling around the room noisily, dropping things in her agitation.

"Then don't tell her," Chloe advised sensibly. "You and Nibblu and the others can soon put everything right. No need to upset your mistress."

Lotta looked sulky. "No—but if it happens again, and again, *signorina*?" she argued. "We must have our sleep. We have never had things like this happen at Santa Clara before."

Chloe sipped her tea. "Oh, well, don't worry, Lotta. I expect your master will see that it doesn't happen too often."

"Indeed I hope so, *signorina*."

Lotta's broad back looked uncompromising as she finished setting things to rights and left the room.

Chloe watched her go with a little grin. Poor old thing, she was probably going to find that a lot of things were different, once Louise got into her stride.

For herself, Chloe had made up her mind to try to avoid crossing Louise. Live and let live. She hoped Louise, for her part, would take the same line.

After she had finished her tea and showered, she stepped out onto the little balcony, to sniff the crystalline air and delight once again in the view.

It was then that she noticed how eaten by rust, how fragile, was the iron railing around the balcony. Touching it, she felt the metal quiver. She peered over it, then drew back with a little shudder. She had never had much of a head for heights, and it looked a long, long drop to the rocks and cultivated terraces below. But no premonition troubled her. She simply thought, as she went back to her room, *I must remember not to lean against the railing*.

She dressed in slacks and shirt and threw a light cardigan over her shoulders, for this was going to be a working day.

When she went downstairs she found Dominic and Mark already at breakfast.

There was fresh crusty bread, smelling deliciously, on the table. There were big yellow cups for coffee, honey in the comb, a jugful of roses adding their fragrance to that of the bread and coffee. She remembered reading somewhere that some famous person—Cicero, she thought—had called Malta "land of roses and honey."

Dominic was reading the *Times of Malta*, but he put it down and got to his feet punctiliously. Mark jumped up to pour her some coffee and hot milk.

They ate and talked in desultory fashion. Nobody mentioned Louise's party. They spoke mainly about the dig.

Nibblu came in after a while, to deliver a message. "The *signora* says please to wait for her, sir, she wishes to go out with you this morning. She has had breakfast in her room. Now she is getting ready."

"Message ends," grinned Mark. "So now what?"

"So we take her with us, as requested. We show her over the dig, every inch of it. We trust that once will be enough."

Dominic's voice was grim. He was angry with Louise, but he wasn't going to play into her hands by losing his temper. He knew her, had her measure. He mustn't let her get under his skin.

Louise showed no outward sign of her late night. As she came in she exclaimed dramatically, "Lord, what a father and mother of a hangover!" But she looked, in fact, as fresh as if she'd gone to bed at nine o'clock.

"Give me some coffee, Mark, my dear," she added. "Black, and hot, and strong. It's the only thing that does any good."

Gravely Mark handed her the coffee. Louise took it and piled sugar into it. She seemed to be waiting expectantly for adverse comments. She was a little on the defensive, perhaps expecting open criticism from Dominic. His bland politeness seemed to take the wind out of her sails. She eyed him warily. Then she laid herself out to be intelligent about what she was going to see at the dig. Chloe's fears of a ruined morning began to die away. *Louise is no fool,* she thought, unaware that already Louise had paid her the same compliment.

When she had finished breakfast, Chloe excused herself and went off to get her photographic paraphernalia, which she had left all ready in the library the night before.

Films, filters, exposure meters, cameras, tripods, flashlight apparatus, notebooks—she checked them over again, then carried them out to the car. Nibblu helped her stow them in the trunk.

"You must take a picture of Dominic and Mark and me when we get to the dig, Miss Linden," Louise said graciously. "We'll send it to the *Prattler*."

"Good Lord, no," Dominic protested. "We certainly won't."

"Oh, but I insist. *'Famous archaeologist Professor Dominic Vining, with his cousin Louise Carlyon, and friend, alongside his latest Stone Age discovery.'* It'll be marvelous publicity for you, darling."

Dominic said nothing, even more eloquently than yesterday when they were entering Mdina's splendid silence.

Chloe didn't have to look at Mark to know he was grinning delightedly again. She fancied he would be particularly enthralled by Louise's "*and friend.*"

AT THE DIG, feverish work was in progress. A gang of men was burrowing into a long, tunnel-like passage leading downhill. The members of Dominic's team were supervising or sorting piles of pottery, ornaments, bones, statues of grotesquely fat males and females, or making notes and sketches.

Dominic made quick work of introducing them. Toby French, plump, bald and enthusiastic. Hugh Warren, a lean and canny Scot. Dr. du Plessis, a South African with a strong Afrikaner accent and a tough look to him. Harry Lemon, a friend from Mark's Oxford days. Walter Fiennes, the oldest member of the team, and the only married man among them.

Dominic didn't give Louise time to go into action. He hustled his party without delay into the sanctuary. For Stone Age families it had been first a place of worship of their pagan gods and then a place of burial, he told them.

Chloe looked around her with keen professional interest. She began assessing the problems involved in underground color photography. She started mentally planning her work, the scope of which Dominic had already explained. She saw that it was going to be very novel and exciting.

They passed through a semicircular forecourt into a large chamber, elliptical in shape. This was divided by a central passage from a similar chamber.

The passage led into other chambers. Dominic named them. The shrine of the presiding deity. The altar room for animal sacrifices. The place of the oracle....

They stared in wonder at the vast blocks of stone that had been used in their construction—colossal slabs, tooled as precisely as dominoes, precisely fitted together.

"And by people who didn't know the use of metal tools," Dominic said.

"Fantastic. And what's that booming, menacing noise—like a ghostly voice—all around us?" Louise wanted to know.

"Actually, it's *my* voice. The acoustics of this place are very strange indeed. In some way the male voice—though not the female—is magnified. The oracle *had* to sound superhuman, you see."

He halted at a flight of wide, shallow steps leading down into a lower set of chambers. A chalked notice said Danger—No Entry.

"Down there are the chambers where they kept their treasure," he said. "Now watch this."

He knelt down on one of the upper steps and pressed down heavily on one of those below him. At once it canted and rose smoothly on end.

"That's a trick step. It was meant to send intruders to their death."

They leaned over to peer at the wide hole, with blackness beneath it, that the raising of the step had revealed. "What a horrible idea," Chloe exclaimed.

But Louise thought it fascinating. "Show me how it works, Dominic." He explained that it was done by counterweights, and she watched him press it back into place. "Fascinating," she said again.

They emerged at length, by way of a sloping stone ramp on a rocky terrace, fragrant with wild thyme, starred with tiny flowers. The main courtyard of the sanctuary was behind them. Opposite, the tiny island of Filfla rested lightly in the purple blue sea. Below, the gentle swell washed on the ledges of apricot cream rock.

"The cliffs down there are honeycombed with caves. Perhaps when we get to exploring them, we may come across what they've found elsewhere—the skeletons of great pachyderms, bears—extinct species. Humans, too."

"But surely pachyderms and bears never lived on Malta?" That was Chloe.

"No, they came from Africa. Once this group of islands was joined to it, you see. The great beasts came to Malta for fresh water, we suppose. It's...."

"Oh, God, must we go into all that?" Louise broke in rudely. She couldn't bear not to be the center of attention. And she was bored. "Can't Miss Linden take our pictures now, for heaven's sake?"

Chloe looked at Dominic for guidance. He took Louise by the arm.

"Sorry, my dear. No time for that now. Another day, perhaps."

"But I...."

"Now—" briskly "—where would you like to go from here? Mark will drive you."

"I insist...."

"He'll bring the car back here for us, so you can feel free to do exactly as you like. We three won't be back for lunch or tea. So enjoy yourself. Telephone Santa Clara whenever you want to go back, and Nibblu will send a car for you. So long."

His manner had such firmness that even Louise didn't

try to argue. In fact she was seated in the car with Mark, and on the move away from the dig, before she had recovered from her astonishment and sense of outrage.

Dominic looked at Chloe. He grinned in boyish triumph.

"And now, C. Linden—to work," he said briskly.

Chloe collected her impedimenta and followed him into the sanctuary. No doubt his new attitude to her meant nothing but that he was delighted to be rid of Louise. But her inner glow of happiness made nonsense of this cautious appraisal. She was convinced he liked her. It was a beginning... .

MARK, DRIVING LOUISE to her Mecca, the Felicia, wasn't nearly so happy. They hadn't gone far before she laid a long, slim hand, scarlet-nailed, on his arm. "Mark, sweetie."

He shot her a sideways glance of suspicion, which she met with a dazzling smile.

"Listen, pet. Will you do a little thing for Louise?"

"Depends what it is."

She held out a paper, but they were driving through a *casal*, and he couldn't spare a glance.

"What's that?"

"My account from the hotel, pet."

"Very interesting."

"They let me go without settling it when I gave Dominic's name."

"Oh. They did, did they? Courteous of them."

"Fix it for me, will you, sweetie? And explain to Dominic."

Mark frowned.

"Explain what?"

"The situation. Financial. Tell him that of course I instructed my bank, before I left England, to transfer my account to their branch in Valetta. But the idiots have let me down. Nothing has arrived. Not a sou."

"Very odd. Perhaps I'd better send them a telegram and find out what went wrong?"

"Oh, no, darling, don't do that. I've written myself by airmail," Louise said hastily. "I'm furious with them."

"But didn't you bring travelers' checks?" Mark persisted. He felt there was something very fishy about Louise's story. Banks didn't let one down. More likely she'd cleaned out her account and there was nothing to transfer.

"Of course. Only the bridge and poker stakes on board got pretty high, and my luck was out. To tell you the truth, I'm broke. You might persuade Dominic to stake me till my money arrives, pet."

"How much?"

She flicked her extravagant lashes at him, but he was looking at the road ahead.

"Shall we say two hundred fifty, poppet?"

"I'll mention it to Dominic," Mark said austerely. Poppet, indeed! And two hundred fifty—just like that. *She's got a nerve,* he thought with strong disapproval.

"My dear, don't you think it's a very good thing I came out when I did?" She was ready to change the subject now she had made her point. "This girl, I mean."

"You mean Miss Linden?"

"Who else?"

"What about her?"

"Of course she's wangled this job deliberately. Hoping to catch him, wouldn't you think? The eligible Professor Vining. That story about having taken some boyfriend's place is too transparent, isn't it? I wormed it out of Dominic—couldn't imagine he'd willingly have engaged a female to work for him. He must have been furious."

"If he was, he isn't any longer. He realizes she knows her job. I bet her work is first-class," Mark said with emphasis.

"Really?" She wasn't interested in Chloe's ability. "Would you call her attractive?"

"Extremely. Who wouldn't?"

"Including Dominic?" Louise's voice was sharp.

"Surely. He's a man."

The blue green eyes flashed.

"Has he told you his opinion of her?"

But Mark had had enough.

"Hadn't you better ask him yourself?" he snapped.

Louise's eyes narrowed, but she laughed and laid a placating hand on his arm.

"There, ducky, don't be cross. I hadn't realized you'd fallen so hard for her. Well, go ahead and have fun, pet."

"Thank you very much," Mark said savagely. "And here we are at the Felicia. If you'll excuse me, I'll go and fix up this unpaid bill of yours."

"Bless you, honey. And later on, when you've opened that account for me at the bank—Dominic won't mind, you know, you can tell him I told you to do it—you may come back and I'll buy you a nice cold martini."

But Mark had gone.

Louise smiled maliciously as she crossed the foyer and made her way out to the courtyard with the tables and umbrellas.

A puppy, she thought, *but he'll soon come to heel. And he'll be useful for heading Dominic off this Chloe Linden....*

CHLOE WAS DOG TIRED when they returned to Santa Clara that evening.

She had had a fascinating day, but the work had been difficult and at times strenuous. She had had no conception, till she began to scramble around them, of the immense scope of the excavations.

She had spent the morning taking notes. Then she had shared a picnic lunch with the team. They had been friendly but casual, treating her as a working unit, like themselves. That had pleased her a lot. She hoped Dominic had noticed. She was still smarting a little from his earlier strictures.

During the day she had watched him at work and thought him an ideal leader. He was tactful with the team, kind but firm with the labor. He was familiar with every inch of ground, every detail of the work. She could see how both team and labor admired and liked him.

She recalled moments when he had helped her over a rough and dangerous place, or laughed with her at something amusing, or made helpful, knowledgable suggestions when she struck some snag.

It'll be enough just to work with him. It'll be all I want, she thought. She didn't let herself wonder if it would always be enough....

As she passed the door—ajar as usual—of Mrs. Vining's room on her way to her own, the old lady's harsh, imperious voice called out, "Is that you, Chloe Linden? Come in and talk to me for a little while."

Chloe sighed. She longed for a hot soak, to rid herself of the day's dust and sweat, a rest on her bed, fresh makeup, clean clothes.

Reluctantly she walked into the vast, dim bedroom, and summoned a smile.

"Good evening, *contessa.* How are you today?"

"No better, no worse, my dear. Don't let us talk about my wretched health. It's a boring topic, anyway. Tell me about yourself. You spent the day with my son?"

"At the dig. Yes."

"Did you enjoy it?" The restless, brilliant eyes were fixed on her with that avid, disconcerting stare. With an effort Chloe went on smiling.

"It was terribly interesting," she said.

"Hmph. *Interesting!* But was it exciting, being with Dominic? My son is handsome, cultured, attractive, surely. Did you enjoy his company? His conversation? Were you happy together?"

For the first time doubt of Mrs. Vining's sanity entered Chloe's mind. Surely a sane person wouldn't talk in this extraordinary manner?

"We were working. Any conversation was about our work—there was no time..." she stammered.

"I asked if you were happy." The strong fingers were gripping her wrist now, hurting her.

"I enjoyed every minute of it," she said with desperate honesty. "It was all new to me, you see. The temple is wonderful, incredible. I'd never imagined....And Professor Vining knows so much—he makes the past live...."

Chloe could see that wasn't at all what the *contessa* wanted to hear from her. Now she had turned sulky. She snapped, "Please don't bore me by talking of my son's work. It is his heart with which I am concerned. Does he seem to like you? Do you think he finds you attractive? Does he seem pleased in your company? Did he. . . ?"

Chloe felt she could stand no more. "Will you please excuse me now, *contessa*?" she broke in. "It was kind of you to talk to me. But I must go now to bath and change. It's very hot and dusty on the dig, you know. And it's been a long day."

"Oh, very well, very well. In a moment you shall go. But you must come and see me often. I want to be kept informed how things are going, you understand."

Her grip tightened on Chloe's wrist. "*Do* you understand?"

Chloe was afraid she understood only too well. She could only hope Mrs. Vining hadn't made her wishes plain to Dominic. She loved him, but she didn't fancy being flung at him in this wholesale fashion.

"I saw *her* today," the old lady went on. "Louise. She dared to come and visit me here, without an invitation. I told her just what I thought of her, coming here, forcing her unwanted company on us."

With a harsh chuckle she went on, "I made it plain I knew why she had come—because she wants Dominic— means to have him. But I sent her away angry. I told her Dominic was hardly likely to look at her, with a young and beautiful girl like yourself here, ready to fall into his arms—"

"*Contessa!*" Chloe tore her wrist free. Her face flamed.

The old lady cackled shamelessly; her dark eyes seemed to snap with delight as she remembered Louise's fury and discomfiture.

"No good your looking shocked, my dear. I like you. I think you would do very well for Dominic. In fact, I'm going to see you married to him—and the sooner the better. I'll make sure he's safe from her, and that there'll be sons to carry on the family name. I'll do it if it's the last thing I do before I die," she finished, with the arrogance inherited from a long line of noble ancestors. She didn't ask whether Chloe wanted to marry her son. She didn't consider Chloe at all, except as an agreeable vehicle for her plans. . . .

Chloe sought for words to express her feelings but

before she could get a single one out, footsteps approached the door, halted. The door opened.

Her color rose again, uncontrollably, as Dominic came into the room. Her heart began to race, her breath to come faster. Nothing in her previous experience had prepared her for these disconcerting physiological discomforts of love.

Dominic bent to kiss his mother's cheek.

"Well, mother—what is this last thing you are going to do before you die?" he asked fondly, with a quick smile—a sort of plea for understanding and tolerance—at Chloe.

But Chloe didn't dare wait to hear his mother's reply. She smiled back at him, fleetingly, and almost ran from the room.

CHAPTER SIX

THE DAYS BEGAN TO SLIP BY in a smooth routine.

Chloe rose early—though not as early as Dominic and Mark, who often breakfasted at the dig. After her own breakfast of coffee, crusty rolls, honey and fruits she followed then in the small Austin Dominic had offered for her use.

It was delightful, driving across the country in the early morning. The Judas trees, pyramids of purple bloom, were in flower along the roadsides. The fields were turning green with the young crops. The warm southern air caressed her skin. She had a sense of extreme well-being.

She soon learned her way through the *casals* along the road to the dig. The people in them got to know her and her little car, and would wave as she passed. Children ran alongside as she navigated cautiously, watching out for the cats, mongrel dogs and toddlers littering the narrow alleys. They offered her bright flowers that had wilted in their hot little hands. "*Sahha*—goodbye," they called as she left the *casal*.

At the dig she worked steadily—and usually alone. She wondered, with wry amusement, if she had to thank Dominic for that. No fraternizing, she thought.

"We never see you," Toby French complained.

"Just as well, I'm awfully forbidding when I'm working," she told him with a laugh.

"So long as you don't forbid *me*...."

She laughed again, but he could see she didn't mean to waste time on him. He sighed gustily. It was a tragedy to be bald and plump and have the soul of a romantic where a pretty girl was concerned....

Chloe was taking black-and-white pictures, as well as color transparencies, of the selected subjects.

She developed these herself, later in the day, in the little darkroom behind the paneling in the library. The color films went to London by airmail for processing, and would be flown back at once for Dominic's approval.

At night, after dinner, she would set up her portable screen and small projector in the library, ready to show her pictures if Dominic wanted to study them. Sometimes he would ask her to show them a second, even a third time.

He was generous with praise when he was pleased, but impatient, even scathing when something didn't come up to standard. She soon made the discovery that in his work he was a perfectionist. It made him an exacting taskmaster, but she didn't mind that. Her pride in her work was stimulated. It was worthwhile enduring a few harsh criticisms to hear his sudden warm, "That's first-class, Chloe. Exactly what I had in mind." Especially when it was said with the smile that never failed to set her pulses racing.

Of Louise, since that first day, she had seen surprisingly little.

"The *signora* sleeps late—often till nearly noon," Lotta told her with sulky disapproval. "She stays out very late, too. Often till two or three o'clock. Nibblu must wake up and go out to open the gates."

Already, it seemed, Louise's days were a succession of dates and social occasions. Chloe wondered if Robert had rallied around as he had been bidden, and seen to it that Louise was "in with the Navy."

She soon learned that Saturday was a half-holiday at the dig. Work on the excavations stopped promptly at noon and the laborers streamed off, laughing and shouting, to the nearest *casal* to buy cheap rough wine, to slake their dust-dry throats.

Chloe drove fast to Mdina and had time to bathe and change into a cool, fresh apple-green cotton sun dress, before the lunch gong sounded through the echoing corridors of Santa Clara.

When she came down to the salon she found Louise—lean and elegant as a greyhound in pale, beautifully cut linen—and Dominic.

Dominic, whom Chloe had grown used to seeing in his

khaki drill working clothes, was completely unfamiliar in white trousers, riding boots and polo shirt.

"There's to be a second match between an island team and the losers of the cup," he explained, seeing her look of surprise.

"You're playing for the island?"

"Yes. I've done so before at odd times when I've been here—I'm half an islander, after all. They called to say they're short one man—fellow broke his wrist in a practice game. And as we'd promised to be there anyway...." He finished with a shrug.

"Of course, Miss Linden would be thrilled to see you play. A pity work won't allow her to be there," Louise put in in her acid-sweet way.

"Nonsense, of course she's going to be there, if she wants to," Dominic said shortly. But when his eyes met Chloe's she caught the gleam of humor in them, and she wondered if he was remembering how he had snubbed her about Robert's invitation—as she was remembering.

"I can't think of anything I'd enjoy more than watching a game of polo," she said demurely.

"Then we'll all go together. Mark can drive us."

Louise looked furious for a moment, then decided to be pleasant.

"That'll be fun," she said, and actually smiled at Chloe.

"Robert just called," said Mark, joining them. "He says there's to be a sundowner dance at the club after the polo. He suggests we all stay on for it, and dine with him afterward. Shall I accept, Dominic?"

Dominic shot an oddly speculative look at Chloe, but her composed expression told him nothing. Before he could speak Louise linked her hands possessively around his arm and answered for him.

"But of course, we'll accept. Blessed Robert, give him my love, Mark. It's years since you and I danced together, isn't it, Dominic?"

"Years," he said dryly. "And I fear it'll be years more before we do again. I don't dance nowadays. But you stay on, of course, if you care to. Mark, too, then he can drive you back. We'd better, in that case, take two cars."

Louise had opened her sea-colored eyes very wide.

"But, darling, you don't mean to say you won't stay and—well, drink or gossip or whatever you like to do after polo—and then have dinner with us? Isn't that rather unkind of you, darling?"

Dominic gave her a level look. "Is it? I don't think so. We'll stay on for a little, if it'll please you. But I have a lot of work to do after dinner. And so, I'm afraid, has Miss Linden. You *have* got those new slides ready to show me tonight, haven't you?" he added, turning to Chloe.

"Yes. I got them ready this morning before I left for the dig."

Louise looked daggers at her. Suspicion, and a dawning jealousy, flamed in her eyes. She dropped Dominic's arm and lifted her slim shoulders in an exaggerated shrug. Finishing her martini, she went over to pour herself another.

As she passed Chloe she gave her a look of frightening malice. "Such a devoted little slave, aren't you?" she said in a savage whisper.

Fortunately the mellow booming of the lunch gong diverted her attention. Chloe sighed her relief. She had been going through her usual sensations of hot and cold, acute discomfort. She hated all this emotionalism. What had she said or done to arouse such dislike in Louise?

However, when she had finished her third martini Louise seemed to decide to be more agreeable. At the lunch table she talked gaily of the match and the dance to follow. She ate greedily—it was her boast that she could eat like a horse and never put on an ounce. Today there was ravioli—she adored it—and fish grilled with fennel— "Utterly divine, your cook is a marvel, Dominic, my dear, and I love this local wine. . . ."

Chloe, still determined not to cross Louise or let anything she said or did upset her, tried to ignore her feelings of uneasiness and resentment. After all, what did it really matter if Louise didn't like her?

When Louise went upstairs to gather hat, gloves and handbag, she followed, but far enough behind to avoid having to talk to her. In her room, she waited till she heard the stilt heels go tap-tap along the marble corridor. A minute or two later, looking young and lettuce-crisp in her pale green dress and shady hat, she went down herself.

THE MARSA WAS A BIG, FLAT AREA given over to polo ground, racecourse, cricket field, tennis courts and the clubhouse, set in its pleasant, verdant gardens and lawns.

Here, on Saturday afternoons, island society gathered to play or watch games, flirt, see and be seen.

Here, today, the sun struck down hotly from a sky of limpid blue onto the stand facing the polo ground. This was already well filled. In front of it, behind the pink geraniums and white rails of the enclosure, a cluster of rapturous young things—alike in shining hair, painstaking suntan, and anonymous sunglasses—cheered on their favorite players and chattered like starlings.

A smell of dust and hot horses mingled with the enticing almond scent of the flowering oleanders, white and rose pink, that lined the drive.

A chukker was in progress as Chloe and Mark followed the other two to the stand.

Somewhere overhead a brisk military voice, rather badly tuned, explained over a loudspeaker the moves of the game. Robert, riding a showy chestnut pony, raced down the field and scored for his side just as they reached the gate. Chloe felt a stirring of excitement—she loved the game.

As the great hindquarters of the ponies heaved up and hurtled past them the young things at the rail applauded deliriously, squealing with delight. When the chukker ended and their heroes rode godlike off the field, the sunglasses came off. The bright eyes were alert to make contact, to register for future dates.

"Heavens, aren't they sweet? How old they make one feel," Chloe whispered.

"Me, too. In the sere and yellow." Mark critically scanned the blue and pink, green, yellow and lavender dresses, the smooth tanned arms and legs, the glossy heads of blond and dark, red and brown hair, and felt elated to be escorting a girl who, in his considered opinion, knocked spots off the lot of them.

He found a couple of vacant places in the stands and they sat down. In a moment the air was full again of the rousing thud of hoofbeats, the crisp smack of stick on ball, the snorting of horses, the shouts, seldom polite, of player to player.

In the interval Chloe found time to look around her. Dominic was nowhere in sight. Louise, at the other end of the stand, was holding court. A tall man in the uniform of the French Navy was bending to kiss her hand with a Gallic flourish. Three younger men hung on her words.

"The Frenchman is one of the top naval brass in NATO," Mark whispered, seeing the direction of her glance. "And the blond chap is an aide-de-camp, who arranges all the palace entertaining. A useful chap to know. So's the dark chap, the flag lieutenant. Louise sure knows how to pick them."

"Miaow!"

"I love being catty. Look, here comes, Robert."

He was trying to join them, but Louise put out her left hand and stopped him.

"You were marvelous, darling. Utterly devastating."

Robert preened himself a little. He had in fact scored twice and was no more averse to a little flattery than the rest of his sex. But his eyes strayed over to where Chloe sat with Mark. What he really wanted was to go along and hear *her* say how marvelous he had been.

Louise may have seen; at any rate she forestalled him.

"Sit down here next to me, my pet. You shall do a running commentary on the next chukker for us. We can't hear a word the announcer says."

Robert glanced ruefully at Chloe, who wasn't, however, looking his way, and with as good a grace as he could muster he sat down next to Louise.

Chloe had just caught sight of Dominic, coming toward her in a purposeful manner. She went through the usual disconcerting moments of heart-swerve, quickened breathing, deepening color. She hoped he wouldn't notice.

"Enjoying it, Chloe?"

"Enormously, thanks." She had herself in hand now.

"Understand the game?"

"Yes—I used to go quite often in the summer to Cowdray to watch them play. I was born not so far away, you know."

"Were you, indeed? I'm a Sussex man myself on my English side."

"I know. Mark told me."

There was a sudden bright ripple of excited laughter from the rails as the teams rode out.

"I see 'the Fishing Fleet' is here in force today," Dominic said, adding dryly, "I'm told polo's a great breeder of romance here."

"Is it?" Chloe answered coolly.

"You wouldn't know?" He sounded amused. "Not interested in the prospects of romance and marriage, Chloe?"

"Are you?" she countered, trying to seem as casual as he was—for how, she asked herself, could she have let herself care so desperately, with so very little encouragement?

"'He that hath wife and children hath given hostages to fortune; for they are impediments to great enterprises, either of virtue or mischief,'" he quoted lightly. "Bacon, in case you didn't know. I must say I couldn't agree more. Look, I'll have to be off. Must get over to the saddling lines. Wish me luck."

"The best. Make sure you score."

He walked off with his long, easy stride and she sat there thinking with mortification of what he had just said.

She had an uneasy feeling that somehow she had given herself away to him. Was he perfectly well aware how strongly he attracted her? And was this his way, oblique but perhaps meant to be kind, of warning her off?

The thought hurt her pride, but then she comforted herself—Dominic wasn't the kind of man to go around thinking women were in love with him, or noticing if they were.

Despite her resolve to try to get over him, when the players rode out for the next match it was for his tall, slim figure that she looked. She saw him move onto the field on a gray, riding easily and well—as he seemed to do most things.

When the umpire threw in the ball and play began she

watched him with such passionate intentness that it was as if her own body was rushing down the field with his. She caught her breath at each crisis in the game; her heart thudded in time with the thudding hoofbeats.

She saw him score brilliantly. When the crowd shouted bravo she shouted too. She was completely carried away. When the chukker ended she found she was shaking all over with the thrill of it.

After the game was over he joined her again and she was suffused with a warm glow of pride and happiness. But she kept it light and casual.

"Well done! You play rather well for an eminent archaeologist—don't you?"

"So-so. I'm a bit out of practice these days," he answered matter-of-factly. His handicap was three, and he had never had any use for false modesty. "Glad you enjoyed it."

"I loved every minute of it."

"Good. Well, let's go and..." he was beginning. But Louise was standing up, beckoning him imperiously. He muttered something unprintable under his breath. He had been feeling grand after the hard exercise and the thrill of victory. Now his face set in taut lines. He didn't want to talk to Louise—but he couldn't snub her publicly. With a sigh he got to his feet.

"Excuse me, Chloe," he said shortly. "Mark will take you to the club and give you tea. I'll see you there later on."

And, later on, when the polo was over and people began heading for the club, Chloe strolled with Mark into the club grounds.

Tennis games were in progress, and through some big trees to the left she glimpsed white-flanneled figures pursuing a cricket ball. In the gardens members ambled around the lawns or sat at small tables, set among the sweetly scented roses, oleanders and frangipani.

"Except for the vegetation, it's really a very English scene, Mark," she exclaimed.

"Comes of our national talent for making any foreign place we occupy 'forever England,'" grinned Mark. "It's what makes other races dislike us so much."

"Do they?"

"Of course, didn't you know?"

She didn't reply. She was watching the approach of Louise and her entourage. Robert was one of them. He lingered behind to whisper urgently to Chloe, "I say, the first dance, please, may I? And see you for tea?"

"Of course."

"Angel," he murmured, and hurried away.

Later in the clubhouse, there were introductions, new faces, lighthearted laughter, happy snatches of talk about nothing in particular. Then tea and buttered toast in a room hung with naval insignia, regimental crests and the flags of visiting yachts, and as full of a nautical atmosphere as was the club in Valetta.

Dominic didn't join them. Later on, when she and Mark were strolling in the gardens again, Chloe saw him talking with an older man. Suddenly he threw back his head and laughed at something his companion had said. Lit that way with amusement, his serious, dark face looked heartbreakingly attractive. She wished she knew how to make him laugh like that.

As soon as the music began for dancing Robert came to claim her. He wanted to get her on the floor before it filled up. He was an expert performer and anxious for her to know it.

He was out for conquest. He had fallen for Chloe in his headlong, facile way—though not with any serious intention, for he considered that a naval career was best pursued without the encumbrance of a wife. He hoped to make the most of the short time left before his ship departed from Malta on exercises—if only Chloe would be cooperative. . . .

Chloe recognized his type, but didn't hold it against him. He was amusing and charming and good to look at, and she enjoyed dancing with him, even though he did hold her rather too close and would have pressed his cheek against her forehead in the American way if she hadn't drawn back and shaken her head at him.

"You dance perfectly. Give me all the rest of the dances," he begged.

"I promised Mark."

"Oh, Mark. He won't mind."

But Mark was waiting to claim her. She slipped out of Robert's arms and into his.

"The next—promise," Robert urged, scowling at his brother in a manner so pregnant with meaning that Mark grinned delightedly.

She had hoped that Dominic might at least sit out a dance with her, but he didn't appear. So she danced with Robert again, and when the music stopped, let him lead her outside onto the veranda.

The swift darkness had fallen by now, and Robert was quick to spot a shadowy corner with a couple of chairs discreetly placed.

"A drink, Chloe? Long, cold one?"

"Please."

He called a passing waiter and gave an order.

"Quickly, before some other fellow butts in," he said. "When may I see you again? Tomorrow?"

"You forget what I told you—I'm a working girl."

"But Sunday—surely your Sundays are free? Vining isn't a slave driver, is he? Let me show you the island. I can borrow a car. We can have lunch somewhere along the coast—I know some good places. A pity it's hardly warm enough for bathing yet—we might have gone snorkeling— and there's marvelous underwater fishing here, too—ever done any?"

"Years ago, when daddy was posted in the West Indies."

"Oh, good. Then later, when we come back from exercises...."

"If I'm still here."

"You've got to be. Anyway, we can picnic tomorrow. And you'd like to come aboard and look over the carrier, wouldn't you?"

He's like a nice child offering me all his toys at once, she thought maternally, and laughed outright.

"Stop, stop," she cried. "I haven't even said I'll come out yet. Truly, I don't know if I can. You remember what Professor Vining said about social engagements. I'm...."

"Don't laugh at me, Chloe, darling. And don't hedge."

He caught her hand and leaned closer. With his lips almost brushing her hair he said plaintively, "Time's awfully short. We'll be off on the spring cruise in no time. I want to spend every spare minute with you."

Still laughing, though gently, she turned her head away from his lips—and felt the gooseflesh run along her arms. For Dominic had come around the corner, and was watching with a look of mocking irony that she found hard to bear.

She could imagine him telling himself how right he had been, at their first meeting on the plane, to say he didn't want her on the dig, stirring up emotional trouble, as he called it, among the team. Here she was, before his eyes and within days, involved in a flirtation. . . .

Robert had jumped to his feet in slight confusion. But he was not unaccustomed to such situations, and quickly recovered himself.

"Oh, hello, sir. Were you looking for someone?"

"For Miss Linden. It's time we were getting back to Santa Clara."

"Oh, but surely you're not thinking of going yet," Robert protested in a voice of doom. "I thought—can't I persuade you to stay and dine with me here?"

"I'm afraid that isn't possible. I believe my cousin and Mark intend to stay on. But Miss Linden and I have a lot of work to get through after dinner."

The steward arrived just then with the drinks Robert had ordered.

"Care for anything, sir?" Robert suggested, playing for time.

"No, thanks."

Chloe picked up her drink and began to swallow quickly. She hoped it wouldn't give her hiccups. She felt acutely uncomfortable, though Dominic's expression when she nerved herself to meet his eyes, was inscrutable now.

She set down her glass and turned to Robert.

"Thanks so much for inviting me. I've enjoyed every minute."

He said eagerly, "But we haven't settled about tomorrow."

She looked at Dominic for guidance, but it seemed he had no intention of helping her out.

"I'm not sure if I'll be free," she said in a tentative way. "Look, call me around ten o'clock, won't you? I'll know by then whether I'm wanted or not, I expect."

Robert brightened at once. "I'll call you after Sunday exercises," he said buoyantly. "Terribly sorry you can't stay on now. See you, Chloe. Good night, sir."

She went and got her hat and gloves, and walked sedately with Dominic to the car under the stars. They were big and bright and seemed very near. The scent of the oleanders and ghost white moonflowers along the drive was overpoweringly sweet.

"Jump in," Dominic said when they came to the car. "I'm sorry I had to tear you away. But you do realize, don't you, that three months is just barely sufficient for all the work there is to be done?"

"I quite understand, Professor Vining."

"Is that formal mode of address meant to imply that you think me a slave driver?"

She said warmly, "Of course not. Naturally my time is entirely at your disposal."

"Sundays, too?"

"If you wish."

She fancied she detected that mocking irony in his expression again. But he drove in silence for a mile or two. Then he said, "I did have an idea that tomorrow I would take you along to look over one or two of the other sanctuaries. Zammit excavated them, you know. I thought we'd see Hagar Qim and Mnajdra. And possibly, if we had time, the Cave of Darkness, Ghar Dalam."

She caught her breath. Was he deliberately punishing her?

"But I'd *like* to do that," she protested. "It sounds terribly interesting."

"Rather a busman's holiday. You really ought to have your Sundays off, I suppose. And I wouldn't want to interfere with your dates with Robert."

Was he—could he possibly be—showing the faintest bit

of jealousy? Exhilarating as the thought was, Chloe rejected it.

"You wouldn't be interfering. I only made a tentative date. And you know very well how interested I am in anything to do with our work. I assure you I'd prefer..." she protested.

His eyebrows quirked upward ironically.

"You really prefer work to play? Admirable girl! In that case, we *will* go out tomorrow. I'll get Lotta to make us a picnic lunch—she's rather good at them—and we'll try to get away soon after ten. Better bring a camera and some color films—there's sure to be something you can use."

He didn't talk much more during the drive back to Mdina. Chloe sat and contemplated with delight the prospect of a whole day alone with him.

"Oh, and you might call me Dominic, as the rest of the team do. We don't go in much for formality on the dig," he said as they were entering the house. She wondered if he had any idea how long she had been thinking of him as Dominic.

"All right, I will," she said. Perversely, her lips refused to utter his name. But he didn't seem to notice—or if he did, he wasn't interested.

"I'll be dining with my mother in her room," he told her. "As the others are out, perhaps you'd like Lotta to bring a tray up to yours."

"Thank you."

"I'll be down in the library to see the new batch of slides a little after nine o'clock."

"I'll have everything ready for you."

She had reached the foot of the staircase and turned, with a hand on the balustrade, to smile at him. But he had already turned away.

She climbed the marble stairs dispiritedly. Illogically all her joyful expectation of the next day was dampened.

Going along the corridor to her room, she almost tiptoed past Mrs. Vining's door. She felt she could not, just this moment, face the sort of catechism to which she had been subjected the last time she paid her a visit.

Guilty but unchallenged, she reached her own door, slipped inside and thankfully shut the door.

WHEN DOMINIC APPEARED in the library at the prearranged time, she saw at once that something was wrong.

"Ready?" he asked brusquely.

"Quite ready."

"Run this lot through quickly—I can't stay more than a few minutes. My mother isn't well."

"Oh—I'm so sorry. Is there anything I can do?"

"Thank you. I think not. Lotta is with her."

He didn't tell her of the scene his mother had made. It had started with reproaches over Louise's continued presence at Santa Clara. When he had pointed out, gently, that Louise had a right to be there, he had been told that he was to blame; if he would only announce his engagement to Chloe, Louise would give up the chase and go.

The argument had ended with tears, hysteria, finally collapse. Lotta had known what to do, the right sedative to give, but he was worried, afraid of one of his mother's heart attacks. As soon as he had seen the slides once he hurried away.

There was nothing for it, after Chloe had put away her apparatus, but to go to her room.

She sat down at the writing desk and began an overdue letter to her mother, but soon found she wasn't in the mood for the sort of gossipy letter her mother enjoyed, and gave it up.

She took a bath and spent a long time over it, turning on the hot tap with her toes as the water cooled.

Afterward she stood out on the balcony in the starlight for a while, cooling off. But somehow the sight of the diamond-sprinkled, velvety southern sky, and the caress of the silky night air, only deepened her feeling of depression.

Taking up a book on Maltese architecture that Dominic had recommended to her, she climbed into her bed and after a long time managed to read herself to sleep.

The sharp slam of a door, very nearby, woke her an hour or two later.

She sat up and listened.

Someone was moving around in the bathroom next door. Louise, of course, returned from the party. Chloe thought she could detect the smell of the Turkish cigarettes she smoked.

She was on the point of lying down again when the door of her room burst violently open. Louise, still in the evening dress, stood silhouetted against the oblong opening into the lighted bathroom.

There was something oddly baleful in the way she stood there, not speaking, smoking in quick vicious puffs, swaying gently, as if she were a little drunk.

"Good Lord, how you startled me, Mrs. Carlyon," Chloe exclaimed. "What is it? Is there something I can do for you?" She wished she could see Louise's face.

Louise cut in sharply, "There certainly is. Listen, Chloe Linden. Lay off my cousin Dominic, will you?" she said. "You got in here by a trick, didn't you? And now you think you can have them all at your feet—Mark, Robert, even Dominic. But let me tell you right now that Dominic is mine. We belong to each other. We always have. He'll always be in love with me. That's why he's never married. Why he's turned down all the pretty, rich, suitable girls his mother has lined up for him. You're a fool to think you'll ever get him away from me. So quit trying, or else!"

Before Chloe could marshal her wits to frame any sort of a reply Louise was gone, savagely slamming the door between the bathroom and her own bedroom, and pointedly turning the key in the lock.

Chloe stared after her blankly. She was shocked, almost dazed, by the malevolence she had unwittingly aroused.

CHAPTER SEVEN

THE FIRST PALE STARS were already blinking in the darkening sky when Robert returned Chloe to Santa Clara the next evening.

They had spent the day together, as he had intended they should.

At breakfast that morning, Chloe had had a message from Dominic, via Mark. His mother, though a little better, was still unwell. Their plans for the day must, he regretted, be postponed.

"I'd have loved to take you out somewhere myself," Mark said. "But I've been commandeered to take Louise out to a destroyer for a gin party. You could come, too, if you liked. Why don't you?"

"I think not." She was wishing Dominic had thought it worthwhile to tell her himself, and struggled to hide her disappointment. "Actually, your brother will be telephoning...."

"Oh. Will he indeed?"

Mark looked and felt rather piqued. All their lives, Robert, with his superior looks and address, had been whisking charming girls from under his nose.

"After exercises," she said. "He plans to show me the island."

"He does, does he? All I can say is, beware of him, Miss L. He's been a menace since he was in sixth grade."

"I'll be careful," she assured him cheerfully.

She didn't anticipate having trouble with Robert; he should be easy enough to handle, she thought.

In point of fact she thoroughly enjoyed her day with him. The weather was warming up, the sun shone brilliantly, the whole island seemed to sparkle.

Robert had somehow acquired a convertible sports car.

He drove her around the coast road, past the balconied houses of Sliema and St. Julien. On their right the sea, sun-sequined and streaked with purple, sapphire and jade, lapped against the pale shelves of rock.

"Now for a bit of tourist stuff," he said, and showed her one of the square, high-perched Crusader forts that once formed a chain of lookouts against Barbary pirates and other infidel enemies. Further on they looked over one of the vast baroque churches that every *casal* boasted—mute witnesses of man's aspirations toward God.

"The parishioners paid for it," he told her. "For years on end they bring a few eggs, a basket of vegetables, a young goat, a handful of peaches or almonds or figs to the priest. These are sold, and the money goes into bricks and stones. They do the work, too. Fantastic, isn't it?"

They went and inspected the Mosta dome, which held a world record for girth, and the San Anton gardens with palace, fountains, lily ponds and shady bowers.

"They sometimes do open-air plays here, as they do in Regent's Park. I saw them do *The Merry Wives of Windsor*. Rather fun on a fine warm night in this perfect setting."

"It sounds marvelous."

They drove back to the coast road and stopped for lunch at the little fishing port of St. Paul. They ate on the terrace of the harbor inn, right above the water. There were freshly caught fish, stuffed eggplant, figs in syrup and coffee with an Italian liqueur called *strega*.

Across the green blue bay, dotted with painted fishing craft with eyes on their high prows, they could see the statue of the Apostle on the rocky island where he was shipwrecked on one of his missionary journeys.

Afterward they drove over Mellieha ridge to Marfa, a jutting point on the north of the island. Here, Robert said, a ferry left daily for the smaller island of Gozo. Leaving the car, they strolled over low cliffs fragrant with wild thyme and carpeted with tiny flowers. A stiff breeze flecked the strait between the islands with whitecaps, and sea gulls wheeled screaming overhead.

"Promise you'll come over to Gozo with me one day,"

Robert said eagerly. "It's a charming little island. Look, I'll hire a boat and sail you over. There's always a stiff breeze in the channel. Or we could go on the ferry if you prefer. I'll show you the cave where Calypso enticed Ulysses...."

"Have you forgotten? Working girl," she reminded him, unable to help laughing at his enthusiasm.

He let his blue eyes, long-lashed as a girl's, wander slowly and caressingly over her face. Already it had taken on a light golden tan. Her eyes were golden and her chestnut hair had golden gleams where the sun touched it. She looked warmly, vividly alive.

He caught her hand in his and swung it lightly between them.

"Let's make a date now. Next Sunday? Say you'll come next Sunday, Chloe."

But she had no intention of committing herself. Next Sunday, Dominic might be free. He might want to take her to Hagar Qim and Mnajdra and the Cave of Darkness, Ghar Dalam. It would be terrible if he did, and she had to say she wasn't free, she already had a date. Gently she removed her hand from Robert's.

"No promises," she said with a smile. "We must wait till nearer the time. You never will remember that I'm not a free agent, Robert, dear. Professor Vining may suddenly find he needs me." *If only he would,* Chloe thought.

"He couldn't need you half as much as I do, Chloe, darling."

She laughed again—but rather hollowly, thinking how very right he was.

Robert had turned away, rather offended by her laughter, and was holding open the door of the car.

"Glad I amuse you so much," he said stiffly. "Better get on. You're quite heartless."

But when she patted his hand and said amiably, "Nonsense, Robert, merely cautious," he laughed too. He was a sunny-tempered young man, really. He could never stay cross with a girl as pretty as Chloe for long. Experience had taught him that it wasn't often necessary....

They drove on northwestward around to the cliffs above

the blue bay of Ghain Tuffieha. A steep flowery path led
to its golden beach.

Reluctantly, after wading in the edge of the water, they
decided that it was still far too cold for a swim, and
scrambling up to the car, drove on to where a charming
place with towers rose above the lush woods and scented
orange groves of Boschetto. "Verdala, built by a former
Grand Master," Robert said.

Here they found a shady spot and Robert, with the air of
a conjurer, produced a picnic basket with tea and some
very special creamy cakes. Afterward they wandered hand
in hand for a while among the orange trees.

"The Governor has his summer residence here," Robert
said. "It's a blissfully cool retreat when the sirocco blows
from North Africa. A foul, sticky, hot wind that makes
life a misery while it lasts. You'll miss it—luckily for you."

The careless words brought home sharply to her that
soon—in a little over two months—she would have gone
from Malta.

"I'll be back in London, I suppose, nose to the grind-
stone," she said flatly.

"And I'll be at sea, thousands of miles away from you,
worse luck," Robert said with pathos. "I'll be miserable
when you've gone, Chloe, darling."

"Cheer up, you'll find 'the Fishing Fleet' waiting to
welcome you back."

He put his arms around her. "I don't want 'the Fishing
Fleet,' I want *you*," he said ardently. "Kiss me, Chloe."

But she only laughed and patted his cheek, and led the
way firmly back to the car.

"Home now. It's getting chilly, don't you think? Or perhaps it's because we're in deep shade. It's been a lovely
day, Robert," she added warmly, seeing how piqued he
looked. "And there'll be time for others before you go
away—mmm?"

He seized on that with flattering eagerness. "Promise!"

"Cross my heart."

With that he had to be content. She wouldn't agree to
dine with him in Valetta.

"I've got to catch up on my letters. I haven't written to

my mother, or my godmother, the one I live with in London.''

"Couldn't they wait one more day?"

"Perhaps. But I've got work to prepare for tomorrow, too. Honestly I have.''

"Oh, all right." He could see that she wasn't going to be persuaded. Her resistance inflamed his ardor.

They said goodbye in the open door of Santa Clara. With his arm around her waist, and his lips very close to her ear, he begged, "You'll come out very soon—the very first time you're free? You'll call me? On the ship-to-shore telephone? Promise, Chloe, darling?''

"Of course—only I don't know how soon it'll be.''

Even as she spoke she saw Dominic descending the marble staircase. He *would* come just at this moment, she thought vexedly. Even if he hadn't heard, he had certainly seen. His ironic expression told her that. *Bother and blast,* she thought, *and all those other words I heard at boarding school. What will he think of me?*

"Goodbye, Robert, and thank you very much for a lovely day," she said firmly ushering him outside.

"I say, that was bad luck," he whispered.

"Foul. Go now, please.''

He murmured, "Goodbye, darling," and ran down the steps. She turned to face Dominic.

"I—how is your mother? Better, I hope?"

"A little, thank you. She has asked for you several times during the day."

Chloe felt miserably guilty, though there was no reason at all why she should. He had said there was nothing she could do—his mother had Lotta with her. Even so. . . .

"I'm so sorry," she stammered. "If I'd known I—we drove around the island. I didn't think. . . .''

"There's no need to apologize. Of course you couldn't have known. But perhaps you'll look in on her on your way up."

It was an order.

"Of course," she agreed meekly.

Hurrying to her room, she tidied herself, after the long day in the sun and wind. Then reluctantly, full of misgivings, she went along the corridor and tapped on Mrs. Vining's door.

Lotta let her in and, at a sign from her mistress, went out into the corridor.

Chloe walked over to the vast bed. She saw that Mrs. Vining was indeed looking ill. Her cheeks looked hollow; her eyes were enormous and unnaturally bright.

"I'm so very sorry I wasn't in when you asked for me, *contessa*. I wouldn't have dreamed of going out had I guessed you might want to see me. How are you now? A little better, I hope?" she asked gently.

The *contessa* made a gesture of impatience.

"A little better. Don't let us talk of my health. Tell me where you have been all day. I wanted to see you."

"I'm so sorry," Chloe said again. "I was being shown the island."

"Ah. And what did you think of it?"

"It's very pretty just now, with all the spring flowers and blossoms."

"Wait till the summer heat burns everything up. It's arid and ugly enough then."

"But the architecture will always be lovely."

Again that gesture of impatience. "Who drove you?" The *contessa* let her suspicion show in her voice.

"I went with Mark's brother, Robert—the one in the Navy."

"That debutante's delight? You prefer his company to that of my son? I thought you had more sense," pronounced the *contessa* with asperity.

Chloe felt the color rush into her cheeks.

"Of course I don't," she protested warmly. "Professor Vining had arranged to take me to see some of the other archaeological finds, but you weren't well, he didn't want to leave you...."

"Call him Dominic, can't you? Surely you don't think he looks like a stuffy professor?" his mother said testily. Her brilliant eyes searched Chloe's face in that embarrassing way they had. "Tell me, are you in love with him yet?"

How do I answer such a point-blank question, Chloe thought.

"I—I . . . ." Not a very good effort.

The eyes lit with a gleam of triumph.

"You are. Of course you are. Wouldn't any girl be? All that money and looks and fame? He could have married a dozen girls, all pretty and suitable. But no. He didn't wish to be *involved*. Involved. One of these stupid modern words."

"I'm very sure, *contessa*, that he doesn't want to be involved now. Certainly not with me."

"Nonsense. He likes you very much. He admires you— he told me so. Oh, I grant you he's not in love—yet. But use your wits, girl. Play your cards well and he'll ask you to marry him yet. Louise will drive him to it. He'll ask you if only to get rid of her. Never fear, my dear. . . ."

"But I don't *want* him to ask me, if he doesn't love me," Chloe said desperately. She looked wildly around the room, feeling trapped. She longed to get away, but couldn't think of an excuse that would sound plausible.

Someone tapped at the door. Lotta's voice came through. "Your dinner, *contessa*." *Saved*, she thought.

A maidservant followed Lotta in, carrying a laden tray set with fine linen, silver, a rose in a crystal vase.

The *contessa* scanned its contents with an interest that suggested she was feeling considerably better.

"I'll leave you now to enjoy your dinner, *contessa*," Chloe said quickly. "I hope you'll feel stronger tomorrow. Good night."

As there was no answer she slipped quietly out of the room. Her cheeks were still hot. Her emotions were in a turmoil. She wondered distractedly what sort of a report on their conversation the *contessa* would make to Dominic.

I'll have to leave Santa Clara, and go live somewhere else, if this sort of thing is to happen, she thought. *It's so frightfully embarrassing. I can't stand it. And how am I going to face Dominic?*

That evening after dinner, and for the next few days, she made a point of avoiding him. When he spoke to her, his eyes naturally seeking hers across the dinner table, she felt herself flushing and thought she detected a flicker of amusement in his expression.

When he asked to see the latest slides on her projector, she made an excuse—rather lame, but the best she could do—that it was out of order, needed taking apart, cleaning, perhaps. Anything to avoid being alone with him, giving a chance to bring up a subject she certainly didn't want to discuss. *Supposing his mother tells him she's sure I'm in love with him,* she thought, aghast.

"I hope your projector isn't going to be out of order long," Dominic was saying.

"No, I'm working on it. Perhaps a day or two," she said, not looking at him, keeping her eyes lowered to what was on her plate, and wishing she were anywhere else.

Once or twice she caught Louise watching her with derisive malice.

I will leave here. I'll move into a hotel, she thought fiercely. But how to produce convincing reasons—reasons that would satisfy Dominic—for moving?

She couldn't, of course, avoid him forever. On Friday evening, when she had bathed and changed after a long, hard day at the dig and had come down to the salon to wait for dinner she found him alone there. She hesitated in the doorway, but it was too late, he had seen her. Besides, she disliked running away.

He was standing with one elbow leaning on the mantelpiece of the carved stone fireplace. She felt his presence as a sharp, physical thing.

When he stood upright she noticed that he was wearing tails. He looked very handsome in them, but his expression was morose, as if whatever occasion had called for them offered him little prospect of pleasure.

"Oh—hello, Dominic," she said hesitantly. Then, she said, with more confidence as he pulled forward a chair for her, "Grand gala? You're dining out?"

He nodded. "Escorting Louise to a dinner party. No avoiding it—invitations from the Grand Palace are a royal command. I'd have got out of it if I could—I've got urgent work to do. However...."

For something to keep the conversation going she exclaimed, "How I should love to see the Grand Palace!"

"I'll take you one day," he promised surprisingly. "It's

certainly worth seeing. We'll take a day off and do Valetta
sometime soon. Mustn't work you *too* hard, must we?''

"Oh—I'd love that.''

He smiled then, his warm, disconcertingly charming
smile.

At once all the turbulence that had been seething inside
her since that last fantastic talk with his mother clamored
for outlet. She needed to talk to him as woman to man—to
the one man.

She wanted to ask him a hundred questions—about his
likes and dislikes, his past, his war experiences, his childhood, his loves. She wanted—as a woman in love does—to
know every last little thing about him.

I'm crazy, she thought, pulling herself together. Because
although he had been looking at her rather intently, his
eyes going from the top of her head to the tips of her gray
suede shoes, he was saying nothing more romantic than,
"Let me get you a glass of sherry.''

She was taking it from him, carefully avoiding touching
his fingers, when the door opened. Louise swept into the
room, followed by Mark in a casual dark suit as usual—
evidently he hadn't been bidden to the dinner party.

"Martinis, Mark,'' Louise demanded. "We must get the
party spirit before we leave, my pet. You look rather as if
we were on our way to a funeral.''

She herself looked anything but funereal. She was wearing a low-cut gown of stark white heavy lace that flattered
her greyhound thinness and the gorgeous suntan she had
already managed to acquire. She looked, with her one-
sided hairdo and original jewelry of big colored stones set
in chunky gold, like a model at a first-class design show—
the not-so-young model who shows the sophisticated
clothes.

Dominic eyed her morosely. Mark gave Chloe his usual
delighted grin, and went to fill up Louise's glass from a jug
of ice-cold martinis.

"M'mmm. Delicious. You've got a real flair,'' she told
him when she had tasted it.

"Drink up, Louise. It's high time we were off,''
Dominic cut in impatiently.

"Mustn't keep His Excellency waiting," Mark said.

Louise flashed a brilliant smile. "Ready, sweetie."

Tossing off the last drops, she set down her glass and thrust her arm through Dominic's. With a triumphant glance at Chloe she drew him with her out of the room.

Unashamedly Chloe wished she were in her place—dressed in her best, going to a glamorous party on Dominic's arm. She gave a sharp little sigh—a Cinderella sigh that turned into a laugh at herself.

"Let's take ourselves out, too, after dinner—there's a village *festa* that might be good, over at Birzebuggia," Mark suggested, looking as if he were feeling a little flat, too. "Rather fun with the right person."

With the right person—yes, she thought. But Mark wasn't the right person, much as she liked him. Better spend the evening catching up on her work. She smiled and shook her head.

"Sorry, Mark. I'm behind with my cataloguing. Another evening, later on, perhaps."

"Rather. Whenever you give the word."

"I'll have my dinner sent up to my room—then I'm going to work in the library."

"All right, I won't disturb you. But bang on my door if you feel the need, later, of a little human sympathy. I'm awful sympathetic," Mark said with his cheerful grin.

She didn't guess that already she was causing him a heartache. *Dear Mark*, she thought vaguely; it never occurred to her to take anything he said seriously. She laughed when he added, "I can't invite you to see my etchings, but I've got some awfully good records, if you'd like to hear them anytime."

"Thanks, I'd love to. I'm a collector myself at home. We'll compare notes—but not now, please."

"Okay. Whenever you say."

Dear Mark, Chloe thought again. *He's really rather a sweet.*

In the library after dinner, she went behind the enormous screen and turned on the dark-shaded lamp whose powerful bulb directed a bright pool of light onto the desk, leaving the rest of the big room in dimness.

She spread out her things around her and set to work. Now and then she got up and vanished behind the half-open door in the paneling—the secret door leading to her darkroom. It was very quiet and peaceful. The only sound that interrupted the silence was the regular harsh chiming of the cathedral clock. Soon she was so absorbed in her work that time passed unnoticed.

SHE CAME TO with quite a start as simultaneously the cathedral announced the hour of midnight and the lights in the library snapped on.

She had just time to think, *it must be Dominic. I'll keep quiet, and he may go away without noticing my light is on, too.*

Then his voice, sounding very cold and controlled said, "If you must make a scene, Louise, do it in here, where there's no danger of the rest of the household overhearing."

She knew then that she was trapped. She shrank down in her chair, hardly daring to breathe.

She could hear Louise sobbing angrily. When at length she stopped and spoke, her voice sounded distraught.

"How can you treat me like this, Dominic? So cold, so utterly unloving. You're heartless. You're driving me crazy."

Then Dominic's voice: "Louise. Please!"

"It's no good your using that icy tone with me. We're going to have this out now."

"Have what out?"

"You used to love me. You were mad about me. Weren't you?"

"If it's any satisfaction to you, I was."

"And you swore you always would be, till you died. What has changed you? What? *What?*"

"It was you who chose to end everything between us, wasn't it, Louise? I'm afraid the answer is that for me, it did end, finally, when you married my cousin Dick."

"But you knew I only did it out of pique. I was disappointed, heartbroken because you insisted on throwing away the lovely amusing life we might have had if you'd

stayed on in the diplomatic service. I was nearly off my
head. But you know very well it was you I really loved—
only you.''

''You chose a strange way of showing it.''

''I know I did, darling. I've told you—I was nearly off
my head.''

Chloe looked around desperately, seeking a way of
escape. She had never felt so embarrassed in her life. If
only the window had been possible—but it was guarded
outside, she knew, by the usual iron grille. Nothing doing
there.

Gooseflesh ran over her skin at the thought of being discovered behind the screen listening in, however unwillingly.

In a panic she moved from her chair and crept, catlike,
into the darkroom. At least, even if they noticed her light
was on, they might not think of her being in there.

She pulled the paneling as close as she could. She dared
not close it in case the small click the lock made should give
her away. Sitting there, rather chilled and utterly scared,
she could still hear every word that was said in the library.

''Of course I know you're angry with me for coming.
You think I'm just a gold digger, don't you? I suppose
when Mark told you about my hotel bill, and that my
money hadn't arrived at the bank, you thought it was just
a stunt. You thought I'd come because I was broke.
Because I'd run through everything in Dick's account, and
meant to live on you instead. That's it, isn't it? That's why
you've been so cold and unfriendly, almost from the first
day I arrived.''

''Don't be absurd, Louise. You had every right to come
here if you wanted, you know that. I admit I think it would
have been—better—if you'd let us know, in the ordinary
way, that you were coming. Also you might have told me,
honestly, that you needed money. As you were Dick's
wife, naturally whatever you needed would have been
forthcoming.''

''As I was Dick's wife? Even though he stole me from
you?'' Louise asked with ill-judged coquetry.

''Naturally.'' Dominic spoke in a voice of ice, but
Louise didn't seem to notice.

"Then you do love me still. Darling, I knew it," she cried.

If only I could get out, Chloe was thinking desperately in the darkness. *If I needn't hear. . . .*

"I knew you hadn't changed. I knew you couldn't not remember what we once were to each other."

Dominic said, "Louise, please!" again; Chloe guessed she had moved closer to him, trying by physical contact, perhaps, to touch his heart.

"Listen, Louise. You're welcome to whatever you need to see you through till Dick returns."

"If he returns."

"If he—doesn't, naturally, there will be other arrangements to be made. A settlement. That, of course, must be done."

"Thank you, darling."

"But you mustn't give up hope yet, in spite of the radio reports. The party may simply have lost radio contact."

"Dick may come back from the Antarctic, but he won't come back to me."

Dominic went on as if he hadn't heard her.

"Wouldn't it be better, certainly more amusing for you, if you were to leave Santa Clara? You like the Felicia—wouldn't you prefer to stay there? I'll arrange it if you would like it. You must realize—with my mother's health as it is—we *must* live quietly here. And this sort of scene, too, mustn't happen again. You must please understand that whatever there was between us is finished, over, forever."

He had schooled his voice in kindness, but Chloe noticed that it shook a little, as if he were under a great strain.

She sat still as a statue, petrified lest through a movement, or even a sound of breathing, they should suddenly discover she was there.

There was a little silence. Then Louise gasped, "You don't mean it, Dominic. You can't!"

"I'm afraid I do, Louise."

"Then there must be someone else. Who is it?"

He didn't reply.

"Is it true—what your mother told me?"

"My mother?"

"She said it was this new girl, Chloe Linden. You aren't interested in her? You wouldn't be caught by that old trick, pretending that young man had asked her to come in his place—simply to catch you. You wouldn't be so simple as to fall for that?"

When again he said nothing she almost shouted, "It isn't true, is it? You can't be in love with her!"

With a sense of utter unreality Chloe heard his calm reply. "Why not?"

"You mean you are?"

He evaded a direct answer.

"Can you give me any good reason I shouldn't ask Miss Linden to marry me?" he asked coolly.

Chloe stifled a gasp. She could hardly believe her ears.

"But you can't marry her, not when *I* still want you," Louise stormed. "Listen to me. I'll get a divorce. Our marriage was all washed up, anyway, when Dick left me. That's why he went. If he's dead now, I don't care. If they don't assume his death, I'll soon be able to get a divorce for desertion. I can stay on here with you, can't I, till then? And when I'm free, we can be married. Everything can be just as we meant it to be before. You want that, don't you, darling, as much as I do? Of course you do. Admit it!"

Chloe held her breath.

"I'm sorry, Louise." Dominic spoke wearily but inflexibly. "I'm sorry you care so little about what's happening to Dick, and whether he's dead or alive."

"I do care—I hope he's dead," she flung at him.

"Even if he were, I'm no longer in the market for you," he retorted, his voice hard.

"So just to spite me, you'll make a fool of yourself and marry this little nonentity," Louise raged. "If you do, I'll *kill* her—I swear I will!"

"Louise, you can't know what you're saying."

"Can't I? I'll show you. Don't imagine I'll let you pack me off tamely to the Felicia, and leave the field clear for her. This place belongs to Dick as much as to you, don't forget that. I'm here, and here I'll stay just as long as it suits me. Is that clear?"

Chloe heard Dominic's sharp sigh of exasperation.

"Very clear. I agree you have the right to stay here. But please understand that if you make any more scenes like this one, Louise, I—and Miss Linden and Mark—will move over to the camp. But my mother will still be in residence here—and in charge. You wouldn't like that, would you?"

There was a long, long silence, broken by the scrape of a match. Chloe smelled the Turkish cigarette Louise must have lit.

Suddenly Louise laughed. With a complete, astonishing change of front she cried gaily, "For the love of Mike, darling, let's play down the drama, shall we? If you want to marry your little camera girl, why, go ahead, with my blessing. Of course she'll jump at you...."

"Perhaps," Dominic agreed coolly. Chloe felt the hot color flame in her cheeks. So he knew. She *had* given herself away.

Louise laughed derisively.

"Like that, is it? Girl meets boss, falls for boss, wins boss. Romance as it is in the love magazines. Well, darling, come and let's have a final drink in the living room, to wish you luck—and then I promise I'll behave."

"Very well."

Dominic still sounded exasperated but relieved, too, that the scene appeared to be over. Chloe heard the lights click off, the door open and close. There was silence and dimness in the library again.

When she unclenched her hands she found the palms were wet. She was shaking all over. The scene had completely unnerved her.

But the need to get quickly to her own room before the other two left the living room spurred her on. She turned off her lamp and groped her way to the door. Opening it cautiously, she peered out. Not a sound to be heard. Taking her shoes in her hand, she sped noiselessly up the marble staircase and along the miles of corridor.

The *contessa*'s door was ajar as usual, and a light burned dimly in her room.

Chloe sped past her door without pausing in her headlong flight. Reaching her own door, she opened it sound-lessly and slid into the welcoming darkness. It was minutes before she switched on the lights.

She was nearly in tears. Wild, chaotic thoughts chased each other half formed through her head—the result of strain and shock. Heart and mind were in turmoil.

Sometime soon—very soon, perhaps, after tonight's showdown—Dominic was going to ask her to marry him. And he didn't love her. She knew that from the way he had evaded Louise's direct question.

Then why? To thwart Louise? Or—more likely—to please his mother?

Whatever the reason, how could she say yes? But how say no, when she wanted him so much?

Restlessly she walked up and down the room, trying to calm herself.

Lotta, knowing she was working late, had left a Ther-mos of hot milk and some cookies beside her bed. Lotta must have taken a fancy to her, she thought, touched.

Or was it just that she was taking her cue from the *con-tessa*, whom clearly she adored? Her impassive manner certainly hadn't shown any feeling at all, other than what any good servant would display toward a guest in the house she served.

Sitting on her bed, Chloe absently sipped the hot milk. She was still bemused by what she had heard. She put down the glass and walked around again, feeling restless, upset, unable to settle.

I'll take a hot bath, she decided at length. Louise hadn't come up yet.

The warm scented water helped to soothe her nerves. When she had dried herself she put on a dressing gown and stepped outside onto the little balcony.

Away to the south she could see lights, and an occa-sional rocket burst in the sky. She wondered briefly if it was the *festa* Mark had wanted them to visit.

She leaned for a moment at the parapet. Its damp cold-ness felt unpleasant against her bare forearms, and she drew back, remembering, too, that it was unsafe. Refusing to think any more about her own affairs, she stood trying to identify the constellations that looked so near and emphatic in the sky's dark bowl.

A whiff of Turkish cigarette smoke brought her out of her astral speculations. She turned around to find Louise standing beside her. Her eyes looked enormous, and seemed to blaze with fury. She took a step toward Chloe, as if she meant to strike her....

AFTERWARD, CHLOE FOUND she had only a confused and fragmentary recollection of what had happened.

She remembered shrinking away, and feeling the rail of the balcony against her body, cold through the thin dressing gown.

She knew she had listened, with stunned amazement, to a violent tirade of abuse; but no memory remained of what had actually been said.

She remembered trying to leave the balcony, get out of reach of the venomous voice. Evidently she hadn't succeeded. Her next memory was of a hand pressed hard, irresistibly, against the middle of her back.

Someone had shrieked. Whether it was herself or someone else she didn't know. Then there had been the terrifying sensation of losing balance, of flailing her arms to retain it, of feeling the balcony rail give way, of falling....

Then there was another, wilder scream....

She had found herself standing shakily beside what was left of the parapet. Lotta's enormous hand grasped her arm in a grip that hurt. Lotta's face wore a look of grim satisfaction.

Shock had held her speechless for a while. She remembered how when she had recovered a little she had gasped, "What happened, Lotta? Where is Mrs. Carlyon?"

Most vividly she recalled Lotta gesturing with her free hand. "Down there."

"Fallen? You mean—the railing gave way and she fell? But that isn't possible. It was I who was falling."

Lotta said sullenly, "The *signorina* can see that the rail had broken. I was in the corridor. I saw her come along. I followed her—the *contessa* had warned me she was dangerous. I am glad she is gone. I hope she is killed,"

Lotta finished simply. "So my *contessa* will be at peace again."

At that Chloe's scattered senses had seemed to return to her.

"We must do something quickly, Lotta. You must go and call...."

But before she could finish the door of the bathroom had burst open and Dominic had walked out onto the balcony.

From this point on her recollection was as clear as crystal.

"I thought I heard a scream—two screams. Are you all right, Chloe? What's happened?"

His eyes went from her face to Lotta's. Lotta was still grasping her arm. Chloe faltered. "The railing gave way. Mrs. Carlyon fell. She's down there...."

"But what were you doing, the pair of you, out here at this time of night?"

He had thrust them both aside as he spoke, and was looking down over the edge of the balcony.

"Louise, Louise! Where are you?"

Louise's deep voice answered at once. It sounded very angry indeed. "I'm here."

"Are you hurt?"

"No thanks to that murderess who pushed me over if I'm not. I could have broken my neck!"

"Then you're all right?"

"I'm alive, anyway. I had the luck to land in a tree."

Chloe was peering down over the edge of the balcony, too, though it made her sick to do so. She thought she could make out the pale blob of Louise's upturned face, and the larger blob of her white dress.

"Look, there she is," she gasped, pointing.

"For God's sake *do* something," the angry voice went on. "I daren't move for fear this branch gives way under me."

"Keep still," Dominic called. "I'm coming down there just as soon as we can find a rope."

Over his shoulder he told the silent Lotta, "Run and get Nibblu. Tell him to bring a long, strong rope from the garage. See that he hurries. And then go and make some strong coffee—a lot of it."

Lotta went out muttering, and he turned to look at Chloe.

"How did this happen?"

"I—I don't *know*..."

"Don't talk nonsense, Chloe. You must know. You were here, surely?"

"Yes. But I can't tell you. You must ask Lotta—or Mrs. Carlyon," she said wildly. Let him think what he liked. How dared he question her in that tone, as if she were guilty of something?

I'm getting out of Santa Clara tomorrow, she thought. *It's too much. Did Louise mean me when she said that murderess? She told Dominic she'd kill me. Was it she whose hand tried to push her over? Was that what Lotta meant?*

When Nibblu brought the rope Dominic lashed it to the foot of the heavy bedstead in her room and fed it downward over the sill of her window, with pillows from the bed placed to prevent the rough stone from chafing it. When all was ready he lowered himself nimbly, and disappeared into the darkness.

It wasn't very long before he was back, climbing agilely into the room again. Then he and Nibblu hauled in the rope hand over hand, very slowly and carefully. After what seemed a long time Louise's head appeared. The two men helped her through the window. She was holding one arm with the other and groaning.

"I've sprained my shoulder," she said. "I can't lift my arm. I suppose—" with a sudden return of venomous anger as her eyes fell on Chloe "—you wish you'd pushed harder. I might have been dead then."

Chloe stared at her aghast.

"You're daring to suggest that *I* pushed *you* over?"

Louise laughed derisively.

"Who else? And we don't need to ask ourselves why she did it, do we, Dominic, dear?"

Dominic was looking at Louise with grim distaste—but the look seemed, to Chloe, nervous and overwrought as she was, to include her, too. Perhaps he was thinking again how right he had been, the first time he met her, to say that women brought trouble.

Perhaps, even, he believed Louise. He was speaking to her gently.

"Please go to your room, and get into bed. Lotta is making coffee. She'll bring you some up, and some aspirins. We'll get the doctor out first thing in the morning, and meantime, I'll fix your arm in a sling."

"Do, darling. It aches rather."

"And you, Chloe—better turn in, too. You can talk things over when you're both calmer."

"There's nothing to talk over," Chloe protested hotly. "You can ask Lotta. She'll tell you exactly what happened, and who pushed whom."

"Ha! A servant! D'you think Dominic is going to take her word against mine?" Louise retorted with insolent confidence. "Come along, Dominic, darling, and do my arm. And lock the door from the bathroom. I'll feel safer that way."

Just for a moment, as Dominic's eyes rested on her face, Chloe caught the gleam of ironic humor in them.

It was as if he were trying to tell her he understood, that she mustn't worry. She wanted to respond with a rueful grin, but she found she couldn't make the effort. She didn't have a grin left in her.

With a hopeless shake of her head she turned away. When they had all left her room she shut and locked the door, and drank Lotta's coffee with two aspirins. She wasn't given to crying as a rule, but tears rolled down her cheeks. She flung herself down on the bed and let them come.

After a while she began to feel better. She got up and went into the bathroom, and washed her face in cool water. When she turned off the switch, no crack of light showed under Louise's door.

Was she asleep? Or lying awake brewing fresh wickedness, like a medieval witch?

You needn't bother, Chloe muttered, addressing the

closed door. *You've won. I'm leaving Santa Clara tomorrow, and Malta just as soon as my job is finished....*

For the second time she wished she had never met Ronnie Fairfax, never let herself be talked into taking on this assignment in Malta.

CHAPTER EIGHT

WHEN LOTTA CAME IN with the early tea next morning she found Chloe on her knees, packing one of her bags.

After a wretched night during which she had milled over and over everything that had happened since her arrival at Santa Clara, she still felt she couldn't bear to stay on there another day.

Lotta stood for a moment grimly watching her, then set the tray down with a disapproving thump, and noisily rattled back the curtains, letting in the usual flood of light.

Then she stood over Chloe with feet apart, hands on ample hips, looking positively truculent.

"The *signorina* is packing?"

"As you see, Lotta." Chloe rolled a pair of cobweb fine nylons without looking up.

"The *signorina* is leaving us?"

"Yes. Today."

"But why? You are not comfortable at Santa Clara? We haven't pleased the *signorina*?"

"Of course you have, Lotta. I couldn't be more pleased with the way you've looked after me."

"Then where? Not back to England, surely?"

"Not at once."

"Somewhere in Malta, then?" Lotta persisted, with the familiarity of a privileged and valued servant.

"That is my business," Chloe told her gently.

"But, *signorina*, what will the *contessa* say? She is so happy you are here. She wants you to stay always," Lotta burst out. "She is hoping...."

She stopped short, biting her upper lip between her big teeth, knowing she had said too much. Her broad peasant face, usually so impassive, betrayed her agitation and unease.

After a pause she went on coaxingly, as if she were persuading a refractory child, "Perhaps the *signorina* would feel happier in another room, further away from *her*. I will ask the *contessa*. The *contessa* knows very well what good reason there is to be afraid of *her*. It can easily be arranged. There are many other rooms here that the *signorina* might like."

Chloe snapped down the locks of the second bag and stood up. With a smile for Lotta, she went and poured herself a cup of tea and sipped it.

"You mustn't worry the *contessa* about me, please, Lotta," she said. "It isn't necessary. Everything is arranged."

That wasn't true, of course, but she didn't feel up to any more argument. Later on, after she had seen Dominic, she would walk over to the hotel in Mdina, which like Santa Clara was built into the ramparts. She would take a room there. Surely nothing could be simpler?

Lotta retired, muttering that the *contessa* must hear of this at once, she would know how to deal with it.

Chloe watched her go. A worried frown creased her forehead. She hoped the *contessa* wouldn't be upset. She hoped, too, that Lotta would have said nothing about last night's fantastic happenings. After a while she swallowed another cup of tea and started to dress.

She wished she might leave without seeing Dominic. But she knew that wouldn't do. He was her employer as well as her host. She would have to face seeing him.

She expected he would be seriously annoyed with her. He would want to know how she proposed to manage without the darkroom and the car. She must be ready with something practical, as well as a plausible reason for leaving Santa Clara.

Since she had no intention of telling him, in so many words, that it was Louise and his mother between them who were driving her away, she'd better let him believe her reasons were entirely frivolous ones. He didn't love her, and wasn't likely to. So it could scarcely matter one way or the other what he thought of her motives.

Even so, she was shaking with nerves when, after break-

fasting alone and without appetite, she went along to the
library to wait for Dominic.

It was Saturday and she knew he wasn't going to the dig.
He had asked her whether she was ready to project the first
batch of slides, which had just returned by air from London.

She got her screen and projector ready and settled down
to wait. She felt more jittery with every minute that passed.

When at long last, over an hour later, the door opened,
her heart jerked. But it was Mark who came in, not
Dominic.

"Why, hello, Chloe. How calm and cool you look, after
all the fuss there's been around the place all morning."

Startled, feeling anything but cool, she repeated,
"Fuss?"

"Lord, yes. Didn't you know? Mrs. Vining has had
another of her attacks."

"Oh—how dreadful!"

"Apparently Lotta went and told her something that
upset her thoroughly. Don't ask me what, I haven't been
told yet. I've been haring around the countryside looking
for Dr. Galea. I just brought him in from San Anton."

"What does he say?"

"Don't know yet. He's with her now. You may as well
put all that gear away, Chloe. Dominic will be fully occupied. He told me to tell you not to wait."

Chloe couldn't help feeling a guilty sense of reprieve.

"Was it a serious attack?"

"I'm afraid it was, rather. In her state of health, any attack is bound to be serious, poor dear. She has a form of
angina, you know. Might die any day, or equally, might
live to a ripe old age. Awful anxiety for Dominic. He
adores her. She was a wonderful woman before she
became ill. I've heard she was a famous beauty. She's still
handsome, isn't she? I wonder what Lotta said to upset
her. Have you any idea?"

Chloe said slowly, "I think I have." Lotta had told her
about the balcony incident, of course. Perhaps, too—
almost certainly—she had told her about her own decision
to leave Santa Clara. Either would have agitated her—been

enough, perhaps, to bring on one of her attacks, Chloe thought unhappily.

"Come on, then. Come clean. Tell Mark."

She shook her head. She would have liked to confide in Mark. He knew all about Mrs. Vining's obsession, and about Dominic and Louise. But she couldn't bring herself to repeat, even to Mark, the conversation she had unwillingly overheard in the library.

She could tell him about the balcony incident, of course. But her own recollection was so incomplete; and anyway, the whole affair was so fantastic. She could no more bring herself to accuse Louise of having tried to push her over the edge than to blame Lotta for Louise's fall. She couldn't imagine anyone believing her if she did. Any more than she could really believe that Dominic had credited Louise's version of her accident.

The whole thing was a mess. The only conclusion she could come to was that the sooner she got out of Santa Clara the better.

"I'd rather not say anything," she told Mark. "I expect you'll hear plenty. You must form your own conclusions. What I am going to do, Mark, is leave here."

His face fell comically. "You mean throw up the job? Leave Malta?"

"No, no. I mean leave Santa Clara."

"But what on earth...?"

"Please, don't ask me to explain, Mark."

"But there must be some reason. Perhaps I can help...."

"No, Mark."

"Is it Mrs. Vining? I know she wants to line you up with Dominic....?"

"I said please don't ask me, Mark."

"Oh, all right. But I wish you could manage to laugh it off—whatever it is—and stay on. I'll hate you to go. It's been heaven, Chloe, having you here."

The real emotion behind the light words surprised her.

"Bless you, Mark. But I honestly feel I must go. It's all become somehow complicated and difficult. I'm not going far, though. I thought of moving to the hotel here—then I could still, I hope, have access to the office and the dark-room."

"Oh, well, in that case..." Mark allowed. That way, he saw a chance of enjoying rather more of her undiluted company that he ever did at Santa Clara. "I know the management there. Like me to telephone about a room?"

"Please do."

"But Dominic isn't going to be pleased, you know. I wonder what he'll have to say when he hears," Mark said as he lifted the telephone.

As she thought of what Dominic might say all Chloe's nervous fears rushed back to overwhelm her.

Mark, it seemed, wasn't having much success.

"Bad luck," he told her as he replaced the receiver. "They've nothing vacant till the end of the month."

"Then I must try to get some place in Sliema or Valetta."

"Rather far from your darkroom and gear, isn't it? And how about transport? Dominic's going to object strongly, I don't mind betting. Besides which he's bound to conclude that you yearn for the bright lights, the social round, the fleet. He'll probably blame my brother."

"I know. But what else can I do?"

"Stay on here," said Mark. He picked up the receiver again as the telephone rang.

"Oh, it's you, is it?" he remarked austerely to the voice at the other end. "Yes, she is. She's here with me now, actually. I'm not sure I want her to talk to you. Oh, all right. Hold the line."

Chloe took the receiver from him. She was laughing in spite of herself.

"Robert?... Yes...no, I'm afraid I can't manage Gozo today.... No, but you see I'm leaving here.... No, not the island, just Santa Clara. Yes, today if I can find a room to go to.... Never mind why, that's my business, I can't possibly tell you. Look, will you be an angel and come up here now? And then run me down to Sliema and Valetta and help me find a place to live? I expect you know all the best ones. Not the Felicia, nothing so grand, I'm a working girl, remember.... What?... In Sliema? Why, that sounds as if it might be wonderful. Could we go and see them this morning?... Yes, I'm ready right now....Of course I will. You really are an angel, Robert. What? Oh, nonsense, my dear. Goodbye."

Her face looked happier as she turned to Mark.

"Robert knows of a room. He says he has some friends who have a big apartment in Sliema and want to rent their spare room to somebody congenial. They had his sister—the husband's, I mean—for a while, but she's just sailed for home. He likes his wife to have company when he's at sea."

"That'll be the Soameses, I expect. Nice creatures. If anybody but my young brother had suggested it—no doubt for his own fell purposes—I'd say it was the very thing."

"Me, too. I think I'll risk the fell purposes," Chloe said, laughing again. She knew very well that beneath all the banter Mark thought the world of Robert.

"Hmm. But I still wonder what Dominic's going to say." *Just let me get it settled,* Chloe thought, *and does it matter much what he says? He can't force me to stay on here. And a fait accompli's an awfully hard thing to do much about.*

When Robert turned up, half an hour later, he was clearly gratified at the warmth of his reception. So delighted did Chloe seem at seeing him that perhaps he could be forgiven for connecting her sudden, unexplained decision to move from Mdina with himself. His amatory experience had shown him no reason why not.

"I've called Freda Soames, and she says they'll be delighted. She said to take you around for a pink gin and see if you could bear each other. If you can, your room's ready anytime. You can discuss the business side over the pink gin. I say, Chloe, it's going to be wonderful having you there—so much more available."

Chloe gave him an absent smile.

She was thinking how much more satisfactory it was going to be, when she explained to Dominic that she proposed to cut short her stay at Santa Clara, if she could say that friends had invited her to live with them in Sliema....

"I'm all ready," she said, picking up her handbag. "Shall we go?"

FREDA AND ALARIC SOAMES were a tall, fair, blue-eyed pair with such a family resemblance that Chloe wasn't surprised to learn that they were second cousins.

They took one frankly assessing look at her, then hailed her with enthusiasm and said she was an answer to prayer.

Their apartment was on the third floor of one of the tall balconied stone mansions that lined the Sliema waterfront. The furniture that had come with it was shabby—armchairs and settee with sagging springs, faded curtains and carpet, scratched tabletops—and rather sketchy. But the pleasant front room they offered Chloe looked out on the sparkling sea and the entrance to Marsa Mxett harbor.

A warm, salt-laden breeze fluttered the curtains. On the promenade with its wind-slanted pink-flowered tamarisks people strolled, children and dogs romped, cars sped by and sea gulls swooped and squawked.

A few hardy characters were bathing off the shallow ledges of rock below the promenade, where the sea lapped pale green and very clear. Away across the water, four corvettes moving in line laid a foaming track on the blue.

"The furniture in these rented apartments is generally a bit grim," Freda said. "But at least our bath is always piping hot. And we have rather a decent old cook, so you won't starve."

"I love this room," Chloe told her.

"Good. Then if you think you could bear to come and live as one of the family, why, we'd love to have you."

"Thank you very much," Chloe said warmly. They talked finances for a while, and came to a satisfactory agreement. "May I come right away, this very afternoon?" she asked.

"But of course. As soon as you like. We're going on board the submarine depot ship for cocktails this evening—Alaric's in submarines, did you know? So you and Robert had better come along with us."

From her cozy way of saying, "you and Robert," Chloe could see that she was already romantically linked with him in her hostess's mind. But did it matter? Robert would be away to sea in a week or two. And she would quite likely have left the island before he came back. Meanwhile, this was likely to be far pleasanter than any hotel could possibly be.

"Thank you, that'll be fun," she said amenably, and refrained from correcting any mistaken impression Freda might have about Robert and herself. Plenty of time for that when she knew her better.

Afterward over the pink gins, she was as gay and lively as she could manage to be, considering that at the back of her mind there was still this nagging worry over the unavoidable interview with Dominic.

It was a pity he was in the courtyard, seeing off an elderly man with a black gladstone bag who must surely be Dr. Galea, when Robert took her back just before one o'clock to Santa Clara. She saw the ironic lift of his black brows.

Hurriedly she told Robert, "Please don't wait. Mrs. Vining is ill—excuse me if I don't ask you to come in. I'll be ready any time after four o'clock. Goodbye till then—and many, many thanks."

"So long, darling. Till then," Robert answered in rather too possessive a tone. Luckily, Dominic couldn't possibly have heard.

When both cars had gone and they were alone, she asked him nervously, "How is your mother now?"

"A little better. She's resting."

"Oh—I'm so glad. I—may I speak to you, Dominic?"

The gleam of humor lightened his eyes.

"If it's as serious as you look, can we let it keep till after lunch? There's the gong now. Come along in. I'm hungry."

To Chloe's relief Louise didn't appear, and neither Mark nor Dominic referred to the events of the previous night; she didn't even know whether Mark had heard the story or not.

The talk was exclusively concerned with the dig. A new burial chamber had been found under the sanctuary. It was now being opened up, and the earth with which it was packed was yielding a rich haul of jars, implements, small statues and bones. The team was having an enthralling time with it.

"By the way, if you can spare the time we might take a

look at those color slides this afternoon,'' Dominic suggested when they reached the coffee stage of the meal.

"Of course. I'll go now and get them ready.''

As Chloe set down her empty cup she noticed that her
hand wasn't quite steady. She wondered where all the poise
on which generally she prided herself had gone since
yesterday. The balcony business must have been more of a
shock than she had realized.

She projected her color slides without mishap, however.
Dominic was pleased, and praised them warmly. She
started to dismantle her projector and pack the slides in
their box.

"Well, now that's over, would you like to 'speak,'
Chloe?'' Dominic asked with the flash of warmth and
charm that was his smile.

"Please.''

"Well?''

She felt herself turn pale. "It's—I wanted to tell you
that I'm leaving Santa Clara.''

"Indeed? Why?''

"Well—as a matter of fact I'm going to stay with friends
in Sliema. Th-thank you very much for having me here.
They've asked me to go this evening,'' she told him in a
rush.

"I see.''

Oh, heavens, he's furious, she thought. "Do you—
mind?''

She hadn't meant to ask him that, so baldly, but the
words had spoken themselves.

He gave her a coldly considering look.

"Naturally I mind. I asked you to stay here for a special
reason, as you know. This sudden departure is likely to
cause me considerable inconvenience—and you, too, I
imagine. However, you seem to have made your plans.''

Avoiding his eyes, she spoke quietly—though her heart
was hammering so that she feared he must hear it. "It's
been very kind of you, letting me live here. But you see I
would prefer to feel quite free and—independent during
the rest of my short time in the island.''

"It isn't necessary to elaborate. You've decided to leave

Santa Clara, and I certainly can't prevent you," Dominic said. "Have you thought about how you'll get to the dig?"

"I thought I might rent a car from one of the garages."

"H'm. Expensive. You'd better take the Austin and park it near where you're staying."

"Thank you very much."

"And what about the darkroom, your projecting work?"

"I thought I could still use the one at Santa Clara. And I would be here to project the slides whenever you wanted, of course."

"It all sounds unnecessarily complicated. However, with the Austin I suppose you can come and go as required."

She said diffidently, "I promise you I won't let this—change of residence interfere in any way with my work."

"I'm glad to hear it."

She was divided between relief at his making it so comparatively easy for her, and fear that there might be more to come. A sting, as it were, in the tail.

There was. It came a moment later.

But it wasn't, as she feared it might be, a reference to the events of last night.

"You spoke of going to stay with friends," he said, rather brusquely. "I was under the impression that when you came to Malta you knew no one in the island."

"No, that's true. I didn't."

"These, then, are new friends? People you've met since you came here?" he asked. He wasn't looking at her. He was fiddling with the box of slides, turning them over, holding first one, then another, up to the light.

"Yes."

"Do I know them, I wonder?"

"They're called Soames. Lieutenant-Commander and Mrs. Soames. He's in submarines. Mark knows them. They're friends of . . . ."

Her small flash of defiance tailed off. She particularly didn't want to tell him whose friends they were. But of course he had guessed. She knew by the mockery in his eyes.

"Friends of . . . ?"

"Of Robert Tenby."

"Ah. I understand."

Something caustic and cynical in his voice stung her to anger.

"You don't. You don't understand at all," she flashed. "Or care!"

He said nothing, only looked at her, eyebrows raised.

"I beg your pardon," she said at length. "I'm afraid I'm a little—upset. I shouldn't have said that. But does it really matter very much if I live elsewhere? I'm twenty-three. Old enough to look after myself. And if my work doesn't suffer—I've already promised you it won't—you won't really mind, will you? You won't, please, insist on my staying at Santa Clara?"

When she lifted her eyes to meet his again, she was relieved to see that he was smiling.

"Don't look so tragic, Chloe, please. I understand a good deal more than you think—though I would prefer not to discuss, now at any rate, what has happened here. But as long as your work continues to be efficient I agree I have no other claim on you. You must do exactly as you choose."

She had the sensation of her heart dropping down, down.

Instead of being delighted that she had got away with it so lightly, she was illogically miserable because he showed no sign of wanting to force her to change her mind.

Nothing, she thought, could have shown more plainly how little he cared about her—herself, as distinct from the work she did for him.

"You mustn't think . . ." she began, then fell silent—for what more was there to say?

He surprised her by grinning.

"I'm not thinking—except that Nibblu had better tune up the car before you leave. Then Carmel can drive you down to Sliema, and find somewhere near your apartment where you can park it."

"It's very, very kind of you."

"Is it?"

She preferred not to tell him that Robert had been com-

ing to fetch her. Better telephone and put him off, and go
with Carmel as soon as the car was ready.

She held out her hand.

"So long, Dominic. Thank you for having me here."

He let that pass. "See you on Monday, then, Chloe?"

"I'd like to send a message to your mother—to wish her
a quick recovery."

"I'll say everything necessary on your behalf."

"Please do—and give her my love."

"She'll miss you, Chloe. And so will I," he added with
the smile that had been her undoing from the start. Her
heart was beating fast, too fast. Her hand, she found, was
still in his, held fast.

"Oh..." she cried and, dragging it away, without
another word turned and fled from the library.

Any more of that, she thought wildly as she ran up to
her room, *and I'd have been in his arms, telling him I'm in
love with him. If he asks me to marry him I will jump at
him....*

Which was the last thing she wanted to say to a man who
thought women were merely "an impediment to great
enterprises...."

As she passed Mrs. Vining's door she saw that for once
it was closed. Angina, she thought soberly; poor, poor
contessa. Guiltily she wondered if her running away like
this would upset Dominic's mother further. Remorsefully
she promised herself to make time to visit her regularly, as
soon as she was well enough for visitors.

Quickly, now, she packed her remaining possessions
into the small overnight case she had carried with her on
the plane. When everything was in she took a quick regretful look around the charming room that had been hers,
went to the window for a last glance at the breathtaking
view of island and sea and went downstairs to telephone
Robert, arranging to meet him later at the apartment.

Only Mark was there to see her off when Carmel
brought the Austin around to the door.

CHAPTER NINE

DARKNESS FALLS SWIFTLY in Malta. One moment the sun is striking sparks off the horizon. The next it is sliding rapidly down toward the horizon, tinting the golden stone fortifications and buildings and turning the water to blood.

Then the shadows gather swiftly; the sea turns wine dark, then indigo. . . .

It was already dark—but the darkness was luminous, silvered by the light of a bright moon—one evening when Chloe stood at her window, looking out at the scene. She had been some time at the apartment now and felt like one of the family.

She had just come from her bath—something to look forward to more and more, now that the weather was warming up, after the long dusty day at the dig. She was cooling off before dressing, as she liked to do.

The night was calm and windless, and agreeably warm. This was as it should be—for the aircraft carrier, due to depart shortly for an unspecified desination, was *en fête*, returning the hospitality its personnel had enjoyed during their time in the harbor.

A batch of invitations had been sent out for a supper and dance on board. Robert had sent cards to Chloe and the Soameses as well as Dominic, Louise and Mark.

Chloe's feelings were a mixture of excitement and vague foreboding—of what, she couldn't have said. She tried to forget the foreboding and concentrate on the glamorous evening ahead.

"It'll be good," Freda had assured her. "These rather grand naval affairs, with the admiral-in-chief and all the top brass there, usually are."

Chloe had a new dress for it, one she had brought out with her and not yet had a chance to wear. It was a dream of amber chiffon and fine lace that fitted her figure closely and swirled into fullness below her hips.

There were slender stilt-heeled sandals to match and for jewelry an exquisite necklace and earrings of topaz, golden brown like her eyes, that had been Lady Stanton's birthday present last year.

She couldn't help knowing, as she studied her reflection in the mirror, curtsying to it so that her skirt billowed around her, that she had never looked better in her life.

She hoped, shamelessly, that Dominic would be there to see her. But then again she felt that sense of foreboding. She couldn't forget he had told Louise, though not in so many words, that he meant to ask her to marry him. And that it wouldn't be for love she was well aware.

If it should happen tonight, what would she say or do? She had absolutely no idea how she would react. It would depend on him—how he spoke, looked. No good getting worked up about it now. Perhaps it wouldn't happen, anyway....

In the sitting room she found Alaric mixing a preparty cocktail.

"Here you are," he said, filling a glass for her. "Just to put us in the party mood. It's fairly harmless."

"It's lovely, Alaric."

Freda looked her over.

"My, my! And who is all this radiance in aid of?"

"No one. It's just that glorious feeling of not knowing what the evening may bring forth. You look pretty radiant yourself—doesn't she, Alaric?"

"Not bad," he allowed, with a fond look that belied the tepid praise. "In fact my women do me credit tonight. It'll be chilly going out in the launch, Chloe. You'll need your mink."

She laughed and picked up her camel's-hair coat. "This'll have to do instead."

Freda, she saw, was wrapping herself into a rather ancient fur.

"I keep this old heirloom for parties on board," she explained. "It's known throughout the fleet as Freda's bit of vermin."

Gaily they bundled themselves into Alaric's car. Chloe, in the middle, made herself small and gave herself up to wishful thinking.

At the harbor they found dozens of parked cars and a crowd of well-wrapped guests, waiting for passage in the trim launches that were ferrying between the carrier and the shore.

Across the water the carrier's immense bulk, brilliantly outlined in lights, glittered like a showboat. It was duplicated in the smooth surface of the water. The launches, coming and going, shattered its reflection into golden fragments that leaped and danced and came together again.

Robert was waiting to greet them at the head of the gangway. He dealt with their coats and shepherded them on deck. His blue eyes studied Chloe ardently, from the top of her shining head to the tips of her sandals.

"You look marvelous. There isn't anyone here to touch you," he murmured as he took her arm.

"Flatterer!"

"No, I mean it."

"Hmm. You chaps are doing Malta proud tonight, my lad," Alaric told him judicially as they mingled with the crowd.

"Had to do something to knock you submarine characters in the eye," Robert retorted. After which grade-school exchange the pair grinned amiably at each other. Honor was satisfied.

Chloe looked eagerly around her, bright-eyed with delight.

For her the vast improbable vessel moving gently beneath her feet had a dreamlike quality. It was elegantly festooned with multicolored lights, and there were awnings to keep the night air from the hundreds of guests. Its spotless quarterdeck was ready for dancing. Its blue-jacketed band fiddled and blew with muted gusto behind banked roses and hydrangeas.

The captain, gold-braided, with rows of medal ribbons on his broad chest was chatting affably with a group of exalted persons—His Excellency and his lady, the admiral-in-chief, an imposing Maltese matron in sapphire satin and diamonds and the little dark baron, her husband.

A monocled Frenchman was kissing hands all around with Gallic grace. Chloe saw him hurry over to greet Louise, who had just made an entrance, a little later when the crowd had thinned somewhat, with Mark. She was in her favorite flame color, and wore her "wicked lady" look with telling effect. The Frenchman lost no time in leading her off on his arm.

Around the fringes of the dancing floor male guests, in vastly becoming uniforms or conventional tails, tossed down whiskeys and pink gins. The women, in summery evening gowns, sipped delicately at their cocktails and looked questingly around them.

A group of pretty young things clustered around the flag lieutenant and the governor's aide-de-camp, suave young men who could be relied on to effect the right introductions and see that no one lacked a dancing partner or someone to flirt with.

Robert brought Chloe a glass of her favorite dry sherry.

"Your eyes are exactly the same color—and about twice as intoxicating," he told her.

She laughed.

"Why, Robert, what's come over you? Such a pretty speech!"

He thought it was, too. He felt in form tonight.

"It's true," he assured her. "Look, I've got three or four duty dances I must do now. Keep all the rest for me, won't you?"

"Wouldn't that be rather indiscreet?"

"I don't care. Chloe, we sail in less than forty-eight hours. I must have a proper chance to talk to you before we say goodbye. It's important. You must promise. All the dances after the fourth."

She laughed and said lightly, "Run along and do your duty dances, and then we'll see."

As she moved onto the dance floor with Mark, who had hurried to claim her, her eyes roved in search of a tall, slim figure, a dark head, quizzical gray eyes in a deeply tanned face. Alas, there was no sign of him.

"Didn't Dominic come after all, Mark?" she asked at length.

"Indeed he did—quite took me aback. It's most unusual for him. I bet the Fishing Fleet are agog."

"I don't see him anywhere."

"You won't—not on the dancing floor. He doesn't dance nowadays—thinks it's a moronic occupation for adults. It is, of course—but fun, too. Actually, he was being taken below by some elderly VIP when I last saw him."

So he was here. That was something, even if he wouldn't dance with her. She caught sight of him as the dance with Mark came to an end, and her heart gave its now familiar swerve. But he hadn't seen her; he wasn't looking for her. He was moving off again, deep in talk, now, with His Excellency. She was sadly disappointed. Despite the glamour and gaiety of the occasion, she felt a sense of flatness spread around her.

She danced next with Alaric, then with two of his friends whom she had met in the submarine depot shop. Then Robert claimed her for number five.

It was a pity that when Dominic came up on deck and at last saw her, she should have been whirling in Robert's arms, with Robert's lips against her hair, murmuring something ardent.

She saw Dominic's black brows go up in that maddeningly ironic quirk.

She thought with helpless exasperation, *this would happen. Oh, damn!*

She managed a gay smile and an airy wave of the hand that rested on Robert's shoulder.

Robert said jealously, holding her closer "Who's that you're waving and smiling at? You're to keep all your smiles for me, understand?"

"Silly! I'm enjoying myself so much I've simply got to smile at everyone tonight. Think of it. It's the first time I've ever danced on one of Her Majesty's ships."

"If I have anything to do with it, it won't be the last," Robert growled.

At the end of the waltz he piloted her firmly away from

the crowd. With her arm tucked in his he led her to a quiet corner well beyond the festooned lights.

"I marked this place down early, and established my claim to it," he told her with naive satisfaction. "Anybody else who comes here is to be told it's reserved for His Excellency and partner."

"Robert!" She laughed.

"You don't really mind, do you? You know why I did it. You must know. . . what I want to tell you, Chloe. I'm mad about you. I'm in love with you, really and truly. I want us to be engaged before I leave."

She was taken by surprise. She hadn't imagined Robert would go as far as this. Light seduction, she had fancied, was more in his line than marriage.

He had put an arm around her, and was trying to draw her close to him. She evaded him adroitly.

"Haven't you forgotten something?"

"Forgotten? What on earth do you mean?"

"Didn't you explain, the first time we met, that a young naval officer travels the fastest if he travels alone?"

"I know, but. . . ."

"And that getting tied up with a woman early in your career can be a serious drag?"

"I was a fool," he exclaimed. "I barely knew you then. I'd no idea I was going to fall so terribly in love with you."

After a moment he added naively, "Besides, you've got a career of your own, haven't you? You wouldn't be a drag."

She laughed out loud at that, and with a muttered exclamation he seized her in his arms.

"Stop laughing," he ordered roughly. "I tell you I want to be married, now."

She disengaged herself neatly once again. He was by no means the first ardent young man with whom she had to deal.

"But not to me, Robert."

"Of course to you. Who else?"

"Listen. You're going off on this cruise or whatever, and by the time you come back, I'll be gone. And there'll be a new batch of lovelies waiting to spoil you. Won't you feel thankful, then, that you're still footloose and fancy-free? Much better than being tied to an absent fiancée you've already half forgotten—right?''

He said sulkily, "Of course, if that's how you feel. I can see you don't care a rap for me. Only for the good time I can give you here.''

"That's a little unfair, Robert.''

He tried to hold her to him again.

"I know, darling. Please forgive me, I didn't mean it. But are you sure you won't?''

"Quite sure, thank you, Robert.''

Kissing him lightly on the cheek, she stood up and shook out her skirt.

"How about some supper?'' she suggested. "I'm starving. Would you like us to have it together?''

"I don't want any supper.''

"Oh, come on. You must keep up your strength, as my old nanny used to say. We'll join the Soameses and make a foursome. It'll be fun.''

"Fun!'' Robert echoed bitterly.

But he was a little mollified by the way she tucked her hand under his arm, as well as by a sneaking feeling that perhaps she was right about memory fading. It usually did when he got well away to sea, he had found.

Mark and Louise joined their party for supper and, a little later, so did Dominic. When he sat himself down next to her Chloe tried to be casual and indifferent, but her treacherous heart performed its usual antics.

She thought he looked put out, but whether with her she couldn't tell.

She had seen very little of him in the past week or two. He had been much at Santa Clara, even deserting the dig in order to sit with his mother, who was still very unwell. In the last week, too, he had made a quick plane trip to London. Mark had told her that some learned society of archaeologists had invited him to lecture on the progress of the excavations, which were causing great interest.

She herself had hardly spoken to him. He had mapped out her program and given it to her in writing, so there had been no special reason he should seek her out, or she him.

But before she left Santa Clara he had frequently come to watch her at work, to offer suggestions and sometimes to help. She had been afraid his present aloofness meant that at heart he was angry at her deflection.... If so, the mask of polite indifference he wore when they did meet was her only clue.

Louise and Alaric, both in sparkling form, were sparring gaily while the others listened and laughed. Under cover of the noise Dominic leaned forward and spoke to Chloe in an urgent undertone.

"Can you spare me the next dance? I want to talk to you. Something rather important."

"I'd have spared you one long before this if you'd asked me," she answered impulsively.

He gave her an enigmatic look.

"Would you? You seemed to me to be rather heavily committed. The fact is that I only came here on the chance of having a talk with you."

Her heart began to race. Was this it?

"But surely you know all my time is yours?"

"Your working time, yes. But I couldn't very well bring up the matter in question on the dig."

"Oh. Well, there's the music now. I've finished supper—have you? Shall we go?"

"Wait a little."

But as soon as Robert had gone off to dance with Freda, and Alaric with Louise, he got up. In the most natural way in the world he held out his hand, tucked hers under his arm and led the way.

"But not to dance," he told her firmly. "Do you know any place where we can get right away from the mob?"

She gave a little spurt of laughter.

"Why should you think I do?"

"Do you?"

"Actually I know the very spot."

He didn't make the ironic comment she expected, and disengaging her arm she led the way to Robert's secret corner. It was unoccupied, and no one appeared to shoo them away. They sat down, and he lit a cigarette for her and took one himself.

"Now that I've got you here I hardly know how to begin," he said ruefully, after a silence in which she had felt sure he must hear the pounding of her heart.

"And as I don't know what it's all about I can't help," she pointed out. "Is it something about my work, Dominic?"

"No." He threw his cigarette down and crushed it out with his foot. "Look here," he went on brusquely. "What I want to know is—are you free? You're not engaged to anyone, are you?"

She shook her head.

"No, I'm not. Why, Dominic?"

"In that case, will you consider becoming engaged to me?"

So this was it? But what a proposal!

The color drained from her face, but she kept her eyes bravely on his as she asked carefully, "Are you telling me that you love me, Dominic?"

She saw his expression change. His eyes looked wary, withdrawn.

"I admire you more than any girl I know."

Her heart sank, though she knew it was what she should have expected.

"The word was love," she insisted.

"Is love of such paramount importance? I respect and trust you. We have interests in common."

She looked away from him. The lights seemed to blur and swim together, a lot of little multicolored haloes. She blinked her eyelids hard to keep back the tears.

"To me, love is more important than all the other things you mention."

He gave her that wary look again.

"You mean you wouldn't consider an engagement, however suitable, without love?"

She felt her control going.

"I mean I wouldn't promise to marry any man who didn't love me enough to live or—or die for me if he had to—as I would for him if I loved him," she said in sudden furious rush of words, losing her head and her temper together. Her bright eyes challenged his, defying him.

She could see he was very much taken aback.

What sort of girl does he think I am, then, she wondered angrily.

"It's obvious you're a romantic," he said, his mouth sardonic. "You sound like a character created by a female novelist. Tell me: is there, in point of fact, anyone for whom you would be prepared to—er—live or die, Chloe?"

"You've no right to ask that."

"No right, agreed. But I'm very anxious to know."

She was silent. Indignantly silent. At length she said in a small voice, "Well, in point of fact there is."

His eyebrows shot up.

"You said you were free."

"I said I wasn't engaged."

"I see. Of course I have no right to ask this, either—but does this fortunate chap know?"

She lost her head again. "For heaven's sake—I've no idea if he knows. I haven't told him, nor has he asked me. Now must we go on discussing my love life? Unless you're thinking of asking me outright who he is?"

He said with a quirk of his dark brows, "No. I don't suppose you'd tell me that."

"Then can't we change the subject?"

"No, Chloe, I'm afraid we can't. You see, I've got a most urgent reason for asking you to be engaged to me. One that I beg you to think about before you refuse."

He got up then and walked around restlessly. The music had started up again. A waltz, "Someday I'll find you," slow and nostalgic. She could have wept.

She said shakily, "Please—I'd like another cigarette."

He lit one for her.

"I had a talk with Galea yesterday. He takes the gravest view of my mother's condition. He fears she's unlikely to survive this last attack. It has left her very weak—undermined what little strength she has. He won't commit himself, but he thinks perhaps two months—not much more."

Chloe saw the pain in his eyes.

"I'm terribly sorry," she said in a low voice.

"I blame Lotta for the attack. She rushed in and told my mother her version of what happened on your balcony.

She insisted Louise was trying to get rid of you—because of me. All highly fanciful, I suspect—but my mother has given me no peace. She's set her heart on my marrying you. Oh, it's difficult to explain—but I believe she'll die happy if we announce our engagement.''

"But we...."

"Listen," he broke in. "Since this other fellow doesn't seem to have entered the lists yet, couldn't you agree, for the sake of my mother's last few weeks of happiness, just until...?"

He didn't finish. She saw that he couldn't. Until she dies, he meant, of course. Sympathy wiped out every trace of annoyance and humiliation she had felt. She only remembered that this was Dominic, and that he adored his mother.

"I know it's a lot to ask of you," he went on in a quiet voice, without a hint of his usual arrogance. "But I'll be everlastingly grateful. And of course—afterward—you'll be perfectly free...."

Free to insist that you keep the bargain, she wondered with sudden wry mirth.

He was standing over her, looking down at her anxiously. She knew she could refuse him nothing.

"Well, Chloe?"

"You must let me think it over."

He frowned.

"That means you've decided against it."

"No, I haven't—I...."

Impulsively she laid a hand on his arm. Her eyes, lifted to meet his with a look of worry and distress in them, brightened as she caught the gleam of humor in them.

"Would it be so terrible, Chloe?" he demanded, with the flash of charming warmth she could never resist.

It'd be all I'd ask of life—if he loved me, if it were real, she thought.

Suddenly her resistance collapsed completely.

"All right, I'll do it," she said quickly. "As long as there doesn't have to be a lot of publicity. As long as we can keep it more or less in the family."

He looked doubtful, though he thanked her warmly.

"I'll do my best to pipe down on the publicity. But I'm afraid my mother may want to announce it with some éclat. She'll want everyone to know—all her innumerable relations.... I don't quite see how...."

"Oh, all right." In for a penny, in for a pound.

"I may tell her tomorrow?"

"I suppose so."

"She'll be very happy."

"I'm glad."

He smiled suddenly. "I must get you a ring."

"It's usual, isn't it?" she agreed, with a little laugh that just managed not to give her away by turning into a sob. She was only beginning to realize all the implications of the position into which she had let herself be talked.

"Perhaps we'd better go back now. I suppose you don't want me to tell anyone here yet?"

She looked panic-stricken. "Heavens, no."

"All right. One thing—you'll come back to Santa Clara?"

"Must I?"

"I think so. My mother will certainly want it."

"But—Mrs. Carlyon...?"

"Louise will behave herself—or go. She's in no position—financially—to make trouble."

"All right. I'll move back tomorrow. But in fairness to Freda and Alaric Soames, I must tell them why."

"If you feel you must. I suppose you can rely on them not to talk. Don't tell anyone else. Except Mark, of course. To all the rest it must be a genuine match. Until...."

"Until you've no further need for me, and I can vanish back where I came from," she finished for him brightly. "You've got it all neatly worked out, haven't you, Dominic?"

He gave her a glance that made her feel ashamed of herself. It was cheap, she thought remorsefully, to taunt him that way, when only his concern for his mother had driven him to take this certainly distasteful step.

But she didn't retract her words as she fell into step and walked, with a quiet composure she was far from feeling, at his side.

She felt him take her arm and give it a sudden warm pressure.

"I do hope you know how grateful I am, Chloe," he said. "I know it isn't going to be easy—especially for you. But I'll do my best to see you don't regret your kindness. And for a start," he went on in a lighter tone, "we'll take a day off from the dig to see Valetta. I promised, didn't I?"

"I'll love that, Dominic."

"And if it's a suitable day—calm sea, no wind—I'd rather like afterward to take a boat around and have a look at those caves underneath the dig."

"It sounds fun."

"I've got a theory I'd like to test out."

She saw that his face had come alive. *That's his real love,* she thought. *Archaeology.* Would it always be so?

As they drew near the dance floor she began to panic again. *I was a fool to agree to this. I'll never be able to carry it off. If I didn't care a hoot it might be easier. But it's going to be grim, pretending I've had the one thing I've dreamed of handed to me on a plate—and knowing all the time it's phony.*

A little smile twitched at the corner of her mouth.

Perhaps I'll do it so well, pretend so convincingly, that when the time comes to end the engagement, Dominic won't want to, she thought. But she knew it was wishful thinking.

Eyebrows quirked, Dominic wanted to know what the joke was.

"No joke." She smiled. "Just a thought. Here's Robert. I think this must be his dance. Excuse me."

And she went gaily, without a backward look at him, into Robert's eager arms.

"You've been gone for an age," he grumbled. "Do you know you've missed a whole dance? What on earth were you doing?"

"Oh, you know how Dominic likes to talk shop."

"Shop! On a night like this—and sitting with a girl like you! Poor chap."

He held her close and looked down at her with those very blue eyes. She thought with a touch of irritation that he was really just a little too complacent. He wouldn't say "poor chap" quite so smugly tomorrow, when he heard the news—as she supposed he must.

That sobered her—the thought that tomorrow the engagement would be made public, everyone would know. She would have to go back to Santa Clara and face the *contessa*, Mark, Louise—to say nothing of Dominic himself. Panic seized her again.

But all at once, while Robert swung her expertly between the other couples on the crowded deck, her fears left her. Her chin lifted. The little smile twitched at her mouth again.

For better or worse, she was going through with this thing.

What was more, she was resolved to enjoy it. She was a newly engaged girl. Very well, she would *be* a newly engaged girl, as happy and radiant as everyone would expect her to be.

She'd play the part for all it was worth. She'd carry Dominic along with her, make him play his part convincingly, too. No half measures.

That way, when it was all over, at least she'd have something to remember....

CHAPTER TEN

It WAS CHILLY, crossing the harbor again after midnight. A light, keen wind had sprung up, ruffling the dark water and blowing cold on her their faces.

When they got back to the apartment Freda made a pot of tea and they drank huddled in their coats around a small heater.

"Good party. Very well done, didn't you think, Chloe?"

"Wonderful, Alaric." She sipped at her tea for a while, steeling herself. At length she said, "I—I've got something to tell you two," she said.

The Soameses looked at her, then at each other.

"Don't tell us," Freda begged. "Let me guess. You're engaged. Robert proposed, and you said yes."

Chloe shook her head.

"Not Robert."

"Then who? Not Mark?" She could see they were agog.

"Not Mark, either. Dominic. Professor Vining."

"What?" Their astonishment was genuine. They could hardly believe their ears.

"But, my dear, this'll be a sensation," babbled Freda, the first to recover. "Why, he's been the hope and despair of successive Fishing Fleets for ages, I'm told. He's been the perennial bachelor. But what a scoop for you. My dear, I do congratulate you and wish you the most marvelous happiness. Just imagine, Dominic Vining falling in love at last."

"Not that one blames him," Alaric added gallantly.

If Chloe suffered a bitter pang, she had enough pride and spirit not to show it. She laughed gaily.

"Oh, but you're mistaken. I'm afraid it isn't like that at all," she told them.

"Isn't like what?"

"He hasn't fallen in love with me."

"Then why on earth . . . ?" Freda demanded, round eyed.

"Freda, my love, remember the curious cat."

"I don't care. How can I help being curious? You know you are yourself. Do tell, Chloe—please!"

"Of course I'll tell you. But you must swear not to breathe a word to anyone."

"Of course we swear, don't we, Alaric?"

"Then . . . the thing is . . . ."

Briefly she explained what had been going on at Santa Clara since her arrival there. She kept the telling matter-of-fact, as if there was nothing particularly odd about the contessa's obsession or Louise's unheralded visit.

Some things she left out.

She couldn't bring herself to talk about the balcony incident. It seemed to her now so farfetched, so incredible, that she almost wondered if she had dreamed it. Nor did she mention the conversation she had overheard that night in the library.

And not by word or look did she give away the fact that she was in love with Dominic.

Even so, the Soameses found it an absorbing story.

"It's as good as a play," Freda declared. "But I must say, Chloe, I think it's awfully sporting of you to take this on."

"You're a brave woman," Alaric said, looking at her admiringly.

"Actually I'm scared stiff," she confessed. "It'll be so easy to make a blunder and give the whole thing away. I go cold when I think of it. And then there's Louise. I wish I could be sure she won't see through me. I'm not a good liar. And I must admit she rather frightens me."

"She'd frighten me, too. She strikes me as the ruthless type," Freda declared. "But I don't see why she should object to having you as a cousin-in-law. *I* wouldn't, I know."

"Thank you, Freda," Chloe said, smiling at her. "Anyway, it can't be for long."

"But supposing the old lady lasts longer than her doctor expects?" Alaric suggested bluntly.

Chloe frowned worriedly. She had already thought of that.

"I don't know. I can only take that fence when I come to it."

"But she might linger. She might even recover. Doctors aren't always right," Freda insisted.

"I don't know," Chloe said again. "Dominic, of course, would do anything in the world for her. . . ."

"Mm. That's all right from his point of view. But it's not quite the same thing for you. I do hope," Freda said seriously, "that this isn't going to make difficulties for you."

Chloe gave her a quick glance. Had she any inkling of the truth? From her innocently anxious expression, it didn't seem likely.

"The worst part of it all," she said quickly, "is that Dominic insists I must go back at once to Santa Clara. It seems that his mother was very upset when I left. I'm so sorry—I've loved being with you."

"We've loved it, too."

"Been grand having you," Alaric assured her warmly. "And of course you must come back to us, if by any chance this thing doesn't work out."

"Oh, I will. Thank you both. As it is, I suppose I'd better go back after breakfast tomorrow. Dominic has already given me my orders for the day," Chloe said with a little laugh.

Freda gave her a shrewd look.

"It'd be amusing if you ended by falling for each other, you and Dominic."

"Very humorous."

"I wouldn't mind taking a small bet—would you, Freda?"

"Not with me, thanks, Alaric," Chloe said.

Pretending to yawn, she stood up. She had had quite enough of this conversation.

"I'm for bed. Don't forget you're not to tell anyone else the engagement is phony—you won't, will you?"

"Not a word, Chloe, we swear."

"Bless you both, I know you won't. Good night, then. Sweet dreams."

She could hear the murmur of their voices, still talking it over in a cozy marital way, as she wandered between bathroom and bedroom before turning in. She wished she knew what they really thought of it.

BY TEN O'CLOCK on Sunday morning she was sounding her horn discreetly outside the big gates of Santa Clara. The porter opened them for her and she drove into the flowery courtyard with its tingling fountain and high, many-windowed walls. As on that first day, Lotta came out to take her bags.

"Welcome back, *signorina*," she said warmly, her broad impassive face breaking into an unaccustomed smile. "My *contessa* will be very happy."

"How is she, Lotta?"

"All the better for the news she had from *il conte* last night, *signorina*."

"I'm so glad."

"So are we, *signorina*, we are all pleased." The other maids, and Nibblu and Carmel, now came crowding around the car, eager to show their delight and approval. Chloe smiled and thanked them.

Lotta picked up the bags and led the way up the marble staircase and along the corridor between the portraits and suits of armor. Chloe felt as if she was coming home.

She found herself tiptoeing past Mrs. Vining's door. She didn't feel quite up to facing her yet. Perhaps the *contessa* was asleep—no imperious voice called out as she went by.

When she had arranged her things in the mausoleum of a closet again, and set out her toilet things, she stepped to the window for a moment to renew her pleasure in the shimmering view—and to gather her courage together. Then she went downstairs and opened the door of the library.

"Why, Chloe—nice to see you back."

"Thanks, Mark."

"Dominic's upstairs—Galea's here. He'll be down soon." For a moment Mark appeared to be struggling with himself, then he added gruffly, "He told me, Chloe. The whole story, I mean. Thank God it isn't real. I had the shock of my life when he said you were engaged. I could have died."

She looked at him in sudden concern. Was he serious?

"However, as long as it isn't a real match. But remember, as soon as it's over, I'm in the lists again."

"Oh, but Mark...." How tell him it was useless? "I didn't know."

He grinned in his old cheerful way.

"Forget it. Just one of those things. Meanwhile Dominic has briefed me to aid and support you. Things are bound to be tricky now and then. By the way, I called Robert's ship this morning and broke the news. Told him the fiction, of course, not the truth."

"What did he say?"

"He said he would *not* be communicating with you before they sail."

"Oh!"

"He was a trifle Byronic."

Chloe refused to take Robert's heartaches too seriously.

"He'll be recovered by the time he comes back," she prophesied.

Mark grinned again. He knew his volatile brother well enough to agree that she was probably right. They heard voices outside the door.

"That's Dominic seeing Galea off."

Now she would have to face him. She panicked a little, caught Mark's interested eye and said lightly, "He talked of taking the day off to show me the sights."

"Sort of celebration? Very right and proper. Only I wish it were me."

The door opened.

"Ah, there you are," Dominic said coolly, and came and stood by Chloe and slipped his arm through hers. Her heart leaped, careless though the gesture was.

"Hello, Dominic. How is the *contessa*?"

"Better, thanks. Feeling brave? Ready to come up with me and see her?"

Now for the big act. "Of course," she said with a bright smile.

"Let's go, then."

He held open the door and she went ahead of him up the marble staircase. In spite of her resolve her heart was thumping, and at Mrs. Vining's door she stood stock-still, unable to take another step forward.

Dominic said gently, "Not scared, are you? You needn't be."

The door was ajar as usual, and already Mrs. Vining's voice, surprisingly strong, was calling, "Who is it? Lotta? Dominic?"

Dominic took Chloe's arm again and escorted her into the room.

"I've brought Chloe to see you, mother," he said.

"Ah. Come here, my dear. Let me look at you."

Chloe walked over to the bed. She saw at once that the *contessa* was better. The hand that took hers was firm, curiously alive.

"You may kiss me," the imperious voice said, and Chloe bent and put her lips against the thin, wrinkled cheek.

"I'm glad to know you are the sensible girl I took you for," the old lady went on. "You have made me very happy, Chloe. It's high time my son married. And I feel sure you'll make him the right sort of wife."

"I'll try, *contessa*," Chloe said, putting a note of hope and eagerness into her voice, trying to play the part as it should be played.

Dominic had an arm around her shoulders now, holding her close. With a laugh he bent and kissed her, his lips just brushing the corners of her mouth.

She thought rather desperately, *I hadn't bargained for this*. She was afraid he would feel her trembling. But perhaps he would simply put it down to nervousness.

"Of course she's going to make me a wonderful wife, mother," he said with affectionate gaiety. "After all, she was your choice as well as mine."

The *contessa* reached for Chloe's hand again.

"I confess it. The first moment I talked with her, I knew she would be just right for you. Bring me that casket from the top of the dresser, my dear. I must give Chloe her engagement gift."

"Oh, please!" What a sad farce all this was.

"Nonsense, my dear child. Of course you must have a jewel to mark the occasion."

She took the casket from Dominic and set it down on the bed in front of her.

"Now don't tell me you don't love jewels. Any woman who *is* a woman does. And what about a ring? Dominic, of course Chloe must wear an engagement ring. Look."

She had opened the casket with a little key she drew out from under her pillows.

"There are several rings here. Choose one, Dominic. Put it on her finger."

Chloe gazed in astonishment at the heap of jewelry now lying tumbled on the counterpane. Brooches, rings, bracelets, necklaces, earrings, a string of exquisite, milky pearls. Even in the dimness of the room the diamonds and sapphires, rubies and emeralds winked and flashed in their old-fashioned settings of heavy gold. A fortune in jewels, she thought wonderingly.

"Well, Chloe? Any stone you especially like? Choose one," Dominic urged. He was putting up a good performance, too, her mind acknowledged wryly as she shook her head.

"No, you must choose for me. I'd rather you did." Did she sound impossibly coy? Evidently he didn't think so. He picked up her hand and looked at her third finger for size. Then he pondered for a while, turning the rings over, carefully examining them as if the choice was a matter of great importance.

Chloe noticed how eagerly his mother was watching him, enjoying every minute of the little play he was making for her benefit. She felt a sudden warm tenderness for them both.

At length Dominic picked out a ring whose stone was a big square topaz exquisitely set in filigree gold.

"This one, then. Just right for you," he said with decision. "Do you like it?"

"It's beautiful."

"Then let me put it on."

Picking up her hand again, he slipped it on her finger and held it out to show his mother.

"Perfect, my dear. The very one I had in mind. Your father brought it back for me from Ceylon, thirty years ago. And now, give these to Chloe, too," she went on, lifting the pearls.

"Oh, please, no. They're much too valuable. I can't..." Chloe began, feeling that the situation was quite out of control.

The *contessa* leaned forward to pat her hand. Her face was quite transfigured with pleasure.

"Not too valuable for my son's wife," she declared. "And so right for you. Put them on now, my dear. They'll go beautifully with that dark linen you're wearing. Fasten them for her, Dominic."

Obediently Dominic took the string of pearls from her. Standing behind Chloe, he put them around her throat, bending his tall head to examine the clasp.

It was rather an intricate, tiny affair and took him some time. His fingers brushed unavoidably against her neck, sending swift fire through her veins.

"There, I've done up the safety clasp, too," he said at last.

"They suit you," the *contessa* said decidedly. "You must wear them constantly. Their luster will increase from day to day. Pearls are like that. They need the life and warmth of the human skin to be at their best. It's years since those have been worn."

They stayed and chatted for a little while longer and Chloe couldn't but be aware of the change in the *contessa*. Her voice was still imperious, but the harshness had gone from it. The dark eyes were brilliant as ever, but had lost their searching restlessness. Her whole face and manner were softer, gentler. She looked really happy. Chloe's sense of guilt and apprehension deepened.

Dominic kissed his mother.

"We're going to leave you now, mother. I want to take Chloe out—I have some places to show her. We'll come and tell you about it this evening, if it won't tire you."

"I shall rest all day, to be ready for you, my dears."

Outside in the marble-floored gallery, Dominic gave Chloe's elbow a quick squeeze.

"Bless you. You were splendid," he said warmly.

"But, Dominic, you must see I can't accept these valuable gifts," she protested, fingering the pearls.

"Can't you? Not when you see how much pleasure your accepting them gives her?"

"I—oh, yes, I do see. But I can't help thinking of what will happen if she finds us out."

"We must make very sure she doesn't. Don't worry, Chloe. Don't feel guilty. You've made her happy. That's what matters."

She said no more. What was there to say? What—to him—did her feelings and misgivings matter, so long as his mother's last remaining weeks were lightened by an illusion of happiness?

"We'll meet at the car in half an hour if that suits you," Dominic went on briskly. "I'll call Lotta and get her to bring our lunch basket along."

Chloe was already dressed for the day's outing, and only needed a hat to protect her from the sun, which now was often too hot for comfort in the middle of the day.

She fetched a shady straw from her room and went down to the courtyard, swinging it in her hand.

The pearls lay coolly against her neck where Dominic had put them. She could still feel, with a tremor of delight, the brush of his fingers against her skin.

CHAPTER ELEVEN

DOMINIC WAS LEANING AGAINST THE CAR when Chloe came down into the courtyard. He came around and opened her door for her.

"Did I keep you waiting?"

"No. You're punctual to the minute."

She saw that he had changed into gray flannels, a becoming blue shirt with a scarf at its open neck, a light jacket. He was hatless and seemed in a holiday mood.

"Nice," he said approvingly, looking her up and down as she got in the car and bending to tuck her pleated skirt out of harm's way.

"Nice, too," she said, greatly daring, eyeing him in turn.

He laughed and slid in beside her. She liked the look of his long brown hands on the wheel. She liked his clean, strong profile, the arrogant way he carried his head, the dark hair. She stole bemused glances at him as he swung the car dexterously along Mdina's narrow alleys, passed beneath the archway and over the drawbridge, negotiated the clamorous square with its panting red buses, donkeys, hawkers and loungers and turned off onto the coastward road at the bottom of the hill.

"What a wonderful day," she exclaimed spontaneously as the sea came into view. The water was blue green and very clear. It rippled gently and seemed to stretch to endless distances. A tiny breeze fluttered the marigolds and poppies that grew thicker than ever alongside the road and in the flat, stony fields. The crushed almond scent of oleanders filled the car whenever they passed a clump of them, rose flowered or white.

"Heaven," Chloe said, sniffing through the open window.

"What? We're taking the coast road so I can let the car out a bit. I hope you don't mind speed."

"Love it!" The sun dazzled on the sea and she screwed up her eyes.

What a pleasant, easy person she is, he said to himself. *She enjoys everything, she isn't temperamental, she's interested and appreciative. And as clean and fresh as a spring morning.* She made him feel lighthearted in an unaccustomed way. *I ought to do this sort of thing oftener,* he thought.

"This is St. Paul," he told her, and pointed out the figure of the apostle, perched up on the island that was his undoing. She didn't tell him she'd already been there with Robert. Instead she commented happily on the painted fishing boats rocking in the bay, the villagers sunning themselves at open doorways, the charm of the little harbor, the comic figure of a stout priest walking under an open parasol.

"And old aunt of mine lives here," Dominic said. "She grows the best roses on the island. There—that big pink house behind those tall trees. Aunt Rosa-Maria. I used to be terrified of her when I was a boy. She has a mustache."

Chloe's happy young laughter rang out.

She wanted to ask him more about when he was a boy, but he put on speed as they left the village behind. The road became very wide, with an excellent surface. The needle crept up to fifty, sixty, seventy.

She smiled to hear him singing under his breath as they swooped around the wide curves. She thought, *I love you, I love you, I love you.* She felt like singing, too.

Close in, the sea was streaked with gorgeous jewel colors, jade, amethyst, sapphire. Here and there fishermen hopefully cast their lines into it. Goats, grazing on the flowery verges, lifted their demon heads to stare with startled yellow eyes as the car zoomed past.

At St. Julien they slowed to a more decorous pace. Here there were English children, Maltese nannies, dogs. On the Sliema seafront the traffic thickened, they shared the road with gleaming cars, buses, cyclists, donkey carts.

Chloe looked up at the windows of the Soameses' apartment, at her own room—but without real regret, though she'd loved being there. She didn't want to be anywhere else but where she was, this minute....

"Valetta now," Dominic said. "The Grand Palace first. After that we'll see."

"I'm looking forward to it."

Kingsway was packed as always. The sidewalks overflowed with Maltese who had nothing to do, it seemed, but stroll and argue heatedly with each other—politics, was the number one topic, Dominic said. Shoppers bargained keenly in doorways, patrons crowded the open-air cafés, a brass band and half a dozen radios, turned up loud, added to the steady clamor of voices.

Evidently a *festa* was imminent, for benevolent saintly images were being hoisted into position against lamp posts, lavish bunting fluttered overhead and draped the stately buildings, electric light bulbs outlined balconies, gables and pediments. An occasional premature rocket exploded overhead with shattering effect.

The side streets that slipped down from Kingsway to the sea, so steeply they broke now and then into a scamper of steps, were similarly decorated and nearly as crowded.

"What is it all about?" Chloe asked. She almost had to shout to be heard.

He shrugged indifferently. "Some saint's day tomorrow," he shouted back, and she remembered that his family was not Catholic.

The car threaded neatly through the traffic and came to rest among the dozens of cars parked in the square between the Royal Library and the Palace.

Sentries of the guard paced back and forth, slapping their rifle butts, high stepping on the turn, rigid with nervousness or importance. One of them so far forgot himself as to wink at Chloe as he did his goose step. She smiled back. He was young and nice-looking and must be excruciatingly bored, tied to his beat on a morning of such sunshine and fun.

She delighted in the Grand Palace. Such a plain-looking building outside, but so full of treasures. Acres of gorgeous Gobelin tapestries, brocade hangings, frescoes, splendid dark portraits of former Grand Masters and dozens and dozens of suits of armor of different designs, all standing around realistically among innumerable weapons.

"But they're so small," Chloe exclaimed, meaning the suits of armor. "Were the men really as short as that in the age of chivalry? I mean, *you* would never get into one those."

"Those are what they got into—and fought in."

"Another illusion shattered," she said sadly. "I imagined all the knights gloriously big and broad and handsome."

He showed her the elaborate gold inlay on some of the suits.

"Dandy little men, too," he said.

Going down the graceful curving staircase to the street again, he showed her how the steps had been made especially shallow so that the knights in their ponderous metal equipment could more easily mount them. The little detail seemed to bring it all alive for her. *He's wonderful to be with,* she thought. She could hardly reconcile this Dominic with the one on the plane who had said so implacably, "I make it a rule never to have a woman on a dig," and who had snubbed her so unmercifully during that lunch at the club.

Does he really like me better now, she asked herself. *Or does he merely feel under an obligation, and is he repaying it the best way he can?*

She didn't know, didn't even care. She let him take her arm and lead her back to the car in the blinding sunlight of the square.

"It *is* a wonderful day," he said. "What if we leave the Cathedral and the Auberges for some other time?"

She nodded happily. She was content to do whatever he suggested. He threaded through the traffic again and swung out of the tunnel beneath the ramparts.

"Right. First of all we'll make for the other coast and eat our lunch on the clifftop. I know rather a good spot."

He drove for a while after that in silence. He broke it to say, "Did you notice how much better my mother is already?"

She nodded soberly. The question brought back to her all the falsity of their relationship.

"Yes. I did."

"You're not—worried about things?"

She hesitated, then decided to tell the truth.

"I am, rather."

"Why?"

"I don't like lies...deception...."

"Not when you know they are for someone's ultimate good, and immediate happiness?"

"Y-yes, but...."

He waited, slowing down a little but not looking at her.

With an effort she went on. "I get scared, Dominic. What if one of us made a slip, and she found out the truth? Wouldn't that set her back again—undo all the good...?"

"We mustn't."

"No. But we could so easily."

"We won't," he told her with calm confidence.

"I do hope not."

She spoke so doubtfully that he exclaimed, "Chloe! You're regretting your promise?"

She shook her head. "Not really. That is, as long as *you* believe it's all right to—to fool her."

He turned his head. For a fleeting moment his level glance held hers.

"I believe it's right for her. The doctor agrees. He's known for a long time how she was worrying over my failure to marry. It seemed to prey on her mind. It certainly aggravated her condition. After this recent attack he warned me to do something to set her mind at rest. He told me time was short—it could only be a palliative. But you can see how it's worked. She's a different woman."

"I know, Dominic. I can see a great change for the better."

He put his left hand over hers.

"Then don't worry. We're justified by her happiness. And I take full responsibility. You can leave all the worrying to me."

She made herself smile and say cheerfully, "All right. I'll try not to worry. I expect I was being a bit morbid.

I promise I'll do everything I can to make things go well."

He fell in with her altered mood with obvious relief. She thought with rueful amusement that he wasn't the kind of man to suffer female emotionalism gladly.

Soon they came in sight of the sea again. What little breeze there had been had died down, and left the water as smooth as glass. It broke in the lightest of lacy foam on the apricot cream ledges of rock.

They had long ago left the highway for a dirt road, dusty and rather stony. Now they turned off this onto a rough cart track along the top of the cliffs. Presently Dominic pulled over and switched off the engine.

"Out you get. This is the place."

There was a clump of fig trees, a stretch of dry, close-cropped turf. Far below the sea lapped, a wonderful pale green, infinitely inviting.

Dominic brought the picnic basket and opened it.

Lotta had halved and grilled a young chicken, and there was a crisp green salad, dewy and cool. French dressing to go with it, crisp crusty rolls. Fruit, too, a bottle of white wine, ice cubes in a wide-necked Thermos to chill it, another Thermos of black coffee.

Chloe enjoyed setting out the plates, glasses, cutlery and napkins on the linen tablecloth Lotta had included. She took the food out of its containers and set it out, too.

"Hungry?" she asked, when all was ready.

"Starving. Looks good, doesn't it?"

"Scrumptious, as Mark would say."

He twirled the wine bottle in the ice, opened it and poured some into their glasses.

"Try that," he said. "Nice?"

"Lovely." But everything was lovely on this lovely, lovely day.

They ate half sitting, half lying on the close turf, with the sun beating down on them, drawing out from somewhere near them a hot, aromatic fragrance of wild thyme, and glittering on the sea.

"This glorious sun," Chloe said, reveling in it. "At home it's been frost and fog and frost and fog all winter. I feel I can't soak up enough of this heavenly warmth."

"You're getting a tan. They'll envy you at home when you go back."

"Yes." Why did he say that, remind her that this was purely temporary? Her spirits sank.

He lit a cigarette for her and another for himself.

He said suddenly, with the air of one who has just made a discovery, "You're a nice person to be with, Chloe."

Her spirits rose again, volatile.

"So are you, Dominic."

He looked surprised and rather pleased.

"Bit of a martinet."

"Only sometimes."

They laughed with mutual pleasure in each other. He leaned back on his elbows, relaxed, at ease.

She was vividly aware of him beside her, not looking at her, watching the gently breathing sea with his eyes narrowed under their dark brows against the brilliant light.

Her look, an unconscious caress, lingered on his face. He didn't notice. He seemed lost in some dream. The smoke from his cigarette curled delicately upward in the still air.

When it was finished he stubbed out the butt and jumped to his feet, stretching himself.

"I'll fall asleep if we don't move. Ready?"

She got up, too, and smoothed her dress down.

"Where next?"

"To look at the dig from the sea. And explore those caves underneath."

"Fun," she said.

"I've got a theory. Like to try it out?"

Anything you say, my love, she thought. Suddenly she began to feel excited, as if she were on the brink of something tremendous. The feeling persisted as they packed and carried the things back to the car. Sunlight dazzled from its roof, and the metal was hot to the touch. They stowed everything and drove on along the cliff top till they came to a small village.

It was just a cluster of flat-topped, whitewashed cottages, a derelict-looking store, a few men and women and several children and some animals.

There were fishing nets and lobster pots strewn around a small quay, and a dock. Three of four of the usual gaily painted boats with eyes on their prows were drawn up on the quay.

The villagers seemed to know Dominic. The children crowded around, staring at Chloe, while he went and chatted with two men who were languidly mending nets. They began dragging one of the boats into the water.

"Come on," he called, and she joined him on the dock. One of the men held on the boat and put out a brown, rather dirty hand to help her in. She stepped down neatly and sat in the stern.

Dominic went over to the car and came back with a big flashlight and a pair of binoculars. He sat down beside her and pointed along the coast to their right.

"That way, Pauli," he said.

Pauli rowed easily, standing up facing the bows. The water chuckled delightfully as he drove his boat strongly through it.

"Blue grotto," he said presently, airing his mite of English for Chloe's benefit and turning around to flash his enviable teeth at her.

"Not now. Dawn's the time for that. Tourist stuff—but I'll show you it some time if you like," Dominic said, and waved Pauli on.

Chloe gave him a smile of dreamy pleasure. She was pretending hard to herself, making the most of this blissful interlude. She leaned out and trailed a hand in the water.

"Ugh! How cold it is!"

"Didn't you know the Mediterranean is really a chilly sea? That hot blue look doesn't mean a thing," Dominic told her. He still wore his relaxed, contented look. She hadn't known him like this. He seemed younger, far less serious. She wished the day could go on forever.

Now he was studying the cliffs through his binoculars.

"Look up there, Chloe. See the beginning of our digging?"

He handed her the glasses and she looked through them and nodded, giving them back to him.

"We're just about opposite the entrance to the sanctuary now," he said a short time later.

He said something in Maltese to Pauli, who at once
changed direction and rowed in toward the base of the
cliffs. There were the usual shallow ledges of rock at the
base. Above them the rocks rose, smooth and perpendicular, for about thirty feet. There were several openings in
them, low down, which looked as if they might lead to
caves. Dominic was studying these through his binoculars.

"We'll have a look at that one," he decided, pointing to
a roughly oblong gap on their left. "It's just about in the
right spot I'd say."

The right spot for what? He didn't explain. He was talking to Pauli again, gesturing with a hand. The boatman
nodded and began to propel them slowly and carefully
nearer to the rocks.

"I want him to take us right inside the cave, if it's big
enough," Dominic said.

Quietly the high-prowed boat nosed its way to the opening, which seemed a good deal bigger now they were near
it. At least fifteen feet across and over half as high.

They slid easily through it into a very large, roughly circular cave. Some small birds, swallows or swifts, fluttered
out above their heads from nests clinging to the inside
walls near the entrance, tucked against some small stalac-
tites.

"Go on, Pauli, right in," Dominic urged, switching his
flashlight on as they moved further from the outside light,
and playing its beam around. Chloe saw walls shining with
damp and quite smooth, without hand- or footholds. Like
the cliffs outside they looked unscalable, perpendicular,
even overhanging in places.

The light dimmed the farther they went, till they were
almost in darkness except that the water, which seemed to
cover the entire floor of the cave, had an intense, magical
blue luminosity. The oars, dipping gently into it, came up
dripping with phosphorescent bubbles.

Dominic took an oar from Pauli and used it to test the
depth of the water. Pauli sculled him around and around,
but nowhere could he touch bottom.

"It's deep everywhere—can't tell how deep exactly, I'd need a lead. It's icy cold, too. Feel it."

"I'll take your word for it."

At one side, that farthest from the opening, they came on a series of shallow ledges like those outside. They seemed to go up and up.

"Like a primitive staircase," Dominic said. "That's interesting. I wonder...."

"Listen," Chloe said.

She became aware of a high squeaking, coming from above.

"What can it be?"

"Bats, I think," he said carelessly. Just then a couple detached themselves from wherever they had been hanging and went blundering out toward the light. Chloe suppressed a shudder; she had always dreaded bats. She would never forget a hair-raising battle between herself, armed with a tennis racket, and a vampire bat one night in the West Indies. Dominic didn't seem to mind them at all.

"Pull close in, Pauli."

Pauli plied an oar and they drifted up against the lowest shelf. Dominic fended the boat off with one hand, and with the other shone his flashlight upward.

"Look, take this and shine it just ahead of me. I'm going up," he said. "This all agrees with my theory." He added perfunctorily, "You don't mind?"

"No. I'll shout if an octopus or a bat or whatever attacks us," she said more amiably then she felt.

"Good girl. I won't be long."

She hoped he wouldn't, but kept quiet; he was so obviously enjoying himself.

She played the beam of the flashlight for him as he scrambled agilely up from ledge to ledge. She could see that the ledges got steeper farther up. More bats, alarmed at this invasion of their privacy, flew toward the opening, squeaking shrilly. Pauli muttered something and crossed himself. *I don't like this much, either,* Chloe thought, and wondered if sinister sea creatures lurked below the strange luminosity of the water.

She was beginning to feel irritable; at last Dominic called

down with annoying cheerfulness, "All right. I can't get any farther. Shine the flashlight straight up."

She did so. Its beam seemed to disappear in the shadows. She couldn't see what he was peering at, up there among those loathsome bats. Her arms began to ache. She and Pauli had to wait quite a while in the eerie dimness before his cheerful hail reached them.

"Coming down now. Guide me, please."

He made short work of scrambling down to the boat.

"Gosh, thousands of bats up there," he said. "The staircase is merely a natural phenomenon. It peters out up there. I hoped it might go right up. But it helped. I found what I expected. Guess what."

"No idea. Tell me."

"Remember that trick step in the flight leading down to the treasure chambers? I found its mechanism. A primitive system of counterweights—but effective, as you say. It's right there overhead."

Chloe stared upward in dawning horror.

"You mean anyone treading on that step would fall down here?"

"And drown. That was the idea. Cold, deep water, unclimbable walls, perpendicular cliffs, a deserted coast. Pretty!"

"Horrible," Chloe said, shivering uncontrollably. Afterward she was to wonder if it had been some premonition that had set her limbs trembling.

"You're cold," Dominic said, suddenly aware of her. "I ought to be shot, keeping you here so long in this chilly dampness. Damned thoughtless of me—I'm afraid I got carried away. We'll get out at once. Come on, Pauli, row."

Once out of the shadow of the cliffs they were in full sunshine again. It struck hot and gratefully on their chilled bodies. Chloe stopped trembling and began to wonder what had frightened her. The boat glided swiftly over the glassy sea toward the dock in the little port.

When it touched there, Dominic jumped out and held out a hand to her.

"Still cold," he said, and kept her hand in his, warmly

enfolded, all the way up to the car. Chloe felt suddenly glowing and happy again. The chill sense of foreboding she had experienced in the cave quite disappeared.

Dominic talked about other traps to catch intruders, in other prehistoric ruins, all the way across country to Mdina. He was far more interested in that, she saw, than in her. Would it always be like that? Would archaeology always come first? It seemed a dreary prospect.

The sun had set when they crossed the drawbridge. Its rosy afterglow made a fairy-tale magic of the domes and towers, palaces and romantic rooftops of the Silent City.

"Well, did you enjoy your outing, Chloe?"

"So very much, Dominic."

"I'm glad. I did, too."

He put his hand over hers and gave it a squeeze—but it was the friendly squeeze of a fellow conspirator, not in the least a lover's caress.

"My mother's going to love hearing you tell her all about it," he said.

She murmured something, but he was tooting his horn outside the gates of Santa Clara and paid no attention. He slipped from the car in the courtyard and came around to open her door.

Something in her expression—a touch of sadness or frustration—seemed to strike him. He put one finger under her chin, tilted her face up and dropped a light kiss on the corner of her mouth. She stayed very still—but that was all. He stood aside while she got out of the car.

"Not to worry—about anything," he told her with kind firmness. "Leave all the worrying to me."

"All right. I won't—and I will," she agreed at her brightest.

He watched her thoughtfully, a little puzzled, unaccountably a little disturbed, as she walked with her light, graceful step into the house. *Women,* he thought irritably as he followed her in.

In her room Chloe changed quickly, did her hair and face and put on the pearls again. She noticed how golden her skin looked against their milky paleness. How lovely they were! She mustn't get attached to them. Naturally she would have to hand them back to Dominic when...if....

She shut off her thoughts, not wanting to believe, any longer, that it could be true that the *contessa* was going to die but not wanting, either, to face the question of what would happen if she lived.

She was going to visit her in a moment, when she had dealt with a fingernail that had chipped. It was a thing she had set herself to do—partly out of that insistent sense of guilt, partly to please Dominic—to spend an hour with the *contessa* every evening before dinner. That was the time, Dominic had said, that his mother found most tedious if she were alone.

She had clipped the nail and was smoothing it with an emery board when someone tapped on the door.

"Come in." Lotta?

Not Lotta. Louise, in a short, very smart black cocktail dress, carrying her mink cape. Wearing her most engaging smile.

"Oh, hello, Mrs. Carlyon," Chloe said warily.

"Come off it, ducky. Louise is the name," the visitor said gaily. "Now we're to be cousins by marriage, shouldn't we be a bit less formal—Chloe?"

"Yes, I suppose we should." Chloe was polite but not enthusiastic. She mistrusted this sudden volte-face. She couldn't believe it was genuine.

To her surprise and confusion Louise leaned forward and kissed her on both cheeks.

"My congratulations. You've certainly given us all the surprise of our lives, sweetie. None of us dreamed...."

Liar, Chloe thought dispassionately. Aloud she said, "Neither did I—Louise."

Louise shot up her eyebrows disbelievingly. She picked up Chloe's perfume from her dressing table and squirted its precious contents onto her wrist.

"Mm." She sniffed voluptuously. "'L'Heure Bleu,' isn't it? Very, very seductive."

She sprayed herself behind the ears with it and smiled meaningfully.

"Clever little thing, aren't you?"

"I don't think so, especially."

"Modest, too. But look at you. So cool and composed. So detached and unforthcoming. And see what you've quietly pulled off. The catch of many seasons. Nice work, my dear."

"Thank you."

Cool and composed Chloe might look, but she was boiling. She would have liked to slap Louise, well and truly.

Instead she forced herself to smile politely and offer her a chair. *Hold everything,* she said to herself. *This is no place for a shouting match.*

Louise sank down gracefully, stretched out her legs and looked at them with satisfaction and lit one of her Turkish cigarettes.

"We must get together more, you and I," she announced. "Now that you've got Dominic where you want him you can relax—mm? Less of this single-minded devotion to his boring old tombs and ruins—though it was a good line, I admit."

"Yes, wasn't it? It worked, anyway," Chloe said pleasantly. *And now put that in your long amber cigarette holder and smoke it,* she thought.

Louise looked quite startled for a moment. Then she grinned. "Even score," she said. "But you really mustn't go on encouraging Dominic in this dreary archaeological nonsense. It's ruining him."

"I don't encourage him. I simply do the job I'm paid for. And I'll go on doing it, I suppose, till it's finished."

"My sweet lamb, you're *engaged* to the man now. You must make him behave normally. He must throw Santa Clara open. But of course he knows that. He knows what'll be expected—by the scores of Valmontez relations, if by nobody else. Gosh, the parties we'll have to throw! Thank heaven I'll at last be able to return some of the marvelous hospitality I've had on the island."

"I doubt if there'll be many parties at Santa Clara while Mrs. Vining is so ill."

"My poor innocent, Aunt Olivia has been enjoying bad health ever since I jilted Dominic. She'll stage a rapid recovery now she's got what she wanted, you'll see."

Chloe gave her a straight look.

"Well, won't it be splendid if she does? Look, I'm due to visit her now—she'll be expecting me. Do you mind?"

"Not at all—" airily "—I'll come with you."

"But she—you...."

"Oh, she'll be pleased to see me now," Louise said, still airily. "My sting's drawn, as it were—so why shouldn't she?"

Chloe had no answer to that. She could only tell herself again that she was no match for Louise—even though to Louise it must seem that for the moment, in the matter of Dominic, she had won. But did Louise mean to let it stay that way? Somehow she could hardly believe it....

Louise was right about the *contessa*, though. For a moment, when her niece by marriage went into her room ahead of Chloe, and ran impulsively to her bedside and kissed her warmly, she did seem to flinch away. But Louise gave her no chance to speak.

"Dear Aunt Olivia," she cried spontaneously, "I just had to come and tell you how delighted I am. You don't know how guilty I've been about Dominic all these years. It's too wonderful he's going to be happy at last—and with a girl like Chloe!"

"It is indeed, Louise," Mrs. Vining agreed uncertainly, her eyes on Louise's face. But its warm sincerity would have convinced a more skeptical woman than the *contessa*, Chloe thought.

"What fun it's going to be," Louise went on. "When the announcement appears in the *Times of Malta* you're going to be overwhelmed with congratulations. You'll want somebody to cope with the letters, telegrams, telephone calls, from everybody who matters in the island. As Chloe insists she's got to go on working at the dig, it'd better be me, Aunt Olivia."

"Thank you, dear. The announcement will appear tomorrow. I suppose all the relations will call."

"In their hundreds, darling," Louise said gaily. "Literally hundreds, Chloe, you've no idea of the ramifications of the family. You must get well, Aunt Olivia. We must get you up in time for the reception."

"Reception?" the *contessa* asked, beginning to be fascinated against her will.

"Of course. To celebrate and to let them all see Chloe."

"Yes, of course."

Louise flashed her wicked grin at Chloe. *What did I tell you,* it seemed to say.

But she was clever enough not to overdo it.

"I must go now, darling." she said. "Chloe will stay and talk to you. And tomorrow, if you feel well enough, we'll begin thinking about the list of guests."

She kissed Mrs. Vining again, and with an airy wave left the bedroom.

"I wonder—have I perhaps misjudged her? I thought she'd be angry, jealous. But she seems really delighted. She's very vivacious, isn't she? What do you think of her, Chloe, dear?"

"I—actually I've seen awfully little of her, *contessa*."

"There was that dreadful affair of the balcony...."

"Perhaps Lotta imagined that. Don't think of it any more, *contessa*."

"No. Lotta loves drama—it's her Italian blood. Perhaps you and Louise may become friends. Poor Louise. I wish she could have news of Dick. Such a tragedy. Perhaps under that bright facade she is really very unhappy. I wonder. I'm afraid I have never trusted her. I must try to like her better."

Chloe murmured agreement and guided the conversation into other channels. She began to talk about the day's adventures. The *contessa* listened absorbedly. Chloe felt again that sudden tenderness. She was beginning to be truly fond of her.

As for Louise, she would play the game her way. If she really wanted to be friendly, Chloe would try to respond. It was her weakness, perhaps, that she would always go out of her way to avoid unpleasantness....

CHAPTER TWELVE

THE ANNOUNCEMENT OF THE ENGAGEMENT between Dominic Valmontez Vining, of Santa Clara, Mdina and Vining Court, Sussex, England, and Chloe Margaret Linden, of London, England, duly appeared in the *Times of Malta* and caused a sensation.

Young ladies of the Fishing Fleet told each other regretfully that there was one of the best chances of all gone—and to a girl none of them had even heard of till she appeared at the polo match that Saturday. Who was she, anyway?

Robert Tenby saw the announcement and gritted his teeth. He had been feeling he wanted Chloe more than ever, now he had lost her to another man. He dashed over to the Soameses for sympathy. They, knowing the truth but under oath not to reveal it, did the best they could. Alaric suggested that probably it wouldn't work out, Dominic was older than Chloe and wedded to his archaeology, perhaps Robert would come back from his cruise and find it had already been broken off.

Robert was willing to believe that. He cheered up and after several pink gins felt sufficiently restored to accompany the Soameses to a cocktail party at the artillery mess in Tigne. He was a volatile young man, easily up, easily down. The Soameses, kindly but clear-sighted, didn't take his heartbreak too seriously.

It was the Valmontez relations who were most excited—Louise had been right there, too. Who was this girl? They must telephone dear Olivia and find out immediately. They must visit her at Santa Clara—if she was well enough to receive them. At least they must leave cards. Soon there would be the wedding present to think of. The ceremony.

A Valmontez wedding. That was something to look forward to indeed.

So—again as Louise had prophesied—the telephone began to ring and went on all day. Messages of congratulation poured in. When Chloe came back from the dig that evening, she could see that the *contessa* was pleased and stimulated. She was already talking about the reception. She looked better—noticeably better.

"You see?" Louise said later in the living room, with cynical amusement. "She'll be up and about for that reception. As Eliza Doolittle said—just you wite!"

Chloe began to believe Louise might be right. How wonderful it would be if the *contessa* did prove her doctor wrong by recovering. Wonderful for Dominic—wonderful for herself, too, because she would have helped and because she genuinely wanted it to happen.

The only thing was—how would they extricate themselves from this tangle of their own devising, without setting the *contessa* back again? It was the question she had tried to put out of her mind, had never brought herself to put to Dominic.

She put it resolutely out of her mind now. Dominic had told her to leave all the worrying to him.

We'll take that fence when we come to it, she reminded herself.

AT THE SANCTUARY, Chloe's colleagues were as friendly and cordial as could be about the engagement, though not quite able to hide their surprise.

"Cagey pair, aren't you? I'd never have believed it of Dominic," Toby French said to Chloe candidly. "Not that I could be more jealous of him."

"Why, Toby?"

"Oh, well—all the delights of a nice, pretty wife *plus* the certainty that she'll understand about being left an archaeological widow half of every year."

Chloe laughed. "I should think you'd better stay a bachelor if that's the way you feel, Toby."

"Oh, I don't know. I'm getting a bit past the age when the usual sort of routine seduction has much appeal.

There's something attractive about the idea of the little
woman waiting at home when I come back from a nice
long absence on a dig.''

"For you, maybe. Hardly for the little woman.''

"Maybe not. I say, when's the wedding to be? Invite me,
won't you? Though it'll tear my heartstrings, I'll be
there.''

"We haven't got as far as thinking about the wedding
yet,'' Chloe said hastily. "Look, I'm busy, Toby. Be a
dear and go away.''

He grinned and left her. The others dropped by, at intervals, to offer felicitations, advice, teasing. They, too,
wanted to know the date of the wedding, and she had her
answer ready now.

"Not till we've finished work on this dig, anyway.''

That satisfied them. They saw, with approval, that
neither she nor Dominic seemed likely to allow sentiment
to intrude during working hours. The days slid into their
smooth routine again, almost as if nothing had happened.

Another burial chamber was being emptied, more
treasures were coming to light every day. When Chloe
wasn't busy at her own job she helped with the sorting and
classification. She was learning a lot, and enjoying herself
very much, as long as she didn't pause to think.

She didn't see very much of Dominic. He didn't suggest
another outing like that first one. Once he played in a polo
match again, and she watched him with the same pride and
excitement. Afterward they dined at the club, but Louise
and Mark joined them and there was no chance of a tête-à-
tête.

Chloe couldn't help noticing how improved were the
relations between Dominic and Louise. Louise was on her
best behavior. She was the affectionate cousin by marriage, devoted to his mother's welfare, helpful, pleasant,
never referring to the past he wanted to forget except for
an occasional mention of Dick.

Manlike, Dominic was thankfully taking her pleasantness at its face value, relieved that there were to be no more
scenes.

Sometimes Chloe felt ashamed of herself for being the

only one who seemed unable to believe in Louise's change of heart. She forced herself to seem friendly, even when Louise, alone with her, betrayed her callous cynicism. To please the *contessa* she joined in the daily discussions of plans for the reception.

Louise had taken complete charge. She had worked up enthusiasm among the servants, who as family retainers felt themselves part of the big event. The house was being vigorously cleaned and polished, rooms long unused were thrown open and made ready, a floor was being prepared for dancing. There would be nearly three hundred guests.

"Dancing?" Chloe asked in surprise.

"Yes, rather. Aunt Olivia agrees with me, don't you, darling? A supper, too, with champagne. Fireworks from the terrace. Grand gala, in fact, pet."

"You're crazy," Chloe said under her breath; but she saw how much the contessa was enjoying it all. She was allowed to sit up a little each day now, in the big wing chair in her room, and to walk a few steps. Dr. Galea wasn't in the least put out at being proved wrong.

"These things happen," he said. "We doctors can only thank God when they do. The spirit conquering the flesh. I've seen it too often not to know it can. But we must take great care. No exertion, no worry—no shocks to the nerves...."

No revelation, when my time is up and I'm due to leave Malta, that the engagement's fake, Chloe thought. She felt desperate. If only Dominic would say something....

But Dominic, having given his mother and Louise carte blanche, as it were, was very occupied with other matters. He had made another quick trip to London, and was due there again in a few days. The rich finds in the sanctuary were causing excitement in serious archaeological circles, it seemed. Chloe often found herself helping to pack up weapons, figures, vases, utensils, human bones, from the daily haul for sending away. When she caught Dominic's eye he would smile at her with a sort of absent approval. Sometimes she cried in bed, out of sheer exasperation and despair.

Mark was her only comfort.

"Not to worry. It'll come out in the wash," he would say, cheerfully, but even he couldn't say how. He plied her with sherry and played his favorite records to her—"Salad Days" and "My Fair Lady" and Danny Kaye and West Indian calypsos and even Liberace. He took her to a *festa* in Rabat, which was so noisy and entertaining, such a dazzle of fireworks and fairy lights, such a clamor of brass bands, singing and rockets, that for a while she quite forgot her troubles and really enjoyed herself.

"I told you *festas* were fun with the right person," Mark reminded her. "I say, Chloe, you mustn't mind my asking, but will there be a chance for me when...if...?"

"Let's not speculate, Mark," she begged him, and let him kiss her a little, on the way home, to salve his disappointment.

Afterward he stammered, "Gosh, Chloe, you're wonderful," and was quite absurdly elated, so that she felt guilty and afraid she'd given him hope where there was none.

Her worst moment came when the *contessa*, during Dominic's absence in London, brought up the question of the wedding date.

"The party is at the end of next week," she said. "I'd like to announce the date then, Chloe, dear."

Chloe suddenly caught sight of Louise's face in the mirror over the *contessa*'s dressing table; she was fiddling with some trinket there, listening to the conversation without, for once, joining in. For a moment an expression of fury passed over it, darkening it as a squall darkens water.

"Don't you agree, Louise?" the *contessa* asked.

Louise turned to her at once with a smile so brilliant that Chloe began to think she must have imagined the fury.

"Of course, Aunt Olivia."

"But, *contessa*, I have to go back to London in three weeks," Chloe said.

"Why, dear? What possible reason?"

"I have commitments—work to do—one or two contracts I entered into before I came here, and can't very well get out of," Chloe said quickly.

It wasn't really true. She had contracts and commitments, yes. But nothing she couldn't get out of if she really must. She musn't admit that. She must see Dominic as soon as he came back. She must see him first, before anyone else did.

The *contessa* was disappointed and only half convinced, she could see.

"And then there's my godmother—I have to see her, consider her wishes," she went on desperately.

The *contessa* nodded. "Of course, Chloe. Dear Lady Stanton. Perhaps she would care to come for a visit. Shall we invite her?"

"I don't quite know... she often goes for a cure at this time... I'll write..." Chloe stammered, conscious that Louise was watching her struggles smilingly. The smile on the face of a tiger, Chloe wondered.

"And of course I do see there is your own mother to be considered," the *contessa* conceded, taking her hand affectionately. "Never mind, Dominic will soon be back. He will decide for us."

Chloe smiled and gladly left it at that. She was determined to be at the airport, waiting for him, when Dominic returned to Malta.

AT BREAKFAST TWO DAYS LATER Mark said, "Dominic's plane is due in at one. Like to come with me to meet him, Chloe? A suitable gesture, don't you think? Eager fiancée awaits lover's return?"

Chloe was spooning honey out of a comb, a sticky, tricky operation. She laid the spoon down.

"Very funny. But actually, Mark, I do want to meet Dominic. By myself, if you don't mind. I can drive his car. I've handled it before."

"But surely I ought to be there, too. The indispensable assistant? Won't it rather be expected of me? Don't you enjoy my company, love?"

"Idiot, of course I do. But I have a very urgent reason for seeing Dominic and talking to him—before he comes to Santa Clara. Before he sees his mother."

"Or our dear Louise."

"That, too. I thought he and I might have lunch together at the airport and I could say my piece and—and sort things out with him.''

Mark was silent while he lavishly buttered a piece of toast and balanced marmalade on it. Then he waved it at her, rather imperiously, and exclaimed, ''As I expected. The situation's getting tricky. Is that the trouble?''

''Yes, it is, rather. Don't let's talk about it, Mark, it makes me nervous. Dominic said not to worry—*he* would cope. Well, the point has been reached where he's got to, unless he wants to find himself tied to C. Linden for better or for worse.''

''How happy could I be with either—either better, or worse, I mean,'' Mark sighed.

''Do be serious. Will you let me go and meet the plane—alone?''

''The trouble with me, girl, is that I can refuse you nothing.''

''Splendid. Then be a lamb and ask Nibblu to leave the car ready at about quarter past twelve.''

''At your service, madam.''

''I'll work in the library, cataloguing, till then. Will you go to the dig?''

''May as well.''

''I'll explain to Dominic for you.''

''Do—I wouldn't want him to think my zealousness—zealousy—was on the wane.'' He finished his coffee and got up.

She said with a smile, ''You're a great comfort to me, Mark.''

Lotta came in then to see if fresh coffee was needed, so he got no chance to reply. Seeing the way his plain, agreeable face lit up, Chloe thought it was probably just as well. This wasn't the time to listen to a declaration.

She enjoyed driving the car and was able to let it out a little on a nice long stretch of highway. But soon she was in traffic and prudently slowed down. Driving it fast had felt a little like riding a charming horse that nevertheless might bolt at any moment.

When she reached the airport there was a plane on the

runway and a lot of noisy people either waiting to depart or seeing off those who were.

Inquiry revealed that Dominic's plane would be an hour late. Fog in southern England and London. Poor London! Here the sun was shining gloriously, as usual, but there was the sort of strong blustery wind airports specialize in. She walked around in it for a while, but when a young man in uniform, with wavy lines of braid on his sleeves, said, "You'll find it more comfortable inside, madam," she took his advice.

She bought a magazine to read and sat down at a table where she would watch the runways.

An attendant came over to ask if she wanted anything and she ordered a lime squash, for her throat was full of airport dust.

Her magazine didn't hold her interest after the first few pages—perhaps she was too keyed up to read intelligently. She put it away and watched the activity going on in and around the plane that was due to depart.

The ground staff was fueling it, loading in luggage and food containers. A pair of legs hung out of an opening in a wing and occasionally kicked the air as if in exasperation. An officer in blue-gray with gold stripes on his arms descended the gangway and strolled over with a handful of documents. A crisp air hostess took them from him reproachfully and sped away on her impractical high heels. Her figure was delicious in its trim tailored suit. Red hair gleamed under her saucy cap. Chloe wouldn't have been surprised if she had gone into a song and dance routine.

Now the ground staff was dispersing, all work done. Air personnel took over. The redheaded hostess tripped across to the plane and up the gangway and was seen no more.

A loudspeaker made an announcement and the airport went into its departure routine. Propellers spun, then became blurry discs as engines roared. Passengers peered through windows as if looking their last on the earth.

The clumsy-looking plane blundered downwind, turned, gunned up its engines to a frightening roar, set off along the runway into the wind with increasing noise and speed, rose and at once was a graceful silver bird winging its way into the blue and out of sight.

A sort of communal sigh went up from the seers off. So *that* one got away all right, they seemed to say. Chloe had sighed, too. As she had told Dominic the first day, she always dreaded the moment when the thing became airborne. Would it soar happily heavenward? Or would it flop back to earth, disintegrate, become a mass of tangled wreckage? She wished she hadn't got this absurd complex about flying.

Looking at her watch, she saw that there were only ten minutes to go before Dominic's plane was due. There would still be the agony of watching it land. Landing was as bad as taking off....

Presently she heard it from far off. The loudspeaker announced it. It came in sight, circled, slid down an invisible slope and touched delicately, bounced gently and came to rest. Thank heaven for that!

The door opened, the gangway slid into place, passengers began to stream across the apron. At last came Dominic, in a dark suit and a hat, carrying a briefcase and talking hard to a man in a brown coat, with a beard, who really did look like a professor.

Chloe stood up and went into the reception hall. Her heart had already missed several beats; she felt rather lightheaded, as if she might faint—though she wasn't the fainting type.

Evidently Dominic had shed the professor person during the customs formalities, for he came out alone. Tall, dark and handsome like the hero of a romance, Chloe thought. *I'm afraid I love you still, Professor Vining.* Pulling herself together, she walked forward.

"Hello, Dominic. Welcome back."

He stared at her in surprise.

"Chloe! All alone?"

"Yes, Dominic. I drove your car—it was lovely. I wanted to talk to you."

The gleam of humor was in his eyes. "Anything wrong?"

"N-no."

"You haven't spoiled a lot of film or dispatched the wrong set of bones to the wrong anthropologist?"

"No."

"Is my mother all right?"

"She's fine, Dominic, absolutely fine. She gets up each day. She's so excited about the party. She's begun to talk of coming downstairs for a little while on the night."

Dominic's warm smile flashed. "Isn't it wonderful, Chloe? I believe old Galea was wrong, she's going to get over this and be all right again—as right as she can hope to be."

"Dr. Galea admits he was wrong. He gloats about it."

"He was always very fond of her. Chloe, I have to thank you for this. I can't thank you. There's no way."

The middle of the reception hall was hardly the place for this sort of conversation, Chloe thought wryly.

"Could we go and have lunch in the restaurant here?" she suggested. "Then I could talk to you properly. You're so tall. It gives me a stiff neck, looking up."

He laughed, looking down at her.

"Of course. Charming idea. You looked worried, Chloe. Didn't I tell you to leave worrying to me?"

"I know, but...."

"Let's find a table, then you shall tell me all!"

When they were seated and he had given the order, he said, quirking an eyebrow at her, "Well, Chloe?"

"I—Dominic, what are we going to *do*?"

"Do?"

"Yes. We've got to face up to it. Your mother isn't going to die—and nobody, let this be clearly understood, could be happier about that than I am. I—I've grown to love your mother. But we got engaged because—you know why, and now the *contessa* is demanding that we fix the wedding date so that she can announce it at the party. I believe she wants to come downstairs to do just that. So you tell me. What are we going to do?"

When he didn't answer at once, being occupied, maddeningly, in studying the wine list a waiter had brought to him, she gritted her teeth.

As soon as the waiter had left them she said desperately,

"Do you realize I'm due to leave Malta nineteen days from now?"

He pretended to look concerned.

"So soon? Oh, no, we can't let you run away so quickly. We'll extend the terms of the contract."

"But I've got *other* contracts. At home. And I told my godmother I'd be home then and she'll be expecting me. Anyway, extending the contract wouldn't solve our problem."

"Which is?"

"Oh, Dominic, must you be so—so...."

"So...?"

"So maddening. You know as well as I do. How are we to tell your mother the engagement is...."

"Off?"

"Yes. How?"

"Must it be off?"

"You said I was to be perfectly free...afterward...."

"But this isn't afterward."

"But I've got to go *away*. I can't go back to England tied to you by this—this phony engagement. How can I?"

"You mean because of this other fellow? The live-and-die man?"

"No—" crossly "—I don't."

"Then...?"

"Oh, for heaven's sake, Dominic, say something constructive. This is your problem as well as mine."

This was becoming a scene—the thing she hated. She felt her cheeks growing hot. She resisted an impulse to run her hands through her hair—she was wearing a hat, anyway.

The wine waiter was showing Dominic a bottle. Receiving approval, he opened it and deftly poured a little into Dominic's glass. Dominic tasted it, appeared to savor it, nodded again. The waiter beamed, filled their glasses and ambled off.

"Something constructive, you want? Well, the best thing I can think of is that you marry me."

"Oh!" It was a gasp more than a word. How agonizing to be offered her heart's desire—and with just about as much feeling behind the offer as if she were being handed a cigarette.

"Thank you. But I hardly think that would work out."

"Why not? We like being with each other—I said so, you said so. You can be extremely useful to me in my work. And as far as my mother is concerned, the earlier the date, the more overjoyed she'll be."

"Your mother, yes, perhaps. But what about me?"

"Still thinking about the live-and-die fellow? Has he come into the picture again?"

"Yes."

"Still in love with him?"

"More than ever."

"And he?"

She lost her head completely then.

"He doesn't care a hoot for me. But till he does, no weddings for me, thank you."

Unconsciously she had pulled off her hat and was running her fingers through the crisp chestnut hair. Dominic flicked one brief glance at it, as he had before, and as before, her hands came down into her lap. She seized her glass with one of them and emptied it at a gulp.

"Careful," he said. "Give you hiccups."

"I don't *care!*"

"Now calm down, Chloe. You won't marry me. Very well, that's agreed. Now we've got nineteen days—it was nineteen you said, wasn't it—to think of something else. Have some of this food, it's excellent."

To avoid argument she took a small helping. She had a suspicion that he was laughing at her, though his face remained serious. His eyes were on his plate—she couldn't see them. She began to plod through her meal, which tasted to her like damp sawdust.

"Tell me about how the plans for the reception are going," he asked, smiling engagingly.

"Louise has those in hand. She's arranging everything."

"So? Chloe, I've got news for Louise."

Her eyes widened. "About her husband?"

"Yes, Poor old Dick. His party got a message through at last. Been trekking for months. Got to a trading post with a radio, and now planes are going out for them. It's quite an epic."

"Oh, how wonderful! We must go back to Santa Clara quickly to tell her."

Dominic said quietly, "You're such a nice child, Chloe."

Chloe was telling herself, *surely Louise will be pleased. She'll go home, to wait for him. Things may work out, if she goes.*

Dominic said gently, "Finish your lunch. A few minutes isn't going to make all that much difference to Louise."

When they had eaten he made her have a cup of coffee and a cigarette. Then he drove her back to Santa Clara. The landscape that had lain so flat and featureless under the stars that first night was pleasantly green and flowery now. Corn and fodder and sprung up, asphodel lilies waved their pink heads. What a pity she would be leaving it so soon. What a pity she felt so very strongly about not marrying Dominic, her only love, because he so plainly didn't return her sentiments. "The best thing I can think of is that you marry me." *No, thank you, Professor Vining*. Not Chloe Linden. She still holds out for love, love, love.

LOUISE WAS WITH MRS. VINING when they got back home. Dominic, holding Chloe's hand as they went in to see his mother, told her the good news right away.

Chloe, watching her face, saw it freeze over, as if an icy wind from Antarctica, where Dick was, had blown over it. But in a second she had recovered herself. The *contessa* said, "Louise dear! It only needed this to make my happiness complete."

"Isn't it wonderful, a miracle, Aunt Olivia?"

"We'll telephone and see about a reservation for you right away, Louise," Dominic said. "You'll want to be in London when they arrive."

The look of fury rippled for a second over the heart-shaped face again—again, like a squall over water, darkening it. Nobody saw but Chloe.

"Make it the day after the reception, Dominic dear,"

Louise begged sweetly. "Dick wouldn't want me to desert Aunt Olivia without seeing that through."

"Perhaps there will be time for Dick to fly out here," the *contessa* said, patting Louise's hand. "Wouldn't that be delightful, Louise, dear?"

"Bliss, Aunt Olivia."

Dominic's face was quite expressionless. He said, "Well, think it over and let me know what you want done, Louise. You look wonderful, mother."

"So much better, dearest. I'm beginning to want to go out, I've been in this prison so long."

"You will, but don't be in a hurry."

"I mustn't miss the spring flowers."

"You won't, I promise."

She began to talk, eagerly, about the reception. Dominic humored her, and then up came the question Chloe dreaded. "We've left it to you to decide a date for the wedding—will you, dear? So that we can announce it then."

He laughed and said soothingly, "Mother, dear, you go a little too fast. We must give Chloe time to go home and consult her own family, mustn't we?"

Somehow he managed to cajole her. *But that doesn't solve the problem,* Chloe thought despairingly. *There is no solution—except, as he says, to marry him. But I won't do it. I won't,. . . . Or only when I'm sure he loves me. He loves me—he loves me not.*

He loves me not.

CHAPTER THIRTEEN

FINDING LOUISE IN THE LIVING ROOM that evening before dinner, alone and waiting for the appearance of Mark and his jug of Martini, Chloe said, "I'm glad, Louise, about your good news."

"Thanks, sweetie. So am I—I suppose. At least we can settle something. But you didn't expect me to go into transports and rush off home to wait for him? Not on your life. Let him come here for me. Not that I'm in the least sure how I'll receive him."

"But he must have had a terrible time."

"So what? He likes that sort of thing, apparently. He could have been a first secretary in some decent diplomatic post by now—but no, he must go on this ridiculous expedition. I sometimes think he must be mental."

She blew out a cloud of Turkish tobacco smoke and added with a grin, "Of course, they may give him a knighthood, like Hillary and Fuchs. That might give me something to think about. Rather nice—Lady Carlyon—don't you think?"

"Very."

"I'll have to give the matter my consideration. Ah, here comes Mark, thank God. Darling, I hope they are very cold."

"Cold as the nether pit, wherever that is," Mark assured her.

"Precious! What should we do without our Mark?"

Mark, standing with his back to Louise as he poured out the large drink she demanded, caught Chloe's eye. His left eyelid dropped toward her in a wink. She knew he was thinking, *good as a play, Louise....*

NEXT MORNING, AT BREAKFAST, Chloe found a note from Louise waiting beside her plate.

"I feel like a day off from entertaining callers and sick-room attendance, ducky. I think I'll come with you to the dig. Wait for me, will you?"

It was high-handed, but Chloe was so relieved that Louise's antagonism seemed to have died—after all, she had no need for it now, now that she could look forward to Dick's return, and perhaps being Lady Carlyon—that she didn't greatly mind waiting. There were plenty of things she could do in the library.

Louise came down, airily unapologetic, at half-past nine in pale corduroy slacks, a light shirt, a brilliant scarf, and her bizarre sunglasses.

She kept up a gay stream of chatter all the way to the dig, mostly about the friends she had made and the parties she'd been to in Malta. She was entertaining and not unduly malicious. Chloe began to wonder if in time she might grow to like her. She looked attractive in her casual getup. It would be a thrill for Toby and the others, anyway.

But Toby and the others, as well as Dominic and Mark, were too busy when they arrived to do more than wave and shout, "Good morning." The laborers were evidently uncovering something exciting.

For once Louise didn't insist on being noticed.

"I'll come down with you," she said as Chloe started carrying her equipment into the sanctuary. "Here, let me take some of that gear."

"Thanks."

"Where are you going to work?"

"In the place of the oracle. Some carvings high up—rather tricky. I'm afraid you'll find my preparations very boring. I'll have to try out my lighting."

"Not to worry about me. If I get bored I'll explore. Or go to sleep on that nice turf in the sun. I mean to have a gorgeous tan to show Dick."

"You've got one already." Chloe spoke absently. Louise's chatter rather distracted her and she wished she would go away and play. "If you explore, do be careful. Keep off where it says Danger."

Soon Louise did go away, and there was peace for a time, broken when she came back to say, "Do come and take a color picture of me outside, Chloe, pet. You never did, that other time. And a black and white for the *Prattler*—they'll eat it up."

"No, really, Louise, I'm just going to start on this...."

"You mustn't be a meanie. Let your work go hang for a bit and do this little thing to please Louise—mm?"

Chloe gave in and spent a tiresome fifteen minutes satisfying Louise's vanity. Then she went back to the place of the oracle, and climbed the small ladder she used for photographing things high up on the walls. It was a little precarious, as the floors of stone slabs had been worn into uneven grooves and hollows by the treading of prehistoric feet. However, she battled on happily—difficulties always stimulated her.

Louise, as far as she knew, was sleeping or sunbathing. A blessed silence wrapped the sanctuary. Faintly, she could hear the voices of the workers and the team, but not so as to distinguish one from another.

The silence was broken some time later—an hour at least, Chloe thought—by calling her name.

"Chloe! Come here quickly! I've hurt myself."

Louise—her voice not quite a scream, but urgent, frightened.

Chloe climbed down to the ground. "Coming. Where are you?"

"Down here."

Chloe hurried—impossible to run on ths rough stuff—toward where the voice came from. Louise was groaning now. The groan came from below. Surely she hadn't ignored the notice that said Danger—No Entry and gone down into the treasure chambers?

It seemed she had.

"Louise!" Chloe called.

"I'm down here. I've twisted my ankle. Can you come and help me up?"

"But, Louise, you knew not to go down here..." she

began. She was thinking about the trick step. Which was it? She didn't. . . .

As if to answer her thought Louise said petulantly, "Don't be silly. I knew about the step. It's the fourth one. Look out for it. The one that opens. And for God's sake hurry. I'm in agony."

"All right. Coming!"

Chloe ran down the wide shallow steps, carefully jumping over the fourth onto the fifth. As she put her weight onto her right foot she felt the step give way. She had a moment of sickening terror, of losing her balance, of hearing Louise's low laugh. She screamed wildly.

Then she was falling, falling. It seemed a long time before she struck the icy water below and went under. . . .

Louise jumped to her feet, ran up the steps past the gaping opening, slipped outside and arranged herself on the turf. A second or two later running figures came in sight, Mark first. She sat up blinking.

"What's the hurry, Mark dear?"

"Somebody screamed. Is Chloe in there?"

"Why, yes. I left her an hour ago, fixing up steps and lights and what have you."

Mark had left her before she finished and was running on. Dominic, Toby French and Dr. du Plessis followed.

Louise narrowed her eyes, grinned maliciously and got up, without haste, to follow them. She wished she had had time to push the step back into place again, then they wouldn't have had a clue where the scream had come from. But who would have thought the girl had such lungs? It had been a question of getting out quick and establishing her alibi. . . .

They were searching now, calling out, "Chloe! Chloe! Where are you?"

Where she won't answer ever again, won't marry Dominic ever, Louise was telling herself. She didn't know there was water below the step. She visualized rocks, and a broken body lying on them. She had spent a lot of time, lately, thinking about how she could use the trick step to get rid of Chloe. She hadn't imagined it would be so easy.

Luck had been with her. It had had to be done, by fair means or foul. . . .

They had discovered the trick step was open. A pity. But of course too late, so what did it matter? She went along the rough passage and stood beside the little group. Mark was on his knees, leaning over, peering, shouting. Dominic said, in a voice she hardly recognized, "Get the flashlight, and ropes." Dr. du Plessis rushed off, pushing rudely against her when she got in his way.

"W-what happened?" she quavered; but no one answered. They were all listening too hard for a voice from below. Only there wouldn't be any voice.

But there was.

Faintly it came.

"Yes, yes, I'm here."

Dominic was on his knees, too, now.

"Chloe! Are you hurt?"

"No."

"Where are you?"

"By the opening. I c-couldn't find the shelves."

Opening? Shelves? Louise wanted to scream in rage and frustration.

"Look out. I'm coming down," Dominic called out. He gave a few rapid orders, then without the slightest hesitation let himself down through the hole, and dropped.

"*Gosh,*" Mark said softly. Du Plessis came running back with Dominic's powerful flashlight and two coils of strong rope. . . .

THE WATER WAS ICY COLD. Chloe had come up gasping with shock and fright. She shook the water out of her eyes and waited for them to get accustomed to the darkness. Instinctively she trod water. She thought, *Louise did this to me. It can't be true, but she did. She told Dominic she'd kill me, but I wouldn't believe it. I thought she was beginning to like me. I thought she'd given up thinking about Dominic.* . . .

Did anyone hear me scream? I know I screamed. But did they hear? Will Dominic remember about this place, when they can't find me? Even if Louise closes down the step, doesn't tell them?

She could see a little now. There to the left was the opening. She began to swim toward it, afraid of getting a cramp and sinking before she reached the ledges outside. She had only gone a few yards when the voices called down to her. They ceased. And then there was a tremendous splash behind her. Arms and legs flailed the water. She felt hands take hold of her, draw her through the opening, pull her up onto the blessed security of a rock ledge.

"You said it had to be someone who was ready to die for you," said a voice bitter with anger. "Do I qualify now?"

"Oh, Dominic, I'm so *cold*."

Strong arms went around her, held her close for a brief moment. Then they shook her, hard.

"You little fool. You knew it was out of bounds, down there. What the *devil* were you doing?"

"I. . . ."

Voices shouting cut her short. Dominic took his arms away and said brusquely, "We've got to swim over to the rock staircase. Look, they're shining the torch on it now. Can you make it?"

Through chattering teeth she said, "Are there—th-things in the water? Creatures?"

"Got to risk that. I'll make a big splash. Come on. No good sitting here freezing."

He plunged in, and she followed. *At least we can die together,* she thought dimly. Somehow the ice of the water turned to fire. They splashed their way through its blue luminosity and Dominic helped her out onto the first of the shelves. The light played on them.

"Now, we've got to climb up. I'll go ahead, then I can give you a hand. Come on. Stand up."

"I can't." Her legs felt as if they were full of cotton, would bend if she put her weight on them. She was cold again, her teeth chattering.

Dominic pulled her to her feet, and she leaned against him weakly. *I can't do it, I'll fall back into the water,* she thought.

Dominic was already on the shelf above her. He held out his hand. He was shivering, too.

"Come on, step lively," he said, in that brisk way of his,

when what she wanted was gentleness, sympathy. But she stepped.

"There, easy, isn't it? Now the next one."

Shelf by shelf they moved upward, the light from above helping them, showing them where to tread. Water dripped from their wet hair and wet clothes. Chloe had lost her shoes; her nyloned feet stepped into the puddles Dominic's canvas ones left. The rock was cold, as cold as the water.

Over their heads the bats squealed, detached themselves, blundered out toward the light oblong at the mouth of the cave. Chloe's scalp crawled—*bats made for your hair, didn't they? They stuck in it and had to be removed by clipping away your hair.* A nanny's story, but she couldn't help thinking about it.

"There. This is where it peters out, Chloe. We can't go farther."

She remained on the top below him peering upward. Faces, unidentifiable blurs, hung around the rim of the hole above.

Dominic shouted, "Ready now. Let the ropes down."

Two thick ropes snaked downward, somebody above set them swinging back and forth like pendulums, and Dominic, leaning far out, managed to catch hold of them and draw them in.

"Now I'm going to be very nautical and make what they call a bosun's chair for you," he explained chattily, bending and looping and tying deftly. "You see—this loop is for you to sit in, this other goes behind your waist. You hang on here and here. Then they'll pull you up. Got a good head?"

"I d-don't know. I've never done this before," she said, trying weakly to make a joke of it.

"You'd better have," he said grimly. He tested everything for strength then made her ready.

"All right?"

"I think so."

"Good girl. All right, hoist away," he shouted to those above. "Now, away you go. If you swing into the rock wall, push yourself off it with your feet. Don't panic, you'll be up in a jiffy."

Terrified, she felt him push her firmly off the ledge. She was swinging now, above the darkly luminous water. *Fatal to look down. Look up, at the faces coming nearer. Fend yourself off the rock wall. Oh, God, that was a bat, there are hundreds of them, hanging upside down like bunches of herbs drying. Up in a jiffy? It was taking hours....*

Then Mark's blessed voice, his hands under her arms, hauling at her.

"I've got you, Chloe. God, what a fright you gave us. Up...you...come. That's the girl. There you are, all safe and sound."

She was sitting on the ground, laughing weakly. Du Plessis was holding out a silver flask he had pulled from his pocket.

"Take a spot of this, Miss Linden. Good South African brandy, overproof. Guaranteed to kill that chill."

"Thank you."

She gulped some, and it flowed down like fire. It warmed her way down inside.

She handed it back with a grateful smile.

"I'd like some, too. Good for shock, isn't it?" Louise's voice, the voice that had said, "I know about the step. It's the fourth one." She had known all the time it was the fifth, or how had she got down there safely herself? Chloe couldn't bear to look at her when she asked, with false concern, "How do you feel, pet?"

"All right, thanks."

"Goodness, what a scare. You nearly gave us heart attacks. Didn't you *know* which step, silly? And why go down there, anyway?"

If I said now, it was your fault, you tried to kill me, would any single one of them believe me, Chloe asked herself. *Wouldn't they at once assume I was light-headed from shock, and rush me off home to bed, and get the doctor to come, and give me tranquilizers or something? Of course Louise knows that. She knows I can't accuse her of attempted murder in front of them all. She knows she'll get away with it. I'm no match for her, never have been.*

But I'm alive. In that way I've won, and she's lost. What must she be feeling?

Whatever Louise was feeling, she didn't show it as she talked away, between drinks of brandy, to Toby and Mark and du Plessis and the others of the team. They were all there now, helping to pull Dominic up.

Now Dominic himself was standing dripping in the center of the group, taking a hearty swig from du Plessis's flask.

"Years since I went up the mast in a bosun's chair," he said cheerfully, and everybody laughed more heartily than the quip warranted, out of sheer relief that nobody had been hurt or lost.

"Now, what about a change of clothing for you both?" suggested Walter Fiennes, the married one of the team. "Toby's for Miss Linden, I should think. They're about of a height, though she'll need to take a lot in at the waist. Mine for you, Dominic, I think they'll fit. I'll organize some dry towels, so you both can get dry. And du Plessis can brew some tea and lace it with his overproof liquor, eh, Hendrik?"

"Yeah, man."

It was Toby who led Chloe tenderly to his tent. Dominic hadn't said anything to her since he came up. Was he angry? Would *he,* if she told him the truth when he asked her again what the devil she was doing down there, believe her? Could she ever bring herself to tell him?

"Here you are, Chloe. Towel, hot water, shirt, shorts, belt. Have a good rub."

"Thanks, Toby."

When he had gone she stripped off her sodden shirt, slacks and underwear and wrung them out as well as she could into Toby's canvas bucket. She took up the rough towel and plied it vigorously till her skin reddened. Then she got into Toby's shirt and shorts, pleated the huge waist around her, belted it in. She had peeled off her torn nylons, and would have to go barefoot. She didn't suppose any of the team took her size in shoes.

Vigorously she toweled her wet hair. It clustered in curling tendrils around her face, drying quickly. She needed powder and lipstick, she thought, looking at her pale face in Toby's scrap of shaving mirror. Her handbag was in the place of the oracle, she supposed. She put her head out of the tent and called to Toby to get it for her.

Dominic came out of another tent, also wearing borrowed plumage.

"It fits you better than mine does," she said, trying a smile on him. But he didn't smile back. He *was* angry— though he'd been kind in the water, and when they were climbing the staircase. When he said, "Do I qualify?" it had simply been a sarcastic quip. *No use building anything on that, Chloe Linden.*

"As soon as we've drunk this tea we'll get back to Santa Clara," he said brusquely. "I should think you'd better take a hot bath, then get to bed."

"Oh, but...."

She didn't go on because his look, his implacable look that she knew from that first day, quelled her; also, she was conscious of a coldness, deep inside her, that the brandy had helped but not defeated.

The tea, hot and sweet and laced and wonderful though it was, didn't defeat it either. Had she caught a chill? Not surprising, if she had—but what a nuisance, what a bore.

"Finished? I'll drive you," Dominic said.

"I'll come with you, darling," cooed Louise, jumping up.

"No, come with Mark, he'll bring Chloe's car in."

"But I'd prefer...."

Dominic ignored her and walked over to his car.

"Come on, Chloe."

Chloe picked up her handbag, thanked Toby and the others warmly and moved after Dominic. He had taken a blanket out of the trunk and tucked it around her.

"Still cold?"

"A little, sort of inside me. Are you?"

"I'm all right. We'll get Galea in to see you."

"Oh, that won't be necessary, I shouldn't think."

"Wouldn't you?"

If I haven't caught a chill already, I'll get one, if you speak to me in that icy voice, she thought wryly.

They started off.

"Perhaps you'll admit now that women do make trouble on a dig," he said after a while.

"You said *emotional* trouble."

"Emotional or not—trouble. Just exactly what *were* you doing, running down those steps?"

Now for it.

"I thought someone shouted for help...Louise...."

"But Louise was asleep on the grass outside."

She had been right. *Nobody* would credit the story.

But Dominic had shot one penetrating look at her, and was now very thoughtful. After a while he said, "All right, Chloe. Let's forget it."

"I'm sorry if I gave you—everybody—a fright."

"That, my dear Chloe, is putting it mildly."

"And I haven't thanked you for rescuing me. I know it sounds corny to say it—but you did save my life, didn't you?"

He turned to grin down at her.

"You should add in thrilling tones, *my hero.* Lucky for us we'd had a look at that cave already, wasn't it?"

"I remember now—I had a feeling then, that day. Pauli crossed himself, and suddenly I shivered and couldn't stop. Not with cold. A sort of premonition. As if I knew even then that something bad was going to happen to me in that cave."

"Was it very bad?"

"I was terrified. That awful drop, the plunge into that icy water, the thought of things reaching up at me from below...."

"Poor Chloe!"

"And you—you deliberately jumped down into it."

"As I said, *my hero.* You forget I knew the place. I knew there was plenty of water under me."

She said obstinately, "All the same, you came and saved me. I was wondering if perhaps nobody had heard me scream, if I would be dead of cold and fright before anyone found me."

She shivered again, and Dominic said, "Stop thinking about it, Chloe. What you want is a hot toddy, hot bath, hot water bottle and a good long sleep."

"I'll be drunk, all that brandy."

"Help you to drop off."

They crossed the drawbridge without her noticing and were pulling up outside the gates of Santa Clara. How fast he must have driven.

The gates opened, he drove in and stopped. He came quickly around to her door to open it and help her out.

"Upstairs with you," he said. "I'll send Lotta to you, she'll look after you. Warmer now?"

"A little." But there was still that core of coldness inside her.

She looked up and said, "You're not still angry with me, Dominic?"

He gave her a long, speculative look.

"Not angry. Just interested to know what really happened to make you do that fool thing. Maybe I'll ask Louise if she can tell me."

"Oh—please don't do that."

"No? Why? She was around...."

"*Please* don't ask her." She was his cousin's wife, had once been his own love. She had failed in her intention. Best leave it at that. "What's the use? I did a foolish thing and gave a lot of trouble, and I'm sorry. You said yourself let's forget it. Can't we, please, Dominic?"

His nod of ironic agreement made her wonder again if he knew—or at least suspected. She said quickly, "Thank you. I promise I'll never go near those steps again," smiled fleetingly and sped away to her room.

CHAPTER FOURTEEN

DR. GALEA CAME TO SEE CHLOE later in the day, and diagnosed shock and a severe chill.

"Bed for a few days, young lady," he said, and was unimpressed when she protested that she couldn't spare the time, must get up and go on with her work.

"Nonsense, nonsense. Dominic will understand, when I tell him what your temperature is, that you can't possibly get up. He won't expect it. It was he who insisted on my seeing you. Now lie down and cover up."

He was writing a prescription, in his illegible doctor's scribble. How did druggists ever know what the spidery marks meant?

"Here, Lotta. Run around to the drugstore." He meant the tiny one in the alley next to the hotel. This shop, a grocery in a recess in the ramparts, an English tea room, a newspaper kiosk and a studio where they painted and gilded saintly images and picture frames, comprised the sum of Mdina's commercial life.

Lotta snatched the paper and ran off with commendable eagerness. She had been told not to speak of the *signorina*'s illness to the *contessa*, but of course she would have to tell her sooner or later. All the servants knew already, and were wondering about the reception—would it have to be put off? That would be a bitter disappointment—they were all keyed up to enjoy it; and besides, they liked the young lady, didn't want her to suffer.

So Lotta ran to the drugstore and arrived there panting. Within a few minutes she was back again with Chloe's medicine, measuring out a dose.

After that Chloe slept and slept. Feverish dreams haunted her. Bats flew into her hair, long octopus arms stretched up and twined themselves around her limbs, when she tried to pull herself out of the water onto the rocks they clung to her and wouldn't let go, and Louise stood there laughing and wouldn't help.

Then Dominic came and said, "What the devil are you doing down there?" and watched her struggles; then he and Louise went up in a bosun's chair together and left her alone, and Pauli crossed himself and began thrashing the water with his oars, and beating the air with them as the boats sailed past.

People visited her now and then—Lotta often, Louise, Mark, Dominic, even the *contessa*. But she was too hot and uncomfortable to want to talk to them. She burned with heat, though an icy stream now and then seemed to run down her spine.

On the third day the fever broke and she woke up to find herself wet with sweat, her nightgown sticking to her drenched body, but her head clear, the sickness gone from her.

She rang her bell and Lotta came running, and said, "Blessed Mary, the *signorina* is better."

"Yes, I am. But soaking wet. Bring a towel and fresh clothes, Lotta."

Lotta was a splendid nurse—she had had years of tending the *contessa*. When she had her *signorina* sitting propped against her pillows, in fresh sheets and nightgown, she exclaimed, "Now I must go and tell the *contessa*. She has been worrying."

The *contessa* herself came in soon after, leaning on Lotta's arm and her own ivory stick, and was installed in the big chair by Chloe's bed.

"I'm so thankful that you are better, dear child."

"So am I, *contessa*. All this wasted time...."

The *contessa* took her hand and stroked it fondly.

"Always so zealous about your work. When you are married to Dominic, I hope you will learn to be a little lazy, as I am."

Chloe evaded that.

"And you? How are you? Still getting stronger?" she asked.

"Every day a little better. You know, there have been so

many messages, letters, callers. Louise has been a great help—I'm not quite up to receiving callers yet. She is competent socially. She has charm, admittedly. I am trying very hard to like her, Chloe."

"I'm glad she was there to help you, since I've failed you," Chloe murmured, thankful that the *contessa* didn't know the truth about her nephew's wife.

"You must get well quickly now. Perhaps we need not postpone the reception?"

"Of course not, *contessa*. There's still nearly a week, isn't there? I feel wonderful, cool, no headache, just a little bit weak, that's all. I expect I'll be up tomorrow."

"Only if Camillo allows you. He is an excellent doctor—you must do exactly as he says, Chloe, dear."

"Of course, *contessa*."

Lotta came back to take the *contessa* back to her room, and when presently Doctor Galea called, he beamed approvingly.

"Ah, the fever is all gone. That is good."

"I can get up tomorrow?"

"For a little. The legs will be weak. But very soon you will be as good as new."

He gave her hand a fatherly pat, wrote out another prescription and left her.

Later on she tried a little walk to the window, and stood there for a few minutes, entranced anew with the wide, shimmering view.

The window was open, and the air flowing into the room was deliciously soft and warm. The island, spread below, was a patchwork of flower colors and green. A string of laden donkeys pattered along a rough track at the foot of the ramparts, carrying their laden panniers easily, tripping on neat small feet.

As Chloe watched, a jet plane came screaming over the citadel of Mdina and landed on the runway near by. It tore along the ground so fast she feared it wouldn't stop, would dash right off the runway and be wrecked. But it pulled up in time, taxied noisily and came to rest.

How incongruous, she thought, *in this medieval island*

with its little forts, its ramparts and crumbling fortifications belonging to the age of chivalry.

At which point Lotta came in with the new medicine and caught her. With a shriek of, *"Madonna mia,"* she bundled her back into bed. Chloe wasn't sorry to go—as Dr. Galea had predicted, the legs were weak. She settled down comfortably, swallowed her medicine and turned over the pages of a fashion magazine someone had put by the bedside. Louise? Probably. Louise would be taking the line that nothing was changed, Chloe had had an unfortunate accident, due to her own carelessness, but she was getting better and the plans for the party would go on, unchanged. Kind Louise would have left the magazine to amuse her....

How can I bear to see her again, talk to her as if we were still friendly, cousins-to-be, Chloe wondered, and hoped Louise would have the decency to keep away.

But Louise came in gaily with Mark that evening, insisting that Chloe drink a martini. "Puts you right faster than anything I know, sweetie," she said, and talked on about the growing list of acceptances for the party and the flower pieces she was going to do for the many rooms that were to be in use.

With her third martini she offered advice to Chloe about what she should wear for the occasion. Nothing sophisticated—it wouldn't fit the part. Something about halfway between virginal and smart. She had the very thing—would lend it if Chloe liked. Chloe thanked her politely and said she had already decided what to wear. "Oh, very well," Louise shrugged, and sprayed herself lavishly behind the ears with Chloe's *L'Heure Bleu.*

Mark, knowing nothing, listened and occasionally joined in with his usual cheerful gusto, which being in love with Chloe didn't seem to diminish except when he allowed himself to ponder on how unworthy of her he was—no looks, no money, no distinction....

He did, however, notice when she began to tire, and removed Louise with surprising firmness. They were going somewhere after dinner, a party on a destroyer, Louise said over her shoulder. "Too bad you can't come too, poor pet."

Chloe's head was spinning; she sank back on her pillows and closed her eyes. Louise would always get the better of her....

A knock roused her.

"Come in." Dominic. Her heart leaped wildly.

"Oh, hello."

"I hear you're better." His eyes fell on the empty glasses. "Had visitors?"

"Mark. And Louise."

He gave her a long, speculative look and said casually, "I fancy our Louise will be leaving us soon."

"Why? What's happened?"

"Dick was flown into London yesterday. I managed to have a few words with him on the telephone. I was pretty frank with him, and he saw my point. He's coming out here as soon as he's coped with all the publicity hounds, attended to his affairs and so forth."

"Oh, how wonderful!"

She caught the gleam of humor in his eyes and said defensively, "I mean it." She wondered if he knew how fervently she meant it!

"I'm sure you do. Dick's a good fellow. A trifle easy-going—or was. Easily led. But this show in the Antarctic seems to have toughened his outlook. Or so I gathered from our brief talk."

She didn't pursue the subject, nor did he. She thought that this was probably as far as they would ever go in discussing Louise. But she didn't mind. Dominic still felt the pull of an old loyalty, perhaps. On the other hand, she felt sure that he knew—or at least had guessed—everything, and had absolved her from blame.

She wanted to forget the whole sordid business now, forever. Attempted murder—especially for the second time—wasn't a thing to dwell on. She wanted to talk of something else.

"I'm going to get up tomorrow," she said, smiling.

"Splendid. But no work. Promise?"

"All right, I promise."

He gave her news of progress at the dig and she said, "I'll be on the job again, the day after tomorrow."

Suddenly they were both feeling strangely lighthearted. It was as if something evil was on its way out, defeated. As if, Chloe felt, they could now make a new start.

Perhaps Dominic felt that way, too. He said, "Sometime you and I must have a talk, Chloe."

She said eagerly, "Now. Why not now?"

But Lotta came in just then with her dinner on a tray.

"And let all that delicious looking food congeal on the plate? Lotta would never forgive me," he said.

"The *signorina* is tired—too many visitors," Lotta said in the bossy way of a privileged servant who has known her master as a child.

"All right, Lotta, I'm off. Good night, Chloe."

"Good night, Dominic."

So they were going to have a talk, were they? Did that mean that Dominic had a plan? A solution of their problem?

Sipping at her chicken soup under Lotta's stern eye, Chloe asked herself how she was going to wait to hear what it was.

CHAPTER FIFTEEN

CHLOE WOKE THE NEXT MORNING feeling perfectly well, and not only well, but with a strong feeling that somehow, soon, everything was going to be all right—though when she examined the prospects she could find no real reason for such confidence.

Still, Louise would be going away, and maybe Dominic had a plan; and if one premonition of hers had turned out to be right, why shouldn't another?

It had rained a little in the night, and the morning was blue and gold, smelling of fresh damp earth and salt sea. It would be hot later on.

She lay in bed late, lazily planning tomorrow's program of work. She would be behind on her schedule, but no matter, she would soon catch up on it....

Time to get up, dress, call on the *contessa*.

She found her delving happily into her jewel case.

"Good morning, *contessa*," she smiled, kissing her cheek. "Can I help you?"

"No, thank you, my dear. Here is what I was looking for. A little present for you, to celebrate your recovery."

It was a bracelet in filigree gold, beautifully worked, nearly two inches wide—a lovely thing. Chloe clasped it around her wrist and held it at arm's length for the contessa to admire.

"Charming. My husband brought it from India—he was a great traveler, you know."

"It's lovely. You are too kind to me, *contessa*."

She was offered a soft, withered cheek to kiss again.

"Not nearly so good as you have been to me, dear child. I can never hope to repay you."

That brought Chloe up with a jerk. It reminded her that the *contessa* remained unsuspecting of the deception that had been practiced on her; that her precarious hold on life still depended on what she and Dominic decided to do.

Suddenly there were tears in her eyes. They fell down her cheeks; she could nothing to prevent the *contessa* seeing.

"Chloe, dearest, you are crying. What is it?"

"Nothing. Just—your gift, what you said. Please take no notice, *contessa*. I expect I'm a bit weak and wobbly after being ill. There, I've stopped. I must go back to my room and repair the damage."

She helped return the heap of jewelry to the casket and put it back on the dresser.

"Thank you again for the lovely bracelet," she said as she left. The *contessa*'s fond smile followed her to the door.

She was crying again as she ran to her own room. She felt overwhelmed with guilt. She wanted Dominic there, to reassure her, tell her again that they had done the right thing. She wanted Dominic....

When she went down to the living room later on she had covered up all traces of her tears. She was glad she had, for there was a stranger in the room—a tall man in a gray suit with fairish hair, brown eyes, a nose and a look strongly reminiscent of Dominic's. He was looking at a case of miniatures and swung around at the sound of the door opening.

"Oh, I thought it might be my wife."

Chloe held out her hand and said smiling, "You must be Mr. Carlyon. I didn't know you were expected today."

"I wasn't. Finished my chores and picked up an unexpected cancellation. Do tell me—who are you?"

His smile was like Dominic's, too, though it hadn't the same power to disturb her. He was thin, with a look of strain as though he had been through privation—but very attractive.

"I'm Chloe Linden. I'm working on the dig. And I'm—Dominic and I are engaged."

"What? The lucky dog didn't tell me—I suppose there was too much to say in too little time. Well—my congratulations to you both."

"And mine to you on your return to safety. You must have had a terrible time, Mr. Carlyon."

"Dick. We're to be cousins, aren't we?"

"Dick, then. Does Louise know you're here?"

He gave a rueful shrug.

"I sent Lotta to tell her. She isn't up yet."

"Shall I go and tell her to hurry?"

"No. Stay and talk to me. Tell me about Aunt Olivia—the dig—what you've all been doing. I've been away for two long, blank years."

"Was it very awful?"

He looked surprised.

"No, on the whole most enjoyable. Annoying when we got out of radio contact—that's a long story. I'll save it for another time. Nobody died, though we all got frostbite sometime or other."

"Louise thought they might knight you."

He threw back his head and roared with laughter.

"The leader of the expedition may possibly get an M.B.E. if he's lucky. We *did* find out a few useful things. But the rest of us—good Lord, no! Very small fry."

"Very brave fry, *I* think."

"You're very sweet, cousin Chloe."

They were laughing together when Louise walked in on them. She ignored Chloe, put out her hands in that same loving gesture she had used on Dominic, swam toward him and held out her face to be kissed.

Dick kissed her cheek, but she flung her arms around him and said thrillingly, "Darling, how wonderful to have you back!"

So she had decided how to receive him. Chloe watched the touching little scene with inward amusement. She was too thankful that Dick had come, and would presumably be taking Louise away, to bear any malice.

"I see you've met Chloe."

"Yes, I was just telling her how lucky Dominic is."

Fury rippled over Louise's mobile face for a brief instant and was gone. Chloe saw it, but Dick was busy lighting a cigarette.

"I want to hear all about everything, darling," Louise said, with a meaningful look at Chloe.

Chloe said at once, "Excuse me, I . . . ."

Dick interrupted. "Don't go, Chloe, just when we've met. Let's all have a drink—must celebrate, mustn't we, Louise?"

"You used to mix a marvelous martini, darling."

"And still do, I promise."

He went over to the side table and busied himself. Louise said, "You're in time for the reception—to celebrate the engagement, you know."

"Ah. When is it to be?"

"Next Thursday."

He brought them their drinks and shook his head.

"Sorry, Louise. We fly back to London on Tuesday. I've got our reservations."

"But we can't. You must cancel them. I refuse."

His eyebrows shot up—the same way Dominic's did, Chloe thought.

"I'm afraid not. We've no time to waste—and lots to do. I'm taking up my new appointment at once."

Louise gave him a wide-eyed stare. "But aren't those meanies in the F.O. giving you a holiday after all you've gone through?"

"Nonsense. I've had my holiday—two years of it. I'm lucky they have a place for me. It'll be starting at the beginning again, more or less. Third secretary."

"Oh, no," Louise said. In a voice of doom she demanded where.

"Teheran," Dick said carelessly.

"Where on earth is that?" When he told her she said with decision, "Then of course I won't come with you. No, really, Dick...."

"Then where do you propose to live? And on what? I've already disposed of the lease of the London apartment."

Her eyes flashed dangerously. "You fool, Dick. Then I'll live here. It's half yours, isn't it?"

"Was. Dominic has agreed to buy me out," he told her calmly. "I had to ask him, Louise. I needed the cash. You've cleaned me out, my girl."

"I don't care," Louise stormed. "I tell you I absolutely will not go with you to this outlandish place."

"I think you will," Dick Carlyon said gently. "I think

you will.'' His eyes and voice had in them something relentless, implacable. Chloe saw that Louise had met her match, and knew it.

Moving soundlessly—though it didn't matter, really, the other two had forgotten she was there—she slipped away and left them to it.

DICK REMAINED ADAMANT about the day of their departure, and Louise lost all interest in the reception and handed over everything to Chloe.

Before that, Chloe had scarcely been able to bring herself to believe in it. It had seemed unreal—something they all discussed frequently, but was unlikely ever to happen. Something that belonged to the realms of fantasy.

There certainly was something fantastic about it, she thought as she studied the list of guests—everyone in Malta who mattered, Louise said—the arrangements for food, champagne, dancing, fireworks, lavish flowers, extra waiters, all to celebrate an engagement that would be broken off as soon as circumstances permitted.

She would have liked to go to Dominic and beg him to call the whole thing off—but the pile of acceptances daunted her, and besides the *contessa* was enjoying it all so much. She was determined to come down for a little while, to receive her guests. There was no possibility of calling a halt now.

Chloe tried to imagine how it would be. She thought of the big lofty rooms, lit with glittering chandeliers, great bowls of exotic flowers on the tables, the *contessa* in her big wing chair, Dominic and herself standing beside her, waiting for the first guests to arrive. She imagined the big cars rolling into the courtyard, dropping off their passengers, circling the fountain, returning to the cathedral square to park. And then well-dressed people coming in, two by two—nearly all of them strangers to her, all looking at her, the girl Dominic had chosen....

If it had been real—if Dominic loved her, if their engagement were a love match—how different she would have felt. She would have been nervous, of course, but thrilled, radiant, on top of the world. As it was, she looked forward to Thursday night with dread.

Since Dick's arrival she had had no chance to get Dominic alone, so she had no idea how he felt. He and Dick spent long days at the dig and long hours in the library after dinner talking. Chloe had no idea how Louise spent her time. Perhaps she was paying a round of farewell calls—or packing.

On Tuesday, when she was breakfasting before leaving for the dig, Dominic looked in on her.

"I'd like you to come with me to the airport, to see Dick and Louise off," he said. "Will you be ready at twelve?"

"Am I not to go to the dig, then?"

"No, take a break today."

"Very well. I have work I can do in the darkroom this morning."

He smiled and left her. She thought vexedly, *why didn't I make him stay, talk to me, tell me what we're going to do?* The truth was, she was still a little afraid of him....

She found Mark working in the library. She hadn't been able to resist telling Mark about the first meeting between Dick and his wife.

"Teheran!" Mark had hooted. "All those Moslems— and Louise! Fresh worlds to conquer! I wish I'd been there to see her face. The face that launched a thousand quips!"

This morning he had news for her.

"I'm flying home next week, Chloe. My father's not well—needs me to help him run the few hundred acres the family still possesses. Look, here's the address. Promise to let me know as soon as you arrive in London."

She said, "Yes, Mark," and thought that perhaps, when that time came, she might be glad of Mark's cheerful devotion.

When it was time to leave for the airport she found that two cars were waiting. Mark was at the wheel of one, which was piled with Louise's matched set of luggage and Dick's one rather battered suitcase. Her own Austin stood alongside—she supposed he would take her in that.

He came out of the house a minute or two later with Dick and Louise and shut them into the larger car.

"Like to drive?" he asked Chloe. She nodded and got in the Austin.

At the airport they found that the flight would be leaving on schedule; they would only have a short wait.

Louise was sulky; she would have liked a big, impressive send-off by all her new friends. But Dick had been adamant about that, too. He had had enough of that sort of thing since his return to civilization.

When the loudspeaker requested passengers to go aboard he shook hands warmly with Chloe, kissed her cheek and wished her happiness. She said with equal warmth, "You, too. Enjoy Teheran." He laughed and said, "You bet I will." Louise scowled, and Chloe hoped she wouldn't spoil things for Dick again. On the whole she thought not. Louise had clearly seen the red light—and she was no fool.

They watched the plane take off and dwindle to a silver speck against the limitless blue. Dominic and Mark turned to each other, solemnly shook hands; then they both laughed. A weight had been lifted from both their shoulders.

"We'll have lunch," Dominic said briskly. "And a bottle of wine. We'll drink to Teheran."

That was all that was said. By tacit agreement all three of them shed Louise from their consciousness. They had quite a hilarious meal in the airport restaurant. When they had finished, Dominic said, "You take the Austin back, Mark. I'll drive Chloe."

He drove fast, and soon they were bowling along the coast road, approaching St. Paul. The sun shed pools of golden light between its tall buildings. The sea sparkled gaily, but Chloe no longer felt happy. She was nerving herself to say something to Dominic—something that took all her courage.

He pulled over at length beside a stretch of smooth turf overlooking a tiny bay, and turned the car off the road so that they faced the sea.

"Let's skip work for today. Cigarette?"

She took a few quick puffs to calm herself.

"Dominic, there's something I want to tell you—to say."

He looked at her with that gleam of humor. "Me, too. But you first. Say on."

She took a deep breath.

"The other day, you said the best way out of our—difficulty would be to marry you. Did you mean it?"

"Obviously."

"And I refused. Well, what I want to say is, I've changed my mind. I—I want to marry you, if you like."

He turned around to look at her more closely. She gazed straight ahead, unable to meet his eyes.

"Aha! What caused you to change your mind, Chloe?"

She hesitated, then said in a rush, "It was your mother. She gave me this lovely bracelet, she said she could never repay what I've done for her, she was so sweet, so trusting. I could never undeceive her. I've made up my mind to go through with it. Dominic, we must, we can't hurt her that much...."

His eyebrows have gone up. He said, "*You've* made up your mind? But what about me?"

She was utterly taken aback. "But you suggested it. You *asked* me to marry you."

"And accepted your refusal."

The slow color rose in her cheeks. She felt terrible. Shamed.

"But now...."

He gave her a look of mocking irony.

"Now *I'm* going to be the one to say what we'll do, my dear. I created this situation. I'll decide how to deal with it. And I won't marry you till you've seen this fellow...."

"Fellow?"

"This live-or-die man. This man you're in love with...."

"Oh," she said, subdued—but with the beginning of a sparkle in her downcast eyes. Her treacherous heart began to beat fast, faster.

"As soon as your three months are up I want you to go to him. You're to tell him, 'I'm engaged. I'm planning to marry almost at once.' If anything will bring him into line, that will. But if he doesn't react, if he just offers friendly congratulations and things, then you'll know it's no good, he doesn't care. And in that case, you can come back here. There will be no need to... undeceive my mother, Chloe."

She lifted her eyes then and met his. They still held a mocking irony. She took a sudden resolve; another deep breath. Holding his glance with hers she said clearly, "Very well. I agree." And after a tiny pause, "Dominic, I'm engaged, I'm planning to marry almost at once." She waited, trembling.

His face seemed to come alive. He said slowly, "Chloe, you mean—*me*?"

"You, Dominic. Only you."

"But when?"

"That first day—on the plane."

His hands were on her shoulders now. His look was an open avowal. He said softly, "It took longer with me. My resistance was—pretty strong, I think it happened slowly, came to a head when I held you in my arms in the water, down in the cave...."

No summer lightning in his case. She gave her little spurt of laughter.

"All among the octopi and bats and things."

He had her completely in his arms now.

"Darling. My darling." His mouth sought hers, hard, hungry. Sea and sky swung dizzily, rapturously, before her eyes closed....

Time stood still. Sea gulls swooped and planed above them. A goat came and looked at them with demonic yellow eyes. A fisherman carried out his gear to a distant rocky ledge and began casting. They didn't notice.

Finally, Dominic said, "Darling—let's go tell my mother. That we're ready to fix a date, I mean."

"Are we?" Her eyes danced at him.

He kissed her again.

"Aren't we?"

"Yes, Dominic. Just as soon as we can."

"My darling!"

He was singing as they swooped around the wide curves of the coast road, and Chloe sang, too, softly, happily, starry-eyed.

Everything had come right. Louise had gone, Dominic loved her, the *contessa* need never know. Everything was for the best in the best of all possible worlds.

WILD PARADISE

PATRICIA COUGHLIN

WARNER BOOKS

A Warner Communications Company

This book is dedicated with love to my husband, Bill, and to my best friends, Carolyn and Ken Malluck and Julie and Michael Blanchette

CHAPTER ONE

Liz scanned the muddy stretch of road outside her parked car with an uneasy sigh. She would feel better about her part in this scenario if the signal were something more foolproof, the way it always was in the movies. Say a blood-red rose pinned to the lapel of a white tuxedo. But the note delivered to her yesterday by the boy who spent his days shining shoes in front of the village of San Luis's sole hotel, a ramshackle two-story dwelling that gave new meaning to the term "no-frills accommodations," had been considerably less original. It simply instructed her to watch for a man wearing a sombrero. Not exactly the sort of thing to stand out like a sore thumb in a Guatemalan crowd.

"Señorita, le gusta la fruta?"

Liz glanced out the window of the rented Toyota to find an open-shirted man swinging a basket of overripe fruit too close to her nose. Her heart began pumping furiously. Then she lifted her gaze higher and discovered she was face to chest with quite possibly the only man in this small, somnolent village not wearing one of the broad-brimmed straw hats as protection from the sun.

"Le gusta la fruta?" he repeated.

La fruta . . . fruit. He wanted to know if she liked fruit.

"Sí." She smiled, wishing he'd hold the damn basket downwind from her, then rapidly shook her head as he thrust a mushy papaya her way. Of course. You'd think three days of being accosted by native peddlers hawking everything from alligator teeth to dried heads of boa constrictors would have taught her that what he really wanted to know was if she wanted to buy his fruit.

"Non, merci. I mean, *gracias,"* she replied in a tortured blend of high school French and Spanish. "I'm not feeling well. Sick." She frowned and patted her stomach, grappling for the word. *"Enfermo."*

"Ahhh. *Enfermo.* Señorita sick."

"That's right. *Sí."*

"Señorita no want fruit."

"Sí." Liz shook her head. "I mean, no, *gracias."*

The man grinned and shrugged before hoisting the basket to his shoulder and ambling off, leaving Liz to continue her vigil. The señorita definitely did not want fruit. What she wanted was for him, whoever *him* turned out to be, to hurry up and get there. She was beginning to feel a resurgence of last night's panic. Time and again she'd awakened in the cell-like hotel room with its tiny, screenless window that let in too many dime-sized mosquitoes and not enough cool

2

breeze, certain she would never be able to pull this off. Fortunately sunrise had spurred an ascent in her spirits as well. Of course she would pull it off. She was a Fitzgerald, born and raised to conquer whatever life strewed in her path. She would succeed or die trying. Wincing a little at her own determination, Liz prayed that last thought would not prove prophetic.

The daily afternoon deluge of rain had stopped just a few moments before as abruptly as it had begun. It had reduced the dirt road running through the village to a ribbon of mud and puddles and left the inside of the small car feeling like a steam bath. Beads of sweat crawled between her shoulder blades, slithering down her spine and inside the waistband of her white cotton skirt to the silk bikini pants already clinging to her damp skin. Lifting her backside off the hot vinyl bucket seat, she tried to peel them loose, all the while keeping her eyes on the street and praying that she would somehow be able to distinguish the man she was waiting for from every other sombrero wearer in the vicinity.

It was while she was tugging at the stubborn elastic legband that he sauntered into view, emerging from between two thatch-roofed huts across the street from where she was parked. In that instant Liz knew she might as well have saved all her prayers. Sombreros and red roses aside, there was no question that this was the man. He looked wary and dangerous and infinitely capable of putting a bullet through Kirk's head if she didn't fork over the twenty thousand American dollars stashed beneath her seat. Thank God Kirk had told her about the cash he had hidden in his suitcase in case of emergencies.

Her fingers clenched around the steering wheel as she watched him wind his way through the piles of mangoes and pineapples on the other side of the road. He wore his hat tipped low to shield his eyes and a reddish-brown leather vest over his dark T-shirt and jeans in defiance of the god-awful tropical heat that made even her loose yellow cotton blouse feel like a suit of armor. Not sparing a glance in Liz's direction, he approached the local convenience store, with its dusty cardboard display of sunglasses in the window and battered, 1950s vintage Pepsi-Cola sign above the door, and lowered himself to the bench out front. Exactly as the note said he would.

If all went according to plan, a truck would soon approach from behind where she was parked to pick him up before heading north out of the village. Liz was to follow. She had no idea where they would lead her or how long it would take, only that she'd been instructed to have a full tank of gas and to make sure she stayed at least fifty yards behind the truck at all times. Ever since the arrival of the note confirming her suspicion that her fiancé, Kirk Allaire, wasn't simply a little late returning from his afternoon foray into the jungle, Liz had been doing a good job of suppressing the urge to panic. Now, with push about to come to shove, she reluctantly admitted to herself that under the circumstances fear might not be an entirely unwarranted emotion.

The guide to Guatemala she'd read after impulsively badgering Kirk into letting her come along on this mission of mercy had cryptically referred to "sporadic bursts of unrest" and cautioned visitors to check with local authorities before venturing into outlying areas of the country. She had no way of knowing if those holding Kirk were leftist guerrillas, renegade government soldiers who suspected his true reason for being here, or simply a band of the cutthroat *bandidos* who roamed this sparsely settled region.

Actually, it didn't much matter. Whoever they were, Liz had no doubt that they would kill him, and her too if necessary, to get what they wanted. She'd already been in Guatemala long enough to realize that Kirk's warning had been right. Things were different here, more complicated and sinister than you would suspect from watching the village women scrubbing clothes in the stream that ran behind the row of huts or the old men gathered in the scant shade of a mahogany tree to pass a bottle of tequila. There was a fine desperation to life in this country. Liz could sense it even though she didn't fully understand it.

The sudden movement of the man on the bench drew her from her uneasy thoughts as he leaned back, stretching long legs out in front of him in a relaxed pose that was a direct counterpoint to her own mounting anxiety. Her breath was coming twice as fast as usual and still she couldn't seem to draw enough air into her tightened lungs. God, she wished that truck would hurry up so she could get this over with.

She was almost afraid that if she had much more time to mull it over common sense would cause her to have second thoughts. Though she was given to acting on impulse, she was also rational enough to know that the prudent thing would be to ignore the threats in the note as well as the postscript scribbled in Kirk's handwriting imploring her to do as she was told, and dump the whole mess in the lap of the local authorities. But then she thought of the group of refugees hiding in the jungle outside the village, counting on them for safe passage to the United States. The certain knowledge that to call such official attention to Kirk and herself would risk their lives kept her sitting there, waiting.

Except for an occasional sideways glance, she kept her eyes directed away from the man sitting directly across the narrow dirt road. With her blond hair, green eyes, and clothes so obviously *norteamericana* in style, Liz knew her mere presence in San Luis was noteworthy enough. No need to invite further attention by appearing blatantly to check out the village's male population. She felt all the tiny hairs on the back of her neck suddenly lift. Instinct temporarily overrode caution and Liz turned her head to find that the man apparently suffered no compunctions about staring at her. True, she couldn't actually see his eyes beneath the sombrero, only a square chin covered by several days' growth of black stubble, but she could feel his gaze fixed on her, and that was more than enough. For the first time since arriving in the tropics, a chill ran through her body.

The roar of a truck's engine spared her from having to drag her gaze away. It came careening from behind her, lurching around puddles the size of wading pools and sending the chickens who habitually gathered in the center of the road squawking off in all directions, before it finally jerked to a halt near where she was parked. A black tarpaulin was tied over the bed of the truck, covering what she judged to be a heavy load from the way it settled low over the rear tires.

Curled up in a small corner near the tailgate sat a young man who looked to Liz to be no more than seventeen or eighteen. He was dressed in the loose-fitting cotton trousers and shirt worn by most of the local farmers. Despite craning her neck, all she could see of the driver was the totally unexpected dark blue baseball cap perched atop his head. Neither man glanced her way.

Lord, they were cool about this. With a laziness that would have seemed insolent back in Boston but that she'd come to expect in the tropics, the first man stood, stretched, and made his way over to climb into the front of the truck. The peeling paint that covered those parts of the ancient pickup that had not totally rusted away was actually more of a faded orange than the red Liz had envisioned, but this was no time to quibble over aesthetics. When the truck began to move again, so did she.

The dilapidated Toyota barely made it through the first puddle before stalling.

"Damn." Her clammy fingers fumbled on the keys, taking three tries to coax the engine back into some semblance of gasping cooperation. After that she inched forward more carefully, her pace further slowed by the chickens and children who ricocheted directly into her path after being displaced by the speeding truck up ahead. As she passed the hotel near the edge of town, she vaguely noticed Miguel, the messenger boy, sitting in his usual spot on the wood-frame porch out front. He jumped up when he caught sight of her.

"Señorita, señorita!"

Liz slid her gaze to the rearview mirror. Miguel had run to the middle of the road, splashing mud all the way to his knees, and was frantically waving his hands as he continued

7

to shout at her in a rapid stream of peasant Spanish. She automatically lifted her foot off the accelerator, hesitating, looking from the boy now approaching her car at a gallop to the lopsided rear end of the truck rapidly disappearing in the distance. He was still a good twenty feet from the back bumper when she slammed her foot down again, giving the sputtering Toyota enough gas to send it into shock. Whatever the kid wanted would have to wait. If she lost sight of that truck now, she might not get a second chance to save Kirk.

Once they passed the last open field that had been slashed and burned from the jungle by local farmers, the vegetation on both sides of the road quickly became more dense, forming an unbroken tangle of vines and plants taller than she was. Daylight was left behind as they plowed deeper into the remote Petén region near the country's northern border. A hundred feet above her head towering ceiba trees locked branches to form a lacy emerald canopy, pierced at random intervals by crystal shafts of sunlight. The road itself dipped and curved through the overgrown foliage, skirting limestone outcrops and natural lagoons, becoming so narrow in places that Liz felt as if she were barreling along in a stifling hot, green tunnel.

With her heart leaping into her throat at every turn, she struggled to match the reckless pace set by the driver of the truck. Even during those brief snatches when she lost sight of it, she could still hear the growl of its engine up ahead. She did her best to concentrate on the sound, and ignore the other noises surrounding her as the darkness thickened. The shrieks and bird calls she could take, even the occasion-

8

al startling flash of vivid pink or orange as a bird flew low in front of her bug-splattered windshield. They were actually fascinating, in a primitive way. It was the blend of hundreds of less distinct noises that made her skin crawl. On both sides she was engulfed by a glistening snarl of lush foliage, and everything in the undergrowth seemed to rustle and breathe.

The smell only made it worse—that heavy, sickening-sweet smell that after a few breaths made you wish there was someplace you could hang your lungs out to air. Driving to the village from the airstrip that first night, Kirk had explained to her that the odor was a combination of native flora and rotting vegetation. She would get used to it, he'd assured her. Maybe, but Liz knew she'd never get used to being this close to whatever native fauna lurked in all that rotting vegetation. Now, dwelling on it in spite of herself, it seemed to her that the jungle had a sort of collective heartbeat, a muffled pulsing sound that grew steadily louder, becoming its own echo until she felt as if it were closing in on her from all sides.

Tightening her grip on the wheel, she tried to concentrate instead on the very real danger that lay ahead. That was when she realized that while she'd been busy frightening herself with lurid visions of skulking wildlife, she'd completely lost track of the sound of the truck's engine. In a wave of panic she put the accelerator to the floor and forged ahead, whipping through several large puddles fast enough to send water splashing in through the open windows onto her bare arm in hot, coffee-colored drops she was too preoccupied to wipe away. Bouncing around a particularly sharp turn, she

9

stared up ahead and a sickening premonition of disaster broke over her. From this point the dirt track stretched straight for as far as she could see without any sign of the truck. Hitting the brake, Liz brought the Toyota to a complete stop and listened.

Nothing. Only the throbbing of the jungle, which sounded even louder and more overtly threatening now that she was totally alone. Desperately Liz tried to recall the terrain she'd just driven through. She was sure there hadn't been any crossroads, anyplace at all where they could have turned off. And even if there had, wouldn't they have waited to make sure she saw and followed? After all, their purpose wasn't to lose her; it was simply to lead her to a place where the money could be exchanged for Kirk.

They had to be somewhere up ahead. If the road remained straight, then she should have no trouble finding them. And if it didn't... Liz raked her fingers through her hair, dislodging several long strands from the barrette holding it off her neck. If it didn't, she'd have to tackle that problem when it arose. What choice did she have? Even if she wanted to go back she wasn't about to attempt turning around here and maybe ending up stuck in the marshy underbrush that dropped away from the road. Despite its ruts and gullies, Liz knew that the road was at least regularly shored up with gravel to counteract the erosive effects of the rain. She wasn't about to take her chances in the muddy overgrowth that lay beyond this last remaining symbol of civilization.

Even as she sat there deliberating, something black and furry with a long, spiked tail chugged across the road in front of her, slinking beneath a wide, fan-shaped leaf and

10

disappearing from sight. Shuddering, she reached to turn the key in the ignition.

"Hold it, lady. You're not going anywhere."

Liz jumped with a sharp gasp, then froze as a long, muscular arm stretched in front of her to grab the keys. She sat with her eyes straight ahead, her back pressed to the seat, feeling as if the wind had been knocked out of her. The voice, harsh and biting, had sounded awfully close to her ear, and though she'd never so much as seen one close up, she knew with paralyzing certainty that the hard, cold object being jabbed into the side of her neck was a gun.

"Please." It was the only word she could think of to say, and it came out a barely audible whisper.

"Get out of the car," the voice ordered.

She tried, but she couldn't seem to unlock her fingers from around the steering wheel and make them open the door. The gun rammed her neck again, harder this time, making her shoulders jerk with pain.

"I said get out."

Before she could move, the door was ripped open from the outside. Somehow Liz managed to slide from beneath the wheel. She hardly noticed the mud that oozed through the straps of her sandals. She was too busy staring into the fierce, scowling face of the man now pointing the gun directly between her breasts, the same man she'd waited for back in the village. His buddy, the one who'd been driving the truck, was now leaning on the back of her car, a piece of reed clamped between his teeth. The youngest member of the trio was nowhere to be seen. Insanely Liz found herself

11

wondering how in the world they'd managed to get around behind her this way. She was smart enough not to ask.

"Just what the hell do you think you're doing?" the one holding the gun demanded.

He'd shed the sombrero, probably before cutting back through the jungle to get the drop on her, and now Liz could see the lined, angular face the hat had hidden. She'd rather have left it to her imagination. Nothing she could have conjured up would have been as menacing as his grim mouth and the cold, unreadable eyes glaring down at her.

He looked at home in this untamed landscape despite the fact that he obviously wasn't a native. Up close Liz noticed what she hadn't back in the village. Both men were over six feet, taller than most Guatemalans, and as gringo looking as she was. And even in the few curt words barked at her so far, she could detect an American accent.

That knowledge brought a measure of relief she knew was probably naive. Neither man looked the type to be swayed by anything as noble as shared citizenship, but at least now she wouldn't have to worry about the language barrier. How their being Americans affected the situation with Kirk she couldn't be sure. They might well be mercenaries, paid participants in the country's guerrilla war. Or they could be just plain thugs out for an easy score. As she looked at her assailant, anything unsavory and despicable seemed possible.

His hair, as black as the whiskers shadowing his jaw, was too long and looked as if it had seen nothing more energetic than a finger-combing in days. An inch-long scar cut through the bristle on his left cheek, stark against the sun-browned leather of his skin. The angles of his face were hard, uncompromisingly masculine in a way that Liz knew would have made her uneasy even in a far less threatening situation. The only thing close to appealing about him was his eyes, the deepest blue she had ever seen, and even they were narrowed in anger. Although why the hell he should be angry with her when she was simply following his orders Liz had no idea.

"What are you, deaf or something?" he growled as she continued to stand there, eyeing him in wary silence. "I asked you what you were doing out here."

Liz scraped her tongue across her bottom lip, thrown even further off kilter by his question. He of all people should know what she was doing out here. Without warning his finger moved on the gun, causing a sharp, metallic click she recognized from every detective show she'd ever seen on TV.

"I was following you," she replied in a hurry.

If he looked angry before, now he looked furious enough to actually pull the trigger of the gun that seemed frighteningly at home in his grip. Liz's eyes flew from his enraged expression to the vein throbbing wildly in his throat, and she took a lurching step backward. Instantly his free hand clamped on to her shoulder. His fingers bit into the tendons at the base of her neck as he jerked her closer, sending shards of pain shooting down her arm. Wincing, Liz tried to shake him loose.

He ignored her struggling and her soft grunts of pain. Twisting her around so they were face-to-face, with only a gun length between them, he snarled, "Why?"

Why? He meant, why was she following him? Liz real-

13

ized, her confusion mounting, adding to her fear. Was this some kind of test?

"Because that's what the note said to do," she explained, desperately hoping that was what he wanted to hear.

"What note?"

She felt a rush of impatience. "The note the kid back at the hotel brought to my room."

Without releasing her he shot a look over his shoulder to his friend, who simply shrugged. "Tell me exactly what the note said," he ordered, turning back to Liz.

"It said I was to watch for a man wearing a sombrero who would be sitting right where you were and who would be picked up by a red truck . . . just as you were. Then I was to follow the truck. Which I did, and here I am." She tried rotating her shoulder. "Look, you're hurting me. Would you mind . . ."

"Tough," he cut in. "I'm not hurting you half as much as I will if you don't wise up and tell me the truth about why you were following us."

"I just told you the truth," she cried. "Do you think I'd make something like that up?"

With startling quickness his hand shot from her shoulder to her jaw, grasping it roughly, forcing her head back until she was staring directly into his eyes. Slowly he dropped his gaze to the slender gold cross that rested over the pulse pounding in the hollow of her throat, then down the length of her body, finally stopping where her rose-polished toenails peeked through the mud. When he lifted his gaze to her face, the glint in his eyes was mocking and blatantly suspicious. "You wanna know what I think? I think it would

14

take a hell of a lot more than some kid's note and a man in a sombrero to drag a broad like you way out here. Now you start talking—the truth—or whatever your reason was for coming, it'll be nothing but a memory. And so will you.''

Again the gun clicked, a clean, final little sound that scared her more than the jungle pulse ever had. Liz could feel her arms and legs trembling. She wondered if she would even be able to stand if he were to relinquish his painful grip on her chin.

"I told you the truth," she repeated, unable to keep the tremor from her voice. "Listen, I don't know what kind of game you're playing or what else you want me to say, but . . ."

"For starters try telling me who sent you the note," he interrupted.

Liz stared at the intensity in his expression in utter bewilderment, a horrible suspicion beginning to build inside.

"You," she blurted, close to panic. "You sent the note. Or at least someone working with you did."

"Now who's playing games, huh?" He squeezed her jaw harder, using the hold to shake her. "Well, baby, the game just ended, because I don't have the time or the inclination to play right now."

He rammed the gun into her breastbone, the savage light in his eyes coldly proclaiming his intent. Liz could smell the oily metal, feel the terrifying pressure of it against her chest, and her lips quivered. "No . . . please."

CHAPTER
TWO

The pained whimper sounded far away, but Liz knew it had come from her own lips. She fully expected to see her life flash before her tightly closed eyes, to hear the blast of the gun, and feel the acrid sting of gunpowder in her nostrils. She wasn't sure how the bullet would feel ripping through her body; she just hoped it would be well aimed so she wouldn't lie for hours on the wet jungle floor, bleeding to death.

It was taking too long, she suddenly realized. She started to open her eyes, then thought maybe that was exactly what he was waiting for, and stopped. He looked sadistic enough to want her to watch while he pulled the trigger. Still, she couldn't stand there indefinitely with her eyes squeezed shut. If her life hung by that slim a thread, she might as well summon the courage to go out in style.

Forcing her eyes open, she found both men staring at her. The driver, standing closer now, looked amused, and maybe a little sympathetic, Liz noted distractedly. The man with the gun still looked mad as hell.

"You stupid bitch," he muttered, releasing her with a movement as full of disgust as his tone. "Were you just going to stand there and let me shoot you?"

"Perhaps the lady did not have any choice." The other man spoke for the first time. "You know, Zach, it occurs to me that just maybe she's telling you the truth."

"Yeah, I was just thinking the same thing myself." He lowered the gun almost reluctantly, but Liz still didn't move. Even without it, he intimidated her.

"So what now?" the driver asked, drawing an impatient look from the man with the gun.

"What do you think?"

"I try not to. After all, you are the bona fide expert at this cloak-and-dagger business." The driver's speech was a blend of exaggeratedly formal inflections and pure Brooklynese, as curious as his bedraggled appearance. "Of course, if you weren't so hotheaded and had handled this little matter my way to begin with, we'd have no problem now."

His friend made an impatient gesture with his gun. "Yeah, and if you weren't so pigheaded we wouldn't be in this godforsaken country in the first place. But as long as we are, I think a little caution is called for, don't you agree?"

"Ah, the old better-safe-than-sorry routine," the driver drawled, making a show of stroking his chin thoughtfully. His jaw too was covered with a few days' growth, only it was

17

lighter, the same murky brown as the hair sticking out from beneath his cap in thick clumps and one long, thin braid that brushed his left shoulder. "I suppose a little caution can't hurt."

"I'm glad you see it that way. Because if she's working for Sanchez we have a hell of a bigger problem on our hands right now."

"But I'm not," Liz interjected quickly. She'd finally gotten her breath back enough to speak, and listening to the two men had confirmed her suspicion about what was going on. "I think there's been a terrible misunderstanding here," she continued in a rush. "You obviously thought I was following you. And I was, or rather I was following your truck, but I can see now that it was the wrong one. So if you'll just give me my keys, I'll be on my way back to the village and we can forget this whole thing ever happened."

There was a long, strained silence during which the man called Zach, obviously the meaner of the two, stared at her as if she were something smeared on a microscope slide.

Finally the driver nodded, made a slight adjustment in the angle of his cap, and announced, "Sounds perfectly reasonable to me."

"That figures," the mean one snorted, fixing Liz with a nasty stare.

"C'mon, Zach, let's not get all hot and bothered under the collar about this."

"Can it, Jade."

Jade and Zach. Somehow knowing they had names made Liz feel better, as if they might even have mothers some-

18

where too. It made them seem more human and less like anonymous killers. Maybe if they knew her name as well . . .

"I'm Liz Randolph," she blurted without preamble, not caring how asinine she must sound. "From Boston."

The one named Jade appeared to bite back a laugh. Sweeping his hat from his head, he gave a dramatic bow. "Russell Jadach. Jade to my friends and enemies alike. From here and there and all over. My associate here is Zachary McCabe, originally from Brownsville, Texas, as you have no doubt already discerned from his speech impediment."

Liz wasn't sure how to react to his bantering. Before she could do more than succumb to a nervous, strangled-sounding laugh, Zachary McCabe took over.

"You know this is all very entertaining, this little meeting of the Guatemalan chapter of Misplaced Americans, but it's not solving our problem."

"What problem?" Jade countered. "Liz made a little mistake. She's sorry, we're sorry. We're all tourists in a strange country so let's let bygones be bygones."

Liz nearly sagged against the car with relief until the lash of McCabe's voice intervened.

"Are you out of your mind?" He glared at Jade. "Never mind, I retract the question. But just so nobody here misunderstands anything else, let's get it straight. There's no way we can let her go."

"Why not?" Liz demanded on a fresh burst of panic. "I told you it was all a mistake."

"I know what you told me," McCabe countered, his mouth set in a grim line. "But I still don't know for sure

19

that Sanchez didn't send you. And I'm not taking any chances by turning you loose.''

The smile left Jade's face. "I don't see what harm it can do, Zach. She's a woman, for God's sake.''

"All the more reason not to let her go. The second she makes it back to San Luis she'll go screaming bloody murder about what happened out here. In case you've forgotten, the last thing we need right now is some eager-assed *policía* checking up on us.''

"So what's the alternative?'' asked Jade. "I can't see us bringing her back to camp with us.''

"That's exactly what I ought to do," McCabe shot back, "and let you baby-sit her the rest of the time we're here.''

Jade ran rueful eyes over Liz's tense form, his expression reflecting more concern than anything else. "It would take more than a baby-sitter to keep the rest of them off her," he remarked.

"No kidding," came his friend's dry rejoinder.

Their words sent a shiver down Liz's spine.

Jade spit the reed from between his teeth. "So it looks like we've got no choice.''

Nodding, Zachary McCabe lifted the gun that had been hanging by his side. "Right. I'll handle it.''

For the second time in minutes, Liz felt as if the earth had collapsed beneath her. Her mouth went dry and her heart pounded like stampeding cattle inside her chest. This time, though, she refused to give him the satisfaction of cowering with eyes closed. She kept her widened eyes focused on McCabe as he swung the gun up and then, nice as you please, shoved it into the waist of his jeans so it was hidden beneath his vest. Her muffled gasp of relief drew a quick look of contempt from him.

"I'll back her car out of the way so you can get the truck through," he said to Jade. "You and Santiago head back to camp with the supplies. I'll meet you there after I finish things here."

Jade casually voiced the question that reverberated inside Liz. "And just how do you plan to do that?"

"What difference does it make as long as I do it?" Ignoring the other man's frankly skeptical stare, McCabe moved to the open door of the Toyota.

Liz watched him climb into the car, deriving satisfaction from the sight of him struggling to twist his big body into the seat adjusted for her five-foot-five frame. At first, as he gunned the engine, the heavy-duty tires merely spun in the soft earth. When they finally gripped, the car shot backward, spraying mud at Liz, who sprang aside with a shout, and Jade, who didn't even seem to notice.

"I'm sad to say it appears we will be walking." He spoke as nonchalantly as if they were standing on Fifth Avenue and he were apologizing for not being able to find a cab.

Liz paused in the act of shaking the mud off her arms to gape at him in disbelief. "I'm not worried about having to walk. I'm worried about your . . . associate killing me."

"Then you may as well relax. Keep your mouth shut and don't do anything too outrageous and I would bet my gold fillings you come out of this none the worse for the wear."

"Are you saying he won't really kill me?"

"Not exactly. What I'm saying is that I would be greatly surprised if he did. Now, shall we go?"

He turned, obviously assuming she had no choice but to trot along behind, and started walking the short distance to where McCabe had backed her car. Instead of following, Liz glanced around frantically, knowing she should bolt while she had half a chance. But where to? If she stuck to the road, she had no doubt they would run her down in no time. Her only hope would be to plow through the solid wall of jungle growth and find a place to hide. The problem was, she was almost as afraid of plunging into that rustling, verdant world as she was of McCabe and his gun. At least a bullet would be quick. How long, she wondered, did it take to die from snakebite?

"I wouldn't try it if I were in your shoes." Jade had paused about ten feet away. Now he glanced down at her mud-caked sandals, which had once been white, and shook his head. "In fact, most especially in your shoes I would not try it. You wouldn't make it twenty yards in those. Besides which, forcing Zach to play hide-and-seek in the bushes definitely falls into the category of outrageous. He would not be a pleasant man to deal with when he caught you."

"*If* he caught me." She felt considerably more reckless facing Jade than she had McCabe. Just the thought of being left here at the mercy of Zachary McCabe set off a pounding in her head that made it hard to think.

Jade laughed. "You can bank on him catching you. When we were in college his nickname was cheetah, you know, like the fastest animal on earth."

"You two went to college?" That fact amazed Liz far more than hearing McCabe compared to an animal.

22

"Sure did. Old Zach and I were roommates. But that's enough reminiscing. Let's move it."

This time he waited until Liz was in front of him before continuing. With each step her sandals sank in the mud, making a slurping sound each time she pulled loose, the straps rubbing against the backs of her ankles. She'd have blisters there by tonight. That is, if she was still alive tonight. It was all unreal. Jade with his hound-dog eyes and slightly regretful manner, hurrying her along so McCabe wouldn't be kept waiting to kill her. Liz didn't know whether to cry or laugh hysterically. Either would be a relief from the tension, but all she could do was trudge ahead in silent terror.

As they approached the last turn she'd made before stopping, she was surprised to catch a glimpse of the truck through a thick veil of vines. Sprawled on the hood was the third man, a boy actually, who she'd seen with them in the village. From the grin he was wearing Liz knew he'd had a bird's-eye view of the recent drama and had thoroughly enjoyed every agonizing moment of it.

Drawing closer, she saw that the truck was actually parked on a narrow trail which forked off the main road at an angle which made it impossible to be seen by anyone coming from the other direction. So they hadn't even had to bother backtracking. They'd simply pulled off there and waited for her, and she'd played right into their hands by stopping when she did.

With a few curt orders McCabe quickly sent the other two men on their way. Then he turned to Liz. A machete must have been among the truck's contents, because it now swung from a loop on the side of his wide leather belt. The sight of it, the long silver blade gleaming, the carved wood handle scarred from heavy use, sparked in Liz all new visions of mayhem.

His voice snapped like the crack of a whip. "Get in the car."

She started automatically for the passenger side.

"No. You drive. I don't want you jumping out on me so I have to chase you halfway back to San Luis."

Liz slid behind the wheel and shut the door. Even when he climbed in beside her, sitting so close in the small car that his bare arm brushed hers, she kept her eyes straight ahead. His skin felt hot and damp, and she could smell the tang of male sweat. She felt him insert the two-foot-long machete into the narrow opening between the seats, heard him pull the gun from his pants, sensed his eyes riveted on her, and suddenly her hands started trembling on the steering wheel.

Quickly she clamped them between her legs so he wouldn't see how much he frightened her. She'd read an article once about a certain type of psychopathic male who got his kicks from terrorizing his female victims. The more they whimpered, the more he enjoyed it. She made a silent pact with herself that no matter what the next few moments brought, she wouldn't beg this man for mercy.

The silence in the car grew unbearable.

"Now what?" she asked, her voice scratchy.

"God, you really are a brainless broad, aren't you? Now you start the car. Isn't that what you usually do when you drive back wherever it is you come from?"

"Boston."

"Yeah. Right. Too bad for all of us you didn't stay there."

With stiff fingers she twisted the keys in the ignition, wishing with every fiber of her being that she had for once curbed her headstrong impulsiveness and done exactly that.

"Down there," he instructed as she pulled ahead, using the gun to point to the trail where the truck had been parked.

Liz obediently steered the car in that direction. Her throat was starting to ache from holding back tears, but she knew if she started crying now she would never stop. If only she had listened to Kirk or her family or any one of her friends. They had all tried to tell her that the Central American jungle was no place for a twenty-eight-year-old woman whose idea of roughing it was having to manually adjust the temperature on the hot tub.

Despite being irked by what struck her as their collective condescending attitude, Liz had known all along there was some truth to what they said. But that was exactly why she'd been so adamant about coming. For too long she'd felt as if she was gliding through life on automatic pilot. She wanted to feel alive again. She wanted to feel she could do something that made a difference . . . besides signing her name on a check. She'd wanted a baptism by fire. And it looked as if she was about to get it, although not the way she'd planned.

"Can I ask where I'm driving to?" she inquired after several minutes of bumping along the barely navigable trail.

"Straight ahead . . . and watch the puddles. I don't want to have to get out and push."

On impulse Liz gave it the gas, deliberately plunging dead center through the next large puddle they came to.

Immediately the hard barrel of the gun was thrust into her side. Liz gasped with pain and fright.

"I said watch out," McCabe warned in a chillingly soft voice, "not try and hit every one. Remember, if I have to push, I'm going to get rid of all the dead weight before-hand. Want to guess what will be first to go?"

She drove more carefully after that, telling herself such shows of defiance were childish, not to mention dangerous. Even if he hadn't been holding a gun, he was a lot bigger than she was, probably much faster, and definitely meaner. Praying now that they didn't get stuck and thus force his hand, she picked her way around the deepest looking of the mud holes, not an easy task. The trail was barely the width of the car and overgrown in places. Low-hanging branches slapped against the windshield and poked in at her through the open windows. With each second that ticked away, Liz knew they were moving deeper into the wilderness and farther away from San Luis and any hope of running across someone who might help her.

Surprisingly, though, as they drove farther in, the jungle became less dense. The thick cloak of trees overhead still blocked the sunlight, but down below she could actually see scattered patches of bare earth. That brightened the prospect of escape and immediately a plan began weaving in her mind. The trail pitched gradually downhill, which meant that if she jumped out, the car would keep rolling until he

26

managed to maneuver his long leg over to hit the brake. That should give her a head start of at least a minute or so.

Would it be enough? She sneaked a glance at him without turning her head. Although the shaft of the gun was still pointed directly at her, McCabe was staring almost pensively out the front windshield.

Without warning he swung around to face her, his expression once more hardening into a scowl. "What are you looking at?"

The expression in his eyes was as ominous and uncompromising as the hole at the end of the gun.

Liz squirmed on the seat. "N-Nothing. I was just wondering where we're headed."

"None of your business."

"What if we run out of gas?"

"We won't."

She gulped in a deep breath, struggling for self-control, but in spite of her best intentions the words were out before she could stop them. "Are you going to kill me when we get wherever it is we're going?"

"I just might kill you right here if you don't shut up," he snapped.

Liz didn't doubt that a bit, and that was why, despite his blunt warning, talking to him suddenly seemed imperative. Somehow she had to convince him that she wasn't a threat to him, that she could be trusted not to go running to the police if he would only let her go.

"Listen, Mr. McCabe," she began tentatively, fully expecting him to tell her to shut up again, "I think you're making a big mistake here."

27

Out of the corner of her eye she saw his mouth twist in a tight, very disheartening sort of smile. "Yeah, I'm sure you do."

"I don't blame you for being upset with me for following you. But as I told you already, it was a case of mistaken identity."

"And as I told you, I think your story is bullshit."

"I swear to you that it's not. I really thought you were the man sent to meet me. I made a mistake." Her voice rose in time with her leaping pulse. "You can't kill someone for making a mistake, for God's sake."

"I've seen men killed for less."

His indifference was like a torch put to Liz's simmering panic. "Well, I haven't. Can't you see I don't belong here? That I'm not involved in any of this? I don't even know anything about this Sanchez you're so afraid of, or about you . . . and believe me, I don't want to know. I just want to get away from here, back to San Luis. I promise if you let me go I won't go running to the police, that I'll keep my mouth shut."

He gave a short, disparaging chuckle. "Lady, you can't even keep your mouth shut now. Stop here."

Liz's foot was glued to the accelerator as she strained against outright panic. She'd blown it, wasted a golden opportunity—maybe her only opportunity—to escape on the chance that she could reason with this . . . this lowlife, and now it was too late.

"I said stop," he shouted, grabbing the wheel and twisting it at the same instant her foot finally slammed down on the brake.

The car turned sharply to the right and bucked to a halt. Liz held on to the steering wheel tightly to keep her head from whacking into the windshield. McCabe wasn't as lucky, and his colorful oath made her wish there was someplace she could hide from his anger. Glancing out the side window to avoid his thunderous expression, she discovered the reason for his frenzied order to stop. The road, if you could call it that, had come to an abrupt end less than two feet from the Toyota's left wheels. At that point the earth simply dropped away in a steep stretch of rock and brush. At the bottom, a hundred feet below, lay a murky pool of water.

"What are you trying to do? Kill both of us?" McCabe demanded, still shouting loudly enough to make her ears ring.

Liz gaped at him, too stunned by what had just almost happened to point out the irony in his question.

"Stupid, goddamn . . ." He was still muttering a string of deprecating obscenities about her intelligence as he climbed out of the car. "You get out this side too," he ordered. "The ground near the edge there might not hold your weight."

Swinging her legs over the center console, she did as he said, keeping her own black thoughts to herself. Heaven forbid she topple over the edge of the cliff and cheat him out of the sadistic pleasure of killing her.

He reached back in past her to retrieve the machete, giving Liz a searing look of impatience when she flinched away from his touch. "Wait over there," he ordered.

She didn't pause to argue as with a flash of silver blade he indicated a stand of cedar trees about ten yards away. Picking a relatively clear spot to plant her feet, she turned back to watch and weigh the possibility of making a dash for it now. It wasn't a cowardly streak, she told herself, but rather a realistic one that warned against attempting it. While the lighter vegetation would make running easier, it would also provide him with a clear shot at her back as she ran. And some instinct counseled that McCabe wasn't the type to miss, even under much more difficult conditions. She remembered Jade's prediction that she would make it through this all right if she just didn't do anything rash. But even as she clung desperately to that thought, her insides churned with a sense of foreboding.

She was preoccupied with her own thoughts, and it was a couple of minutes before Liz paid much attention to what McCabe was up to. At first she'd assumed they had followed the wrong trail and that he was planning to remedy the situation by turning the car around in the mud. But instead of heading it back the way they'd come, he straightened the car so the nose was once more pointed directly at the edge of the cliff.

Getting out, he circled around to the back of the car and crouched down, putting his shoulder to the rear end. Muscles bulged beneath the short sleeves of his T-shirt and ran in thick cords from his elbow to his wrist. His broad shoulders tensed and even his face was etched with a grimace of pain as he strained against the mud-bound car. From where she stood Liz could see the sweat born of his tremendous effort pouring off him. For a few seconds she watched the display of power as if it were a movie running in slow motion. Then, just as the front wheels began to roll over the edge, the full ramifications of what he was doing hit her and she remembered the money—the price of Kirk's safety—hidden under the front seat.

"No. Wait!" she screamed.

It was too late. The force of his last, grunting shove had given the car enough impetus to send it over. All her frantic scream did was distract McCabe from leaping away in time. When, just as he'd predicted, the earth near the edge of the cliff began crumbling under the Toyota's weight, he went with it. Liz watched in horror as his arms flailed wildly, grasping for something, anything to cling to as he was sucked over the edge.

CHAPTER THREE

The bellow of surprise McCabe let out as he fell ripped through the air, twisting her stomach into a giant knot. "Oh, God, no. Somebody help," screamed Liz, forgetting that there was no one to hear, much less help, forgetting that the man for whom she felt such an instinctive wrench of concern was the same man who'd taunted her, called her a liar, and threatened to kill her, not once but twice.

The resounding splash as the car hit the water was followed by dozens of smaller ones made by the rocks and clumps of mud sliding along in its path. Finally the noise tapered off. With her fingertips clawing nervously at her palms Liz slowly, cautiously, inched her way close enough to peer over the edge.

"Goddamn it all anyway."

The words shot up at her before she got near enough to

see anything. He was alive. A shiver of relief rippled through her and hard on its heels a shudder of renewed panic. What was the matter with her? She would be better off if he were dead, or at least floating safely in the mud-laced waters below. That would give her a nice, long head start getting back to the road. Maybe he wouldn't even have bothered coming after her then.

But he wasn't dead and he wasn't floating somewhere below. He was not too far away and, judging from the fierce tone of his voice, in an even worse mood than before. If that was possible.

"Get over here."

The brusque command froze her right in her tracks. "Me?"

There was a pause. "No. My great-aunt Agnes. Who the hell do you think I mean?" He didn't wait for an answer. "Now get over here . . . and watch where you're walking. All I need about now is to have you go over the edge too."

Liz sidled closer at a point a few yards away from the gouges the car's tires had ripped in the soft earth. The tree growing close by looked pretty solidly rooted, and she wrapped one arm securely around the moss-covered trunk before leaning over to take a look. McCabe was about eight feet down, gripping a thick, protruding tree root with both hands. His tan work boots were dug into the dirt wall that was trickling away even as she watched. The car was nowhere in sight, obviously swallowed up by the deceptively calm-looking waters below.

"What do you want?" she called down to him.

At the sound of her voice he twisted his head around to

see her, even that slight movement sending dirt and rocks around him sliding away at a faster rate.

The look he shot skyward was one of utter disgust. "Why me? It's not bad enough being stuck in this mud hole of a country, I have to end up saddled with the dumbest woman ever put on earth. I want the obvious," he said, looking back at her. "For you to help me up from here."

His nastiness, even when asking for her help, pushed Liz over a different sort of edge. "Are you out of your mind? What in God's name makes you think that I would lift a finger to help you? After all you've done . . . pulled a gun on me, threatened me, dragged me"—she glanced around hopelessly—"I don't even know where."

"I don't expect you to help me in God's name." Unbelievably there was amusement in his gravel-edged drawl. "I expect you to do it to save your own sweet ass."

"What are you talking about? It seems to me that you're the one whose ass needs saving at the moment."

"I'm talking about snakes, jaguars, wild boars, underbrush crawling with ants as big as your thumb. One of them stings you and your pretty little ankles will swell up so bad you can't even walk. Then it's just a matter of laying there and waiting."

He didn't have to go any farther. Even with her eyes squeezed shut to avoid it, Liz could picture what he was suggesting in repulsively vivid detail. What might be exotic and fascinating in the pages of *National Geographic* was now a perilous, living obstacle course between her and safety.

"I don't believe this is happening to me," she groaned.

"And it's all your fault. You're the one who pushed the car over the cliff, stranding us both out here in the middle of nowhere."

"Uh-uh, honey. I'm not stranded. Just momentarily inconvenienced. I know exactly where I am and how to get where I'm going. And I don't need your rustbucket of a car to get me there. Otherwise I never would have deep-sixed it. I also have a gun and I know how to use that machete up there, which I'd be willing to bet this root I'm hanging on to you don't. Wielding a machete is a very useful art in the jungle."

He paused a moment, letting the indisputable truth of that sink in before continuing. "If I have to, I can roll and bounce my way down this embankment and be waiting in San Luis before you make it back there . . . if you make it. But if you force me to do that, I promise you I won't be waiting with open arms. Now, are you going to help me or not?"

"I don't know," she blurted. "If I do, how do I know you'll help me in return by getting me out of here? How do I know you won't still kill me the minute you're safe?"

His harsh laugh raked her already raw nerves. "You don't. I guess you'll just have to trust me. Ironic, isn't it, baby? Your executioner has just become your savior."

As she anguished over what to do, he smiled up at her, white teeth flashing against his dark skin and beard, lending credence to his claim of being only mildly inconvenienced. The truth was he didn't look the least bit frantic over being trapped in a situation that would reduce most men she knew to begging. To Liz that was proof positive that he possessed the skills and temperament necessary to lead her to safety. The question was, would he be willing?

If only she could think of something that would tip the scales in her favor. Something she could offer or promise him that would insure his willingness to help her. It only took her a few seconds. The solution was so obvious she kicked herself for not coming up with it sooner—like while she was still sitting on the twenty thousand dollars that had sunk along with her car. Even without it, though, it shouldn't be too tough to convince Zachary McCabe that it was in his interest to help her. Whatever his reason for being in Guatemala, she knew it was nowhere near as altruistic as Kirk's.

"I'll make a deal with you," she called down to him.

"Not interested. All I want from you is a simple yes or no."

"I think what I have in mind will interest you greatly. Randolph is my married name, so you probably don't know who my family is . . . who I am . . . ."

"Or care."

Liz lifted her chin, determined to make him care. Maybe the name Elizabeth Bennett Fitzgerald wouldn't impress him the way it did most others, but she'd bet she knew something that would. Leaning forward as far as she dared, she glared down at the top of his dark head and drew breath to do that which she'd always berated others for doing.

"McCabe, I happen to be an extremely wealthy woman."

"I'm thrilled for you," he remarked dryly. "Now, if this little discussion of your assets is leading somewhere, I wish you'd get to the point. My arms are getting tired."

"I should think the point is obvious. I'm offering to make it worth your while to take me back to San Luis."

"No thanks."

Liz smiled smugly. "You don't have to play hard to get in order to up the ante, McCabe. Just name your price."

"This may come as a shock to you, sweetheart, but I don't have a price."

"You expect me to believe that? I know that whatever you and your friends are so determined to keep secret must be pretty lucrative. I'm simply offering you the same profit for a lot less effort. Think of it, McCabe, the opportunity of a lifetime. I'm so hot and tired and worn-out from battling with you that at the moment money is no object."

She waited. Just when she was beginning to fidget restlessly, his voice, tight with anger, cut through the silence.

"You got that damn straight, lady. Money is not the object. Now get this. Money is also not my reason for being here, and even if it was, you and whoever your family is don't have enough of it to make me drop what I'm doing here just to play Galahad to a foolish, spoiled brat who doesn't know enough to stay where she belongs."

His words were like a shock wave, ripping her seldom-thought-of but ever-present safety net out from under her. Liz couldn't think of anything to say. When McCabe spoke again a minute or so later, his voice was once more casual, holding that elusive mocking note that kept her constantly on the defensive.

"Hurry up and make up your mind, will you? If I have to go down, I want to do it before darkness sets in."

Liz opened her mouth, on the verge of telling him he

37

could go all the way to hell for all she cared, when a smidgen of common sense intervened.

"You ever seen night fall in the jungle?" His offhand question drifted up to her through the heavy silence. "No streetlights, no moonlight, no lights period. Just blackness all around, and lots of low, creeping noises. And of course, the buzz of all those mosquitoes."

Just the thought of it sent a tremor of fear through Liz. He was right, damn him; the sun would be setting soon. All the trails and roads in the world wouldn't do her any good if she couldn't see the hand in front of her. As humiliating—and probably suicidal—as it was, it looked as if she had no choice but to trust him. And pray that buried somewhere in his acrimonious heart was enough decency to prompt him to repay her for helping to save his worthless life.

"All right," she said finally. "I'll help you up, but first I want to get a few things straight. I may not be as capable at this jungle stuff as you obviously are, but even I know you couldn't bounce and roll all the way down there"—she pointed at the water without looking down—"without breaking a few bones. Or worse."

He grinned. "Believe me, I've done worse."

"Maybe, but the fact that you won't this time is because of my help. And in return I want your promise that you'll at least lead me back to the road to San Luis. Then we can part company and forget we ever laid eyes on each other. Do I have your word?"

Without hesitation he removed his right hand from the root and, still grinning, held up a three-fingered salute. "Scout's honor."

It was ridiculous. She was a fool for even asking. The very word honor sounded twisted coming from that hard mouth. For only the second time in her life it was driven home to her how little the advantages she took for granted really meant. The financial empire her father had built from nothing, the political influence he wielded, the vast, legendary fortune to which her mother was sole heir, none of it mattered at all at this moment. Whether she lived or died depended entirely on a man whose life and values, whose idea of right and wrong were probably the antithesis of her own.

A worried frown dragged at the corners of her mouth as she met McCabe's eyes. "All right. What do you want me to do?"

"First get the machete . . . and for God's sake be careful because it's sharp."

Liz moved slowly, drawing a deep breath before picking up the machete, disliking even the feel of the smooth wooden handle in her palm. She hated knives, especially ones as long and lethal looking as the one she was holding. With small, careful steps she walked back to the tree.

"I've got it . . . but I'm telling you right now it will never reach."

His head shook back and forth slowly. "Then we won't even try. But just out of curiosity, which end were you going to give me to grab?"

Hot color washed her cheeks. "I didn't stop to think."

"That's nothing new. But you damn well better think about what you're doing now." His voice was hard, flat. "I want you to find a vine long enough to wrap a couple of times around the trunk of that tree next to you and still reach me. There're plenty of them trailing on the ground up there. Just nose around until you find one that's long enough.''

"But . . ." A hundred reasons why she didn't want to do it and why it wouldn't work anyway raced around in Liz's head. "What about the snakes and the wild boars and the ants? Won't they be in the bushes where I'll have to go to find a vine?"

"Yup."

"Well, then?"

"You got a better idea?"

She thought. "No."

"Well, then?" he mimicked.

Silently, reluctantly, Liz walked toward the trees where she'd waited earlier. Vines cascaded freely between the branches, but in order to cut one long enough she'd have to climb. One look at the trunk alive with the up-and-down travels of scores of insects eliminated that as a possibility. Had the tree she'd been clinging to a moment ago been similarly inhabited? She was suddenly itchy all over.

With her free hand she scratched her shoulder, her collarbone inside her blouse, the side of her waist, all the time keeping her eyes focused on the ground in search of an accessible vine. Finally she spotted one that looked long enough. Raising the machete, she used her foot to hold the vine taut against the tree and whacked it as hard as she could. She succeeded in making a slit only about a quarter of an inch deep. She swung at it several more times. Her upper arms ached—as much, Liz knew, from the tension in her body as from the weight of the machete. When there were only a few, tough-looking center strands remaining, she reached up with one hand to try and rip it loose.

Concentrating on what she was doing, she at first thought it was another stray vine brushing against her outstretched arms. Then she realized that though it was smooth and slippery like a vine, it was much too dark and it was circled with orange rings at regular intervals. Letting loose with a hair-raising scream, she fell back, instinctively swinging the machete in a wild arc at the same time. The blade caught the snake in the middle of its descending body, ripping it from its perch.

Liz didn't look to see if she'd killed it or where it might have landed. Lurching to her feet, she tore out of the brush, not realizing until she fell to her knees back at the edge of the cliff that she was still clutching the vine that must have been torn free in her frenzy. Shudders racked her body as she knelt there, suffering a sickening rush of panic she'd been too stricken to feel at the time. It was the laconic drift of McCabe's voice that finally snapped the terror gripping her.

"That was quick. Can I assume you were successful? Or did you just get tired of looking?"

Anger flashed inside her. Of all the thoughtless, condescending . . . To think she'd risked her life to save that son of a bitch. Without a word she let one end of the vine slip over the edge where he was sure to see it.

"My, my," he said with mock wonder, "and all without chopping off a hand or a finger in the process."

"Not that you'd care if I had," she snapped.

"I would if you bled to death before getting me up from here. Have you got that other end tied to the tree yet?"

Gritting her teeth, Liz stood and carried the end in question over to the tree. The vine was about an inch and a half in diameter, but nowhere near as pliable as a piece of rope. The simple knot she struggled to tie looked exceedingly untrustworthy.

"I don't know how," she was finally forced to admit.

"Why doesn't that surprise me?"

Liz tore the knot loose. "Maybe because you're too jaded . . . too damned cynical to be surprised by anything."

"Yeah," he responded laconically. "That must be it. Now pay attention; here's what I want you to do."

Liz listened and grudgingly obeyed as he instructed her step by step in the art of securing the vine, first peeling away the slippery outer coat to get a better grip, then wrapping it around the trunk and twisting it over itself so it stayed put. She had to admit that even with her feeble talents the knot that resulted looked as if it just might support a man of McCabe's size.

"Now get a grip on the vine just in front of the knot," he ordered. "You're not strong enough to haul me up, but at least you can take some of the pressure off it."

"All right, I've got it. Now what?"

"Now the rest is up to me."

Liz grasped the vine as if it were her life hanging on the other end. And in a way it was. She didn't want to think of her chances out here alone if McCabe didn't make it. He, on the other hand, sounded as unconcerned as ever. The man had to have nerves of steel and very little fear. In a perverse way she almost admired him for it.

From where she stood with her heels dug into the ground, she couldn't see him, but she knew the instant he let go of the root he'd been gripping and started to climb. The vine went suddenly taut, pulling at the knot in spite of her attempt to bear some of his weight. The sound of rocks and dislodged earth cascading down to the water below was as grating as fingernails dragged across a blackboard. Liz could feel his search for solid footholds, and sweat broke out on her upper lip and between her breasts as if it were she crawling up through the mud.

She kept one eye on the knot, watching it gradually slipping even as the sound of his labored breathing grew closer. Finally she couldn't stand it another second.

"Hurry, you have to hurry, I can't hold it."

His response came in a series of grunts. "You . . . wanna . . . trade places?"

"Damn you," she hissed through teeth clenched so tightly her jaw ached.

Finally his powerful hands and forearms slid into view. They were streaked with sweat and dirt, his muscles and veins standing out in high relief as he inched his way along. Liz couldn't prevent a small cry of relief as his shoulders levered upward in a powerful surge and he swung one leg onto firm ground. Sneaking a quick glance at the knot, she saw it pull loose at the same instant she felt it go limp in her hands. With a scream she bent over, clutching handfuls of his vest for dear life at the same time McCabe threw himself forward, landing on top of her and propelling both of them to safety.

The force of his weight as they landed knocked the wind out of her and she lay gasping beneath him, too shaken to push him off. By the time she'd recovered he'd already rolled to a sitting position by her side.

"You all right?" he asked.

"I . . . I think so."

At her hesitant tone he swung around to face her, his attention quickly dropping from her face to her chest. Liz followed his blatantly fascinated gaze to discover the top few buttons on her blouse had been ripped off, exposing the upper swells of her generous breasts. In this heat she hadn't bothered wearing a bra under the loose-fitting top, and while what was revealed was no more than he would see of her on the beach, the fact that McCabe was who he was and they were where they were, alone, made her more uncomfortable than she'd ever been in a bikini. Self-consciously she tried to pull the edges of the torn cotton together.

He grinned, his gaze hanging steady. "Need a hand?"

She didn't look at him. "No. Thank you. Actually, I think we should get going."

Rolling back so he was sprawled on his side next to her, he braced his head on one hand. Liz braved a sideways glance, shaken to find the eyes she was accustomed to seeing flash with anger radiating a very different kind of heat.

"What's your hurry?" His tone was lazy, the lingering western drawl more apparent than ever.

"I'd like to be back in San Luis before dark."

"Not a chance."

"Well, we could at least make it as far as the road."

McCabe shook his head. "I'm afraid not. You see, I'm not headed in that direction."

"But you said . . ." Liz broke off in disbelief. How could she have been so stupid? "You lied to me. . . . You never had any intention of helping me."

He shrugged with a slight inclination of broad shoulders. "Welcome to the real world, baby. I was also never a Boy Scout."

"You bastard."

If she'd thought first, she never would have done it. In a straight physical contest she hadn't a prayer of holding her own against a man his size and in his obviously top-notch physical condition. But even if she'd been the type to tread cautiously, Liz was at that moment at a point of anger past thinking, past caring, driven only by the need to extract whatever meager revenge she could. She heaved herself at him with a low cry, pounding her fists as hard as she could against whatever part of him she could reach.

The second her flesh connected with his, some basic instinct took over, and though she'd never in her life been in a fistfight before she found herself twisting frantically in an effort to bring her knee into his groin hard enough to do damage. McCabe's reaction was a wide-eyed yelp of pain as she connected, not nearly as forcefully as she'd have liked. At the same time she caught him full in the face with her fist.

"Why . . . you little bitch."

He made a lunge to capture her hands, which she somehow managed to elude, getting in a lucky blow to his Adam's apple in the process. Judging from his sharp grunt, that one hurt worse than the one to his face had, and in a distant corner of her mind Liz registered his expression of all-out fury with some trepidation. An instant later she was brought down flat on her back in the scrub grass as he collapsed on top of her, snapping her head back hard enough to make her vision blur briefly. The suffocating weight of his body quickly brought her to her senses and crushed all the fight out of her.

Instinctively Liz squeezed her eyes shut and raised her hands to ward off the retaliatory blows she was sure would follow. Instead of hitting her, though, McCabe yanked both her wrists together in one of his powerful hands and pinned them to the ground so far over her head her shoulder joints throbbed. From shoulder to hip his body pressed hers into the soft earth, his chest flattening her breasts, one hard thigh wedged between her own.

During the fray her skirt had become twisted around her hips and she was vividly aware of the scrape of rough denim against the soft, sensitive flesh of her inner thighs. But mostly she was aware of his breath on her lips, hot and very, very close. Liz knew exactly what she would see if she had the courage to open her eyes. He was lying there just watching her, waiting. What she wasn't prepared for was the look on his face when she finally dared to look at him.

She expected to find him regarding her with fury or triumph, maybe even a blend of the two. But once she opened her eyes his look was different, slightly surprised and full of a very potent awareness. The kind of awareness only a man stretched out full length on top of a woman can feel. Liz's throat went dry and her eyes widened as the scorching intensity of his gaze drove home to her the new danger she was in. Restlessly she shifted beneath him. That was a mistake. She knew it the instant he bared his teeth in a slow grin.

"You're hurting me." Her voice held a note of pleading, but Liz didn't care if it gained her more sympathy from him than she'd gotten the last time she'd used that line.

"Tough. I'm very comfortable and at the moment I don't much care if you are." A slight movement fitted his hips more intimately to hers, letting Liz feel the hardness below his belt buckle pressing into her belly.

She forced herself to meet his smoky blue gaze directly. "Don't. Don't do this to me. Please."

His eyes narrowed, the heat in them abruptly turning to ice. "Do what?" he demanded.

She shook her head, frightened and frustrated by her own helplessness.

"Do what?" he repeated in that same cold, remote voice, jerking on her arms to prod her into answering. "Say it."

"Don't rape me," she spat.

For a few seconds his whole body tightened with fury. His lips were clamped together. Angry white lines fanned from the sides of his eyes and forged deep creases in his cheeks. Then his gaze swept over her briefly, insultingly, as his lips twisted around a short, disparaging laugh.

"Honey, it's a sure bet you haven't gotten a look at yourself anytime lately. You're sweaty, covered with dirt. Your stuck-up little nose is red and peeling, and your hair's

47

full of twigs . . . and God knows what else. I'm not at all sure I even want it from you, never mind wanting it bad enough to fight for it.''

A humiliated blush heated Liz from head to toe. "Do you think I care how I look to an animal like you?'' she cried, infuriated that his barbs had stung her as much as they had. Instead of feeling embarrassed, she ought to be chanting prayers of thanksgiving that he didn't want her. "The truth is I couldn't be happier—or more relieved—that you feel that way about me.''

"Good. Because all in all I've seen shantytown whores who looked more appetizing.''

"I'm sure you have.'' Her eyes blazed angrily. "Well, now that that's settled, would you mind getting off me?''

"When I'm good and ready.''

She was silent for a moment. Then, with exaggerated politeness: "Is it too much bother to ask what you do plan on doing with me . . . since you're obviously not man enough to honor your word?''

"Obviously.'' He heaved a heartfelt sigh of disgust. "I'm damned if I have any better ideas about what to do with you now than I did an hour ago.''

The meaning behind his words filtered slowly through Liz's tired brain. "You mean you didn't bring me all the way here just to kill me?''

"Hell, no. No matter what you might think, I haven't sunk low enough yet to murder a woman just for being stupid.''

Relief seeped through every muscle and nerve in her body. "But back there on the road . . .''

He made an impatient gesture with his head. "That was mostly for the benefit of our audience. Jade would understand my not shutting you up with a bullet, but not Santiago. And until our job here is done I can't afford to have him stirring up the others with tales of how I'm too soft to deal with a woman who gets in the way."

"What job?" she asked.

He silenced her with a look. "I'd have thought you learned your lesson today about being nosy."

"Is it nosy to wonder what's going to happen to me?"

McCabe's thick brows drew together in a thoughtful frown. "I had planned to just leave you somewhere out here in the middle of the jungle and let you find your own way out."

"I'd never make it," Liz said a little frantically.

"I didn't figure that to be my problem. But now . . ." He shook his head with obvious disgust.

"Now?"

His lips quirked in a grim, mirthless smile. "Call me old-fashioned, but I figure I owe you something for hauling me back up here."

"Does that mean you're going to take me with you?" Liz wasn't at all certain whether that was good news or bad.

"I sure as hell haven't got time to take you back. Even though your presence in camp is going to be one gigantic pain in the ass."

She quickly decided she was far better off tagging along with him no matter how despicable he was. There might even be someone in his camp willing to help her. "I'll stay out of the way," she promised.

"Lady, with twelve hungry men and one woman there is no place far enough out of the way. I'm afraid most of them aren't as discriminating as I am," he added with a nasty smile.

Suddenly Liz had much more important things to worry about than his insults. "They won't . . . I mean you won't let them . . ."

"I'll do my best," he countered. "And not because I fancy myself in the role of protector of your virtue. But any breakdown in discipline will only make my job harder. That's why there can't be any hint in anything you say or do about the real reason I'm bringing you back."

"Why, McCabe? Afraid they'll laugh at you if they find out a woman saved your life?"

"Personally I couldn't care less what they think. But down here machismo *is* a way of life. At the moment I need the trust and respect of those men, and I'll do whatever I have to in order to keep it. Even," he concluded deliberately, "killing you if it comes to it."

Liz felt as if she was on an emotional roller coaster, hitting more highs and lows than she'd known existed. She tried to keep her voice calm. "Then how do you intend to explain your decision to bring me back with you?"

He considered that, staring past her into the bushes. After a minute he shifted his gaze back, eyes hardening as he studied her defiant face, then slipping lower for a good, long look at the now fully exposed ivory globes of her breasts. His unhurried assessment made her want to crawl into a hole and hide.

"I guess it's the only way," he said finally, an unmistakable note of resignation in his voice. "If I clean some of the dirt off you first, I might even be able to stomach it."

She didn't have to think twice to catch his meaning. "Oh, no . . . ."

"Oh, yes. I've got to have a believable reason for dragging you along. One that those men will respect."

Liz hated the quiet determination in his voice and the mocking glint in his eyes. She hated the weight of his body still dominating hers, a less than subtle reminder that, like it or not, she had no choice but to go along with whatever he decreed.

"There has to be something else," she insisted. Unfortunately she couldn't come up with a single suggestion as to what it might be.

McCabe shook his head. "There isn't, so you better get used to the idea. Down here women are only good for two things. And you sure don't look like much of a cook."

CHAPTER
FOUR

The very idea of posing as McCabe's woman made Liz shudder. Of course that was all he had in mind, she tried desperately to assure herself, an innocent pretense. The possibility that he was suggesting something more was too alarming to think about.

"I won't do it," she announced.

Few people who knew her would question anything she said in that tone of cool finality, but Liz fully expected an argument from McCabe. And she was ready for him. To her surprise, however, he simply shrugged and peeled himself off her.

"Suit yourself."

Her feeling of triumph at having stood her ground fizzled as he turned and walked away. Scrambling to her knees, she tugged at her tattered shirtfront, making a feeble stab at modesty by securing the single remaining button. "What does that mean?" she demanded.

McCabe picked up the machete from where she'd tossed it and hitched it onto his belt before answering. "It means if you don't want to do as I suggested, don't. It's your decision."

"And?" she pressed, suspicion coiled inside.

He'd been standing with his back to her. Now he shot her a quick glance over his shoulder and grinned. "And good luck to you in making it back to San Luis alone."

Liz's fingers clenched around the torn fabric. She was no less frightened of being abandoned in the jungle now than she was a few minutes ago. She was poised between the frying pan and the fire, and hanging by a terrifyingly slender thread. Her pride or her life, that's what it boiled down to.

"Wait." She was on her feet, tearing after McCabe, who was already moving through the bushes at a pace Liz found difficult to match with soggy leather sandals hanging from her feet. "You can't just leave me here all alone."

McCabe didn't reply, didn't even spare her a glance over his shoulder this time, but Liz swore she could hear his raspy, smug-sounding chuckle wafting back to her through the humid air.

"I'll follow you, McCabe," she threatened loudly because he was stretching the distance between them all the time. "I'll follow you all the way back to your damn camp, and I'll pay one of your men to take me where I want to go. I'll bet they're not all as immune to bribery as you're pretending to be."

The narrow path they were following suddenly ended as abruptly as the road had earlier. Liz hesitated only a second before putting her squeamishness aside and charging into the undergrowth after him. "And while I'm at it," she continued shouting, "I'll be sure to let them know how you couldn't even deal with a woman. That ought to . . ."

The threat ended with a yelp of pain as she plunged thigh deep into a thorn bush. Only the sight of McCabe's back, a rapidly disappearing speck of tan leather, gave her the impetus to grit her teeth and pull her leg out. It hurt even more coming out than it had going in. She was swept with an overwhelming urge to sit down right where she was and cry.

Bright pinpricks of blood welled up from the scratches that covered her left leg from her ankle to above her knee. Dabbing at them with the hem of her skirt cost her a few more precious seconds, and then she was forced to accept the demoralizing fact that even if she ran as fast as she could, she wasn't going to be able to catch up to him.

"McCabe," she bellowed, for once thankful for the hot, still air that magnified each sound. "All right, McCabe, you win." Straining to see him in the distance, Liz thought he came to a stop at that, but still he didn't turn around. "I'll do it. Do you hear me? I said I'll do it."

Slowly he swung back to face her. He was too far away for Liz to see his grin, but of course she didn't need to. She could well imagine every triumphant line etched in his dark face. Seething with frustration, she started to pick her way through the bushes and trailing vines separating them. He didn't even have the common courtesy to walk back to meet her and accept her surrender gracefully, the way any other man she knew would. And that, Liz bitterly concluded, said it all. She was going to have to remember when dealing with Zachary McCabe that he was not like any other man she had ever known. Or ever wanted to know again.

His grin had faded by the time she fought her way to where he stood leaning against the trunk of a tree. He watched her trudge the last few feet with an impatient frown, arms folded in front of his chest in a way that made his black T-shirt strain across his shoulders and above the swell of muscles in his upper arms. Liz grimaced at the sight. She didn't need any reminders of the man's size, or his strength.

"Let's hear that again," he directed as she came to a halt a cautious five feet away from him. "Just so there are no misunderstandings later."

"I said I'll do it. . . . I'll go along with your suggestion."

A very unsettling glint lit his blue eyes as he smiled in a manner Liz considered disgustingly transparent.

Hastily she added, "What I mean, naturally, is that I'll *pretend* to go along with your suggestion of a pretense. For the benefit of your men, of course."

McCabe squinted at her. "You want to run all that by me again? Real slow this time."

She took a deep breath first to stop herself from rambling nervously. "I simply meant that there won't actually be any . . . any . . ." She waved her hand in the air, hoping he would nod understandingly. Of course he didn't. "Anything between us," Liz finished lamely. "But for the sake of your reputation and order among your men, we'll let them believe that there is.''

"Is what?"

"Something between us."

"For the sake of *my* reputation?"

She didn't like the edge in his voice. "Well, you did say that it would look bad for you if the men were to know you brought me back because I saved your life."

"How many times do I have to tell you that you didn't save my life?" he demanded, a scowl narrowing his eyes. "I was never in danger of dying back there."

"All right. All right. So you're bringing me with you because I *helped* you," she conceded, glaring at him. "Rather than be left out here alone, I agree. I'll go along with it, and then your reputation and your precious authority will be safe."

He took a step closer and jabbed her chest with his index finger. Hard. "And what about your reputation, lady?"

"My reputation?"

"That's right. I can think of a much quicker, less complicated way to protect mine than dragging you back to camp with me." His hand briefly—meaningfully—caressed the gun jammed into the front of his jeans. "But what would your fancy family and friends back home say if they found out you spent your Central American holiday playing musical beds with a dozen very *demanding* men? Because that's what's sure to happen if you manage to follow me back to camp and I *don't* make it clear to the rest of them that you belong to me."

It was suddenly hard for Liz to draw air past the lump in her throat. "You said you wouldn't let . . ."

"I said I'd do my best," he reminded her harshly. "As long as you don't go complicating matters for me. And I never said a word about *pretending* anything. So let's get it straight right from the start. You're the one who needs protecting around here, and I'm the one making the rules. Got it?"

Liz nodded, mumbling a reluctant agreement.

"Louder," he growled.

"I said I've got it," snapped Liz.

He smiled, a totally unpleasant twist of his hard mouth. "Good."

Liz fought the urge to hurl a bitter retort his way. Instead she settled for giving the clump of pale hair that had escaped her barrette a defiant toss over her shoulder. She then proceeded very carefully to smooth it into place, as if her entire appearance, from head to toe, was not one hideous lost cause.

"So," she inquired finally with acidic sweetness, "are you going to tell me what the rules are? Or do you plan to make them up as we go along?"

"There's only going to be one rule," he informed her, the unexpected pleasantness of his tone making her instantly wary. "If you choose to come along with me, it's as my woman. And down here that means you do exactly what I say to do, when I say to do it. No questions, no games, no temper tantrums."

"That sounds as if I'll be more your slave than your

woman," exclaimed Liz, disbelief and dismay mingled in her tone.

"I guess that sums it up nicely," he agreed.

Biting her lip to keep from lashing out at him, Liz was struck by a reckless impulse. What would her chances be, she wondered, if she made a surprise lunge for the gun? Having it in her possession would certainly tip the scales of this nightmare in her favor. She could force him to take her back to San Luis. In fact, if she could just manage to reach the handle of it, she thought, eyeing where it jutted out above his belt buckle, the barrel pointed downward at a strategic angle, she would have him in a very vulnerable position indeed.

"Would you even know what to do with it if you got your hands on it?"

His words were soft, taunting, and Liz jerked her head up to find that he'd been watching her while she studied the front of his pants so intently. Instantly defensive, she blurted, "For your information I wasn't even looking at your gun."

"Oh, no?" His thick black brows lifted speculatively. "Then I'd say that makes your answer to my question even more interesting. *Would* you know what to do with it if you got your hands on it?"

The rawly masculine challenge in his eyes made his meaning as clear as spring water and sent a shiver dancing down Liz's spine.

"You're disgusting," she bit out.

McCabe made a clicking noise with his tongue. "Is that any way to talk to your man?"

"God forbid."

"I'm sure he would," he countered dryly. "But that's still the deal, sweetheart. Take it or leave it."

Liz was hot and tired and filthier than she could ever remember being. If there was any alternative to his proposal, she was in no state to think of it.

"Do I have any other choice?" she grumbled, her voice cracking with frustration.

"Not one any sane woman would make," admitted McCabe.

"Then I guess you could say I accept your . . . your . . ."

"Gallant offer of protection?" he supplied helpfully.

His amused smirk filled her with fury, but Liz refused to add to his satisfaction by letting him see how easily he could get to her. "Let's just say I accept, period."

"Good. Then let's get moving. As it is, we won't make camp by nightfall."

"But then how will we . . ."

He lifted a finger warningly, his expression suddenly stern. "No questions. Remember?"

He turned and resumed walking in the same direction he'd been headed before she called to him, without giving Liz a chance to voice her opinion. She hardly thought questions about where and how they were going to spend the night constituted insubordination. Obviously, however, he did and she burned as she realized that at the moment his opinion was all that mattered.

She hated him. Liz reached that bitter conclusion before they'd traveled twenty yards. And she hated him more with each painful step after that. What in the world had she gotten herself into? The humiliation of having to bow to his wishes was only the tip of the iceberg. McCabe's threats aside, she couldn't believe that any twentieth century American male could seriously treat a woman like chattel. But that was exactly what he was now doing, leaving her to trot ten paces behind as he plowed through the damp, overgrown tangle of green, protected by his leather boots and heavy black denim jeans. She could only think of two possible reasons for him to treat her like a piece of property even before they'd reached their audience. Either he was trying to impress upon her the seriousness of the situation and the importance of their act being convincing. Or else he was just plain sadistic.

The second possibility hung over her like an executioner's ax, making the blisters on her feet and the branches and thorns that slapped and tore at her as she struggled to keep up seem minor inconveniences. What concerned Liz far more than a few cuts and bruises or having to appear docile and obedient to him in public was what sort of physical degradation awaited her when she and McCabe were alone. Would he force her to play the part of his woman in private as well? He'd implied that was exactly what he intended when he berated her use of the word ''pretense'' to describe their arrangement.

Against her will a vividly erotic picture of all that being his woman might entail flashed before Liz, making her stomach twist with horror. Resolutely she pushed the thought away. He hadn't raped her yet, although there was no doubt he could have very easily. In fact, he'd taken pains to make it clear to her that she wasn't a sight to strike lust in any man's heart. Liz's nose wrinkled with distaste as she glanced down at her battered body and ruined clothing and ruefully confirmed that he was right. As uncomfortable as it was, though, her dirty, disheveled state just might be her salvation. If she wasn't physically desirable to McCabe, maybe she wouldn't appeal to any of the other men in his camp either... despite what he said about their being less discriminating than he. Liz smiled to herself. She would just have to take pains to stay looking as grubby as possible at all times. Which shouldn't be too much of a challenge, given that she was God only knew how many miles from clean clothes or a shower. Even the comb and makeup she carried in her purse had gone down with the car.

For a while as they trudged along, Liz derived a small amount of satisfaction from elaborating on her passive plan to protect herself. Obviously she wouldn't be able to brush her teeth anytime soon. That alone should turn off most men. For added effect she would have to remember to scratch whenever anyone was watching. Soon, though, physical discomfort began to drive all other thoughts from her mind. She ached from head to toe, or rather head to heel, where the straps of her sandals had rubbed her flesh raw. On top of that, she remembered that she hadn't eaten since breakfast and identified the cramping in her stomach as hunger pains. And now she also had to go to the bathroom.

They had been traveling on level ground, forging a path more or less parallel to the river that had swallowed her car. Liz had lost track of how many times the seemingly endless jungle growth had thinned and then grown so dense McCabe had to clear the way with powerful swings of the machete.

Now, seeing a long, clear stretch up ahead, she realized that if she wanted any privacy at all while she relieved herself, she'd better speak up.

"McCabe," she called.

"What?" he responded without slowing.

"Can we stop for a minute?"

"No."

God, she hated him. For a few seconds she considered stopping and handling matters on her own, but the prospect of having to move even faster on her abused feet to catch up again afterward wasn't only agonizing, it was probably impossible. Suppressing her pride, she tried again.

"Could we *please* stop for a minute?"

He whipped around to face her, looking none too pleased. Sweat glistened on his forehead, and beneath the vest his T-shirt clung damply to a chest which Liz could see was as firmly muscled as his arms. "What for?" he demanded.

"I have to go to the bathroom," she informed him, feeling as powerless as a kindergartner asking permission.

He regarded her mockingly. "Do you need my help for that?"

"No, I don't need your help. But I have to practically run to keep up with you as it is and my feet are killing me. I'm also . . ."

"Hold it," he ordered, lifting his outstretched palm to silence her. "I didn't ask for a dissertation. You've got one minute to do whatever it is you have to do. Get cracking."

"But I can't . . ."

"Fifty-eight seconds," he interjected, checking the watch on his wrist.

Liz glanced around frantically, looking for a reasonably private spot. She was afraid of moving too far away from him and his gun in case something reptilian should slither out of the undergrowth. Besides, she had no doubt he would hold her to sixty seconds flat. Deciding a narrow tree trunk a few feet away was about as much shielding as she was going to find, she scurried toward it.

"Will you at least please have the common decency to turn around?" she pleaded.

For a second she thought he was going to refuse. Then, with a gruff "What the hell," he did as she asked.

"But if you're shy," he added in a harsh tone, "you damn well better get over it fast. A jungle camp doesn't allow for much in the way of modesty."

Liz would worry about that when she had to. Right now it was heaven to feel just a bit less miserable than she had a moment ago. Hurriedly tugging up her panties and rearranging her skirt, she decided she felt good enough to brave his wrath a second time. She was busy trying to decide on the best way to phrase her next request when she noticed McCabe had finally succumbed to the heat and stripped off his vest and T-shirt. Somehow he'd knotted them around his waist, leaving his hands free and the top half of his body exposed to her curious gaze.

Unconsciously Liz slowed her steps to look at him. His skin reminded her of the color of autumn leaves, a melding of copper and gold. It glistened in the heat. From the solid width of his shoulders to his lean waist, it was marred with an assortment of scars and scrapes that inspired questions she was smart enough not to ask.

"All set?" he inquired, glancing around as she approached.

"What . . . oh, yes, thank you." She quickly marshaled her thoughts. "But I was wondering if we might possibly rest here for just a few minutes longer?"

"Nope."

"I really . . ."

Anger ripped through Liz as he once again moved off and left her with her mouth hanging open. Tears of frustration stung her eyelids, turning the surrounding landscape into a blur of hundreds of different hues of green. Afraid if she tried to say even one more word she would break into tears, she started after him in sullen silence. With the very first step she took she felt a gush of moisture trickle over the back of her heel as yet another blister broke. Halting, she angrily reached down and ripped off first one sandal, then the other. Anything was better than the knifelike feeling of those straps cutting into her.

She straightened to find McCabe stopped about ten feet away, watching her. It appeared he wasn't as oblivious to whether or not she followed as he would have her believe. Her gaze retreated from the unmistakable blaze of temper in his eyes, and instead locked on the only slightly less unsettling sight of his naked chest. A wedge of curly black hair arrowed down from about the center of his breastbone, its tip hidden somewhere below his belt. He didn't carry an ounce of fat, which only made the fine sculpturing of his muscles more noticeable. He looked to Liz more uncompromisingly, intimidatingly male than ever.

"What the hell do you think you're doing?" he demanded.

"Getting rid of these," she retorted. Matching his angry

stare, she defiantly hurled the ruined sandals as far as she was able. "I couldn't stand them another minute. I've got blisters on top of blisters."

"Well, you sure as hell can't walk through the jungle barefoot," he declared in a voice rough with impatience. "Some of these plants are poisonous. If you get an open cut . . ." As he spoke, his gaze had dropped to her bare feet. Now he broke off with a sharp intake of breath at the sight of them. "Jesus . . ."

Liz quickly glanced down to see what had produced such a reaction. Her feet looked starkly white against the coffee-colored mud, and as puffy as marshmallows. They were grossly swollen and branded with bands of red where the leather straps had crisscrossed her insteps. Here and there were patches of dried blood, the rusty color a startling counterpoint to the shimmering rose polish on her toenails. She knew their condition should shock her, but she felt strangely detached from the sight. Strain and exhaustion had taken their toll on her senses to the point where she was able to study her feet as if they weren't attached to the rest of her. In the waning light she noticed a minuscule clear spot on one nail.

"I missed a spot," she murmured absently.

"What?"

"I said I missed a spot on one of my toenails when I polished them. See?"

She wiggled the baby toe on her left foot as he moved closer. The pain caused by even that slight movement made her wince. Heedless of the mud, McCabe dropped to his knees in front of her, reached out, and touched the tops of her feet. His callused fingertips felt rough against her sensitive flesh, yet his touch was so light it was almost a tease.

"Your feet are bleeding," he said quietly, exploring their surface with his strong, tapered fingers, taking care not to touch the raw spots where blisters had formed and ruptured. "The skin's ripped clear to the bone in places, and you're standing there worried about your toenail polish?" He shook his head. "You're even more of a dumb broad than I thought."

Liz would have pulled away at the insult, except this time there was no heat in his words. In fact, his tone sounded strangely gentle, and when he finally looked up, his dark blue eyes seemed to reflect the kind of tender concern she wouldn't have thought him capable of feeling.

"Why the hell didn't you say something before now?" he asked her.

"I tried. I told you my feet were killing me when I stopped to go to the bathroom," Liz reminded him.

His grimace seemed one of self-reproach. "Yeah, but I figured you were just pulling a spoiled-brat act because you were tired of walking. I didn't realize your feet were literally *killing* you. Do you know what will happen if you get an infection in one of these broken blisters?"

"No . . . and I don't think I want to." Liz flinched remembering his graphic description of the damage inflicted by stinging ants. As long as he seemed to be in a sympathetic mood, however, she decided to seize the moment. "Does that mean we can stop here for a while?"

She was hoping for a quick, compassionate yes. Instead

he scowled and peered into the distance consideringly before replying, making her fear her first impression of him as cold and ruthless was on target after all. Finally he shook his head, and Liz's heart sank.

"I can't spare more than a few minutes, and that isn't going to do you any good. It'll only make it worse when you finally have to stand up again." He stared back down at her feet, his expression rueful. "But you sure as hell can't walk any farther until your feet are patched up. So," he concluded, straightening with a resigned sigh, "I guess there's only one solution."

Liz started shaking her head frantically, certain he was about to tell her she was on her own. Her throat went dry with panic, but this time when he turned on his heel he didn't walk away. Instead he crouched a bit and extended his hands behind him expectantly.

"All right, let's go," he ordered. "Up."

"Up where?" Liz countered, not moving.

McCabe hitched a thumb in the direction of his back. "Up here . . . piggyback style." When she just stood there eyeing him with a confused expression, he added dryly, "I trust you're familiar with the concept?"

"Yes, I'm familiar with the concept," she mimicked. "But do you seriously think you'll be able to carry me more than a few steps like that?"

"There's only one way to find out. Now, up you go."

Deciding that anything, even being that close to him, was preferable to walking, Liz obediently straddled his broad back and with a none-too-gentle boost managed to wrap her legs around his waist. His hands gripped her just above the knees and she looped her arms around his neck for balance. The going was much slower with him carrying her, especially when he was forced to use the machete. Liz didn't mind. Once she got over the initial awkwardness of being hauled about on a strange man's back, she didn't care if he had to crawl as long as she was spared the agony of putting her weight on her aching feet. In fact, she told herself, he deserved to suffer a little, this whole thing being his fault in the first place.

After he'd been carrying her for a while, though, guilt prompted her to ask if he didn't think he should take a short break.

"I'm fine," he insisted in a couple of slightly winded sounding grunts.

"I'm not too heavy?"

"You're no featherweight, lady, but no, you're not too heavy."

Liz wasn't sure whether to thank him or feel injured. She certainly wasn't overweight, but being five-five and endowed with more curves than she sometimes wished, she knew she had to be a strain on his back. But McCabe was even stronger than she'd thought. And not just because he could carry her so far over rough terrain, occasionally wielding a machete at the same time. Even more striking to Liz was the latent power she sensed in him, much the way she could sense a horse's strength while riding bareback. With her chest pressed to McCabe's upper back, she was vividly aware of the ripple of muscles there whenever he swung the machete. But it was the sinewy area along the sides of his ribs that intrigued her most. She had never known a man could have such well-developed muscles there. But then, she'd never ridden a man this way before, with the sensitive insides of her bare thighs pressed against him, their mingled sweat sealing her flesh to his. The sensations produced by the close contact were distinctly and, to Liz, disturbingly, pleasurable. And the strong, steady rhythm of his steps wasn't helping matters. She fretted that she must be suffering from either sunstroke or insanity brought on by fatigue for this man's touch to elicit anything other than revulsion.

"Do we have much farther to go?" she asked, eager to put space between them once again.

"No." After a few seconds, he added, "You see those trees up ahead?" He indicated a tall grove of what looked like pineapple trees about a hundred yards away.

"Yes."

"We'll stop for the night just on the other side of them."

He seemed to have forgotten that she wasn't allowed to ask questions, and Liz decided to make the most of the opportunity. "Is that where your camp is?" Perhaps he'd changed his mind about trying to make it back there before dark.

"No." He paused. "It's a friend's place."

Liz was instantly alert. "Does that mean we'll be sleeping inside?"

"With any luck we will."

"I suppose I should thank God for that," she muttered, finding it a strain to be thankful for anything in the midst of this nightmare.

McCabe angled his head slightly to look back at her. "You're a real surprise. You know that, sweetheart?"

His lazy drawl and the suggestive slant of his hard mouth caused all Liz's defenses to spring into place. "What's that supposed to mean?"

"Just that I hadn't expected you to sound so pleased by the prospect of sharing a real bed with me."

"Believe me, I'm not," she retorted, embarrassment heating her cheeks. "The only thing I'm pleased about is not having to spend the night outside, lying awake the whole time praying I'm not attacked by whatever lives under all these slimy bushes."

"Me too. Give me a soft bed and a soft woman over hard dirt and a wild boar any day."

"Now *that's* a surprise," Liz parried, keeping her tone carefully innocent. "I'd have thought a wild boar would be much more your type than any woman alive."

He chuckled, tightening his grip on her legs in a brief warning. "Careful, honey, your ass will hurt even more than your feet do if I accidentally drop you into one of these pricker bushes."

Liz bit her tongue. Self-control might not be as satisfying as verbal retaliation, but she had a feeling it would be a whole lot less painful. They covered the rest of the distance to the trees in silence. On the other side the land sloped gradually down to the river, which was much narrower here. Two tiny huts, identical to every one Liz had seen since leaving Guatemala City, were situated a short distance from the riverbank, at the edge of a roughly cleared field. The charred tree trunks piled nearby revealed that whatever tropical growth had once existed there had been painstakingly hacked and burned away in preparation for planting. Farming in Guatemala was a life for hard workers and eternal optimists.

Stopping a few hundred yards from the huts, McCabe lowered her to the ground. "Hey, Armando," he shouted. "Anybody home?"

The makeshift door of the closest hut, the larger of the two, cracked open, but not enough for Liz to see inside. Obviously whoever was looking out could see them, however, and must have recognized McCabe, for the door was swung wide and two tiny, dark-haired children dashed out. A woman Liz assumed was their mother followed. She was young, slender, with black eyes and burnished teak skin typical of those with Mayan Indian ancestry. She smiled at McCabe and greeted him shyly, both youngsters clinging to her faded cotton skirt.

"*Buenas noches*, Santana," he replied, then lapsed into Spanish that was so rapid and fluent Liz didn't have a prayer of understanding. She recognized a few key words, though, enough to guess that he was inquiring about her husband, Armando. The woman smiled apologetically and said something about three days. McCabe nodded, then continued in Spanish.

"*Sí, Sí*," the woman interjected each time he slowed down. She gestured toward the second hut, nodding vigorously, then followed his gaze to where Liz's feet rested on the ground. Gasping at the sight of them, she murmured something that sounded sympathetic.

Liz smiled and thanked her, ignoring the amused grin her stilted Spanish drew from the man by her side. He and the woman exchanged a few more words, then she turned and hurried back into the hut, shooing the gaping children before her.

"What did she say?" Liz asked the moment she disappeared.

McCabe slanted her a censoring look.

"Oh, then don't tell me," she snapped, folding her arms across her chest in disgust. "Who cares? You'll do whatever you want to do anyway."

"You're learning," he drawled in an infuriatingly condescending tone. Liz's tongue was getting sore from her biting it. After a long enough pause to make it clear that he was telling her on his terms, he said, "She told me her husband and brother-in-law have gone to Morales for supplies and won't be back until the day after tomorrow. We're welcome to use her brother-in-law's bed for the night. . . . That other hut over there is his." He nodded in that direction. "I told her my *novia* would be most grateful for her kindness."

"*Novia?*"

"Fiancée," he translated, his smile mocking. "I didn't want her to think my intentions toward you were dishonorable."

"Despicable is more like it," Liz retorted, torn between joy that she would actually be spending the night in a bed and dread that, barring a miracle, she would have to share it with this insolent swine. Her only consolation was that she looked, and no doubt smelled, even less desirable now than she had a few hours ago. She would just have to pray fatigue didn't cause McCabe to lower his standards any.

The door to the hut opened once more and the woman reappeared carrying a cotton blanket and an oil lamp with a murky-colored ceramic base. She handed both over to

McCabe with a shrug, her smile and tone once again apologetic.

"*Gracias*, Santana, *perfecto*," he replied. "*Té eres una ángelita*."

Noting his easy smile and warm tone, Liz was astounded by the charm he could summon forth when he chose to. It sounded to her as if he'd told the woman she was an angel. Whatever he said apparently thrilled her to the core because she went away with a delighted blush coloring her face, as if she'd been paid a compliment by a king instead of by a disreputable-looking, gun-toting degenerate. Any thoughts Liz was nurturing about overcoming the language barrier enough to enlist the other woman's help dimmed considerably.

"Shall we?" McCabe queried once they were alone, making a ridiculously formal sweep with his arm in the direction of the hut. Their hut. It suddenly looked more like a torture chamber than a refuge.

"You go on ahead," Liz suggested, stalling. "I'll hobble along at my own pace."

His eyes narrowed suspiciously. "No, I don't think that's such a good idea. Here, take this." He handed her the lamp. Before Liz knew what he intended, he'd scooped her up in his arms and was striding toward the hut.

"This really isn't necessary," she insisted, forcing herself not to struggle. Her apprehension swelled as the hut's lopsided door loomed closer.

"Maybe not." McCabe unleashed that wretched, taunting grin of his on her as he shoved the door open with his shoulder and carried her over the threshold. "But who says romance is dead?"

He crossed the one-room hut with two steps and unceremoniously dumped her into the middle of the narrow iron bed that stood against the back wall. Ditching the lamp, Liz quickly scrambled off the bed and moved away, careful to face him at all times as if he were an unpredictable wild animal she couldn't trust not to spring at her if she so much as blinked. She came to an uneasy halt in the sliver of light near the open door. It was dusk outside and the only other light in the room came from the hut's one small open window beside her, leaving McCabe in the shadows.

Even so, Liz could see enough of him to send her heart slamming against her ribs. He appeared huge in the tiny room, huge and menacing. He was still wearing that wicked, unsettling grin, and his glittering sapphire eyes looked hungry enough to eat her alive. Sweat broke out all over Liz's body as she surveyed the hard muscles and hair-roughened skin of his shoulders and chest. Without taking a step he had pivoted to follow her every movement with his eyes so that they now stood facing each other, only a few feet of tension-charged air between them. Her nerves were already as unsteady as a trip wire, and when he reached for her, Liz screamed.

"Shut up," McCabe ordered angrily, reaching past her to slam the door shut.

Belatedly realizing that was all he had intended in the first place, Liz felt her cheeks flame over her foolish reaction. "I'm sorry. I thought..."

"Yeah," he countered derisively when she floundered for words. "I can imagine what you thought. Well, you can relax. I never ravish my women on an empty stomach."

74

That was at least temporarily reassuring, and some of the tension drained from Liz's body. She stood uneasily by the door while he glanced around in the darkness. Grabbing the lamp from the mattress where she'd dropped it, he set it on a wooden crate by the bed and pulled a cigarette lighter from his pocket. Once he had it lit, Liz took a look around the room. There wasn't much to see. Besides the bed and the crate, the only things in the hut were a battered wooden chair and a rickety-looking table holding an enamel washbasin. Above the table hung an unframed mirror, the silver worn off in places. Nearby some men's clothing hung on a row of nails hammered into the wall.

The hut seemed clean enough, but Liz shivered anyway, unable to shake the crawling sensation down the center of her back. She took a cautious step toward the chair, then jumped back with a terrified scream as a black, hard-shelled bug the size of a half-dollar darted from behind one of its legs.

"Quick, it's a bug," she shouted to McCabe, who was unknotting his T-shirt from around his waist.

He paused before hooking it over the nail where his vest already hung, to glance at the insect now edging its way along the wall in her direction, and gave a nod as if to confirm her announcement.

"Well, do something," she ordered frantically.

"Like what?"

"Kill it."

"What for? There's plenty more where that came from."

Liz squeezed her eyes shut with a whimper. "Oh, no. I can't spend the night here. I just can't."

"Suit yourself."

She could almost hear his shrug, and she flicked her eyes open in time to see the smug look that went along with it. At that instant it was a toss-up as to which she'd rather see dead—the insect or McCabe. Defiantly she reached for the enamel washbasin and crouching, slammed it down hard on the bug. The crunching sound of the shell cracking seemed to fill the small room. She jerked the basin back up, catching a glimpse of the splattered bug stuck to the bottom, its black legs still twitching, and with a disgusted cry hurled the bowl across the room. It missed McCabe's head by inches . . . unfortunately, Liz thought when she heard his amused chuckle. Stepping daintily over the mess on the floor, she kept her back to him until she heard the door open. Then her revulsion over the bug was forgotten as she confronted a new fear, that of being left there all alone.

"Where are you going?" she cried.

McCabe regarded her silently, his black brows arched.

"Oh, damn you," Liz bit out in frustration. "We're in this together, you know. I think I have a right to know . . ." She hesitated, knowing that in his opinion she had no rights whatsoever. Then her growling stomach supplied just the excuse she needed. "I think I have a right to know whether or not we're going to eat anytime soon."

"Santana and the kids already ate supper," he replied, "but she said it wouldn't take her long to dish us up some of the leftovers." He shot her a nasty grin. "I'm sure whatever it is won't be quite the sort of meal you're accustomed to."

"Who cares? About now anything would taste good," Liz admitted, surprised by how true that was.

"Yeah. Funny, isn't it," inquired McCabe, his saturnine look intensifying, "how the situation you find yourself in can change your perspective? And your desires. And even your image of yourself. I suspect you'll have plenty of time to learn all about that in the next few weeks."

"Weeks?" Liz's eyes widened with dismay. She hadn't thought about how long she'd be stuck at his camp.

"Two weeks if we're real lucky. That's about how long I expect it to take for us to finish up...unless we hit a snag," he told her.

"Finish up what?"

An enigmatic smile slanted his firm lips. "I think I'll go see if Santana has our food ready."

He returned a few minutes later with two bowls of steaming chili and several pieces of flat bread. While he was gone Liz had moved the chair closer to the bed, positioning the crate in between to serve as a table. Then she'd settled herself dead center on the bed in the hope that McCabe would take the hint and settle for the chair. She should have known better. Handing her one of the bowls, he placed the bread on the table and threw himself down on the foot of the bed with his back propped against the wall and his long legs encroaching on her preestablished territory.

Accepting that any protest on her part would be futile, Liz grudgingly gathered herself into the opposite corner of the narrow bed and attacked the chili greedily. She never ate beans, especially overspiced ones mixed with things she couldn't identify, but tonight she emptied the bowl and was sorely tempted to put manners aside and inquire about the possibility of seconds. Instead she reached for one of the pancake-shaped slices of bread. It was as bland as the chili had been fiery, but it satisfied her taste buds as if it were the most elegant dessert ever concocted. They each ate two pieces of the bread, and Liz was eyeing the third longingly when McCabe claimed it. To her surprise he ripped it in half and held a piece out to her.

"Go ahead and take it," he urged when she hesitated politely. "Walking works up an appetite."

"Then you should have the whole thing," Liz demurred. "After all, you did the walking for both of us at the end."

"Take the bread," he ordered. Then, unfurling a lazy smile, he added, "You're going to need all your strength."

Educated speculation over what he meant by that soured the taste of the bread for Liz. McCabe had his piece wolfed down before she had gloomily nibbled half of her own. Setting his empty bowl on the table beside hers, he ambled across the room to rummage in his vest pocket, returning with a pack of cigarettes. He sank back onto the bed, his expression growing steadily more thunderous as he removed one ruined cigarette after another from the soggy, mud-streaked pack.

"This," he announced in a tight voice, "is all your fault."

"My fault?"

"If you hadn't yelled out to me, I never would have lost my footing and slipped over the edge."

"Ha! I was wondering when you'd get around to blaming me. The truth is that if you hadn't been pushing my car . . ."

"Forget it," he interrupted, finally pulling out a halfway smokeable cigarette. "Just forget it."

"I wish I could."

"That makes two of us."

He managed to get the cigarette lit and took a deep drag on it. For a while the only sounds were that of smoke being exhaled and the rustle of the bugs outside. At least Liz hoped they were outside. The lamp didn't throw enough light for her to be certain. Too exhausted to get very worked up about it, she rested her head against the wall and was thinking she might almost be able to fall asleep right there when McCabe's gritty voice pulled her back.

"What did you say your name was?"

Liz came away from the wall with a jolt. Blinking, she played his question over in her mind to be sure she'd heard it right. Then she had a wild urge to laugh hysterically. This man had threatened to kill her twice, had had his miserable life saved by her, whether he wanted to admit it or not, and had carried her on his back through a hot, muddy jungle, and he didn't even remember her name. The whole mess was ridiculous.

"It's Liz," she replied wearily. "Liz Randolph."

"But Randolph is your *married* name?"

The emphasis he placed on the word *married* tickled the suspicious side of her nature. "That's right."

Without warning he reached over and grabbed her left hand, jerking it—and her along with it—in front of him. She ended up on her knees by his side, her face so close to his she could count the tiny lines that fanned at the sides of his narrowed eyes.

79

"Then how come, Mrs. Randolph," he demanded, "a married lady like you is wearing a diamond but no wedding band?"

"I . . ." Liz stared at the diamond ring on her finger and for the first time since she'd been dragged from her car, Kirk's image filled her mind, forcing all other concerns aside. "Oh, my God," she groaned, covering her face with her right hand and sinking back onto her heels as much as his tight hold permitted.

She'd been so engrossed in the danger she was in she had completely forgotten about poor Kirk and his safety. The price of which, twenty thousand dollars, now rested at the bottom of the river along with the Toyota. A sickening wave of guilt broke over her. No matter how desperate her own predicament, there was no excuse whatsoever for her not even sparing a thought for the man she loved, the man she was going to marry. Liz thrust aside the uncomfortable questions that raised about their relationship and tried to think of a way to salvage the situation.

Was there any way she could get the money back? Certainly not on her own. She slanted a contemplative glance at McCabe from between her splayed fingers. He was watching her with a hard, implacable expression that was distinctly discouraging. Still, if she could find some way to convince him that it would be well worth his while to help her rescue Kirk, maybe . . .

Lord, she definitely had to be either a victim of sunstroke or crazy. He hadn't been tempted by her bribes even when it was *his* life at stake. And she could hardly hope to appeal to his noble instincts or sense of fair play to get him to help save the life of a man he didn't even know. McCabe obviously possessed neither. For all she knew, he was no better than whoever was holding Kirk, and he might well be a good deal worse. Telling him any more than she already had might only put both Kirk and her in greater danger.

His brutal tone slashed through her thoughts. "Well? Have you had enough time to come up with a good answer?"

"I don't have to come up with any answer," Liz protested. "I've already told you the truth. Randolph was my husband's name. He . . ." She swallowed the lump that lodged in her throat at having to plumb painful memories in order to satisfy his bullying curiosity. "He died four years ago," she continued in a rush. "The ring I'm wearing now was given to me by the man I'm planning to marry in a few months."

"Is that so?" He lifted her hand higher to inspect the large oval diamond set off by smaller ones on each side. "Quite a rock," he pronounced. To Liz the apparent compliment sounded suspiciously like bitter condemnation. "But then," he added, "I suppose a woman like you wouldn't settle for anything less."

Her suspicion had been well-founded. At first Liz fought to pull away, stung by the barely veiled insult. But when he tightened his grip on her hand, refusing to free her, all the anger and frustration she'd been forced to hold on simmer all day erupted.

"What the hell do you mean, a woman like me?" she cried. "What do you even know about me? Or why I'm here in the first place? You act like I'm down here on a lark.

What did you call it? Oh, yes . . . a Central American holiday, as if it's all some sort of carefree adventure.''

He lifted one black brow. "Isn't it?"

"No," she snapped, ignoring the fact that desire for adventure had actually been a large part of her reason for coming along. "That's not it at all."

"All right." With her smaller hand still encased in his, he resumed his negligent slouching position against the wall. "Then suppose you tell me what you are doing in Guatemala? Especially this part of Guatemala."

All the fight left Liz in a rush. She felt as if a stone wall had sprung up in front of her. Behind her was another just as insurmountable. She let her gaze shift from the cold expectancy in his eyes to the stone floor.

"I can't tell you," she said softly.

His laughter was harsh. "Wrong, baby. You can and, believe me, you will . . . if I tell you to."

CHAPTER
FIVE

As he watched the soundless straining of the muscles in
her throat, Zach was satisfied that she accepted the truth of
his words. He had no doubt he could force the answer from
her. He also had no doubt it would be a struggle. It had
been obvious to him all day that her stony-faced cooperation
had its roots not in cowardice, but in common sense. Zach
half admired her for it. At the same time he didn't discount
the significance of that defiant gleam that never left her
eyes, no matter what he said or did to her. Even when his
back was turned he could feel it boring into him like shards
of fiery green ice, proclaiming that he was a long way from
breaking her spirit. It was even worse when they were face
to face, like right now. Then the rebellious fire in her eyes
took on a challenging dimension and he got this crazy,
primitive feeling that he shouldn't be the first to back down.

Christ, he'd been living south of the border for too long if he was starting to take all that macho crap seriously.

Deliberately he broke the stubborn lock of their gazes and instead let his eyes drift slowly downward over her tensely coiled body. She was sure to hate his looking at her as much as she hated having to obey him. To guarantee that, Zach let his attention linger a long while on the plump upper swell of breast revealed by her torn blouse. It wasn't much of a chore. He liked looking at her breasts. And no matter what he'd told her earlier, he would like touching them even better, exploring their tempting contours with his hands and his mouth.

Gradually he slid his attention lower, smiling lewdly as he silently admired the rounded curve of her hip and the length of pale thigh visible where her skirt had gotten twisted up under her. Out of the corner of his eye he noticed her free hand twitch in her lap, as if she was fighting the urge to wrench her skirt back into place. She was probably resisting so as not to give him the satisfaction of knowing his perusal bothered her. Actually, at the moment Zach was getting plenty of satisfaction from just looking at her. He was partial to women's thighs, and hers were great. Firm but not sticklike. Skinny women didn't turn him on. Liz Randolph did.

The thought stirred him and irritated him at the same time. After that close call back at the cliff, with the adrenaline still pumping through his veins, he would have liked nothing better than a little quick, physical release. But Miss Rich Bitch had iced that idea proper. She hadn't minced any words either in letting him know how she felt about making it with him. If he had been thinking clearly, he would have realized the smartest thing to do would be to ignore the contempt in her damn cat's eyes and take her anyway, right then and there, so she would understand that he meant what he said about being in charge. Not that it would have been any good. Doubtless she would have fought tooth and nail the whole time, making it a totally pleasureless experience for both of them.

No, he mused, forcing his attention back to the matter at hand, Ms. Liz Randolph wasn't the type to give up her body any more easily than she gave straight answers once she'd made up her mind not to. The question was, did he feel like expending the energy tonight that would be necessary to force out of her the facts about what she was doing here?

"Maybe," he said in a soft, deliberate voice intended to draw a reaction from her, "maybe I *should* make you come clean about why you're down here. Maybe then I'll know for sure whether you're working for Sanchez or not."

"Oh, for God's sake," she said, brushing impatiently at her tousled blond hair with her free hand. "I already told you I don't know any Sanchez and I have no idea what you're talking about."

"Yup. That's what you told me, all right."

Zach eyed her thoughtfully, trying once again to decide if he bought her story. Farfetched as it seemed, there was always an outside chance that she was one of Sanchez's flunkies and that her stupidity was just a clever act. That troublesome possibility had been the deciding factor in his bringing her along. If she was a spy, the safest place to have her was where he could keep an eye on her at all times, making sure she didn't contact anyone else with whatever information she uncovered. It would also be playing it safe, he decided now, not to let on to her that he had his suspicions. If she believed she had him duped, she was much more likely to get overconfident and slip up. Then he would know for sure what she was up to. Not knowing made him edgy.

For the time being, things would stand just the way he'd outlined them to her. He would treat her like his woman and watch her like a hawk. With that in mind, he slid his fingers down to grasp her tightly by the wrist and with his other hand jerked the diamond ring off her finger. Her fingers were long and slender, but she still gasped as it scraped over her knuckle. Releasing her so abruptly she was left clutching at the rough cotton blanket for balance, he shoved the ring into the front pocket of his jeans.

"What do you think you're doing?" she demanded, clearly outraged.

"Taking care of details," Zach told her. "I can't very well go walking into camp tomorrow brandishing you as my woman with you wearing another man's ring on your finger, now, can I?"

"Why don't you just tell them it's your ring?" she suggested sarcastically. "That should prove your devotion to me."

"It's not *my* devotion to *you* I'm interested in proving," he retorted. "Besides, even if there were someplace around here to buy a rock like that for a broad, my men all know I'm not sucker enough to do it."

Maybe it was that damned defiant look of hers that

goaded him. Whatever it was, it compelled him to bait her, to rub her nose in the power he had over her and see her eyes burn with frustration and resentment instead of pure defiance for a change. He was successful. Her now unadorned fingers curled into tight fists as she glared at him.

"I hate you."

"I sort of got that impression." His dry tone seemed to stoke her fury higher.

"I mean I really hate you . . . in every sense of the word."

"Then I hope for your sake that you're a damn good actress, baby. I can tell those men that you're mine, but it's up to you to prove it. You're going to have to convince them that you do things for me that are so special"—he leaned closer and dropped his voice to a suggestive drawl—"so satisfying, that it's worth it to me to put up with all the aggravation of having a woman around. Up till now I'd say you haven't shown a real feel for the part. So you better start practicing."

"Really?"

A small, condescending smile curved her lips, and the lifting of her golden, elegantly shaped brows was almost imperceptible, as if he wasn't worth the expenditure of more than the scantest effort on her part. It was a classic look, one Zach recognized well: cool, composed, bitchy. It brought back memories. Unpleasant memories.

He nodded. "Really."

"And just how," she inquired offhandedly, "do you propose I do that?"

"For starters I propose that you take off your clothes. All

of them." He smiled with satisfaction as a look of shock chased all that annoying composure from her face.

"My clothes? What for?"

His smile broadened. "For practice, of course."

"Listen . . . McCabe, please," she pleaded as he slid off the bed and stood with his back to her, stretching. "I didn't mean to upset you. I was only . . . teasing."

He turned to face her. "I'm not."

There was real fear in her eyes now. In spite of it, though, she straightened her shoulders and brought her chin up with all the defiance he knew was in her. For the second time that day she announced, "I won't do it."

Zach's hand was on the gun and it was out of his pants and pointed at her before he knew it. "Would you like to see just how easily I can wipe those four words from your vocabulary?"

Her chin trembled, but it stayed high. "You're real tough as long as you're the one holding the gun, aren't you? I wonder how brave you'd be if it were in my hand instead of yours."

"Let's find out."

Unconsciously spinning it on his thumb in a move he'd perfected years ago, when such displays of skill had mattered to him, he tossed the gun at her. First she recoiled, taken by surprise. Then she lunged for it and after a few fumbling efforts managed to wrap both hands around the butt and aim it in his general direction. She looked a whole lot more scared than Zach felt. Of course, she didn't share the benefit of knowing that he'd taken the precaution of removing the bullets when he went to get their food. He hadn't wanted to wake up in the middle of the night and find himself staring down a loaded gun barrel with a high-strung, desperate woman at the other end.

Slowly, giving her plenty of time to think, plenty of time to squeeze the trigger if she had the stomach to, he closed in on her. Liz watched his advance with wide-eyed terror. As quickly as he'd produced the gun, he now wrenched it from her fingers and tossed it aside. Curling his hands over her shoulders, he pressed her back to the mattress and went down on one knee beside her. Belatedly she started to struggle, but by exerting pressure on just the right spot near her collarbone he quickly quelled her attempt to free herself.

"See?" he said softly. "I don't need a gun to control you. So why don't we stop fighting a war you can't ever win and make the best of this?"

Never, her eyes screamed, but she kept her mouth shut and somehow her silence robbed the victory of all satisfaction for Zach.

Releasing her abruptly, he twisted to his feet, retrieved his gun, and took a step toward the door. Framed in the doorway he turned back to look at her still lying there as rigidly as he'd left her, aiming all that defiance at the ceiling.

"I have to check on a few things with Santana," he told her. "By the time I get back I expect those filthy rags to be off you . . . and waiting in a pile by the door to be burned." His eyes narrowed to a slanting, wicked stare. "If they're not, I'll read it as an invitation to rip them off you . . . and take great pleasure in doing so."

CHAPTER SIX

The instant the door slammed shut behind him, Liz jumped up as if it were a bed of coals she'd been forced to lie on. Her thoughts were spinning like a carousel out of control. She was pacing nervously across the room when her eyes lit on the machete, standing in the far corner where McCabe had left it. Briefly—foolishly—she contemplated grabbing it and running. Her shoulders sagged as, with a sigh of dismay, she admitted to herself that running was no longer an option. Even if she weren't terrified of being out there alone at night, how far could she hope to get barefoot and with her feet in such miserable shape?

She had no choice but to stick it out with McCabe . . . no matter how much she despised him. And that meant she had no choice but to do as he had ordered and take off her clothes. If she didn't, she knew he would rip them off her upon his return, and that would be a thousand times more humiliating for her. Worse, it would be feeding his perverted taste for power. The only bright spot Liz could see in the situation was that if he did burn her clothes as he'd threatened, he would be forced to replace them. It would hardly make McCabe's life easier if she paraded into his camp naked. And anything he came up with in the way of clothing would have to be an improvement over the ruined skirt and blouse that had been so crisp and clean when she started the day.

Suddenly the morning seemed a lifetime away, and the safe, comfortable existence she'd once taken for granted even farther. She couldn't even bear to think about it. To think about being clean and relaxed, curled up on the sofa with a tall glass of iced tea and a fat, juicy novel full of dangers that she could put aside whenever she felt like it would only make her feel worse. Swallowing her pride, Liz lifted her fingers to the sole surviving button on her blouse and slipped it open. At the same time her attention was caught by the articles of clothing hanging on the hooks in front of her and she broke into a grin. She would obey McCabe's orders all right, to the letter.

When he returned a few minutes later, kicking the door open and dropping whatever he was carrying onto the table just inside, Liz was standing primly by the bed dressed in Santana's brother-in-law's clothes. He couldn't be much bigger than she was, because she'd only had to roll the cuffs up a couple of turns and pull the drawstring waist a bit tighter to make the shapeless cotton pants and matching shirt fit reasonably well. Her own clothes were piled by the door as McCabe had specified, except for her panties, which she had rebelliously decided to keep on.

Without sparing her a glance he snatched up the discarded skirt and blouse and left again, this time without shutting the door. Liz stared after him incredulously. She hadn't wanted him to look at her, but his total lack of interest when she'd expected him to come back in panting and drooling for the sight of her naked body was a little humbling. She was about to slam the door herself when he reappeared, backing in this time and dragging a round metal tub behind him.

It was about four feet wide and two deep, its faded silver-gray sides dented in places. It reminded Liz of a tub she'd once seen in an old western. As she looked on, torn between curiosity and apprehension, he made several more trips back and forth, toting buckets of water which he poured into the tub, ignoring her the whole time. Once, right after he'd left, Liz dashed over and dipped her fingers in to feel the water. It was warm and she was filled with an intense longing to climb in and soak in it until all the day's dirt and sweat and misery were washed from her body.

The level of her anticipation rose along with the water. Glancing at the objects he'd dumped on the table, she discerned at least one towel on the top of the pile and a small bar of soap next to it. Obviously a bath for one of them was what he had in mind. And even if she had to wait her turn until he was finished, it was better than staying the way she was. Of course, Liz mused, she had to take into consideration the fact that being clean would put a hitch in her plan to remain undesirable. As soon as she'd formed the thought, the obvious truth of it backwashed on her like a dam bursting. Of course, that was why he was doing all this strenuous hauling of water. He wanted her clean before he raped her.

She jumped as he strode back in. This time he emptied only one bucket of water into the tub and rested the full one on the floor beside it. Then he closed the door and put his gun on the table. Finally he turned to look at her. The edges of his mouth twitched as he took in the bleached cotton pants and shirt, but Liz couldn't decide if it was with humor or anger. Slowly he circled the small space between tub and bed, inspecting her from all sides, before coming to a halt a foot in front of her. His expression was unreadable, and it took every shred of Liz's already sorely overtaxed willpower to keep from squirming under his silent regard.

"A very fetching getup, Liz," he said finally. The sound of her name rolling off his tongue for the first time startled her. It gave the scene a troubling air of familiarity. "Now do as I said and take it off."

"I did as you said," Liz protested. "You told me to take my clothes off so you could burn them."

"Which I've done," he informed her, "courtesy of Santana's wood stove. But you knew what I meant."

"No," Liz shot back, doing her best not to goad him any more than necessary by sounding as smug as she felt. "I only know what you said."

"Fine. I can see that in the future if I want to get the desired results, I'm going to have to be more specific when giving you instructions. What I should have made clear before I left is that what I want is you naked, without a stitch of your—or anyone else's—clothes covering any part of your body. Do you understand that?''

Liz swallowed hard. She still couldn't decide if the gleam in his eye was more savage or amused. ''I understand. But . . .''

He cut her off roughly. ''No buts. Just do it . . . and make it fast.''

Her whole body trembling from fear and anger, Liz untied the string at her waist and lowered the slacks. Awkwardly she stepped out of them, thankful that the bottom of the shirt fell several inches below her panties. She folded the slacks and placed them on the bed behind her, stalling for time. When she couldn't put it off any longer, she grasped the hem of the shirt with fingers that had gone ice-cold and froze.

She couldn't do it. She couldn't willingly bare herself to stand naked in front of this hard-eyed, brutal stranger, knowing what would happen next.

''Let's go, Liz,'' he prodded.

''I can't.''

McCabe made an impatient noise. ''I thought we'd settled this business of I-can't-and-I-won't a few minutes ago. Now strip for me like a good girl. And on second thought, don't rush. Just take it nice and slow to heighten my anticipation.''

''You bastard.''

Far from getting angry, he let the grin that Liz detected lurking about his mouth break full force. ''Careful, baby, or else I might decide to scrub out your mouth along with the rest of you.''

Liz seized the opening, welcoming any chance to postpone her humiliation. "Is that what you dragged this thing in here for?" she queried, nodding in the direction of the tub. "To give me a bath?"

He tilted his head slightly to one side, his expression wry. "No. I just thought I'd add a little humidity to the air in here. Of course it's for you . . . or rather us, to take a bath."

The vision of them bathing together flashed before Liz. His hard, hairy body rubbing up against hers, both of them slippery with soap, their skin flushed from the warm water. She was suddenly hot all over and her pulse was pounding erratically.

"We'll never fit in there together," she cried.

McCabe chuckled and reached out to cup her chin, his skin scratchy against her softness.

"Hot damn," he muttered. "You're always surprising me. Who'd have even guessed you'd be interested in anything as kinky as us taking a bath together?" Liz blushed furiously as he chuckled again. "But you're right, we won't both fit in there at once. So we'll have to take turns. And we'll just have to save the more . . . ah, adventuresome activities for the lake near camp."

The hand holding her chin started moving slowly downward over her throat, the motion almost a caress. His voice became a soft, soothing drawl. "Now then, seeing as how I've decided to play the gentleman by letting you go first, and you seeming to be having a little trouble getting this off, I guess chivalry demands that I give you a hand with it."

With that his slow-moving fingers caught in the neckline of the shirt and jerked downward, ripping it open from top to bottom. While Liz was still sputtering a protest, he grasped the shirt at the shoulders and pulled it off. Without taking his eyes from her, he tossed it aside. The air in the tiny room had to be at least eighty muggy degrees, and Liz felt weak from the nauseating waves of heat rolling through her body. Yet she couldn't stop shivering as he continued to stare at her in silence.

He seemed fascinated by her breasts. His eyes, as they fastened on the pale gold globes, grew narrow and glittered like moonlit seas. Liz's response to his insolent attention was physical and automatic. Feeling it start to happen, she glanced down in horror and saw that her nipples had puckered under his regard so they jutted out at him pertly. Even their color had changed; the usual pink hue was now a deep, rich rose and the rest of her skin was flushed as well. Liz jerked her gaze back up, not in the least surprised to find McCabe wearing a satisfied smirk. Her attempt to cover herself with her arms was halted by his harsh growl.

"Stand still. You had a chance to do this your way."

With a moan of embarrassment Liz dropped her arms back to her sides and turned her head aside. Even without looking she could trace the slow path of his gaze as it meandered lower, over the tightly clenched muscles of her belly to the golden nest of curls she knew would be clearly visible through her sheer panties. She felt more naked than naked standing there in that ridiculous scrap of white silk and lace. It was degrading, as if she were posing for him, intentionally teasing and titillating when what she really longed to do was grab the machete and plunge it deep into his miserable, decadent heart.

Without warning, the fury she felt flared into blind

recklessness. Hooking her fingers into the panties at both sides she ripped them off and hurled them straight at his face, relishing the look of surprise the action evoked.

"There, have a good look," she cried. "Is that what you wanted?"

He nodded, taking his own sweet time about working his way back up to look her in the eye. "Yup. That's it, all right."

Any satisfaction Liz garnered from the moment was depressingly fleeting. McCabe had caught her hurled panties in midair and now stood there twirling them on one finger like some sort of obscene trophy of war. A war which, as he had so obligingly pointed out, she had no hope of ever winning. Liz would have thrown herself on the bed and hidden beneath the covers except she knew that to even attempt it would give him another excuse to put his hands on her, to roughly demonstrate how utterly and completely she was at his mercy.

Sober-faced, he extended his hand to her in a gesture that was farcically gallant under the circumstances. "May I assist you into the tub?" he offered.

The laughter in his voice made Liz cringe.

"No. Thank you," she replied, shooting him a look capable of freezing flames at thirty paces.

Holding her head high, she stepped around him and into the tub on her own. At first the tepid water stung the cuts and scrapes that covered her feet and lower legs. Ignoring the discomfort, Liz sat down, anxious for even the minimal protection from his eyes provided by the clear water. After the first minute or so, the stinging ceased and the feel of the water was soothing and relaxing. Or at least it would have been soothing and relaxing if he hadn't been standing right there watching her the way a hungry cat watches a cornered mouse.

Deciding to confront the matter head-on, Liz tipped her face up to his. "Do you suppose I could have a little privacy for this?"

His mouth quirked. "You mean, do I suppose that I could wait outside with the mosquitoes and the coyotes and the jaguars?"

She smiled sweetly. "That's right."

"No."

Gritting her teeth, she decided to modify her request. "Then could you at least please turn your back?"

He shook his head slowly. "Uh-uh. I figure I deserve some sort of reward for dragging the tub and all the water in here while you relaxed."

"Relaxed?" Liz echoed, eyes wide with disbelief. "I assure you I . . ."

"Yeah, yeah," he broke in, giving the panties an impatient wave. "You also sure weren't doing any of the work. I did. And now I'm giving you a pretty painless way to pay me back."

Liz stared down at the water and pondered that. It was true that if watching her was the only reward he expected—a pretty big if—then she could endure it. What choice did she have anyway? The answer to that was becoming painfully familiar. No choice at all.

"Then as long as you're going to stand there playing voyeur, do you suppose you could hand me the soap?" she asked.

"Sure." He took a step backward and picked it up off the table, riffling the pile next to it for a facecloth while he was at it. "In fact," he said, carrying both over to the tub and dropping to his knees beside it, "I'm going to do better than hand it to you." His heavy-lidded expression made Liz very uneasy. "I'm going to wash you."

"No," she yelped. Then, gathering her composure: "Really, that isn't necessary."

"It is if I say it is," he declared quietly, dipping the faded green washcloth into the water and slowly rubbing it with the soap until he'd worked up a white, foaming lather. "And I definitely say it is."

She was sitting with her knees drawn up to her chest, partly so she would fit into the tub and partly to shield her breasts from his eyes. Now he slipped his hand beneath one bent knee and straightened it. Liz flinched and tried unsuccessfully to jerk away from him.

"I always start with the feet first," he explained, ignoring her frantic twisting movements. Slowly he ran the soapy cloth over her foot, heedless of the drops of water splashing on the floor.

Liz gritted her teeth. He was doing it again, she thought in disgust. Saying things that made this seem like something different than it was. As if they were here together as man and woman instead of captor and victim. So he *always* started with the feet, did he?

"What a pity," she commented, attempting to hide her nervousness behind sarcasm. "Haven't you ever found a woman you didn't have to wash first?"

McCabe laughed from deep in his chest, looking not the

least bit offended by her intended slur. "There must have been one or two, I suppose. But I don't mind. This is sort of like unwrapping a present done up in plain brown paper on the chance you'll find something special or magical underneath." He had finished washing one leg to the knee and manipulated her stiff muscles to do the same to the other. His touch was light, giving Liz no added pain from her injuries as he brought his face close to hers and asked, "How deep will I have to go to find the magic in you, Liz Randolph?"

Liz stiffened, alarmed by what sounded like a very suggestive question. "I have no idea what you're talking about."

McCabe pulled away slightly, his laughter soft, taunting. "No. I suppose you don't."

Again he tried to maneuver her into the position he desired, but Liz tightened the muscles of her legs so they were nearly impossible to move. She cried out when he retaliated by squeezing her knee painfully.

"Relax," he ordered. "Like it or not you're going to get used to having my hands on your body. I'm going to touch you when I want and where I want, and you're going to learn not to flinch when I do. We're supposed to be lovers, remember? I'll be putting my hands on you quite a bit."

Feeling mortified and helpless to do anything about it, Liz stared fixedly at an insect slowly making its way up the opposite wall. Anything was better than looking at his leering face or at his hands, which were moving higher on her legs all the time. She had no doubt that he was intentionally drawing the experience out to prolong her discomfort. He was worse than an animal. He was a monster, deliberately humiliating her as a prelude to the even worse indignities she was convinced would follow.

"And you'll have to get used to touching me," he added, clearly bent on provoking a response from her.

Liz wished she had the self-control not to bite, but she didn't. She spun her head around to see his eyes flashing like the devil's own. "I'd rather be shot," she spat.

"I'm sure you would," acknowledged McCabe dryly. "Unfortunately I'm afraid your fate in the hands of my men would be considerably more sordid than that."

Liz trembled violently as he slid the cloth higher still, washing the outside of one leg all the way to the hip, then coasting back behind her knees and doing the other leg. "Why don't you just try pretending I'm your fiancé," he suggested in an insinuating drawl. "You do touch him, I assume?"

"That's none of your damn business. Besides," Liz added, somehow managing to keep the tremors racking her nerves from sounding in her voice, "I don't have a good enough imagination to pretend that you're him. You're everything he's not. . . . You are a mean, vulgar, lying, cheating bully who is totally without any redeeming qualities whatsoever."

McCabe whistled between his teeth as if favorably impressed. "So what does that leave for lover-boy?" he asked.

"Everything worth being. Kirk is kind and decent and caring. And he would never, ever force me to do anything against my will,'' she concluded on a slightly desperate note of triumph.

The movements of his cloth-swathed hand had been slow and circular. Now, without preamble, his touch grew firm. As if sparked by her last remark, he swept the inside of her leg with a long stroke that brought his hand high and hard between her thighs.

"Poor Kirk," he murmured, twisting his wrist so his palm cupped the softly furred mound at the apex of her legs. "He doesn't know what he's missing."

Liz gasped. Every nerve in her body started clamoring, flashing a confusion of signals to her brain. She tried to back away from the heated pressure of his hand, but there was nowhere to go in the cramped confines of the tub. Grabbing his forearm, she tried shoving him away instead.

"Stop it," she cried. "How dare you touch me, you bas . . .''

"Ah, ah," he interrupted, grinning broadly. "Never swear at a man who's holding a bar of soap . . . unless, of course, you want to eat it."

His gaze locked with hers, his eyes dark and hot, hers wide and vulnerable. Slowly the grin slipped from his face. His hand stayed where it was, and Liz was vehemently aware of the way all the blood in her body seemed to be rushing to that spot and pounding wildly against him. She was afraid McCabe could feel it as well, afraid of what he might think. Just when she thought she would scream from the silent tension arcing between them, he broke the fiery point of contact, slowly sliding his hand up over her belly, resuming his swirling strokes in a path that crisscrossed her ribs. With his long reach he was easily able to scrub the narrow width of her back without moving from his kneeling position beside her.

Liz shifted her gaze unseeingly to a spot somewhere over his shoulder, but she could feel his eyes still riveted on her, searching for what she could only imagine. Signs of weakening? Of arousal? Was the man such a total Neanderthal he thought she might be excited by the way he was treating her? She locked her teeth shut as she felt the cloth move over her breasts, careful to let her expression reflect her revulsion. But he didn't linger as she feared he might. Instead, with an efficiency of motion, he quickly moved on to wash her shoulders and the back of her neck. And he started to whistle. It was the whistle that really got to her. She was seething from the indignity of what he was doing to her, and he was blithely whistling through his teeth as if it were no more outrageous or important than waxing his car.

Finally, dropping the cloth into the water, he leaned his folded arms on the edge of the tub. "Feel better now?"

Liz angled her head to look at him, scrutinizing his quiet question for some sinister meaning or double entendre, fully prepared to lash out at him. But it seemed straightforward enough, and besides, she had nothing to gain from arguing with him. Finally she shrugged. "Yes." It was true. Despite the circumstances of the bath, it did feel better to be clean. With another small shrug she impulsively added, "Thank you."

For what? the defiant part of her screamed. For not humiliating you as much as he could have? For not brutalizing you? Yet. It was a fine situation she'd gotten herself into when she had to thank a man for such "kindnesses."

"My pleasure," replied McCabe.

The words hung in the air between them. Liz knew she wasn't imagining the sensuous shading his gravel-edged voice had given the words any more than she was imagining the desire that was darkening his eyes to glossy black pools. She told herself she should move away, but she was loath to stand and give him another close-up look at what he'd already handled so freely. There was something else holding her there as well, something besides the precious remnants of her pride. It wasn't anything she could see or touch, but it bound her just the same, keeping her sitting there as the water cooled and McCabe's eyes grew heated and hooded. It was more of an instinct, one far older than she was and well beyond her control. She sensed that ever so slowly his mouth was drawing closer to hers. If she didn't do something fast, McCabe was going to kiss her. She was vaguely surprised that the realization didn't send her flying from the tub in a wet panic. She didn't want to kiss him. Not really. But she couldn't deny the fact that a small part of her was fascinated by the possibility.

She still hated him, but her heart was pounding and the blood was rushing through her head with such force she doubted she could even hear him if he spoke now. And between her thighs there was a tight, tingling sensation that filled her with shame. It had all started when he touched her there. Abruptly Liz gripped the rim of the tub with both hands, renewed determination clearing away her confusion. She wouldn't, would not, let McCabe bully and threaten and manhandle her, then show her a little kindness the way you would throw a dog a bone and have her panting for more of whatever he felt like dishing out.

She set her jaw and eyed him frostily. "If you're quite through, I'd like to get out now. I'm getting cold in here."

McCabe stopped angling toward her. His only movement was the slight, surprised lifting of black brows that sent a wave of elation crashing over Liz. It felt wonderful to be the one to thwart him for a change, especially when he'd obviously been so cocksure she was going to sit as still as a gentled mare for his kiss.

"We're *almost* through," he replied after a short silence. His hand lifted to the back of her neck as he added, "There's only one thing left to wash . . . your face."

Liz stiffened as she felt him start to force her head down, but he was too quick for her, and much too strong.

"No . . . wai—"

The rest of her protest emerged as bubbles as she was bent at the waist and her head totally submerged beneath the soapy water. The instant he released his hold on her neck she came up sputtering, her eyes flashing with rage.

"You . . ." She broke off, too incensed to think of anything rotten enough to call him. "Oooooh."

"Upset?" he queried blandly. He was standing now. "Wait until I tell you that there's no shampoo and you'll have to settle for just a rinse." Without warning, he raised the bucket she hadn't noticed him holding and sent the contents pouring down on her.

The water in this last bucket wasn't heated, and Liz leaped to her feet in shock. She was shivering from head to toe as she raked the soaked clumps of hair back from her face. She was feeling furious enough to kill him if he gave her another chance with that gun. Finally opening her eyes, she found him standing close, too close, the towel in his hands opened invitingly wide.

"*Now* you're done," he announced solemnly, but his eyes were bright with repressed laughter. "Like some help drying off?"

"No. Just get away from me. And stay away." She snatched the towel from his hands and wrapped it around her body before stepping out of the tub.

"Suit yourself," McCabe said to her back as she walked away.

Liz had spied another towel on the table by the door and was reaching for it when he deftly beat her to it.

"Oh, no, you don't, baby. I might take seconds on the bathwater, but my towel is all mine. You know something, though?" he asked, leaning back to gaze at her face consideringly, as if it were the first time he'd seen it. "Once you scrape away all that dirt and grime, that's a pretty fancy face you've got."

Liz turned and walked back across the room without responding. She'd decided not to talk to him. If he wanted her silent and subservient, that's what he'd get. And at the same time she could deny him any pleasure he derived from baiting her. Pressing the cotton shirt she'd worn earlier into service as a towel, she dried her arms and legs, aware of the sounds of him shucking his boots and jeans and climbing into the tub behind her.

"Santana sent over some stuff to take care of your feet,"

he told her as she stood trying to figure out the most strategic way to get her clothes back on without dropping the towel. "It's on the table over there by the door. There are also some clothes there for you to wear ... jeans and some sort of top and an old pair of her sneakers. I told her you probably wouldn't be able to squeeze into them, though."

Liz flinched and had her mouth open to retaliate before she remembered she wasn't going to engage in any more verbal dart throwing with him.

"Of course, if they don't fit you," he went on, "you can always wear what you had on when I came in. That was the sort of getup to really turn a man's head."

She couldn't have cared less about turning his head. But the remark about fitting into the other woman's clothes had smacked of challenge, and Liz impulsively crossed the room and picked them up along with the small bottle of antiseptic and rolls of gauze and tape. The sneakers she could make do with even if she had to leave them untied, and the top, a sleeveless red T-shirt, she was sure would fit. But the jeans, she worried, might be another matter. On her way back to the bed she surreptitiously inspected them to no avail. If there had once been a tag with the size written on it, it was gone.

Even without glancing his way, Liz could feel McCabe watching her expectantly as she sat on the edge of the mattress and took her time patching up her feet. The antiseptic stung, and she bit her lip as she slowly dabbed the liquid on the broken blisters at the back of her heels and sides of her toes. Devising a makeshift bandage that stayed put took longer than she would have imagined. Even so, all too soon she was finished and forced to face the moment of truth. Glancing forlornly at the faded jeans waiting beside her, Liz decided they might glide on more easily over panties than damp skin. She glanced around to see where McCabe had flung hers. They weren't on the bed, or under it. With her eyes safely focused on the floor and away from the half of his body visible above the water line, she circled the tub in search of them.

"Is this by any chance what you're looking for?"

At the sound of McCabe's voice Liz looked up in time to see him hoist her soaked underwear from beneath the water. She nodded.

"I washed them for you," he explained, flashing her an outrageous grin as he twisted the bit of silk in his big hands until all the water was squeezed out. He tossed them across the room, managing to hook them on the back of the chair as neatly as if he'd walked over and hung them there. "They'll be dry for you by morning. For tonight you'll just have to make do without them."

The sight of him handling something as intimately hers as underwear turned Liz's cheeks scarlet. She longed to grab them off the chair and hide them from his eyes by stuffing them under the pillow. But she knew if she did, she'd be the one wearing soggy underwear come morning. Sighing, knowing she'd used up her last stalling measure, she reached for the jeans.

The first thing she did was clamp down tightly with her upper arms to anchor the towel in place. Then she stepped into the jeans and pulled them up. Liz knew as they slid over her hips it was going to be a close call and started to pray. It had to be the prayer that enabled her to get the button fastened—barely—but it didn't work nearly as well on the zipper. Liz stopped praying and yanked. It still wouldn't budge. The two sides were too far apart. She tried again. Nothing. Behind her McCabe cleared his throat. Her fingertips ached from gripping the metal pull tab. She was about to admit defeat and slink into the larger cotton slacks in defeat when she remembered a tip she'd once read in a fashion magazine and in desperation lay down on the bed.

Ignoring the deep chuckle that drifted over from the area of the tub, she held the two sides of the zipper as closely together as she could get them and gave one last, violent tug. The fly closed with a hiss and Liz rolled to her feet as if accompanied by a blare of trumpets. McCabe acknowledged her victory with a grin and a nod, and stared so hard at the too-tight jeans that Liz wondered if she wouldn't have been safer, not to mention more comfortable, in the loose cotton pants after all. Well, it was a little late now. She was half dressed and not about to backtrack. Resignedly she started to squirm into the red T-shirt, inching the towel down as she went. It was snug, but not as bad as the jeans. Even so, she never would have worn such a clinging knit without a bra, regardless of how hot a day it was. The sneakers fit best of all, but she still left the laces loose to avoid aggravating the blisters she already had.

Being clean and dressed in fresh clothes had a positive effect on her spirits. She didn't feel quite so downtrodden and hopeless. In fact, she felt closer to exhilaration than she imagined she could under the circumstances. The bath must have also started whatever creative juices she possessed flowing, because as she draped her wet towel over the other side of the chair to dry, it occurred to her that even without talking to him she could give McCabe a taste of his own medicine.

Slowly, taking delight in every preparatory move, she shifted her panties and the towel from the chair to the wall hooks and then carried the chair to a spot about four feet away from the tub. After carefully wiping any traces of water from the seat, she proceeded to sit down facing McCabe, her legs crossed, her posture relaxed, as if she were waiting for the curtain to go up. Except that it already had, and Liz couldn't wait to see how he liked being ogled and stared at and regarded with a smug parody of a smile while he was engaged in what should be a private act.

She didn't have to wait long. McCabe leaned as far back as he could and hooked his hands behind his neck. He ought to look ridiculous, squeezed into that tiny tub, his knees and elbows sticking out all over. But he didn't, no matter how it galled Liz to admit it. He looked comfortable. And confident. And very male. Water polished his dark skin and sparkled in the black forest of curly hair on his chest and under his arms. He wasn't bad-looking, she decided. Just cursed with the sort of roughly chiseled features which had never appealed to her. All muscle and no brain. Give her an Alan Alda type any day. There was a man who fairly glowed with sensitivity. Actually, that was who Kirk always reminded her of, a blond Alan Alda. She doubted Zachary McCabe could spell sensitivity, much less feel it. Even at those moments today when he'd seemed the least menacing, as when he'd first seen the cuts on her feet, she'd sensed a certain violence behind the gentleness in his eyes, and danger lurking just beneath his smile.

"Enjoying yourself?"

His measured drawl startled her from her critique of his appearance. Just in time she remembered her vow of silence and, instead of fumbling for a witty reply, responded with only a small nod and an even smaller smile.

"Good. Because seeing as you're so interested in my bath, I'm going to give you a real thrill and let you participate."

His meaning hit Liz at the same instant the sopping facecloth landed in her lap, soaking her jeans and shooting water up at her face.

"Scrub my back, woman," he ordered.

A quick glance at his face told her he was utterly serious, and her quick flash of anger faded into trepidation. She held the dripping rag away from her, her head shaking back and forth as her mind flirted with a visual image of what he was asking . . . no, *commanding* her to do. It had been bad enough having to sit there and endure his touch on her body. It would be a million times worse to have to touch him, to have to move her hands over his taut flesh, to wash that broad, hard-muscled back and whatever else he should decide needed washing after that.

"No, please," she whispered. "I can't . . ." The sudden narrowing of his eyes censored her. "I mean, I don't want to do it."

"But you will if I tell you to. You know that."

"I know." She nodded, too appalled to feel resentful. "But I'm asking you not to make me. Please."

"Please what? I want to hear you use my name."

"Please, Mc . . . McCabe."

"Uh-uh. Zach. Please, Zach."

"Please, Zach."

He hesitated and for a minute Liz thought he intended to make her beg and then force her to do what he wanted anyway. Then he held his hand out and after a second of bewilderment she realized he was waiting for her to return the facecloth. She did so eagerly, careful to stay a few safe steps away from the tub.

"Now, why don't you make yourself useful by bringing those dirty dishes back to Santana before I change my mind? You might even offer to wash them for her. That is," he added, a smirk in his voice, "if you have any idea how."

Liz collected the dishes and fled. She was so grateful for the reprieve she didn't think to be frightened of walking the short, dark distance between the two huts alone. Santana opened the door almost as soon as she knocked. Her English turned out to be as shaky as Liz's Spanish, but somehow they managed to communicate with a rudimentary combination of simple sounds and sign language. Santana smiled and murmured *"Gracias"* when Liz rubbed her tummy to signal her appreciation for the food. She quickly swept aside Liz's offer to wash the dishes she and Zach had used, gesturing that her children were both asleep and she was afraid they would wake up if Liz came inside.

Liz longed to confide in the other woman and see if she couldn't suggest some alternative to relying on McCabe for protection. Liz would even be willing to stay here until Santana's husband returned and pay him to bring her back to

San Luis. Just as she was about to attempt to communicate this request, she had second thoughts. It would be nearly impossible to explain in sign language everything that had happened, and if she lingered too long trying, McCabe was liable to come out looking for her. He would make short work of contradicting anything she had managed to get across, no doubt turning on that same melting smile he'd used so successfully on Santana earlier. As indifferent as he appeared to be, insisting that he was dragging her along for *her* safety, Liz suspected he was also thinking of his own and would foil any attempt she made to get away. Besides, she knew that down here the male's power over the female was every bit as pervasive as he'd claimed. She wouldn't want to be responsible for Santana incurring her husband's wrath by being caught scheming against his amigo McCabe.

Reluctantly Liz bid her good night, cringing when she responded with a sly smile that told Liz she had exactly the wrong impression of her relationship with the steely-eyed McCabe. Liz only prayed that would still be true in the morning. Her expression grim, she turned and headed back toward the other hut and the long night still ahead.

CHAPTER
SEVEN

Liz wasn't surprised when she reentered the hut to find that McCabe had already finished his bath and dried off. He was in his underwear, leaning over the tub. Without saying a word she moved away from the door and stuck close to the wall, far from the bed, trying to be as inconspicuous as possible. Not an easy task in such cramped quarters.

McCabe hardly looked at her and said only six curt words: "You want to open that door?"

Liz did . . . quickly. Then she stood by and watched as he emptied the tub. She told herself she was watching because there was nothing else to look at or to do in the hut, but the truth was that his big, barely clad body intrigued her almost as much as it terrified her. She figured him to be about ten years older than she, somewhere in his late thirties. Maybe even forty. But his body was in better condition than many men half that age. Most of the men she knew had muscles that looked as if they were the result of some rowing machine tucked away in the bedroom. McCabe's muscles, on the other hand, looked like the result of life, and a hard-lived one at that.

She suspected it had something to do with the deep bronze of the skin which covered them so tautly. It was the sort of dark, weathered hue you didn't get lounging around a pool on weekends. There was also the matter of the various and sundry scars marring his skin. Her studiously casual observation took in several older-looking ones on his back and legs, and there was evidence of a more recent, more serious looking slash along the left side of his ribs. Liz knew it was crazy, but seeing them filled her mind with visions of knife fights in seamy waterfront bars and dangerous, clandestine rendezvous in the rain. Ridiculous fantasies. But knowing that didn't stop her pulse from quickening with excitement. What *was* Zachary McCabe's business in Guatemala?

He left the tub outside, closing the door behind him with a bang that snapped Liz back to reality in a flash. Reality was that narrow bed in the corner. Reality was the lamplight flickering over the sculptured planes of his chest and the long, muscled legs that stretched from his snug white briefs to the floor.

"I guess it's about that time," he drawled.

Liz stopped breathing and pressed herself more closely against the wall at her back, wishing she could melt right through it and be free.

Oblivious to her efforts to disappear, McCabe ambled

over to the bed and turned down the woven blanket which was neatly tucked under the sides and bottom of the mattress. Beneath it was a clean-looking white sheet.

"Do you want the inside or outside?" he asked.

Forcing each word around the lump in her throat, Liz said, "I beg your pardon?"

"The inside or the outside?" His voice was clipped. "The wall or the edge. C'mon, what's it going to be? I'm not going to stand here all night waiting for you to make up your mind."

"Neither." The single-word answer was so soft even Liz could hardly hear it. She cleared her throat and tried again. "Neither. I don't want any part of that bed."

"Oh, for Christ's sake." He dragged his fingers through his still-damp hair. "I'm warning you, lady, I'm not in the mood for this."

"It's what you *are* in the mood for that worries me," Liz summoned the courage to blurt.

He ran his eyes over her consideringly, making her aware all over again of how tightly Santana's jeans and T-shirt clung to her full hips and breasts. When he finally brought his gaze back to meet hers, it was strangely detached, almost bored.

"It's certainly not *you* I'm in the mood for, if that's what's got you standing frozen in that corner like Lot's wife. I should have made it clear earlier, but I guess I was sort of enjoying that scared rabbit look of yours. It's like this, Liz," he continued in an exaggeratedly solemn manner. "I like my women to be a little more than clean. I like them willing. Eager even. So you can come to bed. I promise I won't lay a hand on you.''

She wasn't gullible enough to fall for that line. That was a bed and he was a man. And while he might, as he kept insisting, find her less than lust inspiring, the fact remained that other than the wife of a friend, she was the only woman around. She wasn't going to make this any easier for him. If he wanted her in that bed with him, he was going to have to drag her there fighting and screaming the whole way.

Fully prepared for that to happen, Liz glanced around for something to defend herself with.

"Oh, I get it," he concluded wearily in the face of her wild-eyed expression. "You think this is all some sort of trick to get you over here."

"No," Liz quickly lied. "No, I don't think that at all. I would simply prefer to sleep over here."

He shrugged and fired the extra blanket at her before climbing into the bed. "You won't get any argument from me. This bed's plenty small as it is." He leaned up on one elbow and lifted the glass globe off the lamp, pausing to glance over at Liz before blowing out the flame. "I would recommend that you choose that chair over the floor, though. No sense tempting any scorpions that might be crawling around. Sweet dreams."

Liz squeezed her eyes shut at the mention of scorpions. When she opened them a few seconds later, the room was in darkness. It had been her intention to spend the night on the floor if she were lucky enough to escape his bed, but the possibility of sharing it with deadly scorpions gave rise to second thoughts. There was just enough moonlight slanting through the open window for her to see the chair, and she cautiously made her way over to it, sat down, and gathered the roughly woven blanket around her. The back of the chair hit her about shoulder-blade level, providing no support for her neck or head. Each time she started to drift off she had the sensation she was falling and jerked upright, wide awake again.

This wasn't going to work. Even if she moved the chair against the wall and somehow managed to get to sleep sitting up, more than likely she would end up falling to the floor anyway, and maybe injuring herself. Sore feet were bad enough; she didn't feel like having to go through the rest of this ordeal with a broken arm too. She was forced grimly to rethink the scorpion situation. McCabe could have been simply exercising his cruel streak again, trying to frighten her. But even if there were scorpions sharing their humble abode, what was to stop one from crawling up onto the chair? Or, for that matter, into the bed in which he was already sleeping so soundly? On that cheerful thought she moved to the floor, wrapping herself as completely as possible in the blanket for protection, and fell asleep to the soft, snuffly sound of McCabe's snoring.

She awoke sometime later feeling cold, surrounded by total blackness. Even the sliver of moonlight had disappeared, and Liz could only guess where the window was located. Outside she detected the steady drone of a downpour, and she suddenly realized why she was shivering; she was soaking wet . . . or at least her legs were. There must be a leak in the thatched roof, and she'd been unfortunate enough to pick the spot directly under it to sleep. There wasn't much she could do about it except move. She certainly wasn't about to risk waking McCabe by fumbling about in the pitch darkness for dry clothes. Swinging around so her legs were pointed in a different direction, she burrowed deeper into the half-wet blanket and wondered how long it would be until morning.

This time the drops of water landed on her chin, a rapid-fire battery of them that slithered down her throat and into the warm valley between her breasts. She'd thought she had moved away from the leak, but obviously she had only twisted so her head was in the line of fire. Shivering, Liz shifted position again, first to the left, then, after feeling a drop land on her hair, to the right. Without light it was hard to get her bearings. For a few seconds she lay still, listening. She couldn't feel anything yet, but she could swear she heard the measured thump of raindrops hitting some part of the blanket. Stretching her arm down past her knees, she turned her palm up experimentally. Sure enough, a cold, wet drop plopped into it dead center. Then another. Feeling her nerves tighten with frustration, Liz rolled over several times, bumping into the chair as she went and coming to a halt up against the door. Now she knew for sure she was at least eight feet from where she'd first felt the leak, and as a stream of water started to trickle downward from her temple, she knew just as surely that the roof above her had more holes than a bag lady's shoes.

She gave up. She'd been manipulated, battered, threatened, bullied, humiliated, and now, when she finally had a few hours' respite from McCabe before facing whatever fresh trauma he had planned for tomorrow, nature had joined the conspiracy against her. She couldn't fight everything at once. In fact, she was sick and tired of fighting, period.

From his bed Zack heard the muffled noise and at first wasn't sure what was causing it. Gradually, as his grogginess cleared, he realized it was the sound of someone quietly sobbing. His mouth twisted in the darkness. Yeah, it was *someone* all right. What the hell was the matter with her now? It had been her bright idea to sleep on the floor, not his. No doubt she'd expected him to beg her to be sensible and take half the bed. No, he amended in disgust, she'd probably thought he would eventually give in an let her have the whole bed while he got a backache sleeping on that stone floor. After all, he'd been sap enough to take pity on her when her feet hurt and lugged her the rest of the way here on his back . . . a foolish act of machismo he'd be paying for in the form of stiff muscles for at least a week. Then he had obligingly stepped aside and allowed her first crack at the tub, just as any well-trained, housebroken male would have. But that was as far as he planned to go and Ms. Society over there had better face it. He'd never been very good at playing the gentleman, even when he used to try. And he'd stopped trying years ago.

Rolling over so he was facing the wall, he pulled the pillow over his head and closed his eyes, determined to sleep through her tantrum. It didn't work. Either his imagination was rolling along in high gear or she was crying harder and louder. Shoving the pillows aside, he levered up on his elbows, squinted in the direction of the noise, and cut right to the heart of the matter.

"What the hell is the matter with you now?"

It sounded as if she was struggling to catch her breath between sobs before she could answer. Finally he heard a creaky "Nothing."

More games. "Then do you mind telling me why the hell you're crying?"

"I always cry when I'm freezing," she snapped. Zach took the flash of anger mixed in with the crying to be an encouraging sign that she was starting to feel more like herself again.

"How can you possibly be freezing? It's September and you're in Central America, for chrissake. Besides, I gave you a blanket."

"Big bloody deal," she cried. Zach heard her moving, but he was still taken by surprise when the blanket whipped across the room and whammed him in the face. She had a pretty good arm for a woman. "There's your blanket," she ground out. "You didn't tell me the damn roof leaked."

Zach ran his fingers down the blanket and found that it was indeed wet. Very wet. Which explained why she was so cold. Although the humidity was still high, the temperature had dropped since they turned in, and trying to sleep on a stone floor with only a wet blanket for protection had to be damned uncomfortable. Of course that didn't explain why she was still lying there in tears. Hadn't he offered to share the bed? There was nothing to stop her from giving him a nudge and telling him she'd changed her mind. Nothing, it suddenly occurred to Zach, except all that stubborn pride of hers. He smiled ruefully. That kind of pride was like a shot of Novocain to your common sense. It could send you marching to your death, shaking in your boots every step of the way, rather than give in. He ought to know.

"Liz, I didn't know the roof leaked," he said quietly. "If I had known, I would have insisted you sleep up here with me."

"I'd *rather* sleep in the rain than with you," she shot back.

Zach's hands curled into tight fists and his teeth clenched on the urge to ask her how she felt about spending the rest of the night gagged and tied to the bed. There had to be a better way to handle this. A way to avoid having it explode into a full-blown confrontation that would prevent either of them from getting any more sleep tonight. Only he had no idea what that way might be.

Feeling around on the crate for his lighter, he finally found it and lit the lamp. The sight of her curled up on the floor by the door hit him harder than he would have thought. Probably because she looked so small all of a sudden, more like a child than a woman. The front of her pants was wet from her thighs almost to her ankles, although the rest of her looked pretty dry. She was facing him, staring down at her huddled arms, and her shoulders were twitching at regular, frequent intervals. Hiccups, he deduced with a resigned sigh.

Throwing the wet blanket aside, he peeled back the covers and walked over to hunker down beside her. Unconsciously he touched her shoulder, whipping his hand away very consciously when she flinched at even that slight contact.

"Why didn't you move when you first felt yourself getting wet?" he asked.

"I did." He had to dodge the sudden, wild sweep of her outstretched arm. "There are leaks all over this place... everywhere I went."

Glancing briefly at the scattered puddles on the floor, Zach acknowledged the truth of what she said, and he felt another twinge of something. Certainly not guilt. It wasn't his fault she chose to play pristine martyr rather than get close to him. Hadn't he given her his word he wouldn't touch her? Of course, what he hadn't given her was any reason to believe his word was worth more than a Confederate dollar.

"There aren't any leaks over the bed," he pointed out. "That's probably why Armando's brother put it where he did. Want to change your mind about sharing it with me?"

"No."

"Listen, Liz, you can't spend the rest of the night here on the floor."

Her only response was another hiccup with eyes averted. At least she wasn't arguing or making wild, impassioned statements about how she would never, *ever* share that bed with the likes of him.

"You'll catch something if you don't get off this floor and get dry," he warned. "Maybe pneumonia." Zach hesitated. She didn't look as if she had much jungle savvy, so he dropped his voice to a more critical note and risked adding, "Or malaria."

She still didn't respond, but he saw an indication of

weakening in the way her teeth began nibbling her bottom
lip.

"I have an idea, sort of a deal," he ventured, improvis-
ing as he went.

She sniffled. "What sort of deal?"

He wanted to say: This sort of deal. You get your ass into
that bed on your own and I won't twist your arm behind
your back and force you into it. But he didn't, and he
wasn't quite sure why.

"Just this," he said instead. "You take the side of the
bed near the wall and get under the covers. I'll take the
outside and stay on top of the blanket. That ought to work
for the couple of hours we've got left before daybreak." He
took a chance and hooked his finger under her chin, exerting
only the gentlest force to get her to look at him. "What do
you say, fancy face? Is it a deal?"

Liz scoured his expression for some sign of the devious
intent she was sure he harbored, but she couldn't find any.
At the moment he didn't look devious, or particularly
threatening. He looked hopeful and about as bone tired as
she felt. There were probably a million good reasons why
she shouldn't trust him, and no doubt in the morning she
would be beating herself over the head with every one of
them. But right now she was cold and exhausted and aching
all over, and the pleasure of snuggling beneath a dry blanket
on a real mattress seemed worth any risk.

"It's a deal," she agreed.

McCabe released a long sigh and extended a hand to haul
her to her feet. "Thank God. I was beginning to think the

only way I'd get any more sleep tonight was to switch places with you."

Liz came up beside him with her eyes gleaming. Maybe she had surrendered too easily. "Would you have?"

Ignoring the question, McCabe moved to pick up the pair of loose cotton trousers which had slid from the bed to the floor. Tossing them to Liz, he ordered, "Put these on . . . I'm not sharing the bed with you in those wet pants. And could we please not make a major production out of it this time?"

"Certainly. If you'll please turn around this time."

He did, muttering under his breath things Liz sensed she was lucky not to hear. She quickly changed into the dry slacks and flung the wet ones over the back of the chair to dry before walking over to stand beside him.

"Well, would you have?" she asked for the second time. "Switched places with me, I mean?"

He cast a withering glance her way. "Of course not. Do I look to you like the kind of noble fool who'd put himself out for a broad?"

He didn't wait for an answer. Leaning in front of her, he flung back the covers and held them while Liz settled in. Then, as promised, he covered her with the blanket, blew out the lamp, and lay down beside her with Liz still turning his question over in her mind.

She thought a lot of unflattering things about Zachary McCabe, but that he was a fool was not among them. As for the other half of his question—was he noble enough to sacrifice himself for the sake of a woman?—wasn't that precisely what he had done by carrying her all the way here earlier? Of course, she still suspected he had his own reasons for keeping her with him, and she was too tired to try and figure out whether technically that made him more noble or selfish. The only thing she was sure of as the heat of his body reached hers through the blanket, helping to ease her into sleep, was that at least this one time her nemesis meant to honor his word.

She woke next morning cradled in the arc of sunlight spilling through the window, warm, comfortable, and to her relief quite alone. Somewhere outside a rooster was crowing and the air was already heavy with humidity. Her first thought was of McCabe and the memory of how she'd finally succumbed and let herself be coaxed into the small bed with him. Technically that probably qualified as a moral defeat, regardless of the fact that nothing had happened. Liz didn't regret it, though, primarily because she'd awakened feeling almost human, a state which at times yesterday she seriously doubted she would ever achieve again. But also because their brief exchange in the dark of the night—his concern, her anger, his overture, her acceptance—seemed to add a new dimension to their relationship . . . if you could stretch the term far enough to call this master-slave scenario a relationship.

It had given Liz further reason to suspect he might not be quite the consummate ogre he went out of his way to act like ninety-nine percent of the time. Of course she'd nursed a similar, fleeting hope after he'd carried her here, only to have it washed away when she was subjected to his humiliating version of rub-a-dub-dub. Just her luck to be stranded with a schizophrenic sadist, constantly throwing her off guard with his random bouts of decency only to zap her with some fresh act of mortification. The best she could do in the way of self-preservation was to try and encourage the Dr. Jekyll side of him every chance she had. Maybe if she acted as if she expected to be treated civilly he would respond by doing so. It was worth a shot anyway.

Sitting up, Liz pushed the blanket aside and stretched, triggering an immediate, all-out protest of yesterday's unaccustomed activity from every muscle in her body. More painful still was the realization that today only promised more of the same. Surely McCabe's camp couldn't be much farther. Otherwise why would he have been so foolish as to send the truck ahead, leaving himself without transportation back there?

Clinging hopefully to the belief that they couldn't have far to go, Liz swung her feet to the floor and gingerly eased her weight onto them. Instantly needles of pain arrowed upward from her blistered feet, making her wince. She had to grit her teeth and force herself to walk across the room, then back. Thankfully, with each step the abraded skin seemed to stretch and loosen so that after a few turns around the hut the pain had dulled enough for her to move with only a trace of a limp.

Her efforts at physical therapy came to an abrupt halt when the door swung open and she turned to find McCabe filling the doorway. Backlit by the morning sun, he looked fresh and well rested. And restless, full of a simmering energy Liz could sense clear across the room. It was different from the sheer danger he'd radiated most of yesterday, but just as potent. At that moment he reminded her of a very big cat on a very flimsy leash. She tried to shake the image. It was ridiculous, just one more fantasy that only served to make him seem larger than life and herself in more dire trouble than she probably was. That restless look no doubt signaled simply that he was eager to get back to . . . whatever it was he did. Think positively, Liz cautioned herself. Think Dr. Jekyll.

She pushed the corners of her lips upward in a big smile. "Good morning. You certainly look as if you had a good night's sleep."

Instantly his eyes creased with suspicion. Perfect. It wouldn't hurt to keep him off balance a bit.

"It wasn't bad," he conceded. "All things considered."

Liz elected to ignore that obvious reference to the night's disturbance. "Well, anyway, it looks like a gorgeous day outside. Sunny and best of all, dry. I wish I could say the same for these." She lifted the still-wet jeans from the chair. "But I suppose the heat of my body will dry them quickly enough."

"Leave them."

"I beg your pardon?"

"I said leave them. They're too tight on you."

"I thought we'd been through all that already?"

"We have and you proved that when your pride is at stake you can wiggle your bottom into pants a couple of sizes too small. But the Central American jungle is no place for tight clothing . . . or vanity either. Without getting too graphic, let me say that without the proper air circulation you'll have fungus growing all over you in no time . . . and there are varieties of fungus down here that will make you wish you could slice the flesh right off your body."

128

Shuddering, Liz knotted her arms across her chest. "Fungus . . . it sounds more like parasites."

He nodded. "There are plenty of those around too, which is why you have to wear something on your feet at all times. Sneakers aren't the best choice, because the spines from palm trees can slice through the rubber soles like a hot knife through butter, but they're still a whole lot better than those foolish things you had on yesterday."

"I didn't know . . ."

He overrode her attempt to explain that she hadn't dressed yesterday in preparation for a trek through the jungle. "Just as those pants you have on now are a better choice than the jeans. Besides," he added, amusement edging his deep voice, "you'll be much less of a . . . disruptive influence around camp wearing them than you would in those jeans."

That smacked of a compliment. Unreasonably flustered by it, Liz glanced down at the baggy cotton slacks. He made sense about their being more suitable. They were more comfortable than the jeans too. She just didn't like being ordered to wear them. "Anything else . . . *sir*?"

Grinning at her sarcastic use of the title, he countered, "No, I guess that about covers it for now . . . except for one slight modification." Producing a pocketknife, he crossed the room in two quick strides and crouched before her.

"What do you think you're . . . ?"

Before she finished asking the startled question, he had the knife flipped open and answered her by slashing away at the rolled-up legs of the pants, hacking them off just above the ankle.

"You'll be cooler this way," he explained, tucking the

knife away. "And there won't be any nooks and crannies for bugs to take up residence in."

Grimacing at the very idea, Liz glanced down to survey the ragged, uneven edges. Never in her life had she been so grateful to be made to look so foolish.

"Thank you," she said quietly, meaning it sincerely. First warning her about the fungus and now demonstrating such concern for her comfort—she could almost believe he was human.

For a moment McCabe appeared startled by her expression of gratitude, staring at her with such intensity it took every fiber of control Liz had left not to flinch. Finally he turned away with a shrug. "No problem. There's a bathroom— of sorts—out back if you need to use it, and Santana has breakfast waiting for you at her place. Just make it snappy," he added, but the gruffness lacked its usual razor edge. "I want to be at camp before full sun."

Before full sun? That sounded promising. "How far is your camp from here?" Liz queried.

"Not far."

That told her a lot. Not far in that they'd be there within an hour? Or not far in relation to the planet of Saturn? She'd learned enough about him in the past day not to risk prodding him to elaborate against his will. Especially now, when they seemed to be establishing an attitude of cooperation, however stilted. She didn't want to backslide and see her pal Jekyll fade while Hyde's fangs descended.

Hurriedly Liz made use of the outdoor facilities, splashing clean water on her face from a bucket outside and pressing a rolled-up corner of the facecloth into service as a crude toothbrush. She didn't even dawdle over breakfast as she would have liked to. The only thing she made time for between sips of the strong, sweet coffee and bites of scrambled eggs and peppers was to return the timid smiles of Santana's children.

The boy especially won Liz's heart, and with a sudden resurgence of that unique pain that never completely went away, she knew it was because he reminded her of Jeremy. It wasn't that he looked like him. He was dark and wiry, while Jeremy had been chubby and as golden as sunlight. But he was a boy, with a typical boy's spark of mischief in his eyes. And he looked to be about six, almost the same age Jeremy would have been now. Liz's appetite suddenly disappeared. Resolutely she pushed the half-eaten plate of food aside and with a final thank-you, left Santana and her children behind, along with the memories they'd uprooted. Not now. Not on top of everything else that had happened to her. Emotionally she couldn't afford right now to let herself linger over memories of Jeremy, to take them out one by one, treasuring and polishing them like the priceless, irre-placeable jewels that they were.

Fortunately she wasn't given much time to reminisce. McCabe was already waiting in front of the other hut when she left Santana's, the pistol jammed into the front of his jeans, machete swinging from his belt. His expression was hard-eyed and impatient, prompting Liz to quicken her step as she wove a path among the chickens and hens pecking in the dirt yard.

"Let's move," he said without preamble as soon as she reached his side.

"Wait."

"What for?" he asked with obvious reluctance.

"I thought I'd straighten up in here first," explained Liz, pointing in the direction of the hut. "After all, Santana . . ."

"It's already been taken care of," he cut in.

"Who . . . ?" Liz's eyes widened. "You? You made the bed?"

"What's the matter, fancy face, surprised I knew how?" His smile was mocking, and this time the twist he put on the nickname was blatantly derogatory. "Well, I do. You might have grown up with servants to do that sort of thing for you, but most of us had to learn to shift for ourselves."

On that placid note of condemnation he turned, crossed the rough clearing, and forged into the jungle beyond. Liz scurried in his wake, annoyed and puzzled by his sudden flash of animosity after she had made a special effort to be pleasant to him this morning. So much for her hopes of strengthening the budding lines of communication between them before reaching his camp. Even if he'd been in a receptive mood, it was difficult to communicate with a man charging a good ten yards ahead of you. A deliberate distancing, Liz was certain. Shooting daggers at his leather-clad back, she felt as if she were trapped in a rerun of yesterday. Her feet might be slightly more comfortable, but everything else was the same: the heat, the humidity, the ominous rustling of the wildlife all around her, pierced occasionally by the shriek of what could be either a bird or someone being strangled to death in the distance.

Not until they'd been trudging along for almost an hour was the monotony broken by a ribbon of brown cutting through the unchanging, textured expanse of multishaded green. Finally! A road, and one that looked exactly like the road she'd taken out of San Luis. Liz couldn't believe how the mere sight of something so narrow and mundane could thrill her to the point of giddiness.

Then it penetrated her euphoria that most roads in this country probably looked exactly like this one and any seedling of optimism about striking out on her own was quickly crushed from existence by the weight of common sense. Even if this proved to be the same road she'd set out on, a very important *if*, she was now so completely disoriented she hadn't the slightest idea which way would lead back to town and which would carry her deeper into the jungle. She didn't waste time even thinking about asking McCabe for directions.

Feeling weighted down with discouragement, she tried to keep up with him as he veered left across the road and followed it a short distance until they came to another one on their right. This one, to her amazement, was paved. Roughly paved, true, with an abundance of ruts and potholes scarring its weather-battered surface, but paved nonetheless. At the corner was a sign, its paint faded and peeling. With one leg broken and the other splintered, it reminded Liz of a person who had been driven to his knees. For some reason the sight of it tottering there made her skin prickle with an odd feeling of apprehension.

As they rounded the corner, McCabe's strong pace seemed to quicken even more, affording her little time to try to read what was written on the sign as she passed. Of the original wording all she could make out was a name, Valdivia. Most likely this was a private drive, which would explain why it was paved. Over the name something had been scrawled in Spanish with a can of red spray paint. And above it all, in black letters that looked official and forbidding, the words *Prohibida La Entrado*. Keep Out.

"McCabe," she shouted, "did you see that sign back there?"

He glanced over his shoulder without stopping. "Sure did."

"Well?" demanded Liz, feeling hot and exasperated and fed up to the teeth with this strong silent routine of his.

"Well, what about it?"

"It says keep out. Given the stories about how the local police force tends to shoot first and worry about sorting out the bodies later, don't you think it would be wise to heed that warning?"

At that he drew to a halt and slowly spun around to face her, waiting until she drew closer before responding. "You know, for an innocent American *turista* you sure know a lot about local police policies."

She should. Kirk had drilled her long and often about what would happen if they were caught in the act of trying to smuggle political refugees out of the country. Executing the elegantly detached shrug that was as much a result of her upbringing as her perfectly straightened teeth and fine-arts degree, she said, "It simply makes sense for one to research the customs of any unfamiliar area before visiting there for the first time."

McCabe nodded with a wry twist of his mouth. "Uh-huh."

"Just as it makes sense not to go traipsing across private property when there's a sign clearly warning against it."

"Ordinarily I'd agree. But we don't have a whole lot of choice. You see, camp is just over that next rise. Right smack in the middle of all this private property."

Liz greeted that news with violently mixed emotions. The next rise was only about fifty yards away. She was dying to stop walking, but not nearly so anxious to face the stares and speculation of McCabe's men. And she was even less eager to risk getting shot for trespassing. Smirking with disgust, she shook her head at McCabe. "What a stupid place to build a camp."

"First of all you don't *build* a camp," he informed her, mimicking her supercilious tone. "And secondly, you might say we have the owner's permission to be here."

"Mr. Valdivia?" Liz queried, her curiosity piqued.

"*Señor* Valdivia," he corrected. "Now, if you don't have any further objections, I've got a job to do."

She couldn't resist. "For Señor Valdivia?"

His eyes turned the color of a storm at sea. "Don't ask. That way you won't risk finding out anything you shouldn't know. And that goes for trying to wheedle information out of my men as well. I expect you to be seen and not heard." The gaze that drifted over her body was coolly appraising. "For that matter, it would be nice if you were seen as little as possible."

A quick gust of anger blew through all of Liz's good, prudent intentions. "What's the matter, McCabe, afraid of a little competition?"

"Could be," he drawled, although the angle of his smile

135

suggested how utterly ludicrous he found the notion. "I've heard desperate men sometimes develop strange cravings."

Liz wanted to retaliate by asking if he was referring to himself or to his cohorts when he used the term *desperate men*, but her courage faltered. They stood eyeing each other in hot, thick silence, like two pit bulls deciding whether to tangle or back off. It was as if last night had never happened. Where was that shred of compassion, of common decency she'd thought she had glimpsed in him? There wasn't even a whisper of anything so civilized in the harsh, intractable expression of the man standing before her now. This was the man who had held a gun to her head and reduced her to a limp mass of terror. She had locked horns with him before and lost, and she knew that if she were foolish enough to attempt it again it would end the same way.

Squaring her shoulders to surrender with dignity, she regarded him with icy composure. "All right, McCabe, I get the message."

"No, I don't think you do. At least not all of it. Try *I get the message, Zach*," he instructed as he had the night before. Only this time there was no hint of teasing in his eyes or his voice.

"I mean it," he added when she continued to glare at him with her lips pressed together in stubborn silence. "Calling me McCabe in that charmingly scathing way of yours isn't going to cut it. I can think of a dozen names I'd rather call you than Liz, and if I can resist, so can you."

"Oh, all right," she snapped, hoping to bring this latest losing round to a quick close. She hated to lose even a small battle, especially when she wasn't a hundred percent certain of the stakes.

"All right, what?" he pressed.

"All right, Zach," she forced through clenched teeth.

"Perfect," he pronounced, a sardonic grin hoisting the corners of his mouth. "That husky purr is a great touch, baby. . . . It ought to convince anybody within earshot."

"Yeah, but of what?" she muttered as he turned away.

She'd thought he wouldn't hear and wouldn't bother responding even if he did. Instead he whipped around, impaling her with his sharp, dark blue gaze. "Of the truth, of course. That I'm keeping you around because you're my own personal, convenient, willing, and eager supply of tit and ass."

CHAPTER EIGHT

After all her frantic worrying, their arrival in camp wasn't quite the nightmare Liz feared. As they crested the slight rise above the camp, she was startled to see below a clearing that was easily twice the size of Santana's farm. This exertion of man's will over nature's wasn't the result of recent efforts, however, as evidenced by the scattered patches where bushes and saplings were already thrusting through the black soil to reclaim their turf.

In the center of the clearing, its crumbled walls laced with trailing vines, sat the charred ruins of what had obviously once been a very large structure. The Valdivia home? Curiosity sent questions streaking through Liz's brain as she tried to absorb the scene before her in a series of rapid-fire impressions and at the same time calm her jitters over the imminent meeting with McCa...Zach's men.

The camp itself was located to their far right, on the very outskirts of the clearing. A city dweller by birth and by choice, Liz was distinctly unfamiliar with anything that smacked of "roughing it" and had been blithely envisioning their destination as a pup tent or so pitched amid the trees and vines. But before her was something more elaborate. Trotting down the hill behind Zach, she counted a half-dozen decent sized tents set in the form of a slight crescent and two more positioned closely behind them. Beyond that the jungle once more rose in a majestic wall of vegetation so that if viewed from the air or at a distance, the green nylon tents would blend with the native color. A pretty ingenious way to handle the problem of camouflage, Liz marveled grudgingly, at the same time wondering who it was they were hiding from.

As they drew closer she identified a whirring sound as coming from an electric generator positioned at the rear of the closest tent. Out in front was a long, low stove, more of a grill actually, with what looked like a propane gas tank at the end. An oversized metal coffeepot sat on a back corner, out of the way of the man busily scraping off burned-on food scraps. Several other men were gathered off to one side, laughing and drinking from shallow tin cups. All of them appeared to Liz to be natives, and all of them were dressed alike, in somber-colored work clothes that had seen much hard use.

One man happened to glance up as they approached, saw Zach, and his mahogany face took on a sudden whitish overtone. He quickly nudged the others, and as they hustled to their feet, Liz noticed a small glass bottle quickly disappear into a pocket. Zach had come to a halt about ten feet away from the group, with Liz at his side. She looked up at him, curious to see if he had noticed the same disappearing bottle, and the thunderous expression on his face told her beyond all doubt that he had. He was scowling as he had never, even at his angriest, scowled at her. The dark blaze of his eyes and the whiskers blackening his cheeks made him look like something spit up from the fires of hell.

"What are you doing here?" he asked the men.

His tone was soft but carried the full weight of a mighty anger, and the men responded by ducking their heads and shuffling their feet in the dirt. Their demeanor at that instant made Liz think of a bunch of harmless schoolboys caught in the act of some childish prank by their teacher. But everything else about them—their appearance, the snatches of bawdy conversation she'd been able to decipher as they approached, and most significantly, their very presence here—told her they were a long way from being either harmless or boys.

"I asked what you're doing here," repeated Zach, "and I want an answer. Carlos?"

He spoke just as quietly as he had the first time he asked that question, but his voice pierced the air with the precision of a dagger, promising an unspoken menace Liz didn't think anything alive—including Carlos, whichever one he was— would dare to ignore. She was holding her breath, as if she were the one facing his wrath, and when one of the men finally lifted his head to meet Zach's cold stare with a guilty shrug, she released it in an audible sigh of relief.

The man began a rapid explanation in Spanish, only to be halted by Zach's uplifted palm.

"In English, Carlos," he barked. "You know the rules. As long as you're working for me, you speak English."

"Perdoname," the man called Carlos mumbled, then quickly grimaced at his blunder. "I mean to say, sorry." He made a feeble gesture with the cup still clutched in his hand. "We were only having us breakfast."

Zach arrowed a glance at his watch. "It's nine o'clock," he pointed out matter-of-factly. "Breakfast was over two hours ago. And all of you should have been at work at the site shortly after that."

Liz snapped up the reference to a site of some sort and filed it away for future consideration. If she gleaned enough such thoughtlessly dropped clues, perhaps she could piece together what they were up to.

"I assume," Zach continued in the same crisp tone, "that Jade and the others are already over there?"

Their heads all bobbed in silence, like those statues of cats and dogs with heads mounted on springs that some people put in the rear windows of their cars. Biting the insides of her cheeks to keep from giggling at the incongruous sight, Liz directed her gaze to the ground as all four men grumbled halfhearted apologies.

"Save it," Zach told them. "I'll simply deduct two hours' pay from each of your accounts when we settle up."

Liz looked up in time to see the men's gazes coalesce into a single, fiery beam of resentment aimed at Zach. If he

141

noticed, he obviously wasn't fazed in the least by their silent display of hostility.

"Next I want the bottle," he announced.

Without hesitation the bottle reappeared, yanked from his pants pocket by a man with obsidian eyes and an evil-looking curl to his long mustache. He ambled over to slap it into Zach's outstretched palm.

"Where did you get it?" he asked the man.

The only reply was a slit-eyed stare that sent shivers up Liz's spine. Zach gave a short, harsh laugh as he shoved the bottle into the inside pocket of his vest.

"Okay, Rodil, have it your way. It doesn't take much to figure out the answer. Aside from myself, the only ones who have left this camp are Jade and Santiago. And there's no way you could talk Jade into sneaking tequila back here against my orders. Still, it's reassuring to see you display such loyalty. I didn't think you had *any* redeeming qualities."

The other man accepted the slur in silence. Only the rapid twitching of the muscle in his cheek hinted at the temper Liz sensed simmering inside him. After a minute he lifted his chin and in stiff English said, "Can we go now, *boss*? I wouldn't want to be deducted another hour."

"No, you can wait for me," instructed Zach. "I have a few things to take care of here, and then we'll all go out together."

This was it. Liz steeled herself as best she could. He had dealt with the problem of his truant crew and now he was going to deal with the problem of her, proclaiming for the benefit of the five men now all watching her with a mingling of surprise, curiosity, and unbridled lust that she was here for the express and lascivious purpose of servicing him in bed.

"Old Juan," he said, turning and for the first time addressing the man who'd been cleaning the grill.

"Yeah, boss," the other man responded. Older than the others, he was still every bit as disreputable looking with his white-whiskered chin and broken, yellow teeth exposed by his crooked smirk.

"Juan, the señorita here will be staying. So I'll need an extra cot set up in my tent."

That announcement was greeted by a murmur of low, knowing chuckles from the others that sent flames shooting through Liz, turning every inch of her skin scarlet. Zach silenced them with a look.

"Any comments?" he invited in a forbidding tone.

They all wisely refrained from making any.

"Good," he observed. "Keep it that way." Turning his attention back to Liz, he loosed a smile that she didn't trust for a second. "Old Juan handles the supplies and cooking," he explained, "so he'll be here at camp with you while I'm working."

Liz pressed her lips together tightly and nodded, attuned to the message behind the words. This aging degenerate was to act as her warden whenever Zach was otherwise occupied. As if to reinforce that, Zach slung an arm around her shoulders to gather her close and addressed the old man again.

"You won't let Liz wander away on me, will you, Juan?"

"No, sir, boss," the old man replied, squeezing the

words around a vulgar crackle of a laugh. "She won't get far from old Juan, you bet."

"You see, baby," Zach drawled, "I'm leaving you in good hands."

His fingers curled around her shoulder as he spoke, turning her in to him, and before Liz fathomed his intention his lips had swooped down to claim hers. She stiffened as if struck by lightning and brought her hands up to shove at his chest. He simply tightened his hold on her, pinning her hands uselessly between their bodies so that she had no choice but to stand there and let him take her lips, sealing a barrage of indignant protests deep in her throat.

His arm felt like a steel coil wrapped around her, lifting her onto her toes as his mouth raked over hers. The rough stubble of his beard stung the soft flesh around her mouth and the grinding pressure of his lips pinched hers against her teeth until she finally succumbed and parted them. He wasted no time claiming the soft, damp territory inside, at the same time maneuvering her so that the others were afforded a clear side view of the evocative pumping rhythm of his tongue. It was a calculated, physical reminder of her helplessness, and tears of frustration stung her closed eyelids, trickling down to salt their wetly fused mouths. This was purely an act of dominance. He was putting his brand on her publicly in a way that no one watching could misunderstand.

Abruptly the kiss changed in a way that was yet another shock to her volleying nervous system. Steeled to endure his brutal display of power, she was caught off guard when his lips and tongue gentled, suddenly seeking to soothe her senses instead of storming them. Liz's mind still screamed a protest, but her physical responses weren't so stubborn or so well governed. Her senses slowly began to thrum with a special awareness of him as a man, a sensation as old as time and every bit as beyond her control. Even as her thoughts reeled in confusion, a tremor of something that could only be called pleasure whipped through her body.

The kiss ended as suddenly as it began. Lifting his head, Zach stared deeply into her eyes, his own a swirl of indigo clouded by a tangle of emotions. Passion? Surprise? Bewilderment? Liz didn't know or care. Upon being freed, she fumbled briefly to regain her balance, infuriated that he hadn't released her more roughly so she could blame her unsteadiness on that instead of what she knew was the true cause. The instant she had both feet back squarely on the ground, her hand lifted and swung in a wide arc toward Zach's cheek, only to be stopped short when he snagged her wrist in midair.

"You bastard," she hissed, blinking back tears.

Maddeningly, he chuckled and leaned closer to brush his lips across her cheek. At the same time he whispered for her ears only, "You shouldn't have done that, fancy face."

Liz wasn't sorry in the least, but she was a little worried about what he might do now in retaliation. She was contemplating the merits of apologizing when the man named Rodil intervened.

"Hey, boss," he shouted. "Your lady don't look so pleased by you. Maybe you should let me try my hand at pleasing her."

"Be honest, amigo," urged one of his friends, "it's not your hand you're thinking about pleasing her with."

As they all laughed uproariously, Zach's eyes bit into hers, proclaiming more eloquently than words could have that this was all her fault. When he turned to face the men, however, he did so with one arm looped possessively around her shoulders and a smile that was slow and easy.

"The lady isn't displeased, just temporarily upset with me," he explained. "She's angry because I've told her I can't spare another day off work and that she'll have to wait until tonight to share my bed. She's impatient . . . isn't that so, my lady?"

Liz barely nodded in response to his asinine question. She was determined not to say or do anything to further encourage the snickers and knowing smiles that made her cringe inside. It seemed as if her breasts, their fullness clearly outlined by the clinging red T-shirt, were a magnet, attracting all eyes.

Giving her shoulder a meaningful squeeze, Zach stared down at her. "C'mon, baby, tell my friends how impatient you are to be back in my bed."

She ran her tongue over her lips, keeping her eyes focused on the dirt. "I . . ."

He squeezed harder. "Tell them."

"I . . . Zach's right. I am looking forward immensely to this evening."

"Good girl," he praised, his laugh-tainted words running over her taut nerves like razors. He was all but drowned out by the reaction of the others.

Their whoops and hollers startled Liz. Her words had

come out in such a high-pitched rush she couldn't imagine that even someone fluent in English could have understood them. Then it dawned on her that these men weren't responding to what she had said. They couldn't care less about anything she—a mere woman—had to say, only that she had spoken on command. Zach had snapped his fingers and she had heeled. That had been the point of this entire scene, she realized, anger erupting full force inside her. All Zach's talk about the necessity of her acting as if they were lovers was just that, talk. One more perverse way to amuse himself at her expense. It wasn't important that these men believe she wanted to be here. Only that they understand that Zach had the power to make her stay whether she liked it or not.

That he wanted her here, that he *wanted* her, period, was the crucial fact. In their recognition and acceptance of her as their leader's personal property lay her safety. It was a massively bitter pill for Liz to swallow. Watching Zach amble over to join the waiting men, she felt as if something had lodged smack in the middle of her throat and that she might upchuck it any second. Even his walk fed her rage. It was as obnoxiously swaggering and self-satisfied and *male* as that of any of the Spanish conquistadores who had once conquered this land. In fact, that's exactly what he reminded her of—a reckless, determined interloper ravaging whatever got in his way. In this case it was Liz who had the misfortune of being the conquered territory.

The men continued to laugh, a couple even going so far as to whack Zach on the back as if he'd just scored the winning touchdown or whatever it was they scored down here. Their disgruntlement of a few moments ago was obviously forgotten, outweighed by this more primal bond of masculinity. Zach was accepting their gibes with a lopsided smile that did nothing to undercut the air of power and assurance he wore the way some men she knew wore thousand-dollar suits.

"Don't be too hard on her, boss," urged the one she remembered as Carlos. "If it is a tiger you want in your bed, you cannot have a pussycat outside it."

"Oh, I'm not interested in pussycats," Zach countered amid a chorus of appreciative chuckles. His gaze sought hers across the narrow distance separating them and held it, his dark eyes once more glittering with amusement. "After all, taming a tiger is half the pleasure." With a wink in her direction, he added, "Till tonight."

Then he led his scruffy band to a jeep parked a short distance away and roared off, leaving her alone with old Juan. Liz watched him go, with her fingertips pressed to her still-puffy lips, dropping her hand instantly when she realized what a sappy-looking pose it was. Anyone observing could easily make the mistake of thinking she was mooning over his kiss. As the sound of the jeep's engine faded in the distance, a sense of reality swept Liz, and with it a wave of uneasiness.

She was stuck here, God only knew how far from the next living soul, with a man who looked as if he'd answered a casting director's call for a lecherous villain. For the next minute or so she and the old man eyed each other surreptitiously. Then, drawing a deep breath for courage, Liz forced herself to put her fear aside. She believed very few nice things about Zachary McCabe—fewer all the time, actually—but she firmly believed that he wouldn't have left her here alone with this man unless he was certain she wouldn't be harmed in any way.

Of course, she had also believed there couldn't be more than one red pickup truck passing through the village of San Luis on any given afternoon, and look where that had gotten her. At the moment, however, her choices were two. She could stand here on her aching feet for the rest of the day, sweating profusely in the only clothes she had to her name and feeding her panic, or she could try and make friends with old Yellow Teeth.

Getting chummy with one of the tents would probably be easier, she concluded almost instantly. As soon as she spoke he turned back to the grill and resumed scraping, leading Liz to believe he might have a hearing problem. On the other hand, he hadn't had any problem hearing Zach when he spoke. Maybe he was only deaf in one ear, the one facing her. Anything was possible at his age, she supposed. Judging from his skin, which was as wrinkled as an old leather handbag, he could easily be ninety. Maybe older.

"I said," she repeated more loudly, "have you been working for Zach long?"

"You don't have to shout," shouted old Juan. "I ain't deaf."

"Then you could have . . ." Liz broke off as she realized she was shouting again and lowered her voice. "Then you could have answered my question."

"Ain't none of your business."

Slapping her arms across her chest, she uttered, "I see.

149

Well, then, do you suppose you might do as he ordered and set up that extra cot?''

"Soon as I finish here."

"Could you at least point out Zach's ... I mean which ... I mean the tent that I'll be slee ... staying in?"

He slanted her a look out of one sparkling eye, still scraping away. "You mean the boss's tent, don't you?"

"I suppose. Could you show me which one that is?"

He was looking at the grill again. "Soon as I finish here."

Liz was filled with an urge to grab the spatula he was using and scrape it across his face. To control it she took a few steps away and stared at the nearby ruins without seeing them. This whole thing must really be getting to her if she could contemplate mayhem against a total stranger, no matter how cantankerous and deserving of it he might be. And she had the horrible suspicion her emotional state was only going to worsen now that they were finally here.

Until now she had at least had the misery of walking and her feelings of apprehension to distract her. What would she have to do all day now except sit in this oasis of slime and worry about Kirk and whether whoever had him would really kill him—or had *already* killed him after she had screwed up so royally. In her spare time she could worry about the anguish her family would be put through when she and Kirk failed to return as scheduled and about whether she would still be alive when whoever they sent to look for her finally stumbled upon this backside of nowhere. Impatiently she turned back to old Juan.

She'd been so engrossed in her thoughts she hadn't

noticed when the scraping ceased. Now he was hard at work rubbing the grill with a rag she wouldn't use to wipe her sneakers. As long as he was doing the cooking, there was no way she was going to eat a bit of anything served. As soon as the thought pulsed from her mind, Liz recognized it for the absurd, inappropriate bit of haughtiness it was. She'd never considered finickiness and cleanliness and physical comfort to be privileges, but they were. And under her present circumstances they were also nonexistent. She would eat whatever old Juan dished out, even if it crawled off the grill, or she would starve. It was that cut-and-dried and she could just hear Zack telling her so in that smug tone that made her temper sizzle.

Finally old Juan finished "cleaning" the grill, tossed the rag into the dirt where it had probably come from, and turned to her with the tip of his tongue twisted into the crevice between two teeth.

"Are you finished?" she asked, forcing her cheeriest smile. She remembered a little about positive reinforcement from her freshman psych class. Each time he made any effort at all to communicate with her she was going to reward him with a smile.

"I s'pose."

She smiled. "Will you show me the tent now?"

"I s'pose."

First he showed her his back, starting off before she had a chance to reward him. His method of movement was more of a hobble than a walk, but then, Liz wasn't up to setting any speed records herself. After standing still for a while, her feet had begun to swell and she was looking forward to settling into Zach's tent and kicking off these hot sneakers. Maybe she would even take a nap. She was almost smiling simply because she felt like it when they reached the flap entrance of the nearest tent and she ducked to follow him inside.

Unlike the rest of the tents, this one had the opaque nylon sides rolled down over the mesh screening so you couldn't see in from the outside. Inside, a piece of black plastic had been slung over a rope stretched across the middle, concealing the rear half of the tent from view. On the side Liz could see were stacked cartons of food supplies, cans mostly. At first she was amazed to note that there was also a small, squat refrigerator among the contents; then she remembered the generator outside. She looked in confusion at old Juan, who was plowing through a mountain of empty cartons in one corner.

"This is it?"

"Mmmgrr."

Was that a yes or a no? Liz wondered. She took a step toward the black plastic divider, thinking perhaps the boss had to share his tent with the supplies. In which case she was definitely going to make it a crowd. "Is this where Zach..."

"No." Old Juan spun around and yelled as she started to move the plastic aside. "Out. Out. Out of supply tent."

He literally chased her from the tent, but not before Liz had seen what was hidden behind the makeshift curtain— wooden crates had been piled everywhere. The lid had been lifted from one, enabling her to see the rifles packed inside. Recalling the number and assortment of crates back there,

152

Liz thought they couldn't possibly all contain guns. Then Zach's warning about finding out things she shouldn't came zinging back to her. She was fairly certain this discovery fell into that category, and she resolved to keep it to herself. Old Juan had no way of knowing if she'd seen anything before he started shoving at her, and she was going to do everything in her power to keep him from suspecting she had. She did her best to look bewildered by his anger as he stood scowling at her outside the tent for a minute or so. Then, apparently satisfied that he'd caught her in time and that she was now out to stay, he reentered and she again heard him shuffling boxes around.

"Who wants to look at your stupid old supplies anyway?" she yelled in at him, not caring if he could hear her over the racket he was making and caring even less that she sounded like a petulant child. She felt petulant, dammit.

He emerged a few minutes later lugging a depressingly spartan looking cot along with a blanket.

"If you had wanted me to wait out here," she informed him with much more neutrality than she was feeling, "you could simply have asked politely."

He glared as he walked past her, not saying a word. Liz glared right back. She wouldn't smile at the old creep now if he recited the Gettysburg Address for her. Come to think of it, a smile had probably been the wrong reward to start with. Something along the lines of raw meat might have gotten results.

In silence she trailed him all the way to the tent at the far end of the curved row. Again he plowed inside ahead of her, letting the flap fly in her face, but this time Liz took the precaution of waiting outside. Through the screen wall she could see him survey the small interior for a place to set up the cot, settling on the spot right next to the one already there. Liz suppressed a snort. She'd remedy that cozy situation as soon as she was alone in there. He had the cot up in no time and dropped the blanket on the foot of it before coming out. Liz was standing directly in his path as he did, forcing him to look at her.

"Thank you," she said, silk in her voice. "I'll ring if I need anything else."

He gave her a look that suggested she'd suddenly sprouted a second head, confirming that her sarcasm had soared clear over his. Liz wasn't disturbed. It felt good to be able to vent her frustration on someone who wasn't likely to vent back.

Zach's tent, she concluded upon entering, had about as much ambiance as the hut they'd shared the night before. Aside from the two cots, there was what appeared to be a makeshift desk constructed of broken-up crates, with a smaller wooden box serving as a seat. One jarring note was the metal lamp on the desk, an *electric* lamp, which must run off the generator. Liz wandered over to yet another of the multipurpose crates, this one tucked away in a corner, and peered inside. Ah, his closet, obviously. Without the least compunction she dropped to her knees and began to rummage through the contents.

She thumbed past another pair of jeans, several khaki shirts, and some lightweight trousers in the same color, all as neatly folded as if they were sitting in an elegant armoire instead of in an empty gun crate in a tent in the middle of nowhere. Beneath them lay a few pairs each of white briefs and tightly balled socks, the white sport style with bright bands of color circling the tops. At the very bottom was another T-shirt, this one white with a familiar cigarette logo and the words "Alive with pleasure" emblazoned in red. Holding the shirt aloft, Liz squinted at it, then, with a shake of her head, dropped it back into the box. It was beyond the power of her usually fertile imagination to picture the fierce, no-nonsense McCabe wearing such a thing.

At the opposite end of the narrow box lay items she found of much greater interest: a couple of neatly folded towels and a bar of soap, along with a toothbrush and a tube of toothpaste precision rolled from the end the way she never bothered to do it. Just the sight of it made her mouth water in anticipation. Best of all, there was a comb. She felt like a kid on Christmas morning, not knowing which toy to play with first. Instinctively her hand went to her hair, plucking at the tangled pale gold mass. She wished he'd brought along a brush as well. It was going to take her forever to work these knots out with a comb. A rueful grin suddenly curved her lips. Of course, it wasn't as if she had anything more pressing to do in the foreseeable future.

By doggedly questioning old Juan and interpreting his responsive grunts, she learned that the well and outdoor toilet at the rear of the ruined house hadn't been affected by the fire. She even managed to harass him into letting her borrow a large kettle to carry water from the well back to the tent. The first thing she did, once she managed to lug the sloshing kettle that distance with some water still inside, was brush her teeth. She lingered over the task, savoring the minty taste of the toothpaste as if it were wine while pondering the fact that only a couple of days ago she would have been repulsed by the idea of sticking someone else's toothbrush in her mouth, no matter how thoroughly she'd scrubbed it first. She and Kirk never even sampled each other's food in restaurants, for pity's sake, which was something she and Jeff had always done.

She paused with her mouth full of spearmint foam. Come to think of it, there were a lot of little intimacies of that sort in which she and Kirk never indulged. It had never struck her before what a puzzling dichotomy their relationship was, in that it was both intimate and distant at the same time. Kirk never pressed her about anything, not even for more than a cursory explanation of the accident which had killed Jeff and Jeremy and destroyed a part of her forever. He accepted whatever she said at face value, which Liz supposed said a good deal about his opinion of her honesty but didn't demonstrate much desire to learn the most private secrets of her soul.

She couldn't imagine Zach permitting such a distance between him and any woman he planned to marry. She surmised that if he loved a woman he would demand everything from her, body and soul, past, present, and future. He struck her as a man who wouldn't settle for less than passion *and* intimacy.

Flinging his toothbrush aside, Liz spit the foam into the pan of water and clutched a fistful of hair at the crown of her head. What on earth was she thinking of? To even attempt to compare a kind, caring man like Kirk with the likes of Zachary McCabe was a travesty. And if she and Kirk hadn't yet developed the full intimacy—or passion—of their relationship, so what? It had more to do with the fact that he traveled as often as he did, limiting their time together, than any failing on his part.

Once she was with him again—and far away from Zach—everything would be just as it was before. Even better, because now she could fully appreciate the gentle restraint that had sometimes made her impatient with him in the past. And she absolutely refused to let her confidence about their bright future be clouded by the possibility that she might never see him again. At the moment she couldn't do anything about that one way or the other, and she could not—would not—torment herself with fears that might well prove false.

She lingered over her sponge bath, changing the water several times until she was squeaky clean and smelling of Irish Spring soap from her hair to the chipped polish on her toenails. The scent reminded Liz of civilization, of home. Instead of filling her with wistfulness, as she would have expected, however, she found herself chuckling, imagining the reaction of her family and friends back home if they could see her now, perched on the edge of an army-issue cot, thrilled to the marrow by the luxury of washing with water she'd had to pump and haul from the well with her own two hands.

Once she was clean all over, her scalp tingling from the painstaking task of working the tangles out of her hair, and had straightened up the tent, Liz decided she'd earned a nap. She woke up hungry, certain she must have slept for hours, only to check her watch and see that it was still midafternoon. Logic told her Zach and his men wouldn't cease working at their mysterious endeavor until their stomachs drove them to it, just as hers was now driving her to tangle with O.J., as she'd taken to calling him one more time. With no small amount of grumbling he produced a lukewarm bowl of something unrecognizable. It smelled spicy and tasted awful, but by swallowing quickly she managed to get enough of it past her taste buds to satisfy her stomach. Hopefully dinner would be better.

She checked her watch again. Only a half hour had passed since the last time she'd looked at it, making her think its presence there on her wrist was both a blessing and a curse. If she didn't have it, she knew she'd go crazy wondering what time it was, but it wasn't much better having a constant digital reminder of how slowly the minutes could move when you were bored out of your mind. She could always take another sponge bath. Just sleeping inside the stuffy tent had left her feeling clammy all over, but what was the use? It was a losing battle to try and feel any other way than clammy and uncomfortable in this climate. Liz wasn't even sure which she hated more, being outside beneath the relentless fire of the sun which now beat down on her without even the scraggliest of trees overhead to diffuse it, or being trapped within the close confines of the airless tent.

She hated being fried alive more, she decided, touching her fingers to the top of her head and fully expecting to hear them sizzle. At least until she could beg, steal, or wheedle some sort of hat, she would have to avoid the sun during midday. Feeling sullen, she headed back to the tent and on impulse helped herself to one of Zach's shirts. Using the pocketknife from his box of goodies, she butchered the shirt to match the pants he'd altered for her that morning. The resulting ensemble might look like something a hobo threw out, but the loose cotton shirt was much cooler than the red knit top and she mentally thanked Zach for coming up with the idea in the first place.

He did have a few meager redeeming qualities, she supposed. At least when he was around she had someone to talk to, even if nine times out of ten he refused to respond in more than a monosyllable. Even his taunts were preferable to this sticky solitude.

In desperation she began poking around the only place in the tent she hadn't explored: his desk. If she was lucky, which she obviously wasn't or she wouldn't be there, there might be something among the tidy piles of papers worth reading. Love letters maybe. The thought had been sarcastic, but once it popped up Liz found she was intensely curious about the possibility of some woman somewhere seeing a different side of Zach than the one she'd been afflicted with, a side that would merit lengthy, flowery declarations on pink, scented paper. But there weren't any letters anywhere on the desk. She didn't want to think about why that should make her feel such a jolt of relief.

So there were no letters. Maybe there was something that would tell her more about his furtive activities, though. She thumbed through dozens of supply lists and invoices for food, tools, and weapons. What, she wondered with trepidation, was he planning to do with five hundred sticks of dynamite and two hundred pounds of grain? It wasn't until she moved the box he was using for a chair in order to sit down that she discovered the leatherbound ledger beneath it. *Hidden* beneath it, she was certain. Plopping down sideways on the seat, she opened it and began reading from the beginning. It was a journal of sorts, chronicling events since his arrival here almost three weeks ago. Something in the tone of his writing and the constant reference to detail led Liz to think it had been written more for the benefit of someone else than as a personal record. Maybe as a report for Señor Valdivia or whoever Zach was working for?

His writing was small and tight—displaying alarming evidence of a pressure-cooker type personality, a handwriting analyst might say—and it took her awhile to decipher the first few pages. Once she figured out that his B's looked like L's, it went quicker. The first pages dealt primarily with their arrival here and the logistics of moving in various equipment, trucks, jeeps, a chopper . . . chopper? Liz reread the references to that several times to be sure it wasn't an error. Where in God's name was he hiding a helicopter?

She read on, becoming more and more confused as he related details of a frustrating search for something or someone called Naj Tunich, complete with references to a map in which Zach obviously did not have a tremendous amount of faith. Naj Tunich, she eventually fathomed after reaching the part of the journal describing their discovery of it, was a place. After that she wasn't sure what he was writing about as the text became almost an unrecognizable form of shorthand embellished with Spanish references completely unfamiliar to her. She persevered anyway, uncoding a few words here and there—Maya, glyph, several mentions of excavation—and gradually things began to click into place. As they did, her eyes started to race over the page searching for more, for proof of what her jackhammering heart already recognized as the truth.

Finally she pushed the book away from her in disgust. She might not be sure of each word and detail reported on these pages, but she knew now what Zach was up to, and it sent a chill racing through her. His reason for being here was the antithesis of Kirk's and her own, and it could be summed up in one of the few Spanish words she remembered well from her hurried, pretrip reading. *Huaquero.* Grave robber.

CHAPTER
NINE

Liz had been right in guessing that Zach would exact from his crew a full day's work. The sun was dipping low in the sky by the time they returned. She was ready for him. For the hour or so before the roar of jeep and truck engines could be heard approaching, O.J. had been rattling pots and pans. Loudly, as if annoyed that she wasn't out there offering to help. Well, he could just stay annoyed. Unlike him, she was an unwilling guest here, a prisoner, if you wanted to get technical, and she had no intention of providing his unprincipled boss with free labor. Especially not now that she knew the sordid details of his work.

She remained in the tent, watching through the screen sides as the men unloaded the red pickup, transporting numerous canvas-wrapped bundles to the two tents set up slightly behind the others. Her expression tightened as she noted the delicacy of their movements. She would move delicately too if she were carrying priceless pieces of ancient Mayan art. Stolen pieces. It wasn't even the dollar value of what they were concealing in the truck that upset her, although Liz knew it had to be astronomical. It was the callousness of the whole thing. Zach and his band of seedy thugs were stealing bits and pieces of culture and heritage from a people who didn't even know they were being ripped off and who wouldn't have the opportunity or means to fight it if they did.

The land where these modern Mayan Indians were valiantly trying to scratch out a farming existence was once the very center of the ancient Mayan kingdom. Great cities and temples had dotted this region before the Spanish conquistadores arrived, bringing "civilization" along with them. Kirk had explained to her that only fifty miles to the southwest were the ruins of Tiskal, the greatest Mayan temple ever built. Now those once grand cities and temples were simply crumbled mounds buried beneath fifteen hundred years of jungle growth. Buried along with them were untold treasures that drew some men the way a dead carcass draws vultures. Men like Zachary McCabe, thought Liz, a strange thread of disappointment woven through her bitterness.

Unconsciously her eyes sought him. He wasn't hard to pick out and not just because the men scurrying around doing his bidding were all shorter and slighter than he. Liz suspected Zach's quiet air of assurance and latent power would set him apart even in a group of physical equals. A hat hid his shaggy dark hair and shadowed those harshly carved features that were burned into her memory. It wasn't the sombrero he'd been wearing when she first saw him but a hat with more shape, a Panama maybe, which she knew would look utterly ridiculous on anyone else dressed as he was. Maddeningly, on Zach it looked rakish instead.

He'd been standing off to the side speaking quietly with Jade while the others worked. Now, apparently satisfied that everything was being handled to his satisfaction, he turned toward the tent, his clear blue gaze homing in on hers even at that distance and through the mesh screening. Given a choice, Liz would have preferred to pretend she hadn't even noticed his return, but it was too late for that. Instead she settled for turning so her back was to him when he entered, and sat stiffly on the end of her cot, now located as far from his as the tent's dimensions allowed.

The tent flap rustled as he shoved it aside. "Honey, I'm home."

His tone was light, a clever imitation of the generic-voiced announcers of television commercials.

Liz didn't answer. In silence she catalogued the already recognizable sounds of him dispensing with his trusty pistol and machete, pulling off his vest and shirt. Then he ambled over to stand by the cot, so close to her that she would have brushed the side of one granite thigh if she leaned just a half an inch to her left. She took great pains not to.

"How was your day?" he asked.

The bantering tone was gone, and Liz thought she caught

an unexpected tentativeness amid the coarse textures of his voice.

When she again failed to respond, he ventured, "I guess maybe I should have tossed my hat in first to test your mood."

"Just taking it off is a vast improvement." The saucy retort slipped from her brain to her tongue before she could catch it.

"So much for wondering about your mood," remarked Zach dryly.

Acknowledging that her vow not to speak to him ever again was irrevocably broken, Liz twisted around on the cot to shoot a defiant glare his way. "Just what kind of mood did you expect me to be in? Soft and sweet and waiting by the tent door with your pipe and slippers in hand?"

"Slippers maybe," he countered. "I don't smoke a pipe. But that soft and sweet part sounds great. Do you think you could manage such a miraculous transformation from the real you, though?"

Liz shook her head with contempt. "You have some nerve."

"You're right," he conceded before she could embellish on that theme. "I do. It's just that I knew you must have had a pretty boring day, and I thought maybe a little teasing would cheer you up."

"Boring?" Her eyes were wide, incredulous. "You think I'm worried about being bored? I . . ."

"All right. All right." He cut her off by raising both palms and drowning her out. "I'm hungry and tired . . ."

"And filthy," Liz followed his lead by raising her voice to get a word in.

He bowed his head, like a duelist conceding a point. "And filthy. And definitely not in the mood to rehash every petty grievance you've been hanging around here all day stewing over."

"Petty?" cried Liz, bolting to her feet to face him with both hands planted on her hips. "Petty?"

"You're damn right petty. You're alive, aren't you? If you weren't you'd have something to bitch about."

"You're unbelievable."

His mouth twisted sardonically. "That's what all my women say."

"Please," she groaned, "spare me."

"I'd love to. . . . Just name a time, baby."

It took a few seconds for Liz to register the lewd double entendre that his suggestive leer told her it was. Once she did, color flooded her cheeks. "That's revolting."

"How do you know? You've never tried it . . . with me, that is."

She arrowed him a small, pointed smile. "It's *because* I know you that I know I wouldn't like it."

His lips thinned and Liz braced herself for a zinger of a retort. Then with a sudden, weary sigh, he closed his eyes and dragged his fingers through his hair.

"Listen," he said a few seconds later, looking at her with a determined expression. "This isn't getting us anywhere. I told myself while I was working out there today that this whole thing isn't really your fault any more than it is mine."

"But it is your..."

"Quiet," he roared. Then, in a softer if somewhat strained tone, "I also told myself I was going to make an effort to be nicer to you...at least in private. And within reason."

"What does that mean?" The inquiry dripped sarcasm. "That you won't threaten to kill me anymore?"

"No, it means that even if you are acting like the first-class bitch you are, I'm going to go ahead and say what I planned to say, just once, then I'm going to clean up and go get something to eat." He drew a rough breath and said quickly, "I'm sorry about what happened out there this morning."

Liz's only reaction was a speculative lifting of her brows. "Really?"

Zach nodded. "Really. I still say it was necessary if we want to be convincing, but I also know it was a little rough for you to take, and for that I'm sorry."

"Well, I'm not."

She saw a glint of surprise in his dark eyes before they narrowed to unreadable slits framed by lashes that were thick and black and longer than any man's had a right to be.

"You're not?" he repeated.

"Not at all. Before that happened I had *almost* made the mistake of thinking you could be trusted to some small degree. That kiss was exactly what I needed to remind me what a disgusting animal you really are."

That wasn't quite the truth. As the day wore on she had been less angry over his kiss than speculative, wondering where those winding paths of sensation he'd created might have led if they'd been alone. Her silly fantasies had only come to a halt when she discovered the despicable nature of the business he was in. And that was something she'd decided she must never, ever let him know that she knew.

"I see," he responded after a lengthy pause. His voice was a lazy drawl, but Liz could read his tension in the taut muscles of his lean cheeks and his throat. He took a step closer, trapping her between the cot and the intimidating bulk of his powerful body so that her eyes were level with his chest. Very gingerly Liz sought to avert her gaze from the furred, well-muscled distraction, keeping in mind that if she tilted her head too sharply her chin would come to rest on his sternum.

"Well, I certainly wouldn't want you to forget a crucial thing like that," he continued in a voice that was quietly savage. "So I'll just have to arrange plenty of similar little reminders for you while you're here."

It was almost as if the backfiring of her clever insult had produced acrid smoke, leaving a bitter taste in her mouth. Deciding to retreat while she could still call this a draw, Liz moved to go around him. His agile, bronze hand shot out to grip her at the elbow, jerking her back in place.

"Where do you think you're going?" he demanded.

"To get some dinner. You're not the only one who's hungry."

"Maybe not. But I just might be the only one who's eating if your attitude doesn't improve in a hurry. Hopefully a little contemplation will do the trick." He smiled nastily.

"So while I'm cleaning up, you wait right here and do a little meditating on your manners. *Then* we'll see about dinner."

The injustice of his dictating when she could and could not leave the tent, and the humbling realization that she had no choice but to obey, released her pent-up anger in a reckless flood.

"At least I *have* manners," she hurled the words at him. "Which is more than I can say for you."

"Oh, you have manners, all right," Zach agreed. "Real fancy ones. But at the moment that's about all you do have. And a hell of a lot of good they'll do you down here. You can't *please* and *thank you* and RSVP your way out of this mess, sweetheart. And whoever your rich daddy is, even he can't help you, because I don't have any strings your old man can pull. As far as I'm concerned, you're nothing but a stinking, spoiled brat, and I've had it up to here with all your whining and sulking."

Liz's eyes were an emerald blaze as she watched him demonstrate how fed up he was by shooting his hand to a point in the air at least a foot above his head.

"Maybe I am a spoiled brat," she shot back. "But you're wrong about my not having anything besides manners. I also have *honor.*"

Even to Liz's ears the emphasis she gave the last word sounded ridiculously melodramatic. She didn't need to have the fact underscored by the taunting smile spreading slowly across his face.

He stood with his weight resting on one foot, regarding

her with amused detachment. "The obvious implication being that I don't?"

It felt to Liz as if she were a bundle of dry timber and his indulgent tone the match. All caution and thoughts of self-preservation were blown into oblivion by the explosion caused by their coming together.

"You're damn right that's the implication," she lashed out. "After all, honor isn't something you can steal from a grave . . . is it, *huaquero*?"

She spat the derisive name at him as if it were a mouthful of bile. If he had in turn erupted angrily or struck out at her, Liz wouldn't have been a bit surprised. In fact, she expected it. It might even have made her foolhardy attack worthwhile. But the only satisfaction she got was another flicker of surprise that he quickly masked. Without moving, he gazed past her to his desk. Liz knew that he would see everything exactly as he'd left it. She'd made sure of that when she decided she wouldn't under any circumstances risk letting him know that she'd stumbled upon the truth. She'd known that to do so would be to put herself in exactly the sort of dangerous position she was in right now.

Slowly he walked over to the desk, bent to remove the journal from beneath the seat, and flipped through it. Watching with mounting anxiety, Liz remembered a movie she'd once seen where the villain had stuck a hair between the pages of a secret document so that he could tell if anyone touched it. It would be just like him to have employed some similar sneaky, precautionary measure. After looking the notebook over briefly, he tossed it on the desk and turned back to her.

Instead of the glittery-eyed, hard-mouthed anger she expected, however, he simply shrugged, his expression rueful.

"I suppose it's my own fault," he muttered. "I should have anticipated that you'd go snooping around. If I'd been thinking straight when I left here this morning I probably would have taken the damn thing with me."

Liz banked down on the urge to ask what had interfered with his ability to think straight. Her own feminine and admittedly biased guess was that their kiss had ruffled his feathers the same way it had hers. She would never have suspected so from his actions at the time, and she marveled again at how adept he was at shielding his thoughts and emotions. She also felt a smile fighting to form at the realization that big, tough Zach wasn't as immune to her as he claimed to be.

"Maybe it's just as well, you know," he theorized, crossing to the rear of the tent where his box of clothes sat. "Someone was bound to slip up and tell you sooner or later anyway. Jade, most likely. I think he already has a soft spot for you."

Another tidbit for her mental file. Perhaps Jade was the weak link in this operation, and just maybe he would be her ticket out of here. As if he had eyes in the back of his head which could read her mind, Zach glanced around at her.

"Don't even think it," he advised dryly. "I'm just as certain Jade won't smuggle you out as I am he wouldn't smuggle liquor in. And you don't have to look at me as if I have horns," he added, that familiar sardonic inflection back in his voice. "Believe it or not, there are . . . extenuating circumstances for my being here."

Liz slanted him a lofty look. "I wouldn't. Believe it, that is."

"Fine," he snapped, his eyes becoming an unreadable wall of hammered steel. "That saves me the trouble of trying to explain."

Liz could have bitten her tongue off. She should have had the sense to listen to his explanation first and then tell him that she didn't believe a word of it. The more he talked, the more she would learn and the closer she would be to figuring a way out of here.

He remained crouched beside the box, rummaging through his clothes in silence for a few seconds longer. Then he said disgustedly, "I see that besides helping yourself to my favorite shirt, you also made yourself at home over here. Tell me, is there anything I own that you haven't mauled inside out?"

Liz toyed with the idea of going into detail about the toothbrush and everything else of his that she'd made leisurely use of, then decided against it. There was no sense in rattling his cage unnecessarily. Lifting her shoulders in a careless gesture, she said, "I was sure you wouldn't mind sharing."

"You were right."

He stood, carrying a towel, soap, and a few other things, and walked slowly toward her. There was something sinister about the gleam in his eye and the set of his bristly jaw that made Liz take two steps back for every forward one of his until she came up against the nylon wall behind her.

"As a matter of fact, I'm glad you raised the subject of sharing," he told her softly. "Seeing as how you don't have anything to do but sit around here and pout all day, I'm going to let you *share* my things in an even more fulfilling way. Starting tomorrow you can take over the chore of doing my laundry. I'm sure old Juan will appreciate the break.''

Liz drew in an indignant breath. ''You must be joking.''

''Not at all. In fact you can start with this.'' He fired his dirty, sweat-stained shirt in her direction. Then, in an infuriating drawl he added, ''After all, washing is woman's work.''

''Not this woman's,'' retorted Liz. ''Do you really think I would even consider washing your clothes for you after all that's happened?''

''I should think that after all that's happened, as you so concisely put it, you'd realize that you'll not only wash my clothes but clean my boots and scrub my back if I tell you to. I also think you should be thankful it's just my clothes you'll be handling and not the whole camp's.'' He pushed open the tent flap and ducked his head to fit through. Once outside he paused. ''I'll be back in a while. If you know what's good for you, you'll stay put.''

Stay put. It was the kind of thing you said to a dog, for heaven's sake. Nothing would have given Liz more pleasure at that moment than to tear every last piece of clothing he owned into shreds and drape them about his tent like party streamers. Only a strong instinct for self-preservation held her back. It also made her heed his command to stay put in spite of the growling of her stomach as she watched the rest of the men line up with tin plates in hand. She knew it had to be wishful thinking, but she could swear she smelled charcoal-broiled steak.

Finally Zach returned, obviously fresh from bathing in the nearby lake he'd mentioned, and dressed in clean khaki slacks and shirt with the sleeves rolled back to his elbow. Liz knew she was gaping as he walked back in, but she couldn't help it. He looked different. Younger. Grudgingly she admitted to herself the truth. He looked gorgeous.

Not male-model gorgeous to be sure. But powerfully, rivetingly, sexily gorgeous just the same. The way his damp hair was combed straight back only emphasized the aggressive lines and planes of a face that was uncompromisingly masculine. His cheeks and jaw had been scraped clean of black bristle, leaving the skin there as smooth as polished mahogany. The tips of Liz's fingers tingled with the urge to discover if it could possibly feel as satiny as it looked. Against the untainted bronze of his skin, his eyes gleamed bluer than ever and his mouth looked excitingly mobile, as if it could turn either sensuous or savage, depending on his mood. Liz couldn't prevent a slight tremble from the overall impact. Never in her life had she been so aware of a man as a man.

"Are you ready to eat now?" he asked simply, his honey-and-hickory tone caressing her senses.

Obviously he wasn't going to press his threat to withhold her dinner, and for that at least, Liz was grateful. With her tongue tied in adolescentlike knots at his unexpected transformation from loathsome to downright sexy, she was hardly up to waging another battle of wits. "Yes."

"Good. Let's go."

He even held the tent flap open for her to precede him out. Maybe clothes did make the man, mused Liz. Then even her fascination with the man by her side was overtaken by her interest in food. To her amazement and delight she discovered her olfactory sense was fully operational. It *was* steak she had smelled. Zach laughed at her wide-eyed expression of disbelief, and this time, for a change, it wasn't an unpleasant sound.

Jade, who was sitting within earshot, piped in to advise Liz to savor each bite, because tomorrow it was back to "mystery meals," obviously his term for the unidentifiable mush she'd sampled for lunch. The steak, he explained, was to celebrate reaching the halfway point in their project. Liz found that revelation sobering, but try as she might, she couldn't feel anything but thankful for this meal, even if it did commemorate the partial success of a deed she considered despicable.

"Believe me, I'm not complaining," she remarked, "but isn't it a little extravagant to lug steak along when you're camping in the middle of nowhere?"

"Not when you have a very generous backer," Jade explained in a dry tone.

The remark made Liz's eyes brighten with sudden interest, but a look from Zach was all it took to stop his friend from revealing anything else of any consequence.

"Besides," Jade continued in his typically bantering style, "the steak was all Zach's idea. You know what they say. You can take the boy out of Texas, but you can't take those simple Texas tastes out of the boy."

A smile slanted her lips at the utter ludicrousness of anyone referring to Zach as a boy. "Well, at least now I know why there's a refrigerator in the supply tent."

Zach hesitated for a split second between lifting a good-sized steak off the grill and plopping it down beside the beans already on her plate. "My, my, you do get around, don't you?"

His tone was offhand, but from the corner of her eye Liz caught the quizzical look he flashed O.J. and her breath stuck in her throat. Of course. He was concerned that when she saw the refrigerator she might also have seen the weapons hidden behind the supplies. She exhaled with relief as the old man responded with a slight shake of his head. Now all she had to do was hold her tongue and not let anything slip the next time he baited her.

Managing his plate and a full cup of coffee with one big hand while it took Liz both of hers and total concentration besides to balance her own, Zach steered her to a spot a short distance away from the sprawled group. He ignored their laughter and suggestive comments as they took note of his spit-shined appearance, and Liz doggedly resolved to do the same. As mortifying as it was to have them all thinking he'd bathed and shaved in preparation for bedding her, the fact that he'd seen fit to do so intrigued her. It couldn't be only for show. She would bet the steak now melting in her mouth that this crew of lowlifes wouldn't have thought anything amiss if he'd dragged her into the tent still covered with the day's sweat and mud. So why had he gone to so much trouble? It was definitely an interesting development.

They sat on two of the flat boards obviously placed on the damp ground for that purpose and ate in silence. Zach polished off his meal before she'd eaten half of hers and went back for seconds of coffee, surprising Liz by refilling her cup for her at the same time without being asked. When he returned, he sat down a little closer so that he could share the rock she was using as a backrest and between sips of the strong, black brew asked questions about her life back in Boston. At first Liz's answers were labored and cautious, but as the questions remained superficial enough, she unconsciously lowered her guard. He chuckled when he learned she was the baby in a family of three children, muttering without rancor, "I should have guessed . . . brat." The snort with which he greeted the news that she'd graduated from Radcliffe was decidedly less good-natured.

"So where'd you meet this guy you're going to marry?"

He zinged the question at her without warning, startling Liz by raising the subject of another man. Then she realized the others were far enough away and too absorbed in their own conversations to hear. Still this line of questioning struck her as more nosy than friendly and she decided to respond in kind.

"So where do you keep your helicopter hidden?"

He didn't even blink. "I asked first."

Her lips pursed thoughtfully. Finally she replied, "In Boston."

"In a small clearing we made about a half mile from here," Zach shot back.

Liz couldn't help smiling. "All right, I met him through my job. I was responsible for making the arrangements for a lecture he gave."

"What sort of work do you do?"

"It's hard to explain. You might say I'm a troubleshooting jack-of-all-trades for the office of the archbishop of Boston.''

His black brows lifted like rockets. "I thought only nuns worked for bishops.''

Laughing out loud at his expression, she replied dryly, "Well, I'm not at all like a nun, I'm afraid.''

The slow drift of his gaze over every inch of her body left Liz feeling as intimately stroked as if he'd put his hands on her. When he was finished, he met her eyes with a scorching half smile. "You're right. You're nothing at all like a nun.''

Liz applied all her attention to the last bit of steak on her plate, cutting and chewing as slowly as if it were all that stood between her and a very real danger.

"Then if you're not a nun,'' Zach ventured, "how did you end up working for a bishop?''

"He's my uncle,'' explained Liz. "He refuses to admit it, but I think he created this job especially for me when I was going through a rough time a few years ago and needed something to hang on to. Since then I've sort of embellished my duties, and now I think he needs me as much as I once needed the job.''

"What sort of rough time were you going through?'' he asked, and when Liz brought her head up she found the look in his eyes just as intense and direct as his question.

She bit her bottom lip, feeling an old, familiar ache pushing at the corners of her mind, and squared her shoulders to push back. "I don't want to talk about it.''

He continued to stare at her, as if weighing the resolve in

her answer, then gave a short nod. "All right. Then tell me more about lover-boy."

"I take it you're referring to Kirk?" she countered with arched brows.

He grinned. "Unless you have more than one lover."

With a haughty shrug, Liz replied, "There's not much to tell."

"That says a lot for the guy." His tone held a dry note of satisfaction. "Dig deep. There must be something interesting about him. What does he do?"

Liz clutched her cup more tightly. "Do?"

"Yeah, do. You know, for a living. I rob graves. What does he do?"

"Oh, he . . ." She hesitated. Revealing that Kirk was the creator and driving force behind an active subgroup of the sanctuary movement was bound to invite speculation on Zach's part. It wouldn't take him long to make the connection between Kirk's efforts to help those fleeing political persecution and her reason for being in Central America, and she still wasn't sure whether his reaction to such news would help or hinder their cause.

She finally settled on a suitably vague explanation. "He's the director of a large charitable organization. That's how we met, when he came to Boston to give a lecture to raise funds."

"Sounds noble."

"He is," snapped Liz, the mockery in his tone making her chin come up defensively. "Not to mention honorable."

If she had any doubt that he'd grasped the point of that brittle comment, it faded as he held his cup aloft and intoned, "Here's to honor," before downing the contents in a single gulp.

She expected him to retreat into his typically sullen silence after that and was once again caught off guard when instead he settled himself more comfortably against the rock and asked, "So what does this paragon of virtue do in his spare time? Ski? Sail? Slay dragons?"

Liz could safely say Kirk had never slain a single dragon, but she wasn't as certain about the other things. "I'm not really sure whether or not he skis or sails," she admitted before she thought about how strange a situation that was for two people deeply in love. "We've never really talked about our hobbies," she added hurriedly, realizing she was only making it sound worse when she saw the speculative tilt of his head.

"Really? Then what do you two talk about?"

"We talk about . . ." she began, dragging the words out as she thought. Unfortunately her mind was suddenly blank. She knew they had to talk about something. Hadn't most of their two-month courtship been conducted via long-distance phone calls while Kirk traveled around the country enlisting support for his cause? "His work. We talk about his work. He's really quite involved in it. And busy. We don't really have all that much time to sit around and talk."

"I'll bet. Being honorable must be very time-consuming." His voice dropped to a husky rasp. "How about you, fancy face? Is he honorable toward you?"

Snapping forward so her spine was ramrod straight, Liz countered, "He's marrying me, if that's what you mean."

"Actually, what I was wondering was whether or not he

ever takes off his damn halo. For instance, how is he in bed?"

Liz glared at him with eyes that were a blaze of emerald fire. "How dare you ask me a thing like that?"

He shrugged. "I don't know. It seemed pretty innocuous compared to some of the things I've said and done to you. So is he? Any good in bed, I mean," he added when she continued to stare at him in shocked disbelief.

"Yes," Liz hissed. "He's fantastic. Incredible. More than any other man could ever hope to match."

She emphasized the words *any other man* and was rewarded by the sight of his fingers clenching briefly around the handle of his cup. Then he unfurled that self-satisfied smile that always made her feel like a country schoolmarm with her slip showing.

"Careful, sweetheart," he warned. "I just might decide to interpret that as a challenge to my manhood."

Liz was about to retort that she wouldn't dream of challenging anything so feeble when the sound of a guitar being tuned diverted her attention. The tuning was being done by the man named Carlos, and listening to the soft, broken strains, Liz said a silent prayer of thanks for the interruption. If praising Kirk's bedroom technique smacked of a challenge to Zach, then ridiculing his own would have been tantamount to tossing down a gauntlet he couldn't ignore. If she wanted to make it through this ordeal without being strangled or raped, she was going to have to learn to keep her mouth shut.

The guitar evidently tuned to his satisfaction, Carlos began to play a slow ballad, singing along in Spanish in a voice that was low and haunting. Next he played an American folk song from the sixties. Liz hadn't heard the once-popular protest anthem in years, but as he sang, the words denouncing a war long since over came rolling back to her. It was another reminder of home, and an intense wave of longing to be back there washed over her. She slanted a look at Zach, curious to see if the familiar words inspired a similar feeling in him, but his expression was strangely hard, almost bitter. He didn't relax again until Carlos had moved on to another love song in his native language.

The music may have succeeded in putting an end to Zach's uncharacteristically chatty streak, but it created a different problem for Liz as she felt his arm stretch along her back to settle around her shoulders. Even though they were sitting away from the others and it had grown too dark for them to see clearly anyway, her first instinct was to pull away. She struggled to curb it, telling herself that to cause a scene, thus provoking him into another show of dominance, was not in her best interest.

Instead, calling on a trick she used to employ back in high school whenever a date got too attentive in a dark movie theater, she stiffened until every muscle in her body was as tight as the coils in a new mattress. Obviously Zach wasn't as sensitive to rejection as the boys of her youth. Instead of retreating to his own space, as they invariably had, he responded by gathering her closer in a subtle show of force that left the side of her body pressed against the warm, hard length of his and his hand resting on the slope of her breast.

Think passive resistance, Liz reminded herself. Sooner or

later he was bound to tire of snuggling up to a block of ice. Only, it was hard to play ice maiden when you were sitting so close to a flame. And that's exactly what Zach's body felt like next to hers, a flame . . . hot, exciting, potentially dangerous. As the moments slipped by and Carlos continued to play, her resistance steadily melted and her muscles relaxed until she was leaning against him, her head nestled comfortably in the nook beneath his shoulder. It felt good. He felt good. Strong and solid, and for the first time in two days Liz felt safe enough to close her eyes without worrying about disaster striking while she wasn't looking. In fact, with her eyes closed her grip on time and space dulled, and they could be anywhere, somewhere clean and bright and pleasant. And he could be another man. Not a *huaquero*, not an unprincipled bandit. Just a man. And she could be just a woman.

As if sensing the vulnerable state of her defenses, Zach slowly began to slide his hand lower. Not tentatively, just slowly, his touch always firm and sure. His palm coasted across her nipple, and even through the rough cotton of her shirt the sensation was so strong it made Liz suck in her breath. Then his fingers curled, cupping her breast fully and sending a rush of pleasure shooting all the way to her toes. He began to stroke her, keeping his touch light, the pace lazy, moving his fingertips in feathery swirls that circumvented the tightly aroused crest until Liz thought she would go mad. She could feel the rapid thud of his heartbeat where her arm pressed against him, telling her his mood wasn't as detached as the unhurried motion of his fingers made it seem. Yet the sweet torture continued. Restlessly she shifted her legs, hoping he would read her impatience in the movement. All she succeeded in doing, though, was to bring her thigh into tighter contact with the solidly muscled length of his, adding to her sensual awareness of him.

Didn't he know what he was doing to her? The knowledge that he most likely did and was intentionally teasing her to a fever pitch didn't quell the mutiny of her senses as it should have. Unconsciously she twisted so that she was pressed closer to him, driven by the slow tendril of desire uncurling deep in her loins. Finally, when she was desperate enough to consider grabbing his hand and showing him how she wanted to be touched, he captured the throbbing bud between his fingertips and squeezed just hard enough to make her gasp softly.

Immediately Zach froze, leaving Liz suspended between desire and confusion. Was that all he wanted? An audible sign of her surrender? Something else to taunt her with? Maybe this was his cruel way of getting even with her for poking through his things and calling him a *huaquero*. Dreading what she might find, Liz screwed up the courage to turn her reddening face up to examine his. Before she could say a word, though, he put his finger to his lips, at the same time removing his other arm from around her.

"Shhh," he cautioned, his expression alert. "I think I heard something out behind the tents." With unnatural speed he was on his feet and moving into the shadows. Almost as an afterthought, he paused and ordered, "You stay here."

More dog commands. Only this time, instead of feeling resentful, Liz found herself worrying about what might happen to Zach out there alone in the dark. Before he disappeared completely into the black night, she had seen his hand slip automatically to the gun at his waist. But what if the noise he heard had been made by more than one man, all of them with guns? Liz was about to make her way over to Jade and suggest that he see if Zach needed a hand when he walked over to her instead.

"So," he said, flopping down beside her, "I notice that you and old Zach have come to terms of sorts."

"No . . . yes." Too worried to stand on principle, she dismissed his conjecturing with an impatient wave of her hand. "Jade, Zach thought he heard something and he's gone out there alone to check it out."

"And you think maybe I should go and have a look-see if he is okay?" he guessed before she had a chance to suggest precisely that. At her eager nod he laughed softly. "Liz, in case it has escaped your attention, allow me to point out that Zach is a big boy. He'll holler if he needs help." Giving a lock of her hair a quick tug, he added, "The only thing my running out there after him is going to accomplish is to give up your game too soon. Mystery equals advantage, Lizzie. You remember that and you'll do all right with Zach."

With a sigh Liz hugged her bent knees close to her chest. He was right, of course. Zach's grin would stretch from ear to ear if he thought she cared enough to worry about him. And she didn't really. She still hated him. It was simply not in her to stand by and let anyone, no matter how worthy of contempt they might be, get hurt if it was within her power to prevent it. Still Jade should know best, and he seemed convinced that Zach could take care of himself out there, even if she wasn't. Liz fidgeted through the final few bars of the song without hearing them, hoping it would be the last one of the evening and the men would soon disperse to their respective tents. If Zach was in trouble, they would be sure to notice then.

The long pause after the song ended led her to believe her wish might be granted. Then she noticed Carlos nodding at whatever the man leaning over him was saying, and his fingers began to move on the strings once again. As the man who had been talking to him straightened, Liz recognized him from that morning. It was Rodil, the one with the slit eyes and the bottle of tequila. The one who'd offered to take Zach's place after she'd spurned his kiss. As Liz watched he started walking toward her, his glassy-eyed expression as crude and easy to read as the graffiti on a subway wall.

Stopping directly in front of her, he grinned, exposing crooked teeth with a wide gap right in the front. "My friend Carlos, he plays this especially for us," he told her. "So we can dance."

Liz could well imagine what sort of dancing he planned to do to the slow, throbbing beat of the song being played. "No, thank you," she said, trying to hide her distaste behind a stiff smile. The idea of touching the man, much less being held close to his body, turned her stomach.

"Maybe you no get my message," he said, losing his grin. He hitched his thumb over his shoulder in the direction of his friend, who sat strumming enthusiastically, with one eye on the drama being played out nearby. "This is special from Carlos so we can dance."

"It appears to me, my friend," Jade interceded, "that

you are the one not getting the message. She said no, thank you.''

"Shut up, *friend*," Rodil growled, with an irritable glance at Jade.

"No, he's right," Liz insisted, coming to Jade's defense as quickly as he had to hers. "I don't feel like dancing."

"Well, I do," insisted Rodil in heavily accented English, and reaching down, he yanked her to her feet. Liz stumbled against him and he held her that way with a strength she hadn't expected in a man of his small stature. Instantly Jade was on his feet at her side. She saw a flash of white as he bared his teeth, followed by a silver glint as he produced a long knife from somewhere. Then they were suddenly surrounded by several other men and all she saw were their backs as they formed a wall between Jade and her. Liz had a feeling the reason he wasn't fighting was because they were as well armed as he.

"You are all making a big mistake," she heard him calmly announce in that distinctive, formal speech of his.

"Not as big a one as the one you'll be making if you move even a muscle," a heavyset man near her countered. "My amigo only wants to dance with the lady."

"You've all seen for yourself that the lady already has a partner."

But where was that partner? And if he walked back in on this little scene, would he come to her rescue? worried Liz. Or would he be the first to find enjoyment in her predicament? She prayed that Jade's obvious reference to Zach might be enough to bring the men to their senses, but it didn't seem to. Or maybe at that moment they were all more concerned with Rodil and whatever he was barking at them in rapid peasant Spanish, than with their boss's eventual wrath.

"McCabe won't mind me showing his lady some fun while he's taking a leak," he said, once again speaking in English. For her benefit, Liz supposed. Giving her his full attention now, he laughed in her face as she trembled against him. The fetid odor of his breath, a mingling of beans and rotting teeth, made her turn her head aside so she wouldn't retch. Grabbing fistfuls of her hair, he forced her face back to his.

"Now," he panted, "now we dance."

What he forced her to do was not even remotely related to dancing. Clamping both hands firmly onto her backside so she had no choice but to arch the lower half of her body into his or fall to the ground at his feet, he swayed without any pretense of moving his feet. They were nearly the same height, permitting him easy access to her neck, and after nosing her hair aside, he planted his mouth there with a slimy, wet suction. Liz cried out as she felt a drawing, burning pressure on that spot and tried unsuccessfully to pull away. He was like a leech, sucking at her flesh, and squeezing her eyes shut in horror and revulsion, she started to cry.

Awash in her own misery she wasn't even aware of the moment the music stopped, but she heard very clearly the sharp, metallic click that pierced the sudden silence that followed. It was the same click she'd heard when Zach had threatened her with his gun. Only this time there was no accompanying feel of deadly cold metal against her skin, and she opened her eyes to see the blue-black gun barrel pressed to Rodil's temple instead.

"The only reason I'm not blowing your brains out, Rodil," Zach uttered in a voice every bit as threatening as the gun in his hand, "is because I wouldn't want them to splatter all over the lady. *My* lady," he added meaningfully. "Now let her go."

Rodil obeyed as quickly as if the order had come from God himself.

"That's better." Without taking his eyes off the man at the other end of his gun, Zach extended his arm toward Liz in an offer of shelter, and without a second thought she flew to him. "Now, I think an apology is in order."

That too came without hesitation, first in Spanish, then, after a look from Zach, in stilted English. Still too jittery to speak, Liz acknowledged it with a nod.

No one uttered a word or made a move as Zach lowered the pistol and stuck it back in his pants in a lazy movement that said more about the extent of his power and confidence than waving it around possibly could have.

"If I do decide to kill you," he said to Rodil, "I'll do it with my own two hands, so the pleasure lasts longer. If you don't want that to happen, I suggest you remember that I don't want other people touching what belongs to me." Flicking a steely gaze of disapproval over the others, he added, "That goes for the rest of you too."

One or two men nodded in response to the warning; the rest said nothing. There was no need to. The silence rang with their acceptance of Zach's dictates. Like children they had banded together to test his authority, and with a minimum of words and effort he had demonstrated that at this time, in this place, his rule was absolute. Liz had never felt as safe, as shielded from anything in the world that could possibly harm her, as she did walking back to the tent in the warm circle of his arm.

"Sorry, Zach," Jade said as they passed him. He was folding away the knife he hadn't gotten a chance to use.

Zach swept his regrets aside. "Don't worry about it. There was no damage done."

First ushering Liz into the tent, he rolled down the opaque nylon sides before following. Once inside he moved unerringly through the stifling blackness to turn on the lamp. It cast only a small circle of pale light onto the desk, leaving the rest of the tent heavily shadowed.

Standing about three feet away, he peered at her closely, his eyes unreadable beneath heavy black brows. "I was right, wasn't I?" he questioned. "He didn't hurt you?"

Liz shook her head. Her neck still stung where Rodil had sucked on it, but she wasn't going to quibble about such a minor infliction now that the worst was over. "No," she said, "he didn't hurt me." Suddenly cold, she wrapped her arms tightly around herself.

Zach's eyes narrowed sharply. "Are you sure you're okay?"

"Yes . . . I'm sure." What she wasn't so sure about was whether her chill was caused by nerves or the removal of his body heat. She only knew that she owed this man whom she'd thought she hated a debt of gratitude. "It was . . . awful out there," she uttered, the words rushing like water through an open floodgate. "All those men staring at me. And his hands touching me . . . his mouth . . ." She shuddered, her eyes briefly flickering shut on the memory. "And I didn't know if you'd come back in time to stop him . . . or if you'd even bother."

Zach reached out and with his thumb blotted a tear from her cheek, frowning down at the glistening spot it left on his skin as if transfixed. Finally he lifted his head and asked, "Why would you think I wouldn't bother to defend you? I made it clear to you what our situation is."

"I thought that maybe after what I said to you earlier . . . the name I called you . . ."

His bewildered expression was shattered by a harsh grin. "You mean when you called me a *huaquero*? Why should that bother me? It's what I am. And I learned a long time ago you can't hide from what you are."

Liz shrugged awkwardly. "I just thought it might have bothered you." She suddenly wished she could think of some way to erase the shadow of grimness that haunted his mouth even when he smiled. It seemed the least she could do in return for his help, except she had no idea how to begin. Something told her the roots of Zach's pain ran deeper than anyone, maybe even he himself, could touch.

"Well, anyway," she said with another uneasy lifting of her shoulders, "it was lucky for me you came back when you did. I don't know how to thank you."

As she uttered the hackneyed expression, Liz was struck by a sudden impulse, and without giving herself time to check it, she stretched onto her tiptoes and brushed her mouth across his. The contact was quick and dry, intended to be friendly, but ended up as irreversible as flicking the first in a long row of dominoes. Liz understood the magnitude of what she had done the second her heels landed back on the ground. She stared into Zach's eyes, feeling as if she were about to be swept into a whirlpool of unknown depth. For a few seconds his face remained dark and unreadable, as if he were waging some private war of will. Then the corners of that savage-sensuous mouth tipped upward and a demonic fire lit his eyes.

"Oh, I don't think you give yourself enough credit, fancy face," he drawled. "I think you know *exactly* how to thank me."

CHAPTER
TEN

Liz ran her tongue over lips that had turned as dry as aged parchment. It was obvious what he had in mind and she knew it should be terror making her heart slam against her ribs this way, but it wasn't. It was anticipation. A soaring, dizzying sort of anticipation she'd never come close to feeling before. It must have lingered after Zach touched her outside earlier, simmering there beneath her worry and her fear. Now, under the heat of his gaze, it bloomed anew, spreading through her like wildflowers across a summer meadow.

''You can't be serious,'' she whispered, the words coming to her from where she hadn't the slightest idea. Not her suddenly numb brain, not her heart, and certainly not from the slowly melting core of her.

Perhaps they sprang from some tenacious sense of propriety. It hardly mattered, because for the first time in Liz's life, her body was speaking louder than her conscience. She hadn't faced danger—real danger—often enough to know if this could simply be a natural reaction to a sudden release of adrenaline. She only knew how she felt at that moment: hot and cold, weak and strong, fearful and brave. She felt *alive*. Zach may have stripped away some of the layers of her dignity, but at least now she was able to see what had been hidden beneath it all these years: freedom. The freedom to acknowledge the way *she* felt, not the way civilized manners dictated she should be feeling.

"Oh, I'm very serious," Zach said in reply to her slightly breathless inquiry.

Lifting her chin with panache, Liz countered, "I can't imagine why. You've made it clear you don't find me at all attractive."

He smiled a lazy, mocking smile. Probably because he knew as well as she did that her objection was prompted not by fear, but vanity. Some instinctively feminine part of Liz wanted to hear him admit what she strongly expected was true. That he found her every bit as attractive as she found him.

"You said you'd seen shantytown whores who tempted you more than I do," she reminded him, deepening his amused look.

"I lied." Stepping closer, he reached out and gently brushed the flyaway strands of spun gold from her face. In the process his fingers barely grazed her, but Liz trembled, sizzling from head to toe as if struck by lightning.

"Would it help atone for my lie," he asked in his slow,

raspy drawl, "if I told you that just looking at you makes me hot as hell?" Every one of her stomach muscles clenched into a giant knot. "Or that all I could think about all day today was you, and how soft you felt in my hand last night? And how much I wanted to touch you that way again?"

Liz felt a sudden pulsing down low in that part of her body he was referring to. "N-No," she stuttered. "I don't think that would help matters at all."

His laughter was soft, beguiling. "What you mean is that it won't help you to say no to me. That is what you're trying to do, isn't it? Convince yourself that letting me make love to you isn't the right thing to do?"

"It isn't the right thing to do." Even to her ears the declaration lacked conviction.

"No doubt. But it's what you *want* me to do, isn't it, Liz?" He lifted a hand to frame her cheek. The rough scrape of his callused skin against her soft flesh was all it took to send desire shimmering through her like light through a prism. "Isn't it?"

Liz remained silent, afraid he'd know if she lied and even more afraid to admit out loud the shocking truth, that he was right. She did want him to make love to her, and she wanted it with a reckless hunger she hadn't known she was capable of feeling. She wanted him to kiss her the way he had this morning, only this time she wanted to kiss him back. And she wanted to touch him the way he had already touched her. Then she wanted him to press her down on the cot behind them and cover her with that hard, bronze body that she was able to see in heart-stopping detail even with her eyes closed, and teach her all the other things about feeling and wanting and needing that no one else ever had.

"Don't bother fumbling for the right answer, Liz," he said quietly. "I already know what you want. I can feel it right here." She trembled as his hand grazed her cheek, coming to rest with his palm flat on her chestbone and his fingertips cupped in the shallow hollow at the base of her throat, where her pulse was pounding erratically. "And you know it too. The only question is, do you have the guts to admit it . . . to me and to yourself?"

"I don't know . . . I'm so confused." A lie really, but it was so hard to talk about this. Why didn't he just grab her as he had this morning and take the decision out of her hands?

"You're only confused because you're not being honest with yourself. You can try to cover up what you're feeling and pretend it isn't there, and you might even be able to fool me. But you can't hide it from yourself, Liz, any more than you can hide what you really are."

If there had been anything the least bit pressuring or seductive in his tone, Liz might have retreated. But his words were like a smooth, steady bridge across her own uncertainty. On the other side he stood waiting, promising never-imagined pleasures. She could cross it and claim what he was offering or not. The decision was hers. He wasn't going to pander to her delicate streak of cowardice by making the choice for her. He also wasn't going to give her all night to think about it, Liz discovered as the laconic drift of his voice ruffled the tense silence between them.

"So what's it going to be, baby? Either you want me or you don't."

Feeling as if she were about to step blindfolded off the top of the Empire State Building, Liz took a deep breath and murmured, "I want you, Zach."

Now, she thought on a wave of relief, now his mouth would claim hers, crushing out any possibility of second thoughts, and she could let herself be swept away in a blaze of passion. Her lashes were lowered, her lips slightly parted, soft and wet and waiting.

Nothing happened.

Her eyes flew open again to find Zach wearing a look of mocking amusement. Far from dragging her into his arms and jerking her against him as she expected—and yes, craved—he broke contact altogether. Dropping his arm to his side so he was only touching her with eyes that were as dark and unsettled as a storm at sea and narrowed with just as formidable a challenge, he said lightly, "Then take me."

"What?" Liz gasped, her own eyes brightening with surprise.

"You heard me. If you want me, you'll have to come and take me."

Slowly the message sunk in. He was demanding from her an honest admission of desire, insuring that there would be no vacillation later and assignment of blame for whatever passed between them. In a way Liz understood and accepted his caution. However, accepting the notion as fair and acting on it were two very different things. Everything she'd ever been taught ordered her to snap to her senses and bid him a curt good night. But something else, something primitive and much closer to her core, was urging her to reach out and grab this moment with both hands.

The cords in her throat convulsed as she attempted to swallow her inhibitions. Taking a determined step closer to where he stood with his feet braced apart, his arms hanging negligently by his sides, she lifted her hands tentatively. They almost made it to his shoulders. About two inches away they halted, hovered, and fluttered spastically into a tight clench at her waist.

"I don't know what you want me to do," she confessed.

"Whining won't help any," Zach pointed out dryly. "I'm sure you've done this before, or maybe I should say, had it done *to* you. How do things usually get rolling?"

Liz thought about it and with a start realized just how passive a role she always assumed at times like this. "I guess with a kiss," she said after a minute.

"Well, then?"

She moved closer, and just as she had a few moments earlier, went up on her toes to reach his mouth, bracing her hands on his shoulders for support. His lips were soft and relaxed as she pressed hers against them, but they didn't press back. She pulled away, bewildered.

"You call that a kiss?" he scoffed in response to the quizzical look she shot him.

Stung, she rallied to try again, determined to administer a kiss that would curl his toes and wipe that indulgent smirk off his face once and for all. Wrapping her arms around his neck, she pulled his head down to her this time, giving herself the added advantage of leverage. She began by brushing her mouth across his, back and forth, slowly, letting the light contact sensitize his lips for when she really got down to business. Her own lips quickly began to tingle with pleasure, and the emergence of her tongue to cool them was prompted as much by instinct as design. It still worked, she gloated, feeling his shoulder muscles stiffen beneath her fingers as some wanton instinct prompted her to lick playfully at the corners of his mouth. She traced the outer rim of his lips, then ran her tongue deeply along the crevice in between, painting him with her own heat and moisture. Loosening her hold just a fraction, she tilted her head to gauge his reaction.

The mockery was gone from his eyes. In its place Liz saw a smoky blue reflection of her own leaping excitement, but his voice, damn him, was still frustratingly casual.

"Better," he allowed. "But do you know how to really *use* that tongue of yours?"

"Do you know how to really *open* that mouth of yours?" she shot back.

He smiled. "I'll do my best."

With a stubborn set to her jaw, she arched her neck and curled her arm around him. As promised, his lips parted in response to the determined urging of hers. Without hesitation Liz thrust her tongue past them into the dark, sleek chamber beyond and immediately reeled from the unexpected intensity of the sensation. It was like plunging into liquid fire and she felt the shower of sparks all the way to her toes.

For just a split second she hesitated, dazed, clinging to Zach's shoulders for support in a world that had started spinning around her and waiting for him to deepen the kiss. Then she remembered that was up to her and slowly she began to move her tongue in a patternless exploration of his mouth.

It took Liz almost no time to discover it was as much fun to take the lead as it was to follow, to act instead of being limited to reacting. Maybe even more fun. She loved being free to take her time and learn all the contrasting textures of him, the roughness of his tongue, the damp, satiny flesh just inside his lips, and the hot, wet sweetness that surrounded her and held her so tightly. This must be something of what a man felt when he buried himself inside a woman. A pale version of it, perhaps, but just the erotic association was enough to unleash inside Liz a trembling impatience. The blood was pounding in her ears and she used that pulsating, evocative rhythm to set the pace as she thrust her tongue into his mouth over and over again.

There was no longer any need for her to check and see how Zach was responding. She could feel the rising level of his desire in the bunched muscles at the back of his neck and in the tension in his hard chest as she rubbed her breasts against him and, most thrilling of all, in that unyielding ridge of heat just below his belt. All that remained to be seen was how long he would persist in forcing her to be the sole aggressor. At least he was finally kissing her back, using his lips and tongue and teeth in a clever, imaginative series of counterthrusts and parries. But his arms remained stubbornly by his sides, signaling that he wasn't yet ready to relinquish the tight rein tethering his passion.

Panting for breath, Liz was finally forced to peel her lips from his, withdrawing her tongue in a slow, unabashedly seductive slither. She looked into his desire-clouded eyes with no attempt to be coy. "Are you starting to feel wanted?"

Zach nodded, his smile noticeably drained. "Not to mention slightly ravished," he added, his ragged breathing a delight to Liz. "And more than slightly overheated. Why don't you see what you can do about getting these clothes off me?"

Liz smiled without missing a beat. The truth was that having warmed to the game and to the new, heady role of aggressor, she was enjoying it. She felt powerful and energized, two feelings she'd never before associated with lovemaking. But then, never before had she made love in a situation so forbidden and dangerous as this one. Or, she acknowledged with a shamefully small measure of guilt, with a man as exciting and dangerous as Zach.

"Let's see," she murmured, letting her gaze drift without hurry over his rangy body. She didn't miss the look of grudging admiration that flickered briefly in Zach's eyes as she assessed him from head to toe as calmly and boldly as he had examined her on more than one occasion.

His black hair had dried to a thick, gleaming pelt that curled over his ears and the collar of his shirt, adding to his maverick appeal. His mouth was stern but relaxed, his lips reddened and slick from dueling with hers. Sweat had dampened the khaki shirt in places so that it clung distractingly to his muscular shoulders and chest. He'd left the top two shirt buttons undone, revealing a swirl of soft black curls that Liz vividly remembered narrowed to a silky line as they neared his belt. Her breath caught as her slowly lowering gaze reached that point of demarcation and confronted the bulging proof of his arousal. It strained against the zipper of his pants, making them pull tautly across his lean hips, and Liz felt her blood start to bubble in her veins. His long legs were braced apart in that arrogant stance all Texas-born males must receive along with their birth certificates and never seemed to outgrow. Her face was flushed as she looked back up at his.

"Boots first, I think," she murmured.

Before he could either command her to take them off for him or make a move to do it himself, Liz crouched and began working at the leather laces of one high-top leather boot with shaking fingers. She really didn't want to know if he would have reacted as gentleman or master. He had demanded proof of her willingness, and something fundamentally feminine inside her had responded, driving Liz to demonstrate it to him fully and completely, and with nothing of herself held back. Cupping her hand at the back of his knee, she urged him to lift his foot so she could slip off the first boot and sock. Then she repeated the chore on his other foot while Zach curled his fingers around the overhead tent support for balance. Putting the boots aside, she ran her fingers over his insteps with a small smile. Even his damn feet were manly looking. His skin there was almost as deeply tanned as on his arms and shoulders, and dusted with fine dark hairs.

Surging back to her feet, Liz found herself standing so

close to him the tips of her breasts brushed his chest. She didn't back off, simply lifted her fingers to the third button on his shirt and smiled. "Now your shirt."

It amazed Liz that she was able to free the buttons so efficiently when her whole body seemed to be quivering with impatience. She mostly kept her attention focused on her fingers, but darting glances told her of the hint of amazement Zach was trying hard not to let show. He was waiting for her to balk, she realized. He probably hadn't expected her to go even this far. There was a hint of defiance mixed in with the shimmering arousal in her eyes as she met his and slowly stripped the shirt down over his compliant arms, letting it slip to the floor at their feet.

The sight of his naked upper torso fascinated her. Wide at the shoulders and heavily muscled everywhere, he was still whipcord lean. His pants rode low on his hips, permitting a teasing glimpse of hard, flat belly. Liz was suddenly struck by a crazy urge to snuggle her nose into the thick cloud of black hair high on his chest. Why not? This was, after all, her show. And if he chose to turn it into something else, well, she was ready.

Tipping her head toward him, she rubbed against his chest, a throaty chuckle bubbling from her as the soft hairs there tickled her nose. On impulse she slid to one side and sought with her tongue the flat nipple hidden among the tufts of hair, nuzzling it with her lips and teeth. A sharp intake of breath and the abrupt acceleration of his heartbeat beneath her cheek told her Zach's iron control was melting quickly. She smiled against his chest and took pains to treat the other side to the same ardent attention she'd lavished on the first. By the time she pulled away, both nipples were tightly pebbled and Zach's breathing was coming in short, rapid gusts.

His hands, she noticed, had curled into clenched fists at his sides, more proof of her unexpected skill. It was a heady feeling to know that she had the power to challenge his control in a way that was so effortless, so pleasurable. Feeling a rush of exhilaration, she pressed her palms flat to his chest, dragging them lower in an unhurried caress that ended with her fingertips hooked snugly inside his waistband. Against the back of her fingers she felt his stomach muscles turn washboard rigid at her touch, and the gleam in his eye was suddenly edged with curiosity. He was wondering if she would really go through with it, now that a buckle and a zipper were all that stood between her and intimate knowledge of exactly how much she had aroused him. It was that hint of smugness in his expression that gave Liz the small added impetus she needed to work open the silver buckle of his belt and the button beneath it.

With her fingertips clutching the pull tab on his zipper, she paused to murmur teasingly, "May I?"

The flare of raw passion in his eyes made Liz tremble. He nodded. "Please."

His throat convulsed around the hoarsely uttered word and slowly, slowly Liz lowered the zipper. The metallic rasp sounded like a drumroll in the hushed interior of the tent. Sheer bravado pushed her past a second of trepidation, guiding her hands to the elastic waistband of his shorts—might as well get it over with in one fell swoop, Liz told herself—and giving her the extra jolt of courage necessary to drag them along with his slacks the endless length of those strong, sun-browned legs with their sinewy cords and sculptured hollows. When they hit the floor, Zach kicked both aside in a movement that was at once graceful and totally artless.

Standing stiffly before him, Liz took one look at his coolly expectant smile and her own wilted a little around the edges. She had just reached the end of her spontaneous seductress act, pulled the final trick out of her hat, and was at a loss as to what her next clever move should be. Even her courage had evaporated, leaving her skittish, reluctant to so much as sneak a glance at the new terrain she'd uncovered, no matter how much the thought of it tempted her averted eyes.

"It's a little late to go shy on me now," Zach remarked.

His tone was gentle, too gentle, causing Liz to lift her gaze to his face with a sinking feeling of dread. If he was wearing that twisted, mocking smile again she would clobber him. She would pick up his boots and aim them right at his thick head. She would . . . but the smile on his face was as free of insolence as the warm, wanting look in his eyes.

"I'm not shy," she insisted, not quite truthfully.

"Good. I'm not either. And I have no objection to you looking at me."

Her nerves clamoring with excitement, Liz accepted the challenge and permitted her eyes to cautiously trace the intriguing line of black hair that divided his chest and sliced across the slightly paler skin of his belly only to bush more fiercely than ever at the juncture of his thighs. Jutting out from it at a forty-five degree angle was the hard spear that had made its heat and power known to Liz even through their clothes. It looked huge to her, a bold, blatant, relentless proclamation of his maleness, and Liz felt a quake of apprehension at the sight.

Apparently catching her reaction, Zach angled her a quizzical look. "You have seen a naked man before, haven't you, *Mrs*. Randolph?"

"Of course," Liz snapped. Then, breaking into a rueful smile at her own defensiveness, she murmured, "Just never quite so much of one, I'm afraid."

A series of emotions flashed across Zach's face in response to her candor: suspicion, then understanding, surprise, and pleasure, ending with a flare of desire so strong it incited a curling sensation deep in her loins.

"Don't worry, you'll be able to handle it," he told her, his tone softly reassuring. "I'll make sure of that, I promise."

Then at last he was reaching for her, hauling her against him in the unyielding show of strength she'd longed for, his mouth swooping down to possess hers with a ruthlessness that bordered on violence. He forced her lips to part for the hungry thrust of his tongue, one big hand anchoring her head still and the other sweeping down to cup her buttocks, forcing her as close as was physically possible to the raging fire in his loins. And unbelievably, shamefully, Liz loved every second of it.

Zach kissed her until she was moaning into his hot, open mouth and her legs had turned boneless beneath her, leaving it to his strong arms to keep her from melting into a puddle of pure sensation at his feet. Liz felt in his devouring kiss all the tension and longing and need that had been building

206

in him while she playfully indulged her fantasies, exercising her unexplored powers of seduction on his passive, willing body.

But now the tide had turned with a vengeance.

His hands were everywhere on her body, their touch practiced and compelling. They stroked and kneaded, at times drawing from her a whimper of longing that sharpened into a frantic gasp as he turned playfully, possessively rough. Magically he dealt with the buttons of her shirt, easing it off so deftly that Liz wasn't fully cognizant of its going until Zach interrupted his plundering of her mouth to look down at her. His already passion-dark eyes turned to jet at the sight of the full ivory globes of her breasts, their pink crests now a deep crimson and peaked with arousal.

Liz shivered with excitement, wanting to grab his hands and guide them to her swollen breasts, begging him to touch her there, to ease the throbbing ache in them. As if sensing the need behind her heaving breaths, Zach reached out and captured one soft mound in his cupped palm, curling his fingers to squeeze it firmly. His eyes wrenched shut, and his hoarse groan was echoed by Liz as the slight roughness of his touch sent shooting sensations from her breast to the pit of her stomach.

His hands continued to caress her as his lips lowered to her neck, inflicting a rapid scattering of love-bites along her collarbone and the high curve of her breast, finally opening wide to draw one tingling nipple into the roaring furnace of his mouth. Liz gasped, unable to prevent the small writhing motion of her hips. Her hands fastened on to his shoulders for support as his teeth and tongue tormented the captured bud, licking, sucking, bearing down just hard enough to make her want to scream with pleasure. He slid over and branded the other tip his as well, making it quiver and pulse as he circled it with his tongue before drawing as much of her smoothness into his mouth as he could, suckling and releasing, then suckling again, the rhythm blatantly and unbearably erotic.

Liz clenched her legs together in an unsuccessful attempt to quell the pressure steadily building there. Her whole body seemed to be melting, turning into a hot, liquid rush that pooled between her legs, waiting, yearning. One of Zach's hard arms was wound supportively around her waist, and through the thick, sensual haze engulfing her she felt his other hand move to untie the drawstring securing her slacks. Once unfastened they fell to the floor unassisted. Impatiently she struggled free, kicking them aside. Her only pair of panties had still been wet when she dressed, so when Zach molded his hand, with fingers splayed, to the gentle curve of her belly, it was flesh-to-flesh contact.

Liz's hands clenched at the exquisite sensations his touch sent washing through her, her fingernails biting into the resilient muscles of his shoulder. Urgently Zach bent her back over his arm until he was looming powerfully above her, making Liz feel small and feminine and utterly dependent on his superior strength. With his mouth still hot and busy at her breast, his hand moved on her in a firm, swirling motion, always edging lower, toward the damp center of her desire. His fingers brushed across her hip and the sensitive area on her inner thighs and then whispered teasingly over the soft thatch of hair between. Liz clamped her teeth down on her bottom lip as tremors of pleasure racked her body.

When she didn't think she would be able to stand waiting even one second longer for Zach to touch her the way she wanted, needed, to be touched, he used the pressure of his legs to nudge her backward toward the cot, easing her down until she sat perched on the edge.

Dropping to his knees before her, he drew her legs apart with hands that were gentle but relentless. He easily overpowered her instinctive urge to clamp them together in order to hide herself from the scorching intensity of his gaze. While she watched, torn between excitement and embarrassment, he moved closer, positioning himself squarely in the V of her parted thighs, his hands bracketing her hips. His eyes caressed her as he murmured soft, disjointed phrases, words of praise and hunger, blunt words that would ordinarily shock her. Now, however, with desire moving through her in swirling, shifting currents, they only served to ease her over her sudden spate of shyness. Gradually, under the patient strumming of his fingers, Liz felt her muscles loosen. The pose still struck her as decadent, but deliciously so, and he had driven her to a point where she was helpless to do anything but yield to the searing need growing inside her.

Amazingly at such a foreboding moment, Zach smiled at her, a lazy, sexy smile that made her heart lurch in her chest. Still holding her wide green eyes captive, he slid his hand along the curve of her hip to her thigh, then over and down, his inquisitive fingers ruffling their way through the bright, soft nest of curls to find and part her intimately.

Liz mewed softly, her head lolling back and her hands scrambling to plant themselves on the cot on either side of her to better support her drifting body. Calluses on the pads of Zach's fingers made them feel slightly coarse, but they moved over her delicate flesh as carefully as if she were a priceless violin and he a master musician. Within her a slow, sweet spiral of pleasure was tightening, tightening. Lightly he pressed one finger against the most sensitive spot on her entire body while another slipped deeply inside her, pushing her toward the brink of some endless abyss.

The fevered rasp of his voice urged her on as he sought to pleasure her fully.

"Ahh, you like that," he murmured when she twisted restlessly in response to the skillful movement of his fingers within her. "Show me what else you like, baby. How hard, how deep." He lifted one of her hands and placed it over his own very busy one. "Show me what feels best."

If Liz had been able to speak, she would have told him that what felt best was exactly what he was doing. In fact, it felt more glorious than anything anyone had ever made her feel before. But all she could manage was a broken moan as she locked her fingers around his wrist, silently imploring him not to stop. She closed her eyes as the firebolts of sensation grew stronger, too dazed to think about the implication of the slow, slippery journey his lips were making across her stomach. Then the warmth of his hand fell away. Feeling suddenly bereft, Liz opened her eyes in time to see his dark head lower. Her next breath was a fevered gasp as his hot mouth replaced his fingers.

Instinctively Liz clutched at his hair. "Zach, wait, no . . ."

"Yes," he uttered, the word carried on a moist, intimate caress of a breath.

"I mean, no, no one ever . . . I haven't . . ."

He lifted his head just enough to meet her eyes, flashing her a look of total comprehension. "I'm glad," he told her roughly.

Then his mouth found her again and Liz was transported beyond protesting, beyond thinking, into a world where she could only feel and trust Zach to take care of everything else. The waves of pleasure that ripped through her now made everything that had gone before seem like wind ripples on a still lake. Higher and higher they surged until finally cresting in a white-hot explosion which left everything Liz was and everything she'd ever believed shattered in a million pieces in Zach's strong arms.

She called out to him, panic and wonder mingled in her voice, and he came to her, his hard body stretching up to cover hers. Keeping his hand cupped protectively around the soft mound between her legs where aftershocks still trembled, he bore her down on her back on the narrow cot. His lips drifted across her lowered eyelids and the delicate curve of her cheek, finally settling on her mouth and taking her in a kiss that was slow and lingering but every bit as urgent as those that had come before.

Liz thought herself spent and was prepared to float through the consummation of Zach's obviously still-raging passion in a state of blissful lassitude. But the movements of his hands and mouth on her body very quickly thwarted that plan. With each caress, each increasingly ruthless possession of her mouth, Zach demanded her participation. He teased and dared responses from her, his tenderness of a moment ago swept away in a surge of mock roughness that Liz thrilled to. Her own hunger rapidly catapulted back to the height where she knew his must hover. She felt the immediacy of his need in the heavy rocking motion of his hips against hers, and she began to twitch beneath him in restless anticipation, signaling her readiness.

Still he held back, lifting his body until it barely grazed hers and rubbing tantalizingly against her until Liz was arching off the cot in search of the fulfillment it was within his power, and only his power, to grant.

"Please," she pleaded, "now, Zach, please."

She was begging. She, Elizabeth Bennett Fitzgerald Randolph, who for her entire life had only to express a passing fancy for something to have it arrive on a silver platter, was begging this man, this stranger, this *huaquero*, to take her in the most complete and fundamental way a man could take a woman. The awareness that he'd been able to drive her to such a state only stoked the flame of her passion higher.

"Please," she whispered again, and at that same instant he entered her with a powerful surge that made Liz cry out loud.

Zach swallowed the splintered sound of her need with a kiss, reining his body to absolute stillness, letting Liz absorb the throbbing, burning wonder of him inside her. He filled her completely, and she wished she could hold him that way forever, to draw him even deeper if such a thing were possible. Then he started to move, pulling almost all the way out, then thrusting forward and starting over, again and again, his strokes slow and slick. Liz's thought processes shut down. A small quivering started deep in her belly, spreading through her like a slow-moving river until his pace abruptly quickened, pumping fuel onto the flames that licked at her nerve endings.

The tent was hot, and the slippery contact of their straining, sweat-dampened bodies amplified the eroticism of each touch. Breathlessly Liz tried to gather him closer to her, clinging to the solid expanse of his back and encircling his hips with her long, slender legs. The frantic back-and-forth twisting of her head on the pillowless cot bore testimony to her growing loss of control, and then suddenly Zach's hands were reaching down to brace her hips firmly, his fingers curling into the soft curve of her bottom. Gripping her tightly, he forced Liz to match the driving rhythm he'd established, bringing a rough, primitive order to the hurricane blowing through her.

Relentlessly he carried them both higher, farther, closer to the edge of fulfillment. And then a volcano erupted inside Liz, sending her spinning off in a hundred different directions. And Zach was with her every step of the way, his arms tightly entwined around her weakened body, his heavy shudders echoing hers, his hoarse, exultant cry mingling with her own soft sound of release.

Afterward Liz lay with her eyes shut, relishing the weight of Zach's body on hers, enveloped in a feeling of well-being that precluded all other thoughts. She gave a small purr of satisfaction as he kissed her lightly, repeatedly, as if memorizing her face with his lips. It was a tender and totally unexpected gesture, and she loved it. She loved his gentleness as much as she loved his relentless passion of a moment ago.

Gradually the magical spell receded. Zach rolled his weight to the side without disturbing the intimacy of their embrace. His arms still anchored her close as her heartbeat slowed to near normal. Once again it felt like blood rather than helium that flowed through her veins. The moment seemed ripe for her to say something, only Liz wasn't quite sure what it should be. What did one say to a stranger after making love with him?

Thank you, that was most enjoyable?

"Most enjoyable" didn't come close to describing what had just transpired. For that matter, Zach didn't seem like much of a stranger anymore either. Liz knew it was crazy, probably just a figment of her temporarily starry-eyed imagination, but it had felt to her as if more than their bodies had collided on this narrow cot. Ridiculous as it sounded, it had felt like a fusion of hearts and souls as well. She certainly wasn't addled enough to call what had just happened love, but it was more than lust. She would bet her life on that. She just didn't know how to go about broaching the subject to the man whose body was still melded damply to hers. Maybe what she should do was forget about trying to come up with some momentous remark and simply say the first thing that came to mind.

"Do you plan on spending the night over here?"

Without lifting his head, Zach angled it so he could meet her eyes. Even in the dim light Liz could see the quizzical arch of his black brows. "Do you have any objections?"

214

Was he kidding? She wouldn't object if he announced he never planned to move again. Yet strangely, in spite of the fact that he had just done things to her and touched her in ways that were as intimate as you could get, and that his fingers were still playing with her lightly, she couldn't bring herself to tell him how she felt.

"No . . . of course I have no objections," was all she said in a pleased whisper. "I just thought it might be too cramped here for you to get comfortable."

"I'm very comfortable."

"I meant comfortable enough to sleep."

"If I can't get to sleep tonight, it won't be the size of this cot keeping me awake." He pulled her closer and kissed the top of her head. "Just don't wiggle around too much or you won't be able to walk in the morning."

"Is that a threat?"

"Wiggle and find out."

Liz suddenly realized that his dry, supremely self-satisfied tone didn't have the same antagonistic effect on her that it once did. Now the effect was more like that of church bells ringing on Christmas morning, filling her with a warm, peaceful feeling heavily laced with excitement. She still didn't chance a wiggle, though. Instinct warned that idle threats weren't Zach's style, and at the moment she was feeling too sleepy to do anything more energetic than breathe. Even that was an effort. Succumbing to a giant yawn, she bent her knees to settle herself more snugly in the warm cove of Zach's body and closed her eyes. Within minutes she was asleep.

* * *

Zach listened to Liz's slow, regular breathing and knew he was close to following her into oblivion. There was nothing like a little sex to insure a good night's sleep. He grinned, thinking he ought to sleep like the dead tonight. Of course, she'd probably been right when she suggested this cot would be tight quarters for the two of them. He just hadn't been ready then to let her go and cross to his own cot to sleep alone. He still wasn't.

Trying not to disturb her, he shifted his arm into a marginally less contorted position. Any minute now he would drift off and he didn't want to wake up in an hour with a cramp. He uncrossed his legs. If he did happen to wake up in an hour or so, he could always go over to his own cot then. With a last, long look at the woman asleep in his arms, he reached up and turned off the light. But in the darkness the feeling he'd been trying to ignore was worse. It wasn't exactly a feeling either. More of a sensation, and not a comfortable one. It was like something crawling along the back of his neck to whisper in his ear that he'd blown it, that he'd handled Liz all wrong tonight. And he couldn't figure out why. All in all the night was a roaring success. Of course, the plan hadn't included laying her, and Zach knew what a mistake it could be to veer from the plan in the middle of a job. But he supposed it had been inevitable. Deep down it was what he'd been wanting to do almost from the start. So why now, deep down, was he starting to feel like a total washout?

Probably, he tried to reassure himself, it was because he wasn't used to having to *handle* a woman in the first place. He was used to enjoying women, paying for them if they charged, and then walking away. And when you got right down to it, wasn't that the scenario here? He had enjoyed every moment of his romp with Liz. He was sure as hell paying for the pleasure in aggravation. And in a week or so he would walk away with a big smile and a few choice memories if tonight was any indication. It was perfect. So why, Zach asked himself as he closed his eyes and ordered himself to sleep, couldn't he shake this sensation that something was wrong?

With the sides rolled down, the inside of the tent heated to an inferno by morning. Zach awoke coated with sweat, a cramp in one arm and pins and needles in the other and knowing exactly what had gone wrong the night before. He had made a major tactical error. The realization brought with it a crushing sense of frustration and self-directed anger.

He longed to get outside and fill his lungs with fresh, slightly cooler air, but his arm was currently being used as a pillow by the woman beside him, and he had a feeling that like a cat, she would pounce to full alertness the second he twitched a muscle. He wasn't ready to face her yet. Idly Zach tried to predict which role she would choose to play on this sultry morning after. The subdued and seduced victim? The stoic but repentant martyr? Actually, he didn't give a damn. All he wanted right now was some time to gather his own thoughts before having to listen to hers.

It shouldn't take him long. In retrospect it was easy to see how the events of last evening had slid steadily downhill until he'd been crushed under an avalanche of his own making.

He had been perversely glad, almost relieved when he

returned from the site and learned Liz had discovered what he and the others were doing in this no-man's-land in northern Guatemala. He had spent the whole day thinking about her, speculating about the two of them spending another night in the same small space, wondering if he would be able to keep from acting on the hunger that seemed to grow stronger each time he looked at her. After the way that kiss he'd staged for the men—at least it had started out staged—had ended, he'd had a strong hunch it wouldn't take a brass band to get her into his bed. But he'd known all along that making it with her would only complicate matters. That's why her stumbling onto his record book had seemed such a blessing in disguise. Surely a woman of her breeding wouldn't share sheets with a filthy grave robber.

Only that's what she had done, and more eagerly than Zach would have dreamed possible under any circumstances. But while her uninhibited responses last night may have temporarily short-circuited his common sense, in the clear light of day he was once again all too aware of what had prompted her sudden willingness. The thought of it left the sour taste of self-loathing in his mouth.

Not that she'd been faking entirely. Oh, she was a hot little bitch to be sure and, besides, no woman was a good enough actress to fake the kind of excitement that he'd felt gripping her when they made love. But it hadn't been a sudden change of heart or mad craving for his body that transformed her from shrew to seductress as he'd been dazzled enough to let himself believe last night.

Rather, it must have finally penetrated her stubborn,

spoiled head that she wasn't going to be able to sulk or argue or buy her way out of this mess, even with all that money she had sitting in some bank vault back at home. Spending the whole day stuck here in the middle of nowhere, with only old Juan for company, must have driven her to the edge of desperation, and that little tussle with Rodil had been enough to push her over . . . not to mention scaring all hell out of her in the process. Compared to that lowlife, he must have suddenly looked like Prince Charming to her calculating eyes, and an ally to be cultivated.

Zach angled a glance down at her. Asleep, nestled serenely against his side, she appeared to be as guileless as a child and beautiful enough to make his mouth water. He immediately redirected his gaze to the green canvas of the tent roof. No way was he going to make the same mistake twice. Last night when he'd returned to find her whimpering and struggling in Rodil's clutches, he felt as if someone had plunged a knife straight into his heart and twisted it. She had looked so helpless, so vulnerable. And maybe, temporarily, she was. But he'd bet everything packed into those tents out back that in her element Liz Randolph was about as helpless and as vulnerable as a fox in a hen house.

And just about as crafty. Look at how smoothly she had changed tactics last night. Accepting that she couldn't buy his services with money, she had cleverly resorted to using her second-most-prized commodity, sex. Of course she probably hadn't planned on blowing her whole wad in one shot. No, if he had allowed it, she would have bestowed only a chaste kiss as his reward for handling Rodil. Then she would gradually have increased the ante as he continued to behave in the manner she desired, always stopping short before things got out of hand, of course. She must have figured that within a few days he'd be panting so hard for it, he'd do whatever she wanted. Then afterward she could always shift the blame onto his shoulders, claiming that he had worn her down, and that technically anything that happened between them was rape.

Too bad for her that he already knew the rules of that particular game by heart and had decided a long time ago never to play it again. It was past experience that warned him to force her to take the lead last night. Every step of the way—up to a point—he'd been expecting her to balk. But she hadn't and Zach had to give her credit for that. It had quickly become obvious that she wanted him as much as he wanted her . . . and God knows, he'd wanted her. And so in spite of knowing that she was trying to manipulate him, to train him like one of Pavlov's dogs, he'd finally figured, what the hell?

And that was what led to his major tactical blunder.

He'd started out determined to retain utter control of the situation by rubbing her nose in her own fierce desire until she wouldn't dare to make any tearful accusations afterward. But instead he had ended up with his own senses scrambled, down on his knees in his frenzy to please her, driven by some mysterious urge to love her in a way that would burn from her mind the memory of any other man's touch. A lingering vision of the scene floated before Zach's eyes, unleashing a new rush of self-reproach and injecting tension into every one of his muscles. The slender body beside him stirred. He was right. The woman slept like a damn cat.

"Good morning."

Her soft, sleep-husked words poured over Zach like raw silk. It took every shred of his willpower to jerk his arm free, letting her head fall back to the cot with a thump, and swing to his feet.

"Is it?" he countered without bothering to look at her. "I hadn't noticed."

CHAPTER
ELEVEN

A sick, panicky feeling welled up inside Liz as she watched him dress. With his back to her, he stepped into a clean pair of briefs and his jeans, then sat down on the other cot to pull on his socks and boots. She couldn't help remembering how different the mood had been last night when he—or rather *she*—had removed all his clothes. It wasn't that she'd expected him to greet her this morning with roses and a proclamation of undying love; she wasn't that naive. But she certainly hadn't expected this from him either, thick silence broken only by a few grunts and a shoulder cold enough to frost the sun.

He could at least acknowledge what had happened. He could express some understanding of the change that had taken place, the sensual bond, the link of sorts, that had been forged between them, however tenuous and temporary.

222

He could show some interest, some sensitivity to what she was feeling. But all he did was methodically tighten his leather boot laces without so much as a glance in her direction.

"Zach?" she finally ventured in as calm and neutral a tone as she could manage.

"Mmmm?" He was now engrossed in picking up the clothes they'd left strewn about the tent. He shoved his own back into the crate with the others. Hers he simply tossed over his shoulder at her.

"Is there something wrong?" There was no sense mincing words when he seemed to want to utter so few to begin with.

"Not at all."

"Then where are you going?"

What she really meant to ask was, Why are you acting this way? But that wasn't what came out and Liz fully expected the sardonic look Zach arrowed her way in response to what had. At least he was finally looking at her. Not that his flinty stare or harsh parody of a smile made her feel any better. In fact, it made her suddenly, excruciatingly aware of her nakedness, and snatching up the wrinkled shirt which had landed by her feet, she struggled into it. Clutching it tightly to her breasts with one hand, she attempted to smooth the tangled web of her hair with the other until Zach silently dropped his comb in her lap.

"Not that I think you really need it," he drawled when she peered cautiously up at him. "You look quite fetching . . . and at home just as you are."

Liz froze with the comb in her hand. Just as she was?

Flushed and tousled from an energetic night in bed with a man she hardly knew?

That had to be the point he was making, but Liz couldn't imagine why he was coldly condemning her for something he'd quite freely encouraged last night. As arrogant and insolent as he was, she hadn't believed him to be the kind of man who would tell a woman anything to get her to go to bed with him and then lose all respect for her once she did. She still didn't believe it. There was something more to his mood this morning than a latent case of adolescent male chauvinism, but she couldn't begin to figure out what it might be.

"As for where I'm going," he continued in a pleasant tone, too pleasant, considering that Liz could feel waves of tension radiating from him, "I have a job to do. Remember?"

"I remember," she replied, knowing full well that he anticipated some acerbic comeback about his "job" and refusing to give him the satisfaction of delivering it. Besides, it probably only confirmed his assessment of her as shallow and selfish, but at the moment she was more distressed over the way he was treating her than she was over some stolen artifacts that she couldn't do anything about.

"I understand that you have to go to work," she began, the calm, steady tone becoming more difficult to maintain by the second. "What I don't understand is the way you're behaving toward me."

"I'll just bet you don't, baby."

Liz flinched from his quiet words as if he'd applied a

whip to her slender back, and for a fraction of a second Zach's confidence that he was right about her wavered. Then he took a good look at her wide green eyes and trembling lips, an expression so provocatively convincing it must have taken her years to perfect, and he once again saw the reality of who she was with bitter clarity.

"I'll bet you were expecting to be treated quite differently by me after last night, weren't you, fancy face?" he demanded. "I'll bet you were counting on me to be gentle and solicitous and real, real manageable."

She shook her head, sending her hair tumbling about her shoulders like silken streamers and inspiring in Zach the unwelcome memory of how it had felt against his skin last night.

"I'm not sure what you mean," she told him.

"Liar," he said softly. "But let me spell it out for you anyway: It isn't going to work. You can't manipulate me with sex. Once—and only once—was I ever fool enough to sit up and beg for sexual treats from a woman, but never again."

Liz gasped, her expression shocked. He had to hand it to her; she was an even better actress than he'd thought.

"I wasn't trying to do that," she cried. "How can you even..."

"Easy," he said, cutting off the protest he didn't have the time or the inclination to listen to. "That's exactly what you were trying to do, and you'd go right on trying if you thought it would work, wouldn't you, baby? Tell the truth, wouldn't you be willing to spend, oh, say, every night for the next week in my bed if you thought that it would persuade me to do what you want? Drive you back to San Luis.''

Only a half hour ago Liz would have been willing to spend the next week in his bed even if it meant spending the rest of eternity in hell. How could she have been such a fool? *Be* such a fool, she corrected herself. Instead of lashing out at him in rage, she was actually trying to think of some way to convince him of the absurdity of his accusations. Did he really believe she would have humbled herself the way she had last night if it were only an act? Some sleazy attempt to manipulate him? She opened her mouth to ask, but Zach spoke first.

''What's the matter? Isn't that the deal you had in mind? All right, I'm willing to barter. Four nights in my bed and I'll have one of the men drive you back instead. What do you say?''

It was with something akin to relief that Zach watched the swirl of pain and confusion in her eyes finally flare into anger. No matter how phony he knew it was, that innocent, shattered look on her face had been starting to get to him.

''No.'' She came up on her feet, suddenly looking very small and fragile wrapped in that oversized shirt, and repeated the defiant word. ''No. That's what I say to your *deal*.''

''You sure? That's my final offer.''

''And you can stick it,'' she snapped. ''No deal.''

''Fine, then.'' He returned her contemptuous stare,

embellishing it with a sardonic grin sure to make her temper
boil. "No sex."

"Fine."

"Fine."

Grabbing the first shirt he laid his hand on, Zach crossed
the tent in two angry strides and ripped the flap aside. He
only wished the damned thing was a door so he could have
slammed it behind him.

No sex?

He must be out of his mind to let her goad him to the
point of making such an asinine declaration. Just who did he
think he was punishing with such a ban anyway? He hadn't
been able to keep his hands off her before; how was he
going to manage it now that he'd had a sample of the
delights her soft, smooth body could yield? He met the
knowing smirks the men flashed him with a black warning
of a glare, grabbing the plate of lumpy cereal old Juan held
out and bolting it down without tasting it. A cup of hot,
black coffee went the same route.

No sex.

He was a jackass. And she was a witch. A powerful one
or she wouldn't be able to make him lose his head this way.
She was living, breathing proof that he didn't have the kind
of cold, absolute control over his actions and desires that he
liked to think. Everything she represented repelled and
disgusted him, yet he wanted her with a fury that swept
everything else aside. Even now he was nearly shaking with
the urge to storm back into that tent and tell her there damn
well would be sex whether she liked it or not. And plenty of
it.

Instead he flung his empty plate and cup into the dirt rather than old Juan's waiting pan of murky dishwater and strode off toward the jeep, leaving the others shoveling in the last of their breakfast in their hurry to follow. No way was he going to crawl back in there and admit to her that he'd spoken too quickly. He'd said it now and it would just have to stand. Even if it killed him.

Liz stayed out of sight until she was sure Zach was gone, his ragtag band of social misfits trailing behind. His cruel verbal attack earlier had all but shocked her into silence, but since then she'd thought of a string of things she would like to say to him. Nothing would give her more pleasure than to charge after him and tell him exactly what she thought of him, and maybe scratch his eyes out while she was at it. But she was smart enough to know that if she tangled with him in public while he was in such a volatile mood it would end in humiliation for her. Not until the only sound in camp was that of O.J. slapping dishes around did she venture outside to roll up the sides of the tent, at last letting some much-needed fresh air inside.

If only it were that easy to air out her thoughts. Her head was so full of anger she felt as if it might explode. She was mostly angry with Zach . . . shouting, spitting, fist-pounding angry. But she was also irritated and disgusted with herself for letting last night happen in the first place. Wretch that he was, he'd given her plenty of time to call a halt. Woven through all the bitterness were even more disturbing feelings— confusion and disappointment and—much as it distressed Liz to admit it—a pale ribbon of wistfulness.

Last night Zach had been so tender, so giving, and

now . . . now he was stomping about like a stallion with one leg caught in a pricker bush. He was acting as if he wished last night had never happened, trying to blame her for the fact that it had, accusing her of starting the whole thing with some ulterior motive in mind, for heaven's sake. He'd stopped just short of calling her a whore, insisting that she'd expected to be paid somehow for going to bed with him. Liz pressed her knuckles to her lips, muffling a soft cry of dismay. What had happened to change him so quickly and completely?

The answer was obvious, and humiliating enough to make her want to crawl under the nearest rock. The fact was he hadn't changed. He hadn't said or done anything last night to suggest that their situation would be altered if they had sex. He'd made no promises about the future or apologies for the past. She couldn't even console herself with the thought that he had seduced her. If anything, she had seduced him. Remembering all she had done—all she had let him do to her—Liz's face burned brighter than the sun creeping up over the trees in the distance. God, she hated that man . . . more now than ever.

A midmorning bath in the tree-shaded lake did little to improve her mood. She was so obsessed with her own misery she barely noticed that O.J.'s treatment of her was a smidgen less surly than usual. At lunchtime he even hobbled over to where she was sitting and held out a plate of grayish mush and a cup of coffee strong enough to stop speeding bullets.

Liz lifted her gaze from the unappetizing sight to meet his. "Lunch, I presume?"

"Yup. From now on if you wanna eat, you eat when I fix the men's food. I ain't your cook."

"Maid," she corrected.

He glared at her.

"I think you meant to say that you ain't my maid."

"Bah."

He turned to go, but not before giving her a strange look. No doubt he was wondering what had happened inside their tent last night to cause his boss to roar out of there like a fast-moving thunderhead and her to sit staring into the endless mud as if some great secret of life were written there.

"Oh, O.J.," she called after him.

He glanced back over his shoulder, still looking a little bewildered by the name she persisted in calling him.

"When do the men eat lunch?"

"Now, same's you're doing."

"I see. Do you bring it to them at the site?"

"Nope. The boss sends someone to come pick it up and they eats it out there." He clamped his teeth together as if he'd already wasted more words on her than she merited and shuffled off.

She must have been napping yesterday when lunch was picked up. Did the boss ever deign to fetch the food himself? Liz wondered fretfully. She would prefer to postpone contact with Zach as long as possible. Luckily, when the jeep roared in a short while later it was Jade driving. He also gave her an odd look, though his was heavily shaded with sympathy, reminding Liz that regardless of what Zach said Jade might be persuaded to help her get out of there.

Someday she was going to have to look into that possibility. But not today. Today she was too busy berating herself for being a fool.

It was close to sundown before the moment Liz had been dreading all day arrived. She was standing by the supply tent getting a drink of water when she heard the approach of the caravan of trucks and jeeps. Without thinking she hurriedly began running her hands over her hair and wiping her mouth on her shirttail, her eyes fixed on that spot across the clearing where tires had left deep gouges in the soft earth as they plowed off this morning. When she caught herself primping, she jerked her arms to her sides, her mouth tightening into an angry line. She took a quick step toward her tent, freezing in her tracks when the first truck pulled into view. She'd be damned if she'd let Zach think she was cowed enough to hide from him, even if she was.

Forcing sips from the cup of water down her constricting throat, Liz observed out of the corner of her eye as Zach swung down from the truck seat with the same lithe, masculine grace with which he did everything, even make love. She felt a sudden rush of pride that she quickly told herself was totally unwarranted. After all, nothing he did or said or was in any way reflected upon her.

Sparing only a flicker of a glance in her direction, he disappeared into his tent, leaving Liz feeling absurdly disappointed. She wasn't sure what she expected upon his return, but to be so coolly ignored seemed anticlimactic after all her apprehension. The rest of the men swarmed around the stove, irritably heeding O.J.'s order to line up if they wanted to eat. Liz had casually slipped into place behind them when Zach reappeared. Something in the aggressive clip of his stride as he approached alerted Liz that she was about to get the confrontation she'd felt cheated out of a few moments ago. Too late she noticed the shirt clenched in his hand. The same shirt he'd ordered her to wash for him today.

"What's this?" he demanded, holding it directly in front of her face.

Beneath the negligent lift of her shoulders Liz's heart was pounding like a jackhammer. "It looks like a shirt."

"A *dirty* shirt," he added tersely.

Liz pretended to look more closely at it and nodded. "So it is."

She was suddenly aware of the breathless silence which engulfed them and wished she'd had the good sense to bite her tongue. The entire line of men was watching them, waiting to see how the boss was going to handle his mouthy woman.

"I thought I told you to wash it," Zach stated, his tone quietly menacing.

"I forgot."

The words came out sounding more flippant than Liz had intended. Zach's eyes narrowed sharply. His nostrils flared in a predatory way and his mouth thinned to a hard, straight line, a reminder of how nasty he could be when he chose. In the blue-black depths of his eyes blazed an emotion Liz couldn't come close to identifying. Hatred? Or grudging admiration? She looked at him standing there, backlit by the fire of the setting sun, and wondered how she could possibly feel even a sliver of attraction for him. Every shred of common sense she possessed told her she should feel nothing but contempt. Unfortunately things like common sense and reality didn't seem to have much bearing on the way she felt lately.

"I'm going to make you wish you hadn't forgot," he told her, his soft tone ominous. "I ought to make you take it down to the lake and wash it now. I'll bet a nice, long swim all by yourself in the dark would do wonders for your memory."

A low murmur of amusement passed through the group of men. Liz caught her breath and held it. She'd been wary enough being at the lake alone in broad daylight. She'd rather die than venture there now, when the jungle was starting to come alive with eerie nocturnal sounds.

"And that's exactly what I would do . . . if I didn't have other plans for you."

This brought a louder chuckle from the men, but Liz was too relieved to pay attention. Then she realized what they were chortling about, and her downcast gaze shot up to Zach's. Had he already decided to renege on his order of no sex, she wondered, cursing the small traitorous stirring of excitement the idea caused inside her. Zach obviously guessed the conclusion she'd jumped to and his mouth twisted in a sardonic grin.

"Cool down, sweetheart," he drawled mockingly. "I don't think you'll find what I have planned for you quite that exciting." Without taking his eyes off her, he called for O.J. "Old Juan," he said when the old man sidled over to them, "meet your new assistant. I'm afraid she doesn't know much about cooking, but she's more than willing to learn, aren't you, fancy face?''

Liz met his gaze levelly. She knew exactly what he was up to. She hadn't forgotten his remark about women being good for only two things in this part of the world. And since she wasn't going to be fulfilling his needs in bed, he was going to make damn sure she earned her keep in other ways. Particularly in a way that he knew she would find degrading, a way that drove home in no uncertain terms how different her position here was from the cushioned, pampered life she led at home. From the silence that had once more descended on the gathering, it seemed she was the only one who did understand Zach's announcement. The others all appeared surprised by his harshness in doling out punishment to his woman for something as minor as forgetting to wash his shirt.

''Tell him how willing you are to learn,'' he repeated. Then, without waiting for her to obey, he added, ''In fact, I think dishing up the food for the men tonight and doing all the cleaning up afterward is a good place for you to start.''

Something snapped inside Liz at his obvious determination to humble her publicly. ''No.''

''No what?''

A glint of satisfaction appeared between Zach's meshed lashes and Liz knew she'd played right into his hands. He'd wanted a confrontation, a chance to once more flaunt his power over her, and she'd stupidly given it to him.

''No, I'm not willing to learn,'' she said determinedly.

"And what's more I doubt O.J. wants me hanging around messing with his things."

"O.J.?" Zach echoed quizzically.

Liz flushed. "It's just a nickname I came up with...because of his sunny disposition."

There was an insinuating quality to Zach's nod. "I see. You'll cozy up to any man who's handy, won't you, baby?" Before Liz could open her mouth to protest, he continued. "Why, I'll bet you'll really enjoy this chance to get close to a whole bunch of men at once." He jerked his head toward the table behind him and growled, "Now get serving."

Liz was vibrating with resentment, making it difficult to talk in an even voice. She shook her head and finally managed a tentative, "No. I never agreed to be your galley slave."

"Maybe not, but you did agree to accept my protection in exchange for the use of your body," he reminded her bluntly. "Which no longer interests me."

Liz felt a suffocating wave of humiliation. There wasn't a sound from any of the men, not a chuckle, not even a sharply drawn breath, but she knew they were hanging on every word of this little melodrama. She would have turned and fled if she thought she had half a chance of escaping the flinty-eyed bully looming over her. It would be even more degrading to be chased down and hauled back to camp than it was to stand there being dictated to as if he were her lord and master.

"And as long as you choose to remain here under my protection," Zach continued in that same damn icy tone, "you'll do what I say...*whatever* I say."

Liz felt her stomach knot and her face flame. "And if I choose not to stay here?" she demanded through clenched teeth.

He shot her a derisive look. "The road's still in the same place it was when you walked in. Just don't take the first crossroads; it leads nowhere in both directions. Head due south into the jungle and San Luis is about two days away." His mouth twisted as he raked her with a critical gaze. "Make that three days for you."

Liz didn't have any idea how to find due south without a compass. And he knew it, damn his black heart. Beneath her anger and her embarrassment she felt absurdly crushed that he could treat her this way after what they'd shared . . . what she had *thought* they'd shared last night. A hot flood of tears pressed at the back of her eyes as she lifted her chin and edged past him, making her way to the spot behind the serving table where O.J. usually stood. Blinking rapidly in an effort to hold her tears at bay, she picked up the ladle from the pot of beans and dumped a scoop into the tin plate of the first man in line. The others filed past rapidly and in silence except for an occasional mumble of *gracias*. She didn't reply or look up until she recognized the lean, jean-clad hips in front of her as Zach's, and even then not until he continued to stand there long after she'd splattered a second ladleful of beans into his plate.

With a resigned sigh she gave in and slowly lifted her eyes to meet his. Just as slowly he raised the hand still holding the unwashed shirt and tossed it at her.

"Don't forget again tomorrow," he warned without a trace of a smile.

In the split second before he turned and stalked away Zach saw her face crumble. It was an indication that he still possessed a shred of decency that he felt a stab of guilt. That he was able to shrug it off so quickly was an indication of how minuscule a shred of decency it was. Stupid bitch. What had she expected when she looked up at him with those wide, luminous eyes? An apology? He gave a rough snort as he dropped to the ground a good distance away from where the others were sitting and shoved in a spoonful of the spicy food without tasting it. It was her own fault. She could have avoided this little scene entirely if she had done as he'd ordered and washed the damn shirt.

For a few minutes he continued wolfing down the contents of his plate, trying to ignore the small voice nagging at him from deep inside. It was a voice he preferred not to listen to . . . especially in matters concerning women. He'd decided long ago that all dealings with women existed outside whatever system of honor a man applied to the rest of his life. It was the only way to survive. And if nothing else, he was a survivor. He was also honest enough with himself to admit the truth, that there was no way in heaven or hell that Liz could have avoided tangling with him tonight. If he had returned to find his shirt washed and neatly folded on his cot, he would have found something else to ride her about. He had been spoiling for a fight all day. Ever since he'd let her goad him into making that absurd declaration about no more sex.

A dozen times during the day he'd been on the verge of recanting. He would start toward the jeep, prepared to drive back to camp and tell her he'd changed his mind, that he wasn't even going to attempt to do the impossible . . . sleep night after night in the same tent with a horny little bitch like her and pretend he didn't want her. He would tell her that he intended to take her whenever and however he chose, starting right then and there. But each time he stopped himself. And each time his frustration and rage had grown until he felt like a pressure cooker heated to the danger point. It didn't help his mood any to have to walk off the hardness he felt whenever he thought about being with her. It was while he was doing all that walking that he planned how to make her suffer the same way he was suffering.

Doing his wash and becoming old Juan's lackey was just the start of it. He planned to keep the lofty Ms. Randolph so busy polishing his boots and seeing to his whims that she wouldn't have any time or energy to spend trying to manipulate him. He would solve that problem and at the same time have the satisfaction of bringing her down a peg or two. The food in his mouth suddenly had a sour taste. The problem was that bringing her to heel publicly hadn't been anywhere near as satisfying as he'd expected. Instead of feeling triumphant when her shoulders sagged and she moved to do as he commanded, he'd felt like a bastard. He still did. He also still wanted her like hell. How on earth was he going to keep his hands off her when she was so close? Just the thought of her body all flushed and warm and writhing under his made him want her as much as he wanted to draw his next breath.

And that, he reminded himself for the thousandth time that day, was exactly why he had to stick to his guns. No sex. Of course there was also the matter of his pride to consider. He'd cavalierly told her he wasn't interested in her body, and he'd be damned if he let her find out how far from the truth that was. No matter how he tried to rationalize it, if he made love to her now, in some indefinable but ominous way she would have won. He would know it, and what's worse, so would she.

And that would be all the encouragement a woman like Liz would need to start plotting and wheedling all over again. He would have to be on guard against her constantly, keeping his defenses up, keeping her at a safe emotional distance, and the disgusting truth of the matter was that he wasn't at all sure he would be able to do that. Something had happened to him when he made love to her last night. He'd come close to losing control. Hell, who was he kidding? He'd lost control. He had totally surrendered to the sensual spell she'd cast. And that was something he never, ever intended to let happen again.

He glanced over just in time to see old Juan starting to help Liz scrape the leftover food into the garbage. Zach got quickly to his feet, then sauntered over and ordered the old cook to take an inventory of the supply tent instead. The look Liz shot him said that she knew exactly why he'd done it—to leave her to deal with the mess all by herself. Forming a smile around the cigarette clamped between his lips, Zach held out his dirty plate and waited pointedly until she took it from his hand. Let her glare. The madder she got, the better he would like it. After all, misery loves company.

It was full dark and most of the crew had already turned

in by the time she'd finished washing and drying the last unwieldy pot. Zach had settled himself close by to watch, knowing it made her uneasy and wishing she would slip up so he could blast her for it. She didn't, though. She didn't even give him the satisfaction of another resentful scowl as she glided past him when she was through and headed straight for the tent. By the time he permitted himself to follow, she was already asleep . . . or pretending to be. He stopped by her cot and flicked his lighter, staring down at her curled beneath the rough blanket. His senses rioted. It was as if it were last night all over again, so vivid was his memory of how she felt and smelled and tasted. Muttering the most vicious oath he could think of, he turned away and moved through the darkness to his cot. But it was a long, long time before he was able to sleep.

The first thing Liz did when she awoke was check to see that it was morning. She'd half expected to be shaken awake some time during the night because Zach decided that ordering her around and humiliating her wasn't as satisfying as having sex with her after all. But it was the safe pink light of dawn filtering through the tent's screen sides. Obviously he'd meant it when he said he was no longer interested. She should be ecstatic. And she was, Liz told herself firmly. At least as ecstatic as she could be while stuck in this hot, slimy, bug-infested place.

The second thing she did was roll as silently as possible to her other side to make sure her nemesis was still asleep. Her luck was holding. She'd prayed she'd be able to be up and out before he awoke. As long as she had no choice about helping O.J. or doing whatever else Zach might decree, she had decided to do so willingly. At least that way she could rob him of the satisfaction he so clearly derived from forcing her to obey. Quietly she slipped off the cot and picked up her sneakers. She had one hand on the tent flap when his sleep-roughened voice halted her.

"Where the hell do you think you're going?" he demanded.

Liz continued to face the wall. "To help O.J. . . . old Juan. Remember?"

"Look at me when you talk to me," he commanded softly.

Banking down on the resentment she knew was self-defeating, Liz slowly turned to face him. She kept her eyes carefully averted from the sight of his broad shoulders and naked chest. No sense stirring up unwanted memories.

"I'm going to help . . ."

"Closer," he interrupted.

"I . . ." She swallowed. "What?"

"I said come closer."

"Why?"

"Because I told you to."

Reluctantly Liz took a few steps toward his cot.

"More," he ordered.

Liz swallowed a disgusted sigh and did as he said. When she was standing only a foot or so away from where he lay with his arms folded casually beneath his head, he smiled. It was a distinctly condescending smile.

"Good girl," he murmured. "You can go now."

Liz felt the all-too-familiar snapping of her self-control.

She tossed her hair back over her shoulder, her chin lifting defiantly. "Why you . . ."

Instantly Zach stiffened. His eyes glittered menacingly as he shot to his feet. Liz reeled backward, certain he was going to hit her. When his hands clamped painfully on her shoulders, she instinctively squeezed her eyes shut. Instead of the blow she expected, however, his fingertips very gently touched the side of her throat close beneath her ear, a spot ordinarily hidden by her hair.

"Did I do this to you?" he demanded in a fractured voice.

Liz opened her eyes to find his gaze riveted on the place he was touching. Her thoughts spun in confusion. She had a feeling he wasn't exactly angry, at least not with her. But his expression was murderous and a muscle at one corner of his mouth twitched convulsively, as if he were fighting for control. It took her a few seconds to comprehend that he must be asking about that spot on her neck where Rodil had left his filthy mark on her. She'd seen it herself yesterday, in the small mirror Zach used for shaving.

"N-No," she said, her voice no more than a throaty shadow of sound. "It wasn't you."

He shook his head and Liz realized that what she saw in his eyes was anguish. And concern.

"Then who . . . ?" He bit the question off, his eyes narrowing to fierce slits as he grasped the obvious. "Rodil did this to you, didn't he?" When she didn't answer immediately, he shook her. "Didn't he?"

Liz gave a small nod.

"You told me he didn't hurt you," he growled in a harsh, accusing voice.

"He didn't really," Liz protested. "It's nothing."

His expression grew even grimmer. "No, it's something, all right. But don't worry, I have every intention of taking care of it."

To Liz's amazement he bent his head and pressed his lips gently to the reddish-purple brand. The contact sent fire sizzling through her, and when he quickly straightened again, she knew Zach had felt it too. She also surmised by the look on his face that the kiss had been unplanned, as much a shock to him as to her, and that he regretted it.

He pulled away from her abruptly, and after a moment of awkward silence, he repeated, "Yeah, I'll take care of it, all right."

Without thinking, Liz grabbed his arm as he made a move to go around her. "How? How will you take care of it?"

"None of your business."

That was answer enough. Liz knew intuitively what he planned to do and her stomach clenched into a giant knot. True, she hated Rodil with a passion, but she still shuddered to think of the price Zach was going to make him pay for leaving that dime-sized mark on her throat.

"Zach, wait," she pleaded, tightening her grip on his arm. "I...I'd rather you didn't do anything to Rodil. If you do, it will only make all of the men resent me. It's hard enough here without that happening."

For a moment he eyed her suspiciously. Please, she prayed, don't let him read something sordid and deceitful into this too. Finally he nodded, yanking his arm free.

"All right."

Liz blinked her lashes, not quite believing it had been so easy to convince him. "What did you say?"

"I said all right. I still think Rodil deserves to have his ass kicked, but as long as you'd rather I didn't, I'll skip it . . . this time. But I plan to make it clear to him that you're responsible for his reprieve and that it won't happen again."

He strode toward the entrance, stopped, and almost as an afterthought grabbed a shirt lying on his desk and tossed it to her. "After you get through with my wash, sew a button on this for me." His mouth quirked at her bewildered expression. "You do know how, don't you?"

Liz looked from the shirt to him. "Actually, no."

"Then I guess it's lucky for you that you've got all day to learn. Because if it's not on right by the time I get back tonight, I'll think up a punishment more imaginative than kitchen duty."

Liz's routine changed from that moment on, evolving in an insidious series of small adjustments and compromises. In spite of her common-sense decision to comply willingly with Zach's directives, her pride usually got in the way. More often than not it demanded that she resist until push came to shove and his face turned a pleasing shade of red. Then she would obey . . . following his orders to the letter. She docilely went about washing his clothes, then abandoned them rolled in a ball in the mud to dry or not. She fetched his meals when he demanded it, merrily dumping his coffee in the same plate as his food and carrying the resulting swill to wherever he sat idly waiting.

At first his anger knew no bounds, but he quickly caught

on to her game and it became something of a contest to see who could remain the most unruffled. Zach would respond to each barely legal insurrection on her part with a remarkable—and thoroughly unexpected—degree of patience. He would simply reissue the order in question in such detail that she was maneuvered into total obedience. Slowly but steadily the thrill of baiting him dwindled, however, and Liz sensed Zach was losing his original enthusiasm for playing slave master as well. In subtle, almost imperceptible ways she found the texture of their relationship changing.

One thing didn't change, however. He never wavered from his ban on sex, although the air between them remained as charged as a nuclear reactor. And Liz caught enough hungry glances when he thought she wasn't looking to know he wasn't nearly as nonchalant about the situation as he claimed. Without physical contact, though, they seemed to draw closer in other ways. She actually found herself looking forward to his return at the end of the day. She rationalized her anticipation by telling herself it was only natural to want someone to talk with after spending hours alone with the mostly incommunicado, still prickly-tempered cook. She was responding as any sane prisoner would to the person who provided her with food and protection, not to mention her only relief from an otherwise tedious existence.

After that first night of KP, he usually waited until she filled her own plate and then sat with her to eat. To lull him into talking, Liz would ask those questions she judged he was least likely to object to answering. She inquired about the wildlife in the surrounding jungle, the politics of Central America, how to tune a truck engine. On those subjects, as well as a host of others, he displayed extensive knowledge and insight . . . to Liz's surprise. As she listened to him talk, she sometimes found herself imagining that they weren't there at all, but instead were sitting in a dimly lit restaurant on Boston Harbor, eating baked stuffed lobster instead of refried beans and bacon scraps. And she allowed herself to wonder how she would have reacted to Zach McCabe if they'd met under different circumstances, if he had been a lawyer or a doctor introduced to her by friends instead of a bandit who had shanghaied her from her car at gunpoint.

She would have liked him, she finally decided one day with mixed emotions. Her feelings were even less clear about a realization that came to her soon thereafter. She was beginning to like him anyway. Not just feel some wayward sexual attraction . . . although that was undeniably present as well. Not just cling to him for protection in an overtly hostile environment. But actually like him as a person, as a friend, as a man. She didn't comprehend just how deeply she was becoming involved, however, until the evening the rest of the crew arrived back at camp without him.

The daily deluge of rain had come late that afternoon, leaving the clearing a treacherous stretch of black slime that Liz sank in up to her ankles as she ran to intercept Jade on his way to the storage tents.

"Where's Zach?" she cried, heedless of the mud oozing over the tops of her sneakers and of the way her fingers were biting into Jade's forearm. "Has anything happened to him?"

The look on his face, as he calmly assured her that nothing had happened to Zach, that he was simply involved in something that he couldn't leave right then, told Liz that he knew as surely as she now did that what she felt for his friend was more than the icy tolerance she so meticulously pretended whenever anyone was around to observe. To her surprise Jade ambled back to the cooking area after her, to wait while O.J. put the finishing touches on that day's culinary nightmare. It was her first chance since arriving at camp to speak with him alone, and not until later did it occur to her that she had blown a golden opportunity— maybe the only one she would get—to feel him out about helping her.

Instead she spent the brief time they had to talk pumping him—quite impolitely, she realized to her embarrassment afterward—for information about Zach. Jade was loyally evasive about most of the particulars of his friend's life, including what had led him to his current sleazy endeavor. But luckily a quick flash of bitterness loosened his tongue on the one topic which interested Liz most, the women in Zach's life. She wasn't surprised to hear there had been a great many of them, but was ridiculously elated by the news that there hadn't been anyone special since he was in college. She was no longer amazed by the fact that he'd actually gone to college, having long since concluded that there was much more to Zach than the scruffy, cynical facade he chose to present to the world in general and her in particular.

The minute Jade launched into his contemptuous soliloquy on the subject of one Amanda Bellingham, Liz knew she had to be the woman—the only woman—who had ever been able to make Zach beg for sexual favors. She also had to be the one who left him with such an attitude toward the entire female gender. A babe with bucks, was how Jade described this woman who evidently had at one time been the love of Zach's life. Big bucks. Gorgeous to kill for, in his words, and about as subtle about getting what she wanted as two tons of nitro in a designer miniskirt. It was a fatal sort of charm she wielded, and she sucked poor Zach all the way in, Jade confided before suddenly seeming to remember that while Liz wasn't quite foe, she wasn't a certified friend either, and clammed up.

After that, Liz screwed up enough courage to attempt to satisfy her curiosity directly, only to be stonewalled by Zach himself. At the same time he made no secret of his interest in learning more about her. He was particularly persistent on the subject of her relationship with Kirk, taking great pains to point out to her each small deficiency he detected in it through her revelations. To his face Liz steadfastly contradicted his claim that she didn't know enough about Kirk to be passionately in love with him. But when she was alone, she wasn't so sure. Over and over she told herself that everything would look different once this ordeal was over.

Day by day, though, so gradually it almost escaped her notice, Liz's fierce desperation to get away from the camp and Zach dwindled. She calculated that she had been there eight days when she was suddenly brought up short in the act of scrubbing the neck of one of Zach's shirts with a bar of gritty brown soap borrowed from O.J. for that purpose. She was standing at the edge of the small, tepid lake, with her baggy slacks rolled to above her knees and wearing the red T-shirt Zach had recently forbidden her to wear without a shirt over it whenever the other men were around. On the bank to one side of her waited a small pile of grimy, sweat-stained clothes and on the other, neatly spread out to dry on the sun-heated rocks, were the shirts she had already washed and rinsed.

She had been humming a haunting fragment of a love song that she couldn't seem to get out of her head lately, and she had been smiling to herself at what her family and friends would think if they could only see her now. Suddenly, as if a protective veil had been ripped aside, Liz knew exactly what they would think, and she saw exactly what they would see if they were to suddenly drop from the sky at that moment.

What they would not see was a prisoner chained and closely guarded. Nor a woman confined to her tent or in any way prevented from leaving this bandit's camp, other than by her own abundance of cowardice. What they would see and be utterly shocked by—just as Liz herself was suddenly shocked and revolted—was exactly what she was . . . a woman who had become enmeshed in her own romantic fantasies. They would see her contentedly scrubbing clothes for a man who by all rights she should loathe. Instead she spent her days tending to his personal needs while he went off to do a job that was wrong, legally and morally and every other way. And by night she shared his tent with him. Granted she hadn't shared his bed again since that first time, but that was small balm for her conscience. Especially since deep down she knew that she probably would if he asked. She, Liz Randolph, a woman who had pledged to be faithful to another man, a man who was her fiancé and who right now could be dead or dying while she played a naughty game of Tarzan and Jane with a common criminal. She'd conveniently put out of her mind the pledge she had made to be faithful to Kirk, along with a lot of other things.

With an anguished cry Liz flung the shirt in her hands into the water, then dragged the others, clean and dirty alike, in as well and ground them into the mud at the bottom of the lake with both feet. What was wrong with her? What kind of deviant flaw in her character would permit her to be drawn to a man as ruthless and unprincipled as Zach under any circumstances?

There had to be some secret wellspring of depravity deep inside her. It would account for the feelings of restlessness and dissatisfaction that had plagued her marriage to Jeff. At the time she had done her best to suppress those feelings, doing everything she could to prove to Jeff and herself and everyone else that being his wife and mother to their son was for her the ultimate happiness and fulfillment. After they died together in a fiery car crash, she'd hidden from her family and friends the tormenting guilt that infiltrated her grief. Had Jeff known, just as she had, that their relationship was lacking in so many ways? Did he go to his grave suspecting that he couldn't satisfy her?

It had taken Liz a long time to find peace, to finally accept that she hadn't betrayed Jeff or their son, Jeremy, by having feelings and needs apart from those she shared with them. It had taken her even longer, four lonely years, to let another man close to her. In Kirk she finally found the noble, dynamic man of her dreams. She was attracted by his intelligence and held spellbound by his tales of the risks he'd taken to smuggle oppressed men and women, some toting small children, across borders in the dead of night. He seemed to Liz a modern-day Robin Hood, and she threw in with his cause heart and soul. She'd envisioned them moving mountains together, charging through life righting wrongs, helping the downtrodden, embracing with reckless nobility the cause of those who had so much less than she did.

Oh, she was noble, all right. So noble it had taken only one night in the arms of a man whom she ought to despise— whom she did despise, she told herself—to make her forget about Kirk and all she had planned and dreamed their life together would be. When she thought of Kirk at all lately, it was with a stab of guilt and then only to wonder if he was dead or alive. How could she have sunk so low?

Defiantly she gave the sodden shirts under her feet another kick. It was being here that had done this to her. Being in this place with *him* was changing her. It was the isolation and the constant, underlying fear, and the total absence of anything familiar, anything normal. It was as if she'd been swept into a whole different world, one where the old rules didn't apply.

But the old rules did apply, Liz reminded herself, her stomach twisting with self-disgust. She wasn't a whore and she wasn't a coward, no matter how much she'd been acting like both. But there was only one way she was ever going to prove that, to herself and to Kirk and to all the others back home whom she would eventually have to face. That was to put a stop to it, right then, by getting as far away as she could from this place and from Zach and the power he wielded over her so effortlessly.

Face red with anger and determination, Liz thrust her wet feet into her sneakers and hurried back toward the tent. She didn't care if it took her three hundred days to walk to San Luis, or if she had to cross quicksand and face snakes and wild boars every step of the way. Suddenly she knew that staying here with Zach was infinitely more dangerous than anything that awaited her in the jungle.

CHAPTER
TWELVE

The sky above Liz was a stretch of ebony velvet, pierced by a scattering of silver stars and a pale crescent moon...none of which cast so much as a glimmer of light on the rustling, musty-smelling world she was trudging through. The beam from the flashlight she had filched from the camp supply tent, along with a knapsack full of food and a gun she had no idea how to use, wasn't helping much either. It illuminated only a narrow strip of earth for several feet directly in front of her, leaving her surrounded on four sides by an opaque wall of darkness. She was rapidly learning the full definition of the word *black*. And of the word *fear*.

She had thought she'd felt fear when she first followed that truck out of San Luis what now seemed like ages ago. And later, when a scowling, hellish-looking Zach had put his gun to her chest and cocked it, and again when the snake had slithered against her arm. But none of that was near terrifying enough to be placed in the same category as what now held her in its grip, this monstrous, trembling fear of the unknown.

Hours had passed since she'd fled the camp. After deciding she had to get away, she had bided her time until O.J. made his regular afternoon trek to the other side of the lake to fish. Then she had raided the supply tent and bolted. Doing her best to follow what she could recall of the directions Zach had once rattled off, she passed the first crossroads and kept the sun, which Liz figured was setting in the west, on her right. That should have meant she was heading due south. The only problem was that once the scorching sun had slipped over the horizon, she lost all sense of direction.

Even then she hadn't despaired. She was so accustomed to having fate on her side that her stubborn, innate assurance that things would somehow fall magically into place died hard. She clung valiantly to the hope that she would stumble upon Santana's farm or some other reasonable bastion of civilization before dark. That hadn't happened, and now Liz was stricken by the hideous suspicion that she was walking in circles...and had been for quite a while. She tried marking her path by breaking a branch every twenty feet or so, but the sound of something hissing at her from the shadow of a bush put an end to that bit of Campfire Girl nonsense. She would just have to keep forging ahead until daybreak and then decide what to do next. No matter how tired she got or how much her legs cramped, there was no way she was going to chance lying down on a patch of smelly, spongy earth that she couldn't see.

Her senses were heightened, and Liz wasn't sure that was a blessing. She was shaken by her newly discovered ability to discern layers of sound in the blackness, not all of them identifiable, but every one of them enough to send a chill shivering along her spine. There was the crunchy, rustling sound of things moving along the ground, and the blood-thirsty buzz of mosquitoes swarming at ear level, and the screeching, whining songs of whatever lived above, all of it overlaid by that distinctive throbbing quality peculiar to a jungle pulsing with life. Together with the smell and the heat, it left Liz suffering from a nauseating case of claustrophobia and scared right down to her tightly curled toes.

What would Zach think when he returned and found her gone? Would he be relieved? Or would he come looking for her? Liz seriously doubted he would bother. He was too practical, too levelheaded, to embark on a search when he hadn't the slightest idea what direction she'd taken. And even if he did mount a token attempt, the downpour that had pummeled Liz soon after she'd set out would have washed away any tracks she'd made and Zach would have no choice but to give up. One thing was certain: he would never let her disappearance hinder the precious job he'd come here to do.

That's what Liz *told* herself. Inside, though, she kept hoping and praying for the unlikely and the impossible—that Zach would come looking and that by some miracle he would find her. By chance she discovered that the ridges on the handle of the flashlight numbered ten, just like a decade of the rosary, and she began racing through the familiar prayers from her childhood, imploring that Zach, who as far as she could tell wouldn't know the inside of a church from a museum, would be inspired by divine intervention to go foraging through the jungle in the dead of night in search of a woman he despised. She was halfway through her third decade when there was a sudden explosion in the branches directly above her. Liz quickly identified the sound as a rapid flapping of wings... humongous wings, but not before she had let out a bloodcurdling scream, accompanied by the frantic waving of her flashlight in an attempt to see exactly what was up there.

Either the bird or she or maybe both of them had set off a chain reaction and the air suddenly hummed and crackled with eerie sounds. Liz broke into a run, making giant, frightened leaps as she fumbled to bring the flashlight back into position to illuminate the path ahead. Before she was able to see clearly, her foot came down in the middle of a slimy knot of vines just to the side of the narrow path. The sudden thought that it might be the coiled body of a snake ensnaring her tore another chilling scream from Liz's throat and started her scrambling madly to free herself. With her unhindered foot she thrashed wildly, stabbing and shoving at whatever it was that had her trapped until that foot was also snagged and she was sent hurtling headfirst to the ground. The flashlight slipped from her fingers as she fell, rolling under a bush about five feet away and throwing her into total darkness.

Liz's heart was pounding so frantically it was a physical

ache in her chest as she groped for the flashlight, both feet still entwined in an awkward position. She leaned toward the bush that hid it, stretching until it felt like the muscles in her shoulder were ripping and one side of her face was pressed so deeply into the mud that a warm, thick flood of it oozed into her mouth with each gasped breath. Crying and fighting the urge to retch, she finally managed to work her fingers close enough to the handle to grab it. As she struggled back to an upright position with it in hand, she was startled to hear a different sort of noise joining the clamor around her.

She sat still, listening. This noise was different from all the others, louder for one thing, and blessedly, wondrously mechanical. The fast-paced whirring sound was unmistakably familiar to an American girl brought up on reruns of *Sky King*. A helicopter! Liz knew there was probably only one person in a two-hundred-mile radius that had a helicopter at his disposal, and tears of joy poured down her face.

"Over here. Zach, I'm over here. Here."

Instinctively she kept shouting, heedless of the fact that she hadn't yet actually sighted anything and that he couldn't have heard her over the roaring clatter of the propeller anyway. Still shouting at the top of her lungs, she raised the flashlight, intending to use it to signal her position, and then froze with it held at an upward angle, illuminating a pair of bright orange coals no more than ten feet straight ahead of her.

She blinked several times. Gradually she was able to make sense of the shape surrounding those sinister, burning eyes. It was a tiger—or something very closely related—crouched in a patch of trampled bushes on the opposite side of the path from where she sat trapped. Vaguely Liz recalled that tigers were striped, and this monstrous-looking cat was instead covered with spots, big dark ones on a coat that could be either gold or orange but which looked pretty mangy even at this distance. The thing was probably half starved and desperate. What had ever made her think she was the least bit lucky?

He was positioned with his belly close to the ground, his haunches tensed, his pointed fangs revealed by his half-opened mouth. He emitted a low, unending growl that wafted over to her through the sudden stillness. Probably every living creature for miles around had fled from this natural predator . . . except her.

She was going to die. Any second now she was going to be ripped to shreds and devoured. But instead of seeing her life pass before her wide-open eyes, all Liz saw was the image of a masculinely beautiful face, dominated by eyes that could darken from sapphire to smoke, and a wide, sensuous mouth that could spur her to fury or passion depending upon the mood. Zach. He'd come looking for her after all. Her prayers had been answered. Too bad she wasn't going to live long enough to thank him. An old saying flitted through her dazed brain, the one about being careful what you ask for because you just might get exactly that. Why hadn't she been smart enough to pray that Zach would find her alive?

Liz clamped her teeth down on her lips until she tasted blood. The helicopter was so close now she knew she would be able to spot it if she dared to turn her head just a shade to the left. But she was afraid that the slightest sound or movement would trigger whatever inner mechanism was keeping the big cat in place. Inside she was quivering like soft-set Jell-O. The urge to scream was like fire in her lungs. The cat appeared treacherously concentrated and totally impervious to the racket overhead.

Abruptly the pattern of that racket altered, as if the copter were hovering in place, and Liz launched another fervent jumble of silent prayers. Maybe Zach had spotted the feeble beam of her flashlight and was coming in for a closer look. Before she managed to angle it a bit higher to make sure he saw it, the helicopter resumed full throttle, clearly moving away again. A wail of despair reverberated inside Liz's head, causing her a second of delay before she comprehended that the whirring had ceased altogether. He hadn't been moving away; he'd been searching for a place to set down.

She had no doubt now that Zach had seen the glow from her flashlight. But without the advantage of an aerial view, how long would it take him to find her? A new fear cropped up as it occurred to Liz that he had no way of knowing what she was facing over here. Would his shouts or the sound of his footsteps be enough to incite the tiger to attack? Maybe she should shout a warning before he walked blindly into a deadly situation. For endless moments she vacillated between risking her own life to warn Zach and the irrational certainty that if she just put her trust in him, he would save her.

The silence was unbearable. The blood was pounding so

forcefully in Liz's head that she felt as if her eardrums might explode any second. Suddenly there was the snap of a branch breaking somewhere behind her. In the next instant she saw the soft-edged triangles of the cat's ears flicker with alertness. Her need to warn Zach, even if it meant her own life, ripped a scream from her lungs.

The cat lunged.

Liz's hands came up in front of her face, catching the terrified shriek that poured from her, and she swore she felt the brush of the big cat's heat and weight just a split second before a gunshot blast ripped through the night and his pulsating body dropped in front of her. He had seemed to stop short in midair, as if he'd slammed into some sort of invisible protective shield that surrounded her. He lay before her, twitching spasmodically, rolling his massive, whiskered head back and forth in the mud until a second shot from close behind her finished what the first had begun.

There followed an instant of shocked silence from Liz. Then she dazedly lowered her eyes and discovered that what she'd thought was mud spraying on her when the body landed was actually blood. Bright red blood, still sticky and warm from the animal's wounds. Her screams began anew, rolling on with shrill intensity, until strong arms lifted her, fighting and kicking, from the ground, expertly hacking away the vines around her ankles with a knife and then cradling her against a chest hard and strong enough to absorb the shock waves of her sobs.

"Shhh, baby, it's all right," Zach murmured over and over, his lips moving through the pale silk of her hair and brushing soothingly across her forehead. "It's all over now. I'm here."

"Oh, God, Zach," she said when she could finally manage a shuddering form of speech. "It was a . . . a . . . a tiger."

"A jaguar," he corrected softly. "Not that it makes a rat's ass worth of difference when you're sitting there eyeball to eyeball with one."

She buried her face in the warmth of his chest, letting her whole body absorb the steady, reassuring thud of his heartbeat. "There was a bird and then I got stuck and the flashlight fell and . . . all of a sudden he was just there," she blurted, "growling at me . . . I thought he was going to kill me."

"She," Zach murmured.

Liz tilted her face up to look at him. She could see little in the dark except for a flash of white teeth and the black diamonds that were his eyes. "What did you say?"

"She," he repeated. "That was a female. And you were right; the odds are she would have ripped your throat out as soon as you moved. I suspect she has a young one or two hidden around here somewhere and you were unfortunate enough to venture too close."

"A mother? Babies?" Liz turned stricken eyes up to meet his. "Oh, no, Zach, I feel awful."

"Don't," he ordered in a voice laced with steel. "It was either her or you. Don't even think about it, not now, not ever again. You can drive yourself crazy wishing things weren't the way they are. Put it out of your mind." When she dropped her head back on his chest without saying a word, he prodded, "Okay?"

Liz sighed. He was right, but knowing that didn't do much to ease the shock of seeing something die in front of her for the first time. "Okay."

"How about you? Are you okay?"

"Fine."

"You're not hurt anywhere?"

"Not unless you count aching muscles from walking and a few mosquito bites that I've scratched raw."

"I don't count them. Which means you're in good enough shape to hear what I have to say." With Liz still in his arms he'd been slowly walking away from the scene of the shooting. Now he stopped and unceremoniously dumped her on her feet in front of him. His hands clamped on to her shoulders to shake her so roughly Liz half expected to spit teeth when he finally stopped.

"Just what the hell kind of a stunt were you trying to pull by running away like this, you stupid little bitch?"

His swift transformation from solicitous and sympathetic to bullying left Liz momentarily speechless. She recovered quickly. "I should think it's obvious. I was trying to get away from a man who screams at me, who thinks communication is a four-letter word, and who makes a habit of calling me a stupid little bitch."

"That's the first time I've called you that."

"Today, maybe."

"Ever." He grimaced. "Well, at least for almost a week." Then, in a fractured groan, "Jesus, Liz, I almost went crazy when I got back and found you gone. At first

I figured you'd head for San Luis, and I wasted hours having the men search in that direction without a sign of you.''

"But I am heading for San Luis," Liz protested in confusion.

Zach peered at her for a moment, his eyes so narrowed his thick lashes meshed. Then he let loose a laugh that was a giant explosion of relief and gathered her to him in a quick, bone-crushing hug. "I'm afraid not, darlin'. San Luis is that way." He pointed beyond where she was standing. "You were heading deeper into the jungle. In fact, the site's only over there a little way." He indicated a spot off to their left.

Liz rested her forehead against the center of his chest, feeling the full weight of her own stupidity. "I guess I would have been walking forever if you hadn't found me."

"Clear into Mexico," he confirmed, laughter in his deep voice. His arms were still looped around her, and now he started rubbing her back, his firm strokes feeling like heaven to Liz's sore muscles. When he spoke again his voice was quiet, sober. "Why did you run away, Liz?"

She stiffened in his embrace, her mind a confused jumble of conflicting thoughts and desires. "How can you even ask me that?"

"I mean why now?" he explained. "Why not a week ago? Or when I first brought you here. I thought . . ." He hesitated. "I thought things were changing."

"*I* was changing," Liz cried. "That's the reason I had to leave. I was becoming someone I don't even know."

"Is that so bad?" His voice was as gentle as the movement of his strong hands on her back.

"Yes," Liz insisted stubbornly. "I'm sure you can't begin to understand this, but I was raised to have certain standards and values and morals. And I was taught that they don't change with the situation . . . no matter how unorthodox that situation might be."

She hesitated, steeled for the stinging retort that didn't come. Zach didn't disagree. He didn't argue or berate her. Instead Liz sensed in him a surprising, unprecedented willingness to listen. Like an untapped geyser, words bubbled up in her throat, evidence of how badly she needed to say them, if only to get things straight in her own mind.

"Earlier today I was down at the lake," she began quietly, "and I suddenly got this vivid, Technicolor image of how it would look to anyone in my family if they could see me standing there scrubbing your shirts for you." She dropped her voice with a sigh. "Not to mention how it would look to Kirk."

"Ah, Kirk."

Liz had her fingers linked behind his neck and she was surprised to feel a rapid tightening of his muscles there at the mention of Kirk's name.

"I take it," he continued, "that Saint Kirk would disapprove of you washing my clothes for me?"

"I think . . . no, I know that Kirk would disapprove of a lot of things I've been doing and thinking and feeling lately."

"Things you've been thinking and feeling about me?" Zach prodded.

264

"That doesn't matter."

"It does to me. It matters because I think maybe you've been thinking and feeling the same things I have for a while now . . . ever since the night we made love."

"And what's that?" Liz countered heatedly. "Lust? That's all it was that night . . . all it ever can be. And that's exactly why it was wrong and why it would be wrong to let it happen again . . . no matter what either of us feels. And it's why I had to get away from there . . . and from you. You have this way of making me weak, and when I'm with you I let myself forget things that I shouldn't forget."

Zach levered back to look at her, squinting to see clearly through the darkness. "What sort of things?"

"That I'm still engaged to Kirk, for one, and that I owe him . . . something." She pulled her hands away from him as if he were too hot to touch, knotting them in her own hair as guilty thoughts of Kirk swamped her. "He doesn't deserve this . . . any of this. He doesn't deserve to have me fall into bed with another man while he's . . . My God, it would never even cross his mind that I could do something like that. He always sees the good in everybody . . . because that's the way he is. Kind and generous and honorable."

"You forgot to mention that you love him." There was a mocking edge to the reminder that brought Liz's chin up defiantly.

"Yes."

"And you hate me."

Her mouth opened, but nothing came out.

"Come on, Liz, say it. Tell me that you hate me. It

shouldn't be so difficult. You've said it plenty of times before."

It was true; she had. And at first she had meant it from the bottom of her soul. When had she stopped meaning it? When had the heat gone out of those words, making it something she snapped out by rote, because she knew he expected such token resistance from her?

I hate you. What she felt for him now wasn't even close to hate, but she was afraid to probe too deeply into exactly what had sprung up in its place. This afternoon she had taken the easy way out by telling herself that whatever she felt for him was absolutely wrong...the result of subtle brainwashing. Now she wasn't so sure.

The mere fact that he was here undercut her opinion about his lack of character. He had come after her when he could have stayed back at camp and let her die out here alone. Surely that meant something. For starters it meant he wasn't as ruthless and unprincipled as she sometimes feared. He wasn't all bad. And maybe, she mused, fragile seedlings of hope pushing through the frozen surface of her despair, maybe that meant that what she was feeling for him wasn't all bad either.

"I knew you couldn't say it," Zach taunted softly as she continued to eye him in tortured silence. "I knew it, because even though you might not be the pure and ladylike creature your fiancé thinks you are...that you *thought* you were, you're no liar."

His rough palms framed her cheeks, tipping her face up so he could read her expression as he spoke. "The truth, Liz, is that you don't hate me any more than I hate you."

Some wayward impulse made her ask the next question, her voice husky with emotion. "What do you feel for me, Zach?"

The words to tell her how he felt were right there inside him. Zach had felt them rumbling around in there at odd, unexpected moments. Like when she squared off against him with that defiant gleam in her eye, determined to make him work for each small victory. Or when he said something that fell within her broad definition of risqué and she responded with an obligatory look of disapproval that eventually dissolved into the slightly conspiratorial smile that had come to feel as if it was attached directly to his heart. The words were there all right, but they were locked behind an eighteen-year-old promise he'd made never to say them to any woman ever again.

"I feel this," he told her simply. Shifting his hands so they bracketed her hips, he pulled her hard against him and lowered his mouth to hers.

He'd only intended to kiss her once, to try to let her know what he was feeling in the only way he knew how. The only way possible without uttering those words he could not . . . *would* not say. But when she opened her lips beneath his, winding her arms around his neck with that small, breathless sound that made him crazy, Zach knew one kiss wouldn't be enough. Not tonight, not ever.

He gave a low, primal growl and opened his mouth wide over hers, driving his tongue deep inside her. Without preamble his hands thrust inside the loose waist of her slacks and the silk panties beneath to stroke the curve of her enticing bottom. Slowly he slid his fingers lower, letting them slip and play in the softness between her legs in a way he knew would start her rocking against him. His hips met the random thrusts of hers, pressing deeply against her, letting her feel the pressure building inside him. Then he moved his fingers in the intimate caress he'd learned could fire her blood in an instant, making her quiver against his palm, which in turn sent a firebolt of desire shooting through him.

With a jerk he pulled his hands from her pants, banking down hard on the urge to take her right where she stood. She wouldn't try to stop him; Zach was sure of that. Even now she was subtly urging him on, slipping one leg between his with a gentle, undulating motion. But he wanted more than a quick release. For some reason he couldn't fathom, he wanted to prove something to her tonight. He wanted to erase all the doubts and fears that had driven her to run from him. He knew he couldn't have her to keep forever, but dammit, he wanted every second of the time they had left together. He clamped his legs tightly around hers, halting its teasing motion.

"Not here," he told her in a voice that rippled with frustration. But where? Not back at camp. As much as he wanted to make this right, he couldn't wait that long.

The solution occurred to Zach almost immediately. Grabbing Liz's hand, he started pulling her at a rapid pace along the muddy trail guarded by limestone outcrops and giant ceiba trees. His heavy-duty flashlight did a good job of lighting the way, but Liz still stumbled over the roots and rocks that dotted the seldom-used path. When she wasn't stumbling, she asked a string of apprehensive questions, to which he gave the same reply: "Wait and see."

It took them ten minutes to reach the site. When the familiar boulder-strewn slope with its crumbled flagstone walls loomed ahead, Zach felt his pulse speed up with anticipation. He quickly led her beneath a wide limestone shelf to a gaping black hole, but when he started through it, Liz balked.

"Zach, I'm afraid," she announced baldly. "There might be . . . who knows what in there. Bats, maybe."

"Bats leave their caves at night. Besides, I'll be with you," he reminded her. "You trust me, don't you?"

What an outrageous question for him to ask her. He knew the second it rolled off his tongue what her answer had to be. But to Zach's amazement, she hesitated only a split second before nodding.

"Yes," she said with a quiet certitude that made him feel as if he could lift the mountain looming over them and hurl it as far as the Atlantic Ocean. "I trust you, Zach."

Oh, Liz, he thought, what are you doing to me? Quickly he turned away, refusing to humiliate himself by replying, only to hear his voice crack around the sudden lump in his throat. With only a curt nod of acknowledgment, he lifted her through the shadowy opening to the inside of the clay-floored cave. He'd thought he had walked off some of his urgency, but her breathless admission of trust was all it took to fire it again, leaving him hungrier than ever for her. Unfortunately he hadn't anticipated that Liz would be so fascinated by the place where he'd been spending ten to twelve hours a day for weeks now. He carefully propped the flashlight where it would throw the most light and turned to take her in his arms, only to be stopped short by the look of rapture on her face as she gazed at the eerie beauty surrounding her.

A rueful smile lifted the edges of his mouth. He wasn't so hungry that he couldn't appreciate what she was feeling. He'd felt just as spellbound the first time he'd walked into this place. It was an awe-inspiring sight. The pale plaster walls stretched to fifteen feet above their heads and were covered with elaborate depictions of ancient Mayan rites painted in a mixture of deep and bright shades. Amid the detailed drawings were double rows of hieroglyphics that had been painstakingly etched into the smooth plaster hundreds of years ago. Fringed curtains of white stone hung from the distant ceiling.

"Welcome to Naj Tunich," he finally said softly.

Liz whirled to face him, her face flushed and beautiful. "This is Naj Tunich?"

He nodded. "It translates to stone house, or cave."

"Then this is where you . . ."

She broke off abruptly, but the unspoken condemnation hung in the air between them like a cloud of putrid smoke on a windless day.

Zach gave another nod, this one curt. He'd be damned if he'd be drawn into a discussion of morals—his morals—that was sure to screw up his plans for the night.

"This is it, all right," he said in a studiedly light tone. "Although technically most of our work has been done on the other side."

"What's it like on the other side?" she asked, her face lit with curiosity.

"It's like what you see here," he told her. That's what it had been like anyway, before he and the others had gone to work searching behind the walls for long-buried treasure. There was no way he was going to let her see the other side the way it was now.

"Altogether this is a three-pyramid complex," he explained as she ran her fingers hesitantly over the smooth stone surface. "They are—or were—linked by what I guess to be about twelve hundred yards of passageways. A number of small galleries and chambers were incorporated into the design, most devoted entirely to a particular theme ... fire, water, life, death."

"I thought it was just a . . ."

"A grave?" he supplied dryly when she faltered.

She turned to him and nodded.

"No, it's much more than that. The Mayans were a very complex culture. Advanced in some ways and very primitive in others. They saw the universe as a flat square of earth. In the center stood the giant tree of life, the sacred ceiba, whose branches extended to the sky and whose roots reached deep into the underworld ... Xibalba. Xibalba was home to the gods of death and sacrifice, and the entrance to it was thought to be through a cave. Of course, caves couldn't be shunned altogether, because they were the only source of water during the dry season. So, to placate the gods, this is how the resourceful Mayans dealt with them."

"It's beautiful," Liz murmured. "I had an idea that it would be ... crude. But it's not."

"No, crude doesn't come close to describing Mayan civilization. Some of the artwork we've uncovered is so beautiful it took my breath away."

Zach saw her eyebrows shoot up in surprise at his impulsive admission, then draw together in a frown as she tried to reconcile it with the fact that he was here to steal all that breathtaking beauty. Or at least, Zach mused uncomfortably, as much of it as he was able to remove with a power saw and truck.

"Cat got your tongue?" he prodded when he got tired of wondering what she was looking so damn pensive about.

"No. I was just standing here daydreaming that any minute you're going to tell me that you're actually an archeologist traveling incognito as a *huaquero*. Or maybe a collector of some sort. Or even an undercover cop investigating an art smuggling ring." With a sigh she concluded, "But you're not, are you?"

Catching the desperation that flashed in her eyes, Zach released a short, bitter laugh. "No, I'm not. Would it miraculously make everything all right if I were? Face it, Liz. No matter how you slice it, what I'm doing here is dead wrong. The beauty of this place isn't something that can be shipped home to some plush penthouse gallery and hung on the wall. That just doesn't cut it."

He stalked across the cave, putting his back to her and bracing both hands on the wall, which was smooth and cool to the touch. "The beauty here is deeper than what you see. It's . . . mystical. You and I stand here and marvel at these drawings and we become linked to the past, to the scribe who stood in this exact spot twelve hundred years ago and carved them into this stone by the light of a torch. You remove them from here and you void that link to time and place. Then all you've got is some rich man's souvenir.''

"Then I don't understand . . . Why are you doing it? I know you can't be the . . . the hoodlum you like to pretend you are. Just as I know that deep down you're honest and decent and caring. And honorable.''

He spun around, propped his shoulders on the wall where his hands had been, and arrowed her a cynical smile. "You know all that about me, do you?''

Zach recognized the stubborn tilt of her jaw.

"Yes. I know it in spite of the way you've been acting ever since I first laid eyes on you. But I can't do anything to prove it. You have to do that.''

"You sound like my Sunday school teacher used to sound when she was trying to motivate me.''

"Did it work?''

He held his hands palms up and grinned. "You've seen me in action.''

"I'm serious, Zach. You're the only one who can turn this thing around, the only one who can stop it.''

She was pleading with him. Zach was amazed that she would even bother. What could it matter to a broad like her if he ripped off all of Central America? He refused to tease himself with the possibility that if he could change, repent somehow, then they might have a chance for something beyond a quick good-bye at the bus stop back in San Luis. They didn't have a snowball's chance in hell of anything, and that was that. He levered away from the wall with a

273

sigh, wishing it were within his power to do what she so clearly wanted him to do.

"I can't stop it," he told her. Moving closer, he reached out to catch a silken streamer of her hair in each hand and wound them over and over, using the hold to draw her against him. "I can't stop it."

"Of course you can. Just stop. Walk away. Send those men home . . . or wherever it is they go to. Prove to yourself what I already know is true . . . that you really are a man of integrity, a man of honor."

"Baby, that's exactly what I'm down here trying to do." With that he lowered his head, intending to silence her the best way he knew how. She squirmed in his arms, but this time Zach knew it wasn't inspired by passion.

"But . . ."

"Not now," he growled against her ear where his tongue was making teasing forays. "No questions. Right now all I want is you, Liz."

"Zach, wait . . ."

"I can't. I can't wait."

His mouth opened over hers, twisting, rubbing, consuming her with a need he made no effort to temper. Or hide. He couldn't get enough of the taste of her or the feel of her soft body clinging to his. It was as if he couldn't kiss her long enough or hard enough to begin to satisfy the desire raging within; he couldn't press her close enough to his body to placate his clamoring senses.

Creating a sliver of space between them, he sent his fingers flicking over her shirt buttons, ripping the top one off with an impatient jerk before commandeering enough self-control to deal with the others in a more civilized manner. His palms swept along the satin terrain of her shoulders and arms, dragging her shirt down with them. Just as eagerly he dispensed with her slacks and panties, as Liz obligingly kicked off her sneakers, and then she was standing naked before him, opening her arms to him, her jade eyes soft with an offer he in no way deserved.

He threaded his fingers through the smooth cloud of her hair and allowed himself the privilege of devouring her with his eyes.

"You are the thing of real beauty here," he told her after a long silence. His voice was revealingly hoarse, and he saw in her eyes her total shock to hear from his usually terse lips words of praise that were long overdue. "Tonight *you* take my breath away. It makes my eyes ache just to look at you, you're so goddamned beautiful."

Her answering smile set off fireworks inside him. He was feeling inspired enough to admit that to her too, but she spoke first, slanting him a provocative look as she tugged his black T-shirt loose from his jeans and swirled her fingertips across his bare chest.

"I just might return those compliments," she whispered, "if you gave me the chance."

Zach grinned. "Is that your subtle way of ordering me to strip?"

"Subtle but effective . . . I hope."

"Damn effective."

He tore off his clothes with none of the care or interest he'd accorded hers. Without waiting for Liz to voice the approval that flared in her eyes as she watched his rangy, scarred body come into view, Zach swept her high in his arms. His lips went wild, kissing her soft mouth and the graceful curve of her neck and the tips of her breasts, which darkened to wet rubies under the ministrations of his tongue. Slowly, gently, he bore her down to the bed of clothes he'd arranged to protect her tender skin from the abrasive clay floor. A muffled clang sounded as she settled in, and smiling, Zach reached over to pull a bottle from his vest pocket.

"I almost forgot. Old Juan sent this along. He figured you'd need a belt after being on your own out here."

Reaching for the small, unlabeled bottle that Zach uncapped and offered her, Liz regarded its dark purple contents suspiciously. "What is it?"

"A local innovation. I think wild plum brandy would come closest to describing it in terms you'd recognize."

She brought the bottle to her lips and tipped her head back, unprepared for the warm rush of liquid that tasted sweet on her tongue, only to explode into white-hot fire the second it reached her belly. Coughing, she thrust the bottle back at a chuckling Zach.

"Ugh. That doesn't taste like any brandy—or any plum— that I've ever tasted."

"That's because you don't do your drinking in the right places," he told her.

Reading his remark as merely one more jab at her lifestyle, Liz countered, "And I suppose you do?"

"Tonight I plan to."

Too late she saw the dark, dangerous flash of mischief in his eyes, and then the liquor that had felt so warm on her tongue was splashing over her in a shockingly cold river that flooded her breasts, then flowed through the valley between them, across her stomach and lower. Zach carefully put the half-empty bottle aside as he moved to kneel between her thighs, spreading them wide to accommodate him. Then, smiling wickedly, ignoring her halted protests that he shouldn't do this, he did.

Lazily he traced the trail of moisture across her trembling body, lapping at each small pool of sweetness and fire, lingering long after Liz knew the brandy must be gone and it was only her essence he was drinking in with such ardor. She arched her neck with pleasure and skittish anticipation as he reached her belly button, exploring it with a slow swirl of his tongue and then licking his way lower. Feeling the ripples of sensation begin to build, she braced her hands on the sturdy width of his shoulders, loving their sleek, muscled contours, glorying in the strength and power she felt poised there beneath her fingertips. She glanced down, finding the contrast of his dark head with her pale thighs wildly erotic. Then his mouth found her, the possession wild and electric, and her eyes closed tight with passion.

The instant his mouth captured the wet satin core of her womanhood, Zach knew she was primed and ready, very close to coming apart in his arms. And tonight that was just the way he wanted her. Relentlessly he drove her higher still, as greedy for the honeyed spice of her as he was for the splendor of burying himself deep inside her softness and letting her catapult him to a place he'd never been without her. Too soon he felt her quaking movements quicken, heard her call his name, the sound no more than a soft gasp, and he concentrated all of himself and everything he'd learned about pleasuring her to bring her to a sobbing climax.

Afterward he stayed with her, waiting until he felt the storm pass away and her shallow, panting breaths turn slow and regular once again before stretching up to cover her vanquished body with his still hard and raging one. Without warning Liz's hands shot up to stop him. With her palms pressed flat to his chest, she pushed with gentle, inexorable force until he allowed himself to be rolled to his side next to her. Still without saying a word, she pressed him fully onto his back. Then, smiling a smile that made Zach suck in a sharp breath of disbelief, she straddled him and reached for the bottle of wild plum brandy.

The shock of it hitting his body in a cold stream was nothing compared to what followed. Her mouth was a hot, sweet invader which left no part of him unconquered. Zach surrendered willingly, excitement like nothing he'd ever known pulsing within him. As her lips and tongue moved over him he wasn't sure if he was in heaven or hell. He wanted the exquisite layering of sensation upon sensation to go on forever, and at the same time it took every shred of his willpower not to roll her onto her back and take her with all the fierce passion she'd unleashed inside him.

Finally the pleasure-pain of being held in her velvet vise toppled completely the wall of self-control he had thought so impenetrable. Murmuring fractured, uncensored words of need and sex and love, he pulled her up, shifting their sweat-sheened bodies until he was on top. With a rough groan he drove his satin-steel heat deep inside her. It took only a few quick, love-violent strokes to send them both soaring on a flight that seemed golden and infinite.

Later Zach wasn't sure if seconds or moments had passed before his anesthetized senses awoke to the realization that someone was moving around just outside the cave. He was off Liz in a shot, lunging for the gun he'd discarded along with his clothes.

"Shut up," he hissed when she came up on one elbow, her smile adorably sleepy, and started to ask why he was shoving bullets into his gun. Later he could apologize for being so ungallant. At the moment their lives might depend on his getting the damn thing loaded in time and her keeping her mouth shut.

"Get dressed," he risked whispering. Without bothering with his own clothes, he levered to a crouch between her and the cave entrance and held his gun steady.

The panic that rose in Liz's throat as she scampered to do as he ordered made it hard to breathe. Clumsily she yanked on her slacks, shoving her underpants into one deep front pocket. It took her several misplaced jabs before she managed to get her arms into the elusive sleeves of her shirt. Instinctively she dropped to her knees to huddle behind Zach's broad back before even attempting the buttons. Her fingers were shaking so much she had only managed to fasten half of them before a pair of black-booted feet dropped through the gaping opening only a few yards away.

Zach cocked his gun in warning, but the wiry Latin male who was wearing the boots along with a mishmash of military fatigues only grinned. The next instant Liz learned the reason for his cavalier attitude as three more men lowered themselves inside, all of them toting automatic rifles that looked infinitely more deadly than the gun in Zach's hand.

"Buenas noches, señor," the first man said in a tone as cold as his smile. His black eyes flicked past Zach to Liz. He gave an exaggerated bow. "Señora Randolph. You are Liz Randolph, correct?"

Zach exhibited no visible sign of surprise at his use of her name, but Liz was able to feel the sudden tensing of the muscles in his back. There was only one way this man could know who she was, and Liz suddenly wished with all her heart that she'd trusted Zach enough to tell him the whole story about her and Kirk and the money. Now it was too late.

"Correct?" the man repeated more firmly.

"Y-Yes. I'm Liz Randolph."

He nodded. "Good."

"Now, how about telling us who the hell you are?" suggested Zach in a voice as smooth and unruffled as lake water.

"Of course, forgive me," he murmured, returning his attention to Zach. "I am Tito Rodrigues. And you will both be coming with me and my friends here. But first, you, señor, may take a moment to dress." Smiling pointedly, he ran his gaze over Zach's nude body on which, to Liz's horror, there lingered purple streaks of brandy. "The night is warm, but the mosquitoes, they can be hell on the sticky spots."

Liz felt her face heat with color. Zach's nakedness left little doubt about what they had been doing. Slowly he stood and, with the hand not clenching the gun, casually reached for his jeans, apparently nowhere near as mortified to be caught in such a state as she was. If anything, he appeared to be a mixture of annoyed and irritated by the whole thing, and with the small portion of her brain not paralyzed with fear, Liz applauded his control.

"I will take that for you," Rodrigues said to Zach, indicating his gun.

Zach hesitated only a heartbeat before relinquishing it.

"And now you will please hurry," ordered their captor. "Señora Randolph has already kept us waiting for a very long time."

CHAPTER THIRTEEN

"Just what is it you've kept these men waiting for, Señora Randolph?" The heavy note of sarcasm in Zach's voice only added to Liz's anguish.

As soon as Zach had finished dressing, Rodrigues, undisputedly the man in charge, demanded the key to the helicopter from him. Smiling sinisterly, he then proceeded to inquire if that was where they had hidden the money.

"No answers?" he'd prodded in the face of Zach's grim silence and her fidgeting unease, then quickly dispatched one of his underlings to search the chopper. "It matters little if you talk now or later. I have no doubt El Tigre will be able to persuade from you what we want to know."

El Tigre. *The tiger.* Liz's stomach muscles had cramped convulsively as they were hustled out of the cave. Pure instinct for survival had warned her not to confess right up front that the money was irretrievably lost. To admit that would be tossing away the closest thing they had to a bargaining chip and, she feared, might be tantamount to signing death warrants for Kirk, Zach, and herself.

In the shadows outside the cave had waited three more men armed with automatic weapons. After halting Liz's frantic inquiries about Kirk's safety with a curt order for silence, Rodrigues signaled one of the others to start off along a narrow, almost impassable trail. With no further explanation about where they were being taken, she and Zach had been ordered to follow.

That was about an hour or so ago, and they'd been walking ever since, their arms bent so their hands were positioned uncomfortably at the backs of their necks. A precaution, Rodrigues had called it in that loathsome tone of feigned regret. Liz called it a case of overkill. What chance did she and Zach have against armed men who outnumbered them three to one? Eventually they reached a road of sorts where the going was marginally easier and there was room to walk two abreast. A voice from somewhere behind roughly ordered Zach to move up next to her. No doubt so they could have a clear shot at both of them if the need arose, Liz speculated. She didn't care. Relief seeped through her aching body at the prospect of at last being able to exchange a few furtive words with her only ally in this nightmare.

Then before she had a chance to say anything, Zach had asked that question in a voice every bit as steely and menacing as the guns trained on them, and she had realized just how coldly furious he was. *Just what is it you've kept these men waiting for, Señora Randolph?*

Hurriedly she began trying to tell him everything at once, the words spurting out in an unordered jumble. She rattled on about Kirk's work with the sanctuary movement and how she had accompanied him down here on what was to have been a routine mercy mission. And about how she had waited behind at the hotel while he ventured into the jungle outside of San Luis to meet with the organizer of the small band of refugees they planned to smuggle out of the country.

She kept her voice low, expecting at any second to hear another order to be quiet. When it didn't come, Liz gradually relaxed a little and took the time to paint in more details, whispering to him about the note and the ransom demand, repeating the same story she'd told him once before about the mix-up with the trucks and ending with the rueful revelation that the money these men had asked about had been in a briefcase beneath the front seat of her car.

For a few minutes after she finished speaking, they trudged along in silence. Finally out of the corner of her eye she caught a slight movement of Zach's head, as if he were trying to look at her, and his deep voice rasped softly through the night air.

"You're telling me that you stood there and let me push that car over the cliff *knowing* there was twenty thousand dollars under the seat?"

"Of course I knew it," hissed Liz. "Who do you think put it there in the first place?"

Ignoring her rhetorical question, he continued, "And that same twenty thousand dollars is the money these guerrillas holding machine guns aimed at us are so hot to get their hands on?''

"I suppose," she countered distractedly. She had been nurturing a hope that their captors might be sane, reasonable men at heart, but his reference to them as guerrillas had started her stomach wrenching all over again. "Zach, do you really think they're guerrillas?"

"No. I really think they're Boy Scouts dressed for a Halloween party. What the hell do you think they are? The Guatemalan Welcome Wagon?''

"There's no need to snap," she snapped.

"Maybe not, but it sure helps pass the time until I can wring your neck.''

"Wring my neck? May I remind you . . . ?"

"No," he interjected, "you may not remind me of anything. In fact, don't even talk to me. You've already got my ass on the line because of your lame-brained part in some bleeding-heart cause that lets you and your fancy friends feel noble and fulfilled while you sit around the health club sipping Perrier. I don't think I can stomach listening to any more of the saga of you and your halo-packing boyfriend. So just shut up.''

Liz pressed her lips together, determined not to stoop to bickering at such a time, but it was like trying to hold back Niagara Falls with a dam built out of Saran Wrap.

"I'll shut up, all right," she told him in a whisper as vehement as a bellow. "In fact, you'll sprout feathers and fly before I ever say so much as one more word to you. Ever. But first I just want to say that my life is as much on the line as yours is. And besides, if you had listened to me at the start and believed what I told you, I wouldn't have lost the money in the first place and none of this would be happening."

"My problem is that I was fool enough to believe anything at all that you told me," Zach shot back. "Yeah, you really trust me, all right." His voice hardened to a contemptuous drawl. "Well, baby, I'd hate to see what kind of secrets you'd keep if you didn't trust me."

All the fight left her. In its place was a profound hopelessness. She had told herself that his coming after her meant something. She had thought that what they'd shared inside Naj Tunich afterward had been a benediction of sorts, elevating their relationship to a new level of trust and understanding. But obviously she'd been wrong. Again. None of it meant anything if given the slightest opportunity Zach would still jump to believe the absolute worst of her.

They continued walking, but now the stiffness that permeated all of Liz's joints felt comfortable compared to the silence separating her from Zach. In a way she felt more alone now than she had roaming around out here by herself. Finally, when she was tired enough to drop in her tracks and let them shoot if they pleased, she glimpsed a light in the distance. It was faint but enough to keep her going awhile longer. As they drew closer, she saw that it was a ramshackle farmhouse, its windows illuminated by the flickering light of lanterns. Around it were several smaller huts identical to the one she and Zach had once shared.

The guerrillas dispersed as they approached the house, a few heading for the smaller huts, leaving only Rodrigues and one other armed man to shepherd them inside. Liz's feeble hope that together she and Zach might stand a chance now that the sides were even fizzled as she stepped inside and saw two more men sitting at a table playing cards, each with a rifle resting by his side. Then her gaze moved past them, across the spartan room to the man sitting on the floor against the rear wall, his hands tied behind his back.

"Kirk." Liz was across the room and on her knees beside him before she even heard Rodrigues's crisp order to halt. Even if she had heard, the wave of relief carrying her forward was too strong to resist. She threw herself across Kirk's chest, her tears intermingled with disjointed phrases of wonder and thanks, until one of Rodrigues's henchmen grabbed her by the hair and painfully hauled her to her feet.

Cupping her hands to her face, she stared down at Kirk, trying to control the muffled sobs that lifted her shoulders in great shuddering spasms. He looked thinner, but he'd always been on the thin side, not the overbearing, muscled, athletic type at all. And he was definitely paler than usual, causing Liz to wonder how often he had been let out of this hot, dirty room during the past week and a half. Judging from the stringy, greasy condition of his pale blond hair, it was clear that he hadn't been afforded the privilege of a bath. But at least he was alive. Liz felt as if the weight of two worlds had been lifted off her shoulders.

"Oh, God, Kirk," she cried. "You're alive. You're really alive."

"No thanks to you."

It was the bitter bite in Kirk's tone as much as the denunciation itself that shocked Liz into sudden, dry-eyed silence. If she'd been able to think at all a few moments ago, she would have attributed his stiff response to her embrace to the fact that his hands were tied. Now she took a good long look at the thin, white line of his lips and the almost maniacal glint in his pale blue eyes and realized that wasn't the case.

"Do you know how long I've been stuck here in this flea-ridden cesspool waiting while you took all your sweet-assed time getting here?" he demanded.

Liz was too flabbergasted to be angry or embarrassed. She completely forgot that this little scene was being witnessed by others, among them Zach. She would rather die than have him suspect that Kirk was anything but thrilled to see her again.

"Of course, I know, Kirk. But you don't understand what happened to me. I..."

"I don't give a damn what happened to you," he broke in harshly. "All you had to do was bring the money...*my* money. That's all. No questions, no problems. But did you do that for me? No. You screwed it up. You'd probably screw up a fucking wet dream if you had the chance."

"You filthy scum..."

Liz recognized the angry tone as Zach's and whirled around in time to see the small room explode into a tangle of shoving, fist-swinging male bodies. Both men seated at the table jumped up to assist their buddy in tackling Zach, who was proving about as easy to take down as a granite mountain. Using his feet and his shoulders, he charged relentlessly forward, obviously bent on getting his hands on a cowering Kirk. With a sudden power surge, he plowed one of the men aside, leaving him sprawled on the floor with a slightly dazed expression, and had his fist primed back to slam into another's jaw when Rodrigues took matters into his own hands by firing a shot at the ceiling.

It worked as well as if this were a movie set and the director had hollered, "Cut." Zach froze, still holding his target suspended in front of him by his shirtfront, and sought Liz with his gaze. Satisfied that she hadn't been in the path of the bullet, he hesitated a few seconds longer, then with a contemptuous shove sent the man he was holding flying backward. An instant later footsteps clattered on the wooden steps outside and the door flew open. Rodrigues hastily assured the back-up squad who'd come running at the sound of a gunshot that he had everything under control, and they obediently filed out again.

"Who the hell is he?" Kirk demanded once the door had slammed shut behind them. Liz noted that now that Rodrigues had things under control, Kirk was eyeing Zach with considerably less trepidation than he had a moment ago.

"Don't you know?" countered Rodrigues.

"Should I?"

The little, dark-haired man shrugged. "He appears to be such a . . . close friend of your beautiful fiancée that I just assumed he was a friend of yours as well."

Kirk volleyed his suspicious glance from Zach to Liz and back. "I never laid eyes on him before he walked in here," he announced. "I have no idea what the hell she's doing with him."

"Ahhh," murmured Rodrigues to the accompaniment of his cohorts' insinuating chuckles. "This touching little reunion grows more interesting by the moment."

"The reunion is over, pal," Kirk declared. "You've got your money. Now untie me and let me go."

"I'm afraid that's quite impossible, my friend." Rodrigues's tone was convincingly remorseful. Only the rather feral gleam in his eye told Liz otherwise.

"What are you trying to pull?" demanded Kirk, struggling to his feet. "You and that cutthroat El Tigre managed to up the price on me once, but if you try it again, you're screwed. That twenty thousand dollars she's got is all there is, the end, finito, friend."

"And there," sighed Rodrigues, "is the heart of our problem." His eyes and his tone turned sharp as daggers. "Your woman does not seem to have the money."

Kirk's eyes widened to disks of watery blue. "What are you talking about?" He jerked his gaze to Liz. "What is he talking about?" Back to Rodrigues. "Of course she's got the money." To Liz. "Tell him you've got the money." Slowly a hint of panic infiltrated his belligerent expression. "You do have the money, don't you, Liz? Don't you? Answer me, goddamn you."

"I...I..." Liz was so nervous her teeth chattered around each halted word. "I *had* the money," she finally managed to get out.

The rapid coloring of Kirk's face made Liz think of a white canvas onto which someone had just dumped gallons of blood-red paint. Rage puffed and distorted his features so that he suddenly looked like a complete stranger to her. She tried to remind herself that everything he was saying and doing was the result of the tremendous strain he'd been under, but it didn't change how she felt. At that moment she was scared to death of him.

She had braced herself for a loud, enraged tirade and was caught off guard when he spoke in a deadly emphatic whisper instead. "You don't have my money?"

Before Liz could summon enough brain-muscle coordination to shake her head, Zach spoke up, his voice soothingly calm. "No. Now I have it."

Rodrigues's snake lips puckered with heightened interest. Confusion flitted across Kirk's face.

"You? You have my money?" he cried. Then, without waiting for an answer, "Then why don't you hand it over so we can all get out of here?"

Liz saw Kirk flinch from the look Zach shot him.

"I'll hand over the money when I'm good and ready," announced Zach.

"What the hell do you mean—"

"Enough," roared Rodrigues. Only Kirk's labored panting broke the silence that ensued. Rodrigues's contemplative gaze skipped from Zach to Kirk several times; then he threw up his hands. "We'll leave it to El Tigre to get the truth when he returns."

"Why wait?" Kirk sputtered like a singed cat. "You just heard him admit that he has my money. You guys are the ones holding the guns here. Make him fork it over."

Liz gasped at what Kirk was suggesting. Granted he'd been under a lot of stress and he didn't know Zach from Adam, but he should at least be giving her the benefit of the doubt instead of aligning himself with the animals who had kidnapped him to begin with.

"*If* this man truly has your money, señor," Rodrigues said to Kirk, "he does not have it on him. And it was not in the helicopter they left near the cave where we found them."

"All the more reason to beat the truth out of him," Kirk snapped.

"No." Liz glared at him, trying to convey with her eyes how crucial it was that he calm down and trust Zach. "Kirk, you don't know what you're saying. Zach is a friend."

Kirk's expression turned even uglier. "Is he now?" he drawled. "Well, suppose you tell me just how good a friend old Zach here is? And while you're at it, how about telling me what you and your *friend* have been doing for the week and a half I've been stuck here waiting? What was going on in that cave, Liz? How about telling me that?" he ended in an earsplitting shout.

Either Rodrigues had tired of the squabbling or he had a soft spot for a woman in tears. With a wave of his hands, he ordered, "Finish your lovers' spat later. As for the money, we'll wait for El Tigre and then see who's hiding what. Now you sit," he barked at Kirk, who slinked back into his place against the wall. "And you," he continued, encompassing both Liz and Zach with his gaze, "may sit as well . . . as soon as you empty your pockets on the table over there." He grinned. "Another precaution."

With a shrug Zach ambled over to the table and methodically tossed a few *quetzals*—the Guatemalan equivalent of the dollar—and coins onto the table. From his back pocket he pulled a flat pocketknife and dropped it on top of the money.

"That's it," he drawled.

"Turn them in and out then, please, so I can see for myself." Once Zach had smirkingly pulled the white fabric of his pockets inside out, proving they were indeed empty, Rodrigues nodded. "Good. I would search your clothes as well, but we have already seen for ourselves that you are hiding nothing, eh, señor?"

Zach ignored his gibe altogether, but Liz couldn't help checking to see Kirk's reaction. He was staring at her with narrowed eyes that held an unsettling speculative glint. She stood by, watching uneasily while one of the men tied Zach's hands behind his back and ordered him to sit.

"And now you, Señora Randolph," prodded Rodrigues. "Your pockets, if you would be so kind."

"I . . . there's nothing in them," Liz explained.

"Then you won't mind showing me, no?" He smiled and rapped his fingers on the table. "Quickly, please."

Liz moved hurriedly to turn her pockets inside out as Zach had done and then halted as the fingers of one hand encountered silk instead of rough cotton. Her panties. She was going to have to pull them out, right here in front of these leering strangers, and in front of Kirk who was bound to think . . . Liz swallowed hard. What could he think but the truth, that she and Zach were lovers? If her face hadn't been a crimson mask of humiliation before, it was then.

Scrunching the scrap of white silk and lace into as tight a ball as possible, she pulled it out along with her pockets. "There was only these . . . this." She put the panties on the table, pressing them down with her palm to insure that they stayed balled, only to have Rodrigues scoop them up and hold them aloft.

"I see, Señora Randolph, that you have very quickly learned the secret of staying cool in the tropics."

Half the room, the native half, erupted into insinuating guffaws, while the three *norteamericanos'* expressions ranged from mortification to scorn to granite-jawed silence. After what felt to Liz like an eternity, Rodrigues at last had his fill of entertaining the troops by twirling the bikini pants on the tip of his baby finger and he carelessly tossed them back on the table. They landed dead center, unfurled like an obscene banner heralding her unfaithfulness.

Not caring if one of them shot her in the act, Liz lurched to snatch them up and jammed them back into her pocket again, her flashing green eyes defying anyone to try and stop her. Gradually, under her glare of righteous indignation, even the dumbest looking of the guerrillas shifted from leering at her to looking sheepishly at his boots.

Rodrigues barked a command in Spanish to the man standing closest to Liz, who then jumped to secure her hands behind her back as he had earlier done to Zach. She almost welcomed the painful distraction of the sisal rope chafing her wrists.

"*Now* you may sit down, Señora Randolph," instructed Rodrigues. "I have other matters to see to, but my friends here will keep you company until El Tigre arrives."

Turning away, he spoke in rapid-fire Spanish to the men who'd been playing cards when they arrived, then he and the fourth man left the house together. The two remaining behind glanced at Liz, who still stood simmering by the table, exchanged a shrug that she interpreted as a fatalistic comment on women in general, and sat down to resume their interrupted card game.

Liz had been carefully avoiding eye contact with either Kirk or Zach, fearing a bitterly accusing look from one and an infuriatingly amused grin from the other. Now, squaring her shoulders, she started across the room to sit and for the first time noticed that Zach had chosen to park himself precisely opposite where Kirk was huddled. Great. Where, she wondered, would Miss Manners decree was the socially proper place for her to plop down? Really it was a moot point, Liz reflected with that wry sliver of humor that refused to be crushed by adversity. As far as she knew, Miss Manners never addressed herself to the sticky problems of etiquette encountered when one was being held prisoner by guerrilla *bandidos*. She was on her own here.

In an attempt to test the waters before taking a plunge, she slanted an awkward sideways glance at Kirk, not at all surprised by the laser of resentment emanating from his eyes. Strangely, and shockingly, Kirk now seemed the stranger to her. But Zach's expression wasn't much more inviting; at best it could be described as coldly detached.

Reluctantly she moved to sit a few feet away from Kirk, telling herself it was, after all, the right thing to do. It was also the story of her life. When the chips were down, those years of training really took over, opening the guilt gates until she caved in and did what was *supposed* to be right instead of what her instincts told her was right for her. Always to be stricken later with second thoughts, just as she was right now. Here she was sitting with the man she was supposed to love, doing her best not to look longingly at the man she was suddenly afraid she really did love instead, even if he did seem to hate her.

"Can't take your eyes off the sucker, can you?" Kirk taunted without bothering to keep his voice low. "Why the hell didn't you sit in his lap if you're that hot for him?"

Liz started to lash out at Kirk, then caught sight of the muscle jumping along Zach's jawline and bit her words back. She welcomed his subtle, unexpected show of gallantry but didn't want to see him act on it when it might well mean a bullet in his back. She was going to have to grit her teeth and find a way to placate Kirk.

"I sat here because I wanted to," she said, turning to look at him. What was one more lie? "We are still engaged," she added.

"Are we?" He shot a look at her ringless left hand. "Not so anyone would notice. Tell me, Liz, did you hand my ring over to him with my money?"

"I didn't have any choice," she said in a quiet voice, hoping her restraint would be catching. It wasn't.

"Oh, yeah? Well, it doesn't look to me," Kirk raged accusingly, "as if you wanted much of a choice."

Liz had as good an idea of how to respond to that as she had of how to handle Kirk in his current mood. The polite, soft-spoken intellectual she remembered was nowhere in sight. If she hadn't seen and heard it for herself, she never would have believed Kirk capable of the rude and cruel things he was hurling at her. Determinedly she fended off his barbs, avoiding altogether his increasingly hostile demands to know what had happened to his damn money. She was afraid that if he found out now, he would use the information to save himself and let her and Zach be damned.

There was, she concluded, absolutely no excuse for his behavior. Granted he'd been subjected to a great deal of strain, but she had too. And so, in a different way, had Zach. Suddenly the contrast between the way the two men were handling the situation eradicated the last of her patience with Kirk. He had been reduced to a crass, whining . . . bastard. While Zach . . .

She gazed across the room at him, marveling at the totally relaxed yet totally alert picture he presented. She knew he had to be every bit as tired and very nearly as alarmed as she was about the danger they faced. Yet you'd never know it to look at him. He gave new meaning to Hemingway's definition of courage, Liz thought with a proprietorial rush of pride. Grace under pressure. Why, why hadn't she had the sense to listen to her heart and sit over there with him?

She was deliberating over whether she dared get up and move over to him now, when Kirk squirmed to his feet beside her.

"Hey you . . . Pedro, or whatever your name is," he yelled at the men playing cards.

The two of them exchanged an exasperated look, then one half-turned to face Kirk, thrusting his chin up in a silent question.

"Take me for a walk out back," demanded Kirk.

The man grimaced, obviously not smitten with the idea of having to interrupt his game yet again. "You can't wait?"

"No. I need to use the can almost as much as I need a

breath of fresh air.'' The look he cast down at Liz before following the guard outside made her feel dirty all over.

The man who remained behind to keep watch made a quick grab for his gun as Zach rolled to his feet with the same fluid coordination he did everything, and started toward Liz.

''Hey, señor, where do you think you are going?''

''Over here,'' Zach replied, already sliding his back along the wall close beside her. ''The sun was in my eyes over there,'' he said sarcastically, nodding at the black window.

''Yeah, yeah,'' the young guard muttered, apparently drawing the wise conclusion that it wasn't worth tangling with the big, hot-tempered American again, especially over something as minor as where he chose to sit. Putting his gun aside, he proceeded to pick up his friend's hand of cards and study them.

''So, fancy face,'' Zach ventured in a tone too damn civil to be trusted, ''what sewer did you have to crawl in to find lover-boy?''

Liz considered pretending she didn't know who he was talking about, then dismissed the notion as too ludicrous. She ran her tongue over her parched lips. ''Kirk's not . . . himself,'' she offered listlessly.

''Not himself?'' echoed Zach. ''Hell, woman, he's not even human. He's a first-class, grade-A bag of scum, is what he is.

''You know,'' he continued in that same easy, conversational tone, ''meeting old Kirk raises a number of interesting questions in my mind . . . I mean besides the obvious one of how you managed to stay in the same room with the man—and I use the term loosely indeed—long enough to accept his proposal. It makes me wonder about things like your definition of the word *kind*.'' Liz's facial muscles tightened in direct proportion to the sharpening of his tone. ''And *generous*. And what was that third sterling quality of his that you've been beating me over the head with? Oh, yes, of course.'' His eyes glittered nastily. ''Honor.''

''He's different here,'' Liz uttered in a half-hearted attempt to defend him. ''He's acting like . . .''

''A dirt bag,'' Zach supplied when she couldn't seem to think of a polite way to describe what he was acting like. ''Which makes me wonder, Lizzie, about your taste in men. I mean, what was your first husband like? Is Kirk-the-worm a step up or down? Honey, I'll bet your first old man is rolling in his grave to see what you caught second time out. Unless . . .''

His black brows lifted speculatively, the eyes beneath them dark and clouded with an emotion Liz couldn't comprehend. It was as if he was determined to pay her back for each and every time she'd lauded Kirk and found him miserably lacking in comparison.

''Unless,'' he said again, ''unless your soft spot for Saint Kirk is what put the poor bastard in his grave to begin with. Is that it, Liz?'' he pressed, heedless of her small sound of shock at how low he was willing to swing to get to her. ''Maybe you hooked up with Kirk while number one was still around and he decided to put himself out of his misery? Is that what happened to him, Liz?''

''No, that is not what happened to him,'' she cried,

finally goaded past all control, past caring that their guard had abandoned his efforts at stacking the deck in order to give them his full attention, past caring about anything but striking back at him.

"That isn't even close to what happened," Liz said again, her temper stabilizing at a setting of cold fury. "Jeff was killed in an auto accident. It was snowing out and he lost control and hit a telephone pole head-on. It snapped and landed on his car. Before anyone could get to him, the car exploded. A freak accident is what the papers called it."

Her voice was an icy, emotionless monotone as she reported the facts of a situation that was so much more than facts to her. It was flesh and blood and screams she wasn't there to hear and a part of her life gone forever. But just reciting the facts would be enough to hurt Zach the way he had hurt her, the way she *wanted* to hurt him.

"Jeff was driving a sports car," she forced herself to continue. "Afterward one of the firemen was quoted as saying that it looked like a charred metal pancake." She heard Zach gulp in a deep breath, saw him open his mouth to tell her that was enough. But it wasn't enough for Liz. She wanted him to hear it all, the way she'd had to hear all his cynical ramblings and accusations. She locked gazes with him, not caring that his was now glassy with reflected pain.

She took a breath. "Jeff was on his way home from picking our son up at his baby-sitter's house. Jeremy was two and a half . . . and he was strapped into his car seat next to Jeff when the car crashed."

Unshed tears were pooled in Liz's eyes when she finished, practically blinding her. Still she was able to see Zach's reaction to her words. His head jerked back as if he'd been sucker-punched in the jaw and his face was etched with sorrow so obviously sincere it drained all the anger from Liz's soul.

His powerful body yearned toward her and she saw him straining at the rope binding his hands as if driven to take her in his arms. "Sweet Jesus, Liz. I'm sorry. God, I'm sorry."

He shook his head, the sudden motion sending a single, shocking drop of moisture spilling from one eye to trickle an indelible streak down his cheek. Liz stared at it as if transfixed until he turned his head away.

"God, why am I such a bastard to you?" he muttered almost too low for her to hear.

It was Liz's turn to strain at the rope, the urge to gather him against her a physical ache. So this is love, she thought, feeling its full potency for the first time in her life. This blinding need to comfort the one you love and the ability to let go of any amount of anger and pain to do it. Zach didn't ask for comforting. He certainly never gave her the slightest indication that he would welcome it. Even now she could sense him withdrawing into himself to repair and refortify the wall that surrounded him, a wall that until a few minutes ago had only cracked when he made love to her. And then only during those final, golden seconds when he cried out to her to hold him, just please hold him. No, he never asked for her comfort or her love, but he needed both more than any man she'd ever known. Of that Liz was certain.

The door flew open, causing all three inside the hut to

glance that way. Kirk stumbled in as if shoved from behind, closely followed by the guard who had escorted him, Rodrigues, and another man. The newcomer had the same black hair and eyes as the rest of the guerrillas, and he too was dressed in mix-and-match olive drab. But there was an unmistakable air of authority about him. Something in the self-assured set of his shoulders and the insolent confidence in his expression reminded Liz of Zach, and told her without a doubt that he was in charge here. She knew he was El Tigre even before the now subservient Rodrigues announced him.

His black agate gaze sliced across the room, moving over Zach with a hint of scorn which sharpened to sexual interest when he reached Liz, lingering long enough to inspect her from her tangled gold hair to her legs beneath the hacked-off slacks, legs which were tanner and firmer than they had been only two weeks ago. Although he didn't make a sound, Liz swore she could hear him smacking his lips in anticipation and instinctively twisted her head to throw Zach a frightened glance. Zach was staring straight ahead with a strange expression, eyeing the guerrilla leader, who was taller and more muscular than most Guatemalans. Zach didn't exactly look relieved or frightened. He looked calculating, she decided.

Liz, waiting breathlessly to see what would happen next, was startled when Zach was the first to speak.

"El Tigre?" he queried, the beginnings of what Liz recognized as a genuine smile twitching at the corners of his mouth. "*You* are the infamous El Tigre?"

"McCabe," El Tigre said. "What the hell are you doing here?"

"Waiting for you, evidently. You never could be where you were supposed to be on time, you miserable blackheart."

The slur was drawled without rancor, and El Tigre received it by throwing his head back and roaring. Zach looked on with amusement, while everyone else in the room gaped at the two of them with a mixture of bewilderment and wariness.

Finally Liz could stand it no longer. "You two know each other?" she exclaimed, directing the question to Zach.

He nodded, still grinning. "Sure do. We worked together in 'eighty-one, building the pipeline from Rubelsanto to the Caribbee coast."

She didn't have the faintest idea what that was, or care. She was too stunned by the chummy way Zach was treating this creep who'd had them captured and now held the power of life and death over them. It was as if they were some sort of long-lost buddies. Not that she should be surprised. Zach's association with the likes of El Tigre was just one more reminder of the unsavory life he led. But in this case at least, it might prove a blessing. Surely he would be able to clear up this whole misunderstanding.

"Does that mean he's going to let us go?" she asked Zach.

"I don't know," he replied, looking straight at El Tigre. "Does that mean you're going to let us go?"

"Oh, McCabe." The other man's smile was extinguished between tightly compressed lips as he shook his head, then launched into Spanish.

Zach shook his head back at him. "Whoa, whoa, *no comprendo*. You have to speak English, remember?"

El Tigre broke off with a cynical lift of his thin brows. "All these years south of the border, my friend, and you still speak no more Spanish than a chicken?"

"Who could be bothered to try?" Zach countered, shrugging. "You people speak so many dialects of the same damn language it makes me dizzy."

Liz, remembering the fluency with which Zach had conversed with Santana, knew his claim of ignorance now was an act. El Tigre's expression told her he knew it as well. Yet when he spoke again, it was in English and she clung to that small victory as an omen.

"I was trying to explain," he told them, "that I find myself in a very difficult position here. My plan, I regret to admit, was to do what I must to ... persuade from you the whereabouts of the money. Then to kill all three of you."

"Tidy," Zach acknowledged dryly.

"But now ..."

Liz held her breath, certain he was about to say that now he would of course release them unharmed.

"Now all that can wait until later," he finished. "First my old friend McCabe and I must share a drink or two."

"Damn magnanimous of you ... El Tigre," Zach said with a sardonic twist of his lips.

"The hell it can wait until later," Kirk stormed, commanding the attention of everyone in the small room. "I've waited as long as I intend to. Old friend or not, I demand that you make him turn over that twenty thousand dollars ... my twenty thousand dollars," he reiterated with an emphatic glare at Zach. "Then I'll just take my . . . my goods and be on my way."

His words confirmed a suspicion that had been nibbling at the corners of Liz's mind ever since Kirk's earlier remark to Rodrigues about the price being raised. It was clear to her now that the twenty thousand dollars she'd been ordered to bring, that she had risked her life to bring, hadn't been ransom at all. She wasn't sure exactly what Kirk was involved in with these lowlifes, only that he was. Obviously his frequent trips down here were inspired by something more complex than concern for the politically oppressed. Liz felt like a fool. And she felt used. But to her amazement, instead of feeling angry with Kirk, she felt free of him. It was as if his unwitting confession had severed the last threads of her obligation to him.

"Your goods are gone, señor," El Tigre informed Kirk with a threatening sneer. "I found another buyer. One without your, ah, cash-flow problems, yes?"

"You can't do that," Kirk cried. "I paid you a hundred thousand up front. And my cash-flow problems only started when you upped the price, you stinking swindler."

"The price was never set in stone, señor. It is always whatever the market will bear. That is the American way, no? And as for your demands," he dragged the last word out, smiling cruelly at Kirk, his eyes glinting with evil intent. With a movement so quick Liz wasn't sure where it had come from, a knife appeared in his hand, the slim blade flashing silver in the flickering lamplight. "I'm not sure I heard them right. Would you care to repeat? Hmmm?" he prodded when Kirk only shuddered silently against the blade now pressed to his throat.

"N-No," Kirk finally stuttered.

"Good." El Tigre removed the blade from his throat, leaving behind a sliver of bright red blood, and turned back to Zach, chuckling as if he'd just finished listening to a good joke instead of threatening a man's life. "Untie him...untie my friend Zach McCabe," he shouted to Rodrigues, who hustled to do his bidding. "And bring us a bottle."

A bottle of tequila appeared along with two grimy-looking glasses. El Tigre spilled a generous amount of the clear liquor in both glasses, then held his aloft.

"To old friends... may nothing as silly as twenty thousand dollars ever come between them."

Zach joined him in tossing off the first shot, then said, "I'm glad to hear you feel that way, old friend. Because this particular silly twenty thousand dollars is sitting at the bottom of the Rio Mopán."

At El Tigre's incredulous look, he delivered a brief explanation of what had occurred. When he finished, the guerrilla glanced over at Liz, then threw his head back in another explosion of laughter.

"Then you understand about the money?" Zach inquired without any sign of a smile.

"Bah. Women... who could understand anything they do? But I understand that something must be done to make up to me for the money." He discarded his pensive look with a sudden wave of his arm. "Later we'll worry about business. For now we'll drink."

306

As he hoisted the bottle, Zach asked, "How about untying my woman too, amigo?"

"*Your* woman?" El Tigre's brows lifted. "I thought she was his woman," he said with a slight inclination of his head in Kirk's direction.

Zach flicked his gaze over Kirk as if he were a fly buzzing annoyingly at the porch screen on a hot summer night. "That's all changed," he said simply.

"Ahh, still a winner with the ladies, eh, McCabe?" He slapped him hard on the back, then his voice grew steely, striking a note of foreboding deep inside Liz. "But no, I'm afraid she stays as she is for now. Another drink?"

Liz looked on in outrage as Zach simply shrugged and held out his glass. He didn't argue on her behalf. In fact, he looked totally unconcerned about the fact that her wrists were bound so tightly they burned. Instead he and his good buddy El Tigre pulled chairs up to the table and made themselves comfy. For Liz the night unfolded with a chilling sense of unreality. She was terrified and exhausted and growing more furious by the moment as she watched Zach and El Tigre swill tequila and swap stories as if this were a damn class reunion.

She tried to listen to what they were saying, but their abbreviated references to people and places unfamiliar to her left her, more often than not, totally in the dark. Kirk was no help in easing her anxiety. When he spoke at all, it was to needle her about her activities of the last week and a half, speculating openly and obscenely about her and Zach. Finally, in retaliation, she hurled at him her suspicions about his real reason for coming to Guatemala. It didn't come as much of a surprise when he laughed in her face.

"So I smuggle a little art along with smuggling peasants," he retorted. "The only difference is in the profit margin."

"Well, you can kiss your profits good-bye," snapped Liz, shocked by his callousness. "As soon as I get home I'm going to blow your respectable cover wide open."

"You just do that," he invited. "I'm planning a little heavy cover blowing of my own." He darted a pointed glance at Zach, then looked back at Liz with unveiled contempt. "I just wish I'd thought to bring a camera along to take a few snaps. . . . You know, to pass around to your friends. The tropics have sure wreaked havoc on your prim-and-proper image."

Liz's lower lip curled with disgust. With a toss of her head she put her back to him just in time to hear her name mentioned at the table. She listened intently, trying to piece together what she had missed while bickering with Kirk. Evidently El Tigre was suggesting that *she* might be suitable compensation for the lost money.

"Man's crazy," Kirk muttered beside her. "No way are you even close to being worth twenty thousand dollars."

"Shut up," Liz hissed at him.

The conversation between Zach and El Tigre evolved into a sort of verbal duel, with Zach protesting—nowhere near vigorously enough, in Liz's biased opinion—that he didn't like to share his women and El Tigre insisting that his honor demanded he receive something of value in place of the money. Both men were slurring, proof that the tequila had taken its toll. For a while they continued to spar clumsily with their words, now eschewing the glasses in favor of passing the bottle directly, and then seemingly out of the blue they both staggered to their feet.

"And he can be the referee," Zach declared, pointing to Kirk with one hand, as the other clutched the table as if it were the railing of a lurching ship. "He's the only impal . . . impal . . . impartial one here."

El Tigre nodded and signaled for Kirk to get up. As he moved to obey, Liz struggled to her feet.

"Referee for what?" she asked him frantically. She had a sickening sense that something horrible was about to happen. "What are they going to do?"

"Don't worry," Kirk assured her with a cruel twist of his lips. "They're only planning a little target practice outside. Best two out of three shots at an empty bottle. . . . Good thing too, because it doesn't look like either of them could stand up long enough for any more than that."

Zach and El Tigre had already stumbled out the door while Rodrigues waited, gun in hand, for Kirk to follow. He did, only pausing long enough at the door to say to Liz, "Oh, one more point of interest. It's winner take all . . . and you, sweet thing, are the prize."

"No . . . wait . . . please. . . ."

As the door slammed shut behind them, Liz made a move to follow, determined to put a stop to this insanity. Gesturing with the barrel of his gun, the remaining guard ordered her to halt.

"Please, señora," he implored laughingly, "El Tigre will blame me if he can only collect damaged goods."

Liz slid back into place, so frightened and angry she couldn't stop shaking. Damaged goods. How could Zach do this to her? The answer was obvious. He had gone and let himself get staggering, stinking drunk; that's how. If he'd cared about her at all, he would have stayed in control of his senses so he could get them out of here. Instead he was entering into some ridiculous macho test of skill. And with her as the prize. It was as if she were his possession, no more important to him than his boots or a good-luck piece he might wager in a poker game. Less, in fact. He hadn't bet his boots that he could outshoot El Tigre. He had no right to do this to her. Tears welled up in Liz's eyes as she realized that, right or not, she had no way to stop it.

The sudden sound of a gun blast made her jump two inches off the packed dirt floor, and she came down trembling. Closing her eyes, she whispered a prayer that they would both pass out cold or shoot at each other instead of the target. Anything to put a stop to the shouts and laughter outside. Another blast fired, followed instantly by the sound of shattering glass and loud whoops of delight. Did that mean El Tigre had scored a point? Liz fretted.

If her hands had been free, she would have jammed her fingers in her ears so that she couldn't hear. As it was, she had to listen to each shot, each resulting explosion of glass. All too quickly there came a raucous cheer, and then the door burst open and Kirk strode in wearing a grin that sent Liz's heart crashing to her heels.

"Surprise," he gloated. "Your hero just lost the war."

CHAPTER
FOURTEEN

At a smiling order from Rodrigues, Liz was immediately hustled off to El Tigre's hut to wait for him to come and collect his winnings. The scene outside was pure bedlam. Men, many of them acting and sounding as drunk as their leader, swarmed around in a mob that she surmised had the two contestants at its center. Liz longed for a chance to come face to face with Zach so she could tell him just what a despicable traitor she thought he was, but it didn't happen. She barely caught a glimpse of his sturdy back before the rest of the men saw her and started calling out to her in loud Spanish. Liz didn't need a translator to understand the implication of their remarks. She kept her eyes focused on the ground as she was pushed along the rest of the way, knowing that if she'd taken time today to eat, she would have thrown up right then and there.

Her escort shoved her into the tiny hut and left without bothering to light the lamp. With her hands still tied behind her, Liz was forced to negotiate her way around the dark interior by feeling with her shoulders and knees. Eventually she bumped into what felt like a cot and perched nervously on the edge to wait. The party outside seemed to go on for hours. Liz listened to the raucous shouts and laughter with a mixture of terror over what was about to happen and cold, raw fury at Zach for betraying her. If El Tigre had to win, she thought bitterly, she only wished he had put a bullet through Zachary McCabe's black, faithless heart in the process. Eventually the noise outside tapered off until she heard only an occasional burst of laughter, and then there was silence.

That's when Liz made the leap from fear to panic. Panic was a pain in her chest and a pulsing in her head. Her mouth turned dry with it and she shook so badly the cot was rocking beneath her. The night was so black she couldn't see when the door opened, but she heard it and a scream poured from her. Instantly a strong hand was slapped over her mouth, choking off all sound. An arm as powerful as a steel cable clamped around her middle, putting a quick stop to her breathing as well. Her lungs were burning and she felt as if they might rupture before it finally penetrated to Liz's terrorized brain that the rough, masculine voice purring close to her ear was Zach's.

Her anger faded into confusion and then into a bone-melting relief that made her go limp in his arms as she nodded frantically, trying to signal her awareness of who he was.

"Okay now?" he whispered.

She jerked her head up and down.

"If I let you go, you have to be real, real quiet. Understand?"

She gave a frantic nod and finally he released her. Liz gulped in air for a few seconds before collapsing against him.

"Oh, Zach. I'm scared. I'm so scared."

"I know, I know, baby," he whispered, telling her over and over that everything was going to be all right.

After a minute or so, she pulled away, trying to peer at him through the heavy shadows. "You're sober," she observed in amazement.

"More or less. I wouldn't want to have to walk a straight line to save my soul, but I think I can manage to get us safely out of here...if you cooperate."

"But what about El Tigre? I thought he won your stupid little contest." The whole scene came flooding back to Liz and she slammed her fist into Zach's chest. "How could you bet me that way?" she demanded. "As if you owned me...and then to let him beat you...."

"Let him think he beat me," he corrected, catching her fist before it could connect a second time. "The one thing I remembered best about Manny Silva was that he never knew when to stop celebrating, pick up his chips, and go home."

"Manny Silva?" she echoed, relief seeping through her, making her suddenly giddy.

"That's his real name."

With supreme satisfaction, she said, "You set him up, didn't you?"

"Sure did, and while he's still happily sleeping off his victory, I suggest we move."

As he slashed through the ropes around her wrists, Liz inquired whether he had any idea where they were.

"Some," Zach told her. "I'm going to head back the way we came and try to make it to the chopper."

"Rodrigues has the key," she reminded him.

"Not the spare I always keep in my boot," countered Zach, and Liz realized all over again how much she loved him and why. He took a minute to rub the feeling back into her wrists before pulling her to her feet. "C'mon, let's go."

As they skirted around the back of the farmhouse, Liz caught a glimpse of a sleeping Kirk through the window, and against her own better judgment she tugged Zach to a halt and pleaded with him to take Kirk with them.

"Why?" Zach countered, his eyes narrowing suspiciously.

"Because we have to. You know they'll take it out on him when they find us gone."

"Right. And he deserves it."

Liz twisted her hands. This was no time for a lengthy argument, and Zach's belligerent tone warned that he wasn't going to be easily convinced.

"Maybe he does deserve it," she whispered, "but I don't deserve to have whatever happens to him on my conscience for the rest of my life. Please, Zach . . . we have to take him with us."

Zach stared at her in disbelief. After all that bastard had done to her, she still cared about him enough to want to save his ass. Not that he should be surprised. Cleaned up and returned to their natural environment, Kirk was still a much better match for Liz than he would ever be. When was he going to learn once and for all that women like her operated on a very different value system than he did?

"Is it your conscience you're worried about, Liz," he challenged, "or your future? Dead men make poor husbands."

Liz frowned in confusion. It took a few seconds for his implication to penetrate her overtaxed brain. "What are you talking about? Whatever was between Kirk and me is over. You can't seriously think . . ."

"What I think doesn't matter," he broke in harshly. "Just like what you decide to do with Kirk doesn't matter. Personally I'd like nothing better than to leave him here to let him take the heat for all of us, but I'm not going to argue about it when any moment someone could wake up and hear us. Wait for me behind those bushes over there." He indicated a thick clump of overgrowth beyond the house.

Liz obeyed, biting back the urge to explain to Zach how wrong he was about her and Kirk. There would be time for that later. Right now they were both past thinking or speaking logically. She had almost chewed her bottom lip raw before he finally reappeared, dragging a sullen Kirk behind him. Zach's face was tight with anger.

"He's all yours," he growled, literally shoving Kirk at her. "Just keep him out of my sight before I kill him too."

Liz reeled with shock, but she knew better than to ask for any explanations right then. They started walking, with Liz carefully positioned between the two men. Although the jungle trails all looked exactly alike to Liz, she had every confidence Zach knew where he was headed. She wasn't the least bit surprised when they sighted the helicopter, looking for all the world like a silver-and-blue piece of heaven on earth. The three of them landed back at Zach's camp about twenty minutes later. What did surprise Liz—shocked her, in fact—was the reception they received.

She expected the men to be glad to see Zach, having learned during her stay that, despite their grumbling, most of them liked as well as respected their tough-as-shoe-leather boss. But she didn't expect them to greet her as if she were a little sister to them all. They streamed from their tents, bombarding her with welcoming shouts and hugs along with a stream of admonitions about the worry she'd caused them. Even Rodil sidled over to give her a sheepish pat on the shoulder, and wonder of wonders, O.J. actually smiled at her. When he learned she hadn't eaten since yesterday morning, he even went so far as to put on a pot of coffee and whip up what passed for scrambled eggs in her honor.

As if sensing he was doomed to be an outsider here, Kirk took his coffee and sat glumly off to the side, while Liz reported the events of the night to a rapt audience, giving Zach the billing he deserved as conquering hero. He endured her storytelling with a faintly indulgent expression, waiting until everyone had finished the impromptu breakfast before standing and gazing at the entire group expectantly until he had their complete attention.

"It's now four A.M.," he announced. "I want you to break camp and make everything ready to be trucked out of here by six. That gives us two hours," he continued over the mutterings of surprise and scattered groans, "and no time for bellyaching."

"May one ask the reason for this haste?" Jade ventured.

Zach hesitated. Then, with a quick glance at Kirk, he explained, "Because I had to kill one of Silva's guards when we were leaving. That will be all the motivation he needs to come after me. I'm not about to hang around here and put all our work on the line to play soldier with a bunch of misfits. We'll take what we've got so far and run. Don't worry," he assured the others, "you'll all get full pay."

"Run how?" It was Jade again. "It will take us four trips with the truck—minimum—to move all that." He indicated the extra tents where each night the men carefully stowed the day's booty. "That will give your pal Silva the tiger plenty of time to track you here."

"We're going to make it in one trip," Zach declared. "We'll use the pickup and the jeeps to carry some of the stuff, and the rest I'll fly to the coast in the chopper."

Jade was shaking his head. "Bad move, Zach. You land that thing anywhere near Livingston and you'll stir up mucho interest among the locals. How long do you suppose before the *policía* come snooping and find you sitting in a chopper chock full of stolen culture?"

"Do you have a better suggestion?" demanded Zach.

He sounded exasperated, and Liz noticed that the lines bracketing his eyes and mouth were more pronounced than ever. She knew at this point he had to be running on adrenaline and willpower alone, and wondered how long he could keep going. She herself was ready to drop from exhaustion.

"Yes, as a matter of fact, I do have a suggestion," Jade told him. "We'll take what we can over the road and leave the rest. I'll handle loading the boat and you fly straight home. You can be back in Mexico in time for supper."

Zach shot him an impatient grimace as he started to turn away. "Forget it."

"No, I won't forget it." Jade moved around so he was standing directly in Zach's path. "Listen to me, man. You're way past thinking straight."

"I'm thinking straight enough to know that Valdivia's not going to cut you a check for half a job. As it is, we'll be lucky if we can snow him into believing we finished early and that he's getting all that was in there."

"Screw Valdivia," Jade hollered. "No check is worth spending the rest of your life in some hellhole of a prison."

"Oh, no?" Zach jabbed his index finger into his friend's chest. "You want to talk about life, buddy? Then let's talk about losing it too. Let's talk about what those Colombians are going to do if you don't come up with the money you owe them. What do you think, Jade? Do you think they'll execute you in front of Cindy and the kids? Or them in front of you?"

Liz sucked in her breath in a horror-stricken gasp. Jade simply turned ashen and looked as if he were fighting not to retch.

Slowly he shook his head. "It's not right, Zach. It's bad enough I dragged you into my mess in the first place. I can't ask you to risk your life for me."

"Who's asking me to?" Zach retorted, and Liz could tell he was trying to sound harsh. "Just get the hell out of my way and let me do what has to be done." As Jade reluctantly stepped aside, he added, "And get these guys to work loading those trucks, will you?"

Within minutes the camp was a kaleidoscope of activity. Only Liz and Kirk seemed at loose ends. Liz had tried in vain to lift one of the boxes. Then Jade ordered Kirk to lend a hand transferring the crates from the tents to the trucks.

"Think again," Kirk sneered in reply. "I don't take orders from men wearing braids."

"You do now," interjected Zach, who had been working within earshot. Hitching his thumb in the direction out of camp, he added, "Take your choice . . . Jade's way or the highway. If you want a ride back to San Luis, you can damn well sweat for it."

Liz swallowed a chuckle as Kirk reluctantly—and quite inefficiently—joined in the group effort. They worked to load the largest truck first, carefully arranging and padding the crates to protect the valuable, irreplaceable contents. Liz finally found out why Zach had brought along all the grain stored in the supply tent. Tearing open the cloth sacks, the men poured some into each crate to conceal what was packed beneath. After watching for a while, she wandered over to sit by a tree well out of their way and watched the sun lift into view above the treetops. Her eyes had just drifted shut when the sound of approaching footsteps brought her head up fast. Her senses must be adapting to life on the edge of danger. When she saw that it was Zach approaching, her heartbeat escalated into a fast-paced flutter that indicated excitement of a different sort.

He hunkered down beside her, his mouth curving in a

lopsided, utterly devastating smile. "Liz, I . . ." He shrugged. "I don't know where to begin."

"I know. I feel the same way." So much had happened. So much had changed. Liz didn't have any idea how to translate what she was feeling into words that wouldn't scare the stuffing out of the physically strong, outwardly hardened man in front of her.

"Then maybe," Zach said, his tone tender, "we shouldn't even try to say anything." He glanced over his shoulder restlessly. "We've almost got the trucks loaded. I'm going to stagger their leaving as a safety measure."

"And the helicopter will go last?"

He nodded.

"Do you have to be the one flying it?"

Liz knew the question was motivated by selfishness, but she didn't care. If somebody was going to get caught red-handed, she didn't want it to be the man she loved. During their flight down here, Kirk had been very eloquent in warning her about the arbitrary practices of the Guatemalan justice system. If caught smuggling, Zach could spend as little as a month in a squalid jail cell, or as long as the rest of his life.

"Yeah, it has to be me. The only other man who could fly the chopper is Rodil, and there's no way I'd trust him out of my sight with something as valuable as a helicopter . . . not to mention what's going to be inside it. Besides," he concluded with quiet certitude, "I'm in charge here; the risk is mine to take."

"What do you think the chances are that you'll be caught?"

He gave a cynical snort. "Who knows? I'll just be glad when this whole thing is over."

She touched his arm lightly. "Zach, what did Jade mean when he said he'd dragged you into this mess . . . *his* mess, he called it?"

"That was just talk," he said, looking away from her.

"I don't think so. But if you don't want to tell me, I can always ask Jade personally. He loves talking about you."

Zach's lips pursed as he slanted her a pained expression. "I'll bet." He sighed resignedly. "Look, Jade needed some fast cash and I owed him a favor. It's just that simple."

"Is somebody really threatening to kill his family?" Liz pressed.

"The people he's messing with don't bother making threats," retorted Zach in a tone as brittle as his expression. "They let their actions do their talking."

"How much money does he owe these people?"

"Plenty." Expelling a rush of air from between slightly parted lips, he stretched his legs out to settle down beside her. "It started when Jade won some bucks at jai alai a year or so ago and decided to make an old dream of his come true by buying a small charter fishing business down in the Keys. He wasn't at it two weeks before some guy shows up and tells him he's required, *required*," Zach repeated with a tinge of disbelief, "to pay a percentage of his weekly take to the organization he represents . . . which turns out to be a local gang of Colombian hoods."

"Sort of like the protection money the Mafia charges small businessmen?"

"Exactly. You pay them a hundred bucks a week and they

won't torch your boat. Only Jade, being Jade, told them to go to hell—only not that nicely, you can bet.'' Briefly an affectionate smile pierced his bitterness. Then the expression in his dark eyes turned lethal. "The first time they only trashed his boat and he was able to get a bank loan to repair it. But his insurance rates suddenly went so high he missed a payment. Then they came back and torched the boat but good. Of course, the fire department arrived before it was a total loss, but no bank in this world would give Jade another loan to fix it.''

"So he went to a loan shark for the money instead,'' guessed Liz.

"You got it. Then once all the money is spent and the boat is ready to float, he discovers that the guy who was so obliging about lending him the money works for the same gang he'd been bucking all along. Now they give him a new choice; he can either make the protection payments along with the installments on the loan or they call the whole amount due in ten days.''

"And that's why you're down here doing this,'' Liz concluded, "to help Jade get enough money to pay them off.''

Zach nodded. "If he doesn't, he'll be paying them and dancing to their tune until the day he dies.''

Reaching out, he ripped up a handful of straw grass and let it sift through his fingers piece by piece. "Jade first met this Valdivia character in a local bar. His family has owned the land all around here for generations. When he fell out of favor with those currently in power, they started to hassle him. After they shot his son and tossed his body on his front porch, he took the rest of his family and ran like hell...burned everything here to the ground before he left so that some fat-ass politician didn't end up living in his home."

"Did Valdivia know the Mayan ruins were on his property?"

"Sure. His family had always known, but they kept their mouths shut about it because they knew that telling anyone would be a fast way to have their land seized as a national treasure. Valdivia asked Jade if he knew of anyone who'd be willing to go in after what was buried there if he provided a map and paid well for the risk involved. Jade knew I was familiar with the country around here, so he asked me and I told him I wasn't interested."

He hurled the last of the grass aside. "Then the situation changed and it was no longer a matter of choice but financial necessity. I told Jade to tell Valdivia that if he paid for a big enough crew and the right equipment to minimize the difficulty and the risks, I'd take a shot at it. By that time Valdivia had approached someone else about it, and Jade and I sort of...cut old Sanchez out."

"The same Sanchez you suspected me of working for?"

Zach nodded, his smile as sheepish as it ever got.

Reaching for his hand, Liz lifted it to press her cheek against his warm, callused palm. "Jade's lucky to have you for a friend."

"Yeah, well." He shrugged, looking embarrassed. "We go back a long way, and I owed him one...a big one."

"I knew it," Liz said with a smile. "I knew all along...well, maybe not all along, but I've known for a while that there had to be a good reason for what you were doing."

"And now you know what it is," Zach countered with an edge of finality. "But I've got to be getting back, so if you want to know any more about Jade's problems, you'll just have to ask him. . . . You two will have plenty of time to chat on the drive to San Luis."

He had been gently untangling his fingers from hers, but now Liz clung tightly to him. "What do you mean? I'm going to be leaving with you in the helicopter."

"The hell you are," he shot back, his quick frown and implacable tone telling Liz not to bother trying to change his mind about it.

"All right," she relented, "I'll go with Jade if that's what you think best, and I'll meet you in Livingston."

The sight of him shaking his head slowly back and forth made Liz tighten her grip on his fingers even further. "I don't understand."

"Sure you do, Liz. This is it. I'm going to Livingston alone and you're going home."

"You can't mean that."

"Of course I mean it," he said, pulling his hand free and leaning away when she attempted to touch him again. "You should be jumping for joy. After all, this is what you've wanted all along."

"Right, it's what I *wanted*," she countered. "But it's not what I want now." She stared straight into his eyes until he turned away with a shrug.

"Too bad, baby, because that's the way it is. And don't look at me like that," he growled, without even looking at her to see how she was looking at him. "You don't go shacking up with a guy like me . . . with a *huaquero*, for

Pete's sake, and expect . . . promises or whatever the hell it is you're sitting there expecting from me now. The sex was great and you're not as much of a spoiled brat as I first thought. That's it. Good-bye.''

The terrible feeling of dread that had started coiling inside Liz when he first dropped the bombshell suddenly began to loosen. As Zach continued talking, his gestures uncharacteristically awkward, revealing how uneasy he was, she found the feeling starting to reverse into one of confidence.

"Hold it, McCabe," she ordered as he made an abrupt move to rise. "I think you should know that you're wasting your breath." Liz felt like laughing out loud at the wary narrowing of his eyes. "That's it and good-bye," she mimicked in a scoffing tone. "You don't fool me with all that macho bluster, and you don't scare me anymore either."

His mouth creased with grudging admiration. "I'm not trying to scare you, fancy face. I'm trying to make you accept the truth. This can't work for us."

"Not if I go home and you go to Livingston alone and get yourself tossed in jail, it can't."

"It can't work, period. You remember what I told you last night in the ruins? About how the beauty there is interwoven with time and place? Well, it's the same with us. Okay, I admit that it was more than great sex. It was beautiful, but it was only beautiful for the here and now. Believe me when I tell you that we're from two different worlds.''

"I don't care."

"You will soon enough. There's no denying there's a strong sexual attraction between you and me. Or that no matter how much of a bastard I've been to you while you were here, I'm still the closest thing to a friend that you've had. I heard you talking about what happened last night and I wouldn't be surprised if right about now I look like some sort of damn romantic hero to you."

Liz lifted her shoulders in a small shrug. That was a fair summation of the way she thought of him. Zach looked appalled.

"Well, the fact is I'm not," he growled. "And you'll see that for yourself as soon as you're back with your own kind."

"You're my kind," Liz insisted.

He released a harsh laugh. "Not by a long shot, sweetheart. I don't know exactly what your family is like or how much money you have, but it smells like a whole lot." He skimmed his eyes over her, warming Liz with the approving glow that she suspected lit in them against his will. "Even with you wearing rags I can tell that everything about you is expensive . . . from your perfectly straightened white teeth, to your snotty little East Coast accent, to that wide-eyed, slightly amazed look you get whenever you push and something doesn't give the way it no doubt always does back home."

"So I have money," Liz countered with an airy wave of her hand. "That doesn't make me any less of a person. Besides," she added, trying to inject a little lightness into a conversation she feared was rapidly spinning out of her control, "didn't your mother ever tell you it's just as easy to fall in love with a rich girl as a poor one?"

He smiled weakly. "Maybe. I never listened to very much my mother had to say."

"Well, you're going to listen to me," declared Liz. Rolling gracefully to her knees so she was facing him, she cupped her hands around his solid biceps. "I love you, Zach McCabe."

His mouth pulled tight, but Liz was too busy watching his eyes to pay much attention to that discouraging sign. And in his eyes skyrockets went off, telling her that regardless of how many obstacles he threw in her path, he liked the idea that she loved him. Maybe, deep down, he was even starting to love her back.

"You don't even know me," he protested in a strangely winded tone.

"I know all I need to know. I know that you took care of me when you didn't have to, when it would have been easier to just walk away. I know that you came after me last night and ended up risking your life to save mine. I know that you did the same for Jade . . . and even for Kirk, for God's sake."

"And you think that's all you need to know, huh? Well, keep dreaming. Have you even given a thought to what your family and friends are going to say when you tell them you're in love with a man who'll rob a grave if the price is right?"

"That's not the way it is," she protested, dropping her hands to her lap with an impatient jerk.

"But it's damn close. How *do* you imagine that I earn my living, Liz?"

The question caught Liz off guard. Actually, she didn't care how he earned his living, hadn't even squandered a thought in that direction. But she wasn't about to admit that to Zach, who would surely use it to bolster his argument that she hadn't thought this through carefully enough.

"Not even able to venture a guess, hmm?" he prodded. "All right, then I'll tell you. I'm a pilot . . . No, don't grin yet, honey. You see, I'm the sort of pilot folks seek out when the commercial airlines don't fit their needs. I'll fly anything, anywhere if my price is met, and I make it a point never to ask awkward questions about things such as what it is I'm hauling or why the client wants it dropped in a particular place in the middle of the night. Get the picture?"

Liz nodded tersely, stalwart in her belief that together they could work out any wrinkle, even the slightly less than legal one he described.

"Before I managed to save enough from working on the pipeline to afford my own plane, I did a little bit of everything." He spoke in quick punches, as if driven by some private demon to keep battering Liz until he saw in her eyes the contempt he so obviously thought he deserved. "Most of the jobs I took back then I'd sooner forget, and a few I won't even admit to. How do you think all that will go over when we're at a party sometime and one of your friends sidles up, tells me he's a data-systems engineer, and asks what I do?"

"Like I said before," Liz told him in a voice that was quiet and steady, "I really couldn't care less. For the first time in my life, what my family or my friends think doesn't matter to me."

She lifted her hand to silence him when he started to interrupt. "No, I want to explain this to you, and then maybe I'll finally understand it myself. Ever since I was a little girl I've had this . . . this sensitivity to what I was supposed to do, and I did it. When I was in college, there were other boys who attracted me more than Jeff did, but I got involved with him because they weren't the right type according to my family's standards, and Jeff was. I knew even before we were married that he wasn't right for *me* at all. I was only twenty-one years old. I wanted to do things, exciting things, things that mattered, and all Jeff wanted was to work his way up to being a full partner in his father's law firm.''

"Then why the hell did you marry the guy?"

Liz made a rueful sound. "Because I was pregnant, and it was the *right* thing to do. Sometimes, before Jeff and Jeremy died, I used to feel so trapped. Then afterward I felt so guilty for ever feeling that way that I couldn't even stand to look at myself in the mirror. It took me a long, long time to accept the fact that I hadn't been betraying them by having needs and desires aside from what I felt for them.''

Liz took a deep breath and stared down at her loosely clasped hands. "After I met Kirk, I kept telling myself that he was the perfect man for me. . . . He was gentleman enough to impress my family, but with a recklessly brave, noble streak that appealed to me.''

"Wrong on all counts," Zach intoned dryly. "You're not a very good judge of character, sweetheart.''

"Maybe not with Kirk," Liz conceded. "Maybe I was just tired of being alone and so I saw in him what I wanted to see.'' Her lips quirked with humorous self-reproach. "And what *he* wanted me to see, I suppose. I cringe to think how much money I've donated to his cause over the past several months.''

With a resolute shake of her head, she cleared away thoughts of Kirk and brought her eyes up to meet Zach's. ''But this is different. I know my instincts are right. In fact, I think they always have been, but I was afraid to risk going with them. So instead I always made the safe choice and did the right thing, the thing I was expected to do. But not this time. This time I've found something worth taking any risk for, and I almost blew it once already, by running away from you because you didn't fit my narrow definition of the right man.''

''Look closely,'' Zach advised. ''I still don't.''

''I've changed my definition. Now all I have to do is convince you.''

''Sorry, honey, I don't have that kind of time to spare.''

He shifted forward on his way to standing, but Liz threaded her arm through his to stop him, glaring at him in exasperation. ''Why do you have to be so damn stubborn?''

''I'm not being stubborn, I'm being a realist. How long do you think you'd be happy with me living in a place like this?''

''You don't live in a place like this,'' Liz pointed out. ''I heard Jade mention that you'd be going home to Mexico.''

''That's right. I work out of a small village in Mexico that's a hell of a lot closer in atmosphere to the spot you're sitting in than it is to Boston. That's reality, fancy face.''

''We could work it out...other couples do. We could compromise.''

''Not unless Tijuana is your idea of a compromise,'' he

uttered. Then, rubbing his fingers across his black-bristled jaw: "Look, Liz, I can't go back to the States with you or for you. Not now, not ever . . . because there's a warrant out for my arrest."

Liz looked at the straight line of his mouth, at the blue eyes that were bleak and haunted, and didn't want to ask. But the question rolled out of its own volition, so hushed it was barely audible. "For what?"

Zach's answer came in a voice that was coolly dispassionate. "Manslaughter."

CHAPTER
FIFTEEN

Zach's sight was foggy, his hearing fuzzy. He jammed his finger helping Rodil shut the door of the overloaded truck and hardly felt it. It was as if he were removed from his own body, floating somewhere above and looking down on everything that was happening here below. Well, not everything, he thought humorlessly, only Liz.

He was aware of every move she'd made since he'd left her sitting at the edge of the clearing, reminding her as he turned to go that Jade's truck would be leaving in ten minutes and she better be in it. He had hesitated only a fraction of a second before stalking away, but he figured that was plenty long enough for her to get started if she'd wanted to say anything. She hadn't said a word, just sat there in shocked silence and looked at him with a broken expression in those huge green eyes.

Ever since then he'd been waiting, hoping, and—much as it shocked even him—praying that she would come to him and demand an explanation of the confession he'd blurted out, or at least ask for a few more details. But she hadn't. She'd lingered awhile where he left her, then had wandered over and said good-bye to each of the men, clearly taking pains to avoid him in the process. She'd spent a hell of a long time talking to Jade, though, and Zach found himself straining at the bit to call his friend over on some pretense afterward and find out what they'd been looking so chummy about. Only his pride held him back. Besides, if anybody could make him sound better than he was, Jade could, and would. It stood to reason that if Liz had meant it when she said she loved him, she'd jump at whatever Jade said in his defense. And then she would come to him herself.

Zach didn't fully accept the fact that that wasn't going to happen until he watched the plume of thick, black mud spray from beneath the tires of Jade's truck as it drove off with Liz in it. He stood there staring until it disappeared, and then for a long time afterward not caring that the men who still remained were eyeing him strangely. He'd had his share of accidents through the years and been in more than his share of fights, but nothing he'd suffered from any of them had ever come close to the pain that spread through him now. It was if a cold, mechanical hand had closed over his heart and was slowly ripping it out of him. The urge to jump into one of the jeeps and go after her was like a fire in his belly. This time, though, it wasn't pride that held him back. It was something else. Something Zach couldn't think about right then.

He might not have Liz's track record for doing what was right, but at least this time when the chips were down he'd managed to pull it off. One way or another he'd had to make it clear to Liz that there wasn't any future for her with him. If she walked away thinking him so despicable she would never suffer a second thought, so much the better. And if what he'd told her about being wanted for manslaughter wasn't exactly the truth, he could live with that. Lying was a relatively small-ticket item in the catalogue of his sins.

Not that Zach was even sure it was a lie. The warrant had certainly been real enough sixteen years ago. He'd never had any reason to check to find out if what Jade told him was true, that the charges against him had been dropped after further investigation of the incident. Even if he could return to the States without standing trial for that crime, which he didn't commit, there remained the little matter of not reporting for active duty in the armed forces, of which he very definitely was guilty. There had been just one time, years ago, when amnesty had been declared for all wayward draft dodgers and he'd been tempted to go back. But the thought of accepting even the token punishment of doing six months' ''alternative duty'' in some veterans' hospital seemed to him a way of forcing him to admit that he'd been wrong and that he was sorry. He wasn't.

He'd been twenty years old when Dan stepped on a land mine in Vietnam and was shipped home without his legs. Dan was more than just an older brother; he was a role model, a hero. All his life he had scrambled to follow in Dan's footsteps, with only marginal success. It was an accepted fact by everyone in the McCabe household—him included—that his football scholarship to UCLA was second best to Dan's appointment to West Point. It was another accepted fact that upon graduation Zach would follow Dan into the service.

Then he'd visited him in the hospital that day, his gaze both drawn and repelled by the awful, permanent flatness of the sheet there below his waist, and he began to wonder if maybe all the signs and demonstrations protesting the war that he observed around campus were right, and that maybe he and his father and his brother, who would never again break into a gallop to receive one of his high-flung passes, were the ones who were wrong. His first mistake had been in voicing that thought in front of his father.

Until that moment he had thought that the two of them had a terrific relationship, something right out of a Norman Rockwell painting, for crissake. He learned in a hurry, though, that his father's pride and praise hinged on how closely Zach adhered to the course he'd charted for him. All the time he'd been growing up his father had told him to think for himself, to stand on his own two feet even if he had to stand alone. Then, in the span of one brief semester break, he'd discovered it was all a farce. The more he and his father discussed the subject of the war, the farther they drew apart and the more determined Zach became to make up his own mind. The night his father told him that Dan, disabled as he was, was more of a man than he'd ever be, was the night he'd left home. He hadn't been back since.

Zach pressed the heels of his hands hard against his eye sockets, trying to clear his head. He hadn't allowed himself to think so deeply about all of this in years. Thoughts about that time of his life invariably triggered memories of Amanda, memories that had the eerie power to reach through time and give him an instant, temple-pounding headache. Trying to forestall it, he began making his way along the row of tents, checking to be certain nothing was left behind that could be traced to any of the men, and through them to him and Jade. Amanda dogged him every step of the way. Amanda Bellingham had been very beautiful, very spoiled, and very involved in the antiwar movement at UCLA. Only later did he realize that she would have been very involved in a movement to elect a sheep President if it had been the cause célèbre of the moment. He had also been a little slow in recognizing the way she doled out passion to him like bonus points. Then again, maybe he did notice, but was just so hot for her he didn't give a damn.

Looking back, he could see that the months between the time he'd cut himself off from his folks and the time he'd fled the country were like a string of fast-falling dominoes that fell faster and faster and with greater and greater ramifications as they went along. Overlaying all the craziness of that period of his life was the hot, sweet sensuality of being in love with Amanda. Just being with her had made him happy, and if going along to marches and sit-ins was what it took to make her happy in turn, then so be it. Anyway, by that time he was convinced that she was right about the war being a very expensive, very lethal joke. As he became more involved in the extracurricular activity of being an antiwar activist, his grades had gone to hell, taking with them his athletic scholarship. At the time he hadn't even cared about that. Classes and practice had interfered with his seeing Amanda as often as he wanted to, which was all the time.

The perfect irony of it all was that the thing that finally sent his life spinning totally out of control was supposed to have been the *peace* movement's *nonviolent* blockade of a munitions train. Instead the train ended up derailed, killing a conductor, and the National Guard ended up in a shooting frenzy. Zach ended up holding a young woman he barely knew in his arms and watching her life pump out of her through a bullet hole, turning his jeans a sodden blackish-red. It had been his first taste of violence and bloodshed. His stomach had gotten a lot stronger since, but back then he'd thought he would never stop puking.

When Amanda yelled at him to run, he did, quickly losing sight of her in the fleeing crowd. He'd felt like being alone anyway, and had walked for hours, thinking. Here he'd been convinced he was making such a profound state-ment, when all he'd really done was trade his father's beliefs for those of Amanda and her friends. Both were equally dangerous, equally self-serving. He didn't want any part of any of it after that, but he had been fool enough to still want Amanda with a passion. He'd finally headed for her place, expecting some understanding and compassion for what he was feeling, and instead found himself in the middle of a victory celebration as they watched the day's bloody events on the eleven o'clock news. With sudden clarity he'd seen that this was just one more social game to all of them, Amanda included. Disgusted with himself for ever being part of it, he'd decided to act like the man he'd thought he was and turn himself in to the police.

Despite a painful all-night session with a couple of energetic cops, he'd kept his mouth shut about who else was involved. They still managed to round up most of the others within a day or so, giving them plenty of reason to believe he had spilled his guts. He would never forget how quickly Amanda's undying love for him had turned to scorn. . . . It was almost as quickly as she and the others were bailed out on reduced charges by high-priced, fast-talking attorneys. That left only him to take the heat as the mastermind of the whole disaster. Somehow Jade had finally managed to come up with the money to spring him, and even the sincere young public defender assigned to his case had agreed with Jade's cynical warning that he was about to learn about the American justice system firsthand by taking the fall for those so bolstered by wealth that they never even stumbled. He had anguished over it for days, then had done the only thing that made any sense at all at the time. He ran. Sometimes it felt as if he'd been running ever since.

Zach waved off the last jeep with the realization that he'd done a pretty half-assed job of managing this final part of the operation. It wasn't like him to lose his concentration in the middle of a job this way. But then, it also wasn't like him to fall so hard for a woman that she filled all the nooks and crannies of his brain until there wasn't even enough room left to fit a thought in sideways. He turned and started toward the chopper when something at the top of the slope overlooking the camp caught his eye. Jesus, he was even worse off than he'd thought if he was seeing things. Then the vague suggestion of a shape drew closer, becoming clearer with each step until there was no doubt that it really was Liz he saw, not some vision conjured up by wishful thinking.

She was barreling down the hill toward him, her hair flying behind her like streamers of fine gold silk. As she came within reach, she lifted her arms to wrap them about his neck and landed against him with all the subtlety of a runaway locomotive. It was a pretty apt comparison, Zach decided, staring into her upturned face, which was radiant with love and vibrant with determination.

He suddenly felt the way you feel when you step outside on a frigid cold night and the wind seems to suck all the air from your lungs. Only the temperature was about ninety-five degrees and there was no wind. His breathlessness was entirely the fault of the woman in his arms, the woman whose body fit his as if they'd been created from two halves of the same mold, the woman whose smile threatened to change his life forever.

"Oh, Liz." The words were more a movement of his lips than a sound. But Liz smiled, and Zach knew that she'd heard and that she understood, and that no matter how softly he spoke, she always would.

He lowered his mouth to take hers in an open, searing kiss, pouring into it all the things he wanted to say. Her once shy tongue sought his, the contact a thunderbolt of sensation. They both trembled from the power of the desire it unleashed, their bodies straining against each other with a hunger born in the soul. When she finally pulled away to drag in a shuddering breath, Zach was left wanting, needing, aching.

"You're supposed to be on your way to San Luis with

Jade,'' he said when he'd recovered enough control to speak.

She'd come back. The thought was spinning inside his head in a never-ending circle. She'd come back. There was no way she would have done that, putting herself in certain danger, risking her own freedom, if she didn't really love him. He knew he ought to beat her for the stupid, headstrong pain in the ass she could be, but at the moment he couldn't even work up enough annoyance to wipe the smile off his face.

"Didn't I tell you I didn't want you coming with me?" he demanded when she just continued to look at him with that utterly defiant, absolutely bewitching smile.

"Mmm-hmm."

"And aren't I the boss here?"

"Oh, definitely."

"And do you have any idea how I punish women who defy me?"

She opened her eyes so that he got a full dose of their sparkling green fire. "No, but I can't wait to find out."

As she moved her hips provocatively against his, Zach snaked his arm lower and held her tight, pressing her firmly against his rising manhood.

"Wanton," he growled against the smooth terrain of her throat as he raked it teasingly with his teeth.

"Mmmm." Her head tipped back with pleasure. "And aren't you glad?"

Zach laughed, spinning her away from him with a quick swat at her fanny. "Frankly, yes. I just wish I had the time right now to explore it more fully."

Her playful look faded. "There'll be time, Zach. Maybe not right now, but we will have time . . . for everything."

He folded his hands into fists as he searched for words. "Liz, I . . ."

"I know," she said quietly when he faltered. "Jade told me all about your brother and Amanda and what happened that day at the train. He also told me the criminal charges against you were dropped years ago but that you're too stubborn to do anything about it."

"Is that why you decided to come back?" he asked, suspicion returning like a bad habit. "Because you figured it wasn't as serious as I let you think?"

"No. I knew I was coming back even before I climbed into that truck. But I also knew that if I didn't wait until every last jeep had left you'd just foist me on someone else."

"Damn right," he interjected, trying to sound stern, which was a difficult feat, as he was grinning from ear to ear.

"I came back," she said, "because I love the man you are now, not the boy you were sixteen years ago. And because I love you enough to stand by you, whether I have to do it in some godforsaken Mexican village or in a court of law while you confront mistakes you made a long time ago."

"The thing with the train was a mistake," he countered, his tone slow and deliberate. "But I'm pretty sure Jade wouldn't steer me wrong about it being settled. Maybe someone else who was there finally came clean and told them I didn't have anything to do with orchestrating that mess. But that doesn't change the fact that I could still end up serving time as a draft dodger."

"That's highly unlikely. Tempers have mellowed since the sixties, Zach. I know people who could help you work it out."

"Amnesty." He nodded and looked at a spot somewhere over her shoulder. Somewhere inside him he felt a wall start to crumble. "I always figured that was the same as crawling back, and I told myself no way would I do that. But I guess I just never had a good enough reason to crawl until now. All right," he said, turning back to her with a smile, "we'll talk about it. But right now all I want is to get to Livingston and get this over with. The sooner I have you safely out of this country the better."

"Couldn't we just fly straight to Mexico and arrange to ship the rest of the stuff from there?"

Zach shook his head. "No. I'm legal in Mexico and I want to stay that way . . . especially now. The Mexican government has some sort of reciprocal treaty with Guatemala concerning stolen artifacts. If I get caught landing there with this stuff, they'll toss me in jail *and* yank my pilot's license. Neither of which is going to help my case back home any. I figure the odds are better doing it this way. I just wish you weren't tagging along."

"Better get used to it, McCabe," Liz quipped.

She expected a sarcastic retort from him. Instead she got an amiable smile.

"I guess that could be arranged," he said, turning and starting toward the helicopter, which was parked at the far side of the clearing where the ground was firmer. "If you give me about forty years or so."

"*Give* you forty years?" echoed Liz as she struggled to keep pace with his long-legged stride. "That sounds like a request."

"Sure does."

"Is that something like a proposal?"

"I'm not sure. I've never had anyone propose to me." He was still walking, a good ten feet ahead of her by now. "You're the bona fide expert in that area. Does it sound like a proposal to you?"

"Very close."

"Then I guess it must be a proposal." He swung open the door on the passenger side of the cockpit and gave her a hand up, lingering afterward with a small, slightly uncertain smile. "So what do you think?"

Liz fluttered her lashes as if bewildered. "Think?"

"Yeah. You know, about the proposal."

"Oh, the proposal." She chewed her lip thoughtfully for a few seconds. Then, reaching for the door handle and pulling it toward her, "I think that all things considered, I've heard better."

"Bitch," he said just before the door slammed shut, a big grin on his face.

Livingston was a fishing village on the country's east coast. Not a whole lot bigger than San Luis, was how Zach described it to her. Liz, prepared for the worst, was delighted when he pointed up ahead at a rambling assortment of white, pastel, and red tile-roofed boxes and shouted over the whir of the propeller, "That's Livingston."

The village sprawled along the ruffled coastline of the Caribbean. Out in the glossy blue waters beyond, boats drifted like giant feathers. Liz wondered at which of the spindly, fingerlike piers in the distance Jade's boat, the *Cindy Ann*, was moored. Instead of flying directly over the village so she could get a closer look, however, Zach made a wide circle and set the helicopter down in a field, sending chickens and hens and a few pigs gathered there scattering in a noisy huff. A couple of ancient-looking cows nearby looked up briefly, then lowered their heads back to the grass without so much as a break in their chewing. What they lacked in interest was more than made up for by the assortment of men, women, and children who piled from the adjacent houses to see what had landed in the middle of their grazing area.

Zach climbed out first, then lifted Liz down to stand beside him as the small group approached. They splintered into factions as they drew close, the children dancing ahead to touch the helicopter with quick, cautious fingers, while the women hung back in a shy cluster. Their tittering, Liz surmised, doing her best to smooth her hair and straighten her shoulders, was over her bedraggled appearance. Only the men stepped boldly forward to confront Zach, their expressions a mixture of curiosity and wariness. After a few minutes of discussion, of which Liz understood only a sprinkling of words, one of the younger men in the group nodded in response to something Zach had said and pointed across the pasture.

Zach turned to her. "He says he has a truck and he's

willing to drive us—along with as much of the cargo he can fit—down to the boat.''

''What about the rest of it?''

''That will have to wait until Jade shows up. This guy's a little leery about getting involved as it is . . . and the others flat-out refused at any price.''

Their young driver quickly brought his truck over, and the rest of the men went so far as to give them some help loading it, with Zach stuffing a few dollars into each of their hands afterward. When the time came to climb into the truck, Zach hesitated with the door half open. ''I don't suppose you could be persuaded to wait here?'' he asked her without much hope in his voice.

''Not a chance.''

''That's what I figured. And as long as there are still crates in the back of the chopper, I suppose it's a case of six of one, half dozen of another whether you stay or come. Vinicio here tells me we'll have to take the long way around the village because there's a street festival going on . . . Guatemala's answer to the Fourth of July or some damn thing. With a little luck the local police will be so busy keeping order they won't notice us.''

Vinicio's circular route brought them close enough to the village center for Liz to glimpse the activity there. It was a picture-postcard scene, with most people dressed in native outfits woven in bright colors and dancing to loud, impromptu street bands. Donkeys with small toys and other treasures strapped to their backs stood at the street corners, reminding Liz of the balloon hawkers who worked the parades back home. The air was filled with a mixture of sweet and spicy cooking scents and the universal sounds of a party in full swing. Liz viewed it all with a comforting sense of normalcy. Celebrations, it seemed, were basically the same everywhere, and for the first time since arriving in Guatemala, she felt insulated from guns and guerrillas and violence that erupted out of nowhere.

The feeling of safety began to ebb as soon as they reached the dock. The *Cindy Ann* was tied up at one of the outermost piers, where it seemed ominously quiet compared to the noisy hubbub just a short distance away. Liz waited in the truck while Zach and Vinicio struggled to transfer the heavy crates to the boat. After successfully maneuvering the first across the narrow gangplank onto a bobbing *Cindy Ann*, Zach paused to hand her the key to the helicopter.

"You better hang on to this," he explained. "If I go for a swim and lose it, we've got big trouble."

"Oh, señor, you got big trouble anyway."

They both followed Vinicio's pop-eyed gaze to the dark-colored jeep rolling to a halt behind the truck and the two men climbing out of it. Both were dressed in the khaki uniforms and wide black belts of the national police force, and both were sporting very nasty, very intimidating smiles. Liz swung back to Zach in time to see Vinicio bolt, darting across the narrow street and disappearing from view. The urge to follow exploded inside her.

As if reading her panic, Zach spoke to her quietly, his lips barely moving. "Stay right where you are."

If he was hoping the policemen wouldn't notice her sitting there, he was soon disappointed.

"Buenas días, señor," the first officer said, stopping close in front of Zach and angling his head to bring Liz into the range of his stiff smile as well, "and señora. How nice of you both to join us for our Independence Day celebration."

Zach didn't say a word. Liz, following suit, listened to the smooth-voiced policeman with mounting despair.

"Alas," the man continued, "you are perhaps not aware that no work is permitted to be done on a national holiday."

"No," Zach responded, "I wasn't aware of that."

"Such a pity. We will have no choice but to impound your"—he hesitated, his smile sharpening—"shipment."

Still smiling, he held his hand out to his partner expectantly, and as if on cue the other man produced a crowbar from the back of the jeep and handed it to him. It took him about half a minute to pry open the nearest crate, and another twenty seconds to plunge his hand through the grain, remove a bundle wrapped in dingy gray padding, and peel it open. Liz felt as if she'd aged fifty years by the time he'd exposed for them all to see an intricately carved fuchsite mask inlaid with shell. The mask was horrifying, obviously something intended to ward off devils in the afterlife, but it seemed benign compared to Zach's expression at that moment.

When the policeman lifted his head again, the smile had fled his face, replaced by a look that made Liz's blood run very cold.

"Obviously," he stated, "you were also not aware that it is forbidden to remove from the country at any time objects of cultural significance. I will, of course, have to place you both under arrest."

CHAPTER
SIXTEEN

The local jail was a two-story adobe building at the edge of town. During the short ride there, Liz listened with mounting dismay to Zach's relaxed attempts to bribe the two arresting officers. The way her luck had been running lately, it came as no surprise to discover they had been apprehended by quite possibly the only honest men on the entire, openly corrupt Guatemalan police force.

Once inside the police station, they were turned over to a fierce-looking officer whose sweat-stained uniform gaped open across his huge belly. In a repeat of the scene in the guerrillas' hideout, he laconically ordered Zach to empty his pockets, his puffy-rimmed eyes lighting like hundred-watt bulbs when he saw the thick roll of quetzals that fell on his desk, landing between the coffee stains and an ashtray that looked as if it hadn't been emptied for at least a month.

After glancing briefly at Zach's passport, he proceeded to sweep the rest of his possessions into a desk drawer with one beefy forearm. Then he ordered the young policeman who'd been standing by eyeing Liz speculatively, as if wondering what she looked like when she wasn't wearing rags and two days' worth of grime, to take the prisoner away.

She instinctively made a move to follow, only to be halted by a brusque command from the officer in charge. He motioned for her to stay put as he reached to answer the telephone. The man escorting Zach hesitated with his hand on the doorknob, his face softening at the sight of Liz's stricken expression. Darting a wary glance at his superior, who was engrossed in a heated argument with whoever had phoned, he took a few seconds to explain that she was to be held downstairs with the women prisoners and that the men were locked on the second floor. If he meant to somehow reassure her with that bit of news, he failed miserably.

Liz took a deep breath, determined to hide the panic bubbling inside her. Zach had enough to worry about without her adding to the list. But although his face remained carefully blank, she saw the desperation in his eyes and the tension in his broad shoulders and realized he knew exactly how scared she was. Just before he stepped through the doorway that opened directly onto a narrow flight of stairs, he twisted to flash her a reassuring smile over his shoulder.

"Don't worry, fancy face," he called to her softly, "I'll find a way to get us out of this."

Liz did her best to smile back, and then he was gone and she was alone with the officer still talking on the telephone. He showed no signs of winding down anytime soon. Liz waited restlessly, crossing her arms and uncrossing them again, then thrusting her hands deep into her pockets. Her eyes widened as her fingers brushed against the key Zach had handed her earlier. After a quick check to make sure that she wasn't being observed, she slowly inched her foot high enough to slip the key under the innersole of her sneaker. Somehow the bulge of it there beneath the ball of her foot made her feel a little better. Not that the key was going to do them much good in here, but if they did somehow manage to get out...

With an uneasy sigh Liz paced a few nervous steps to the window. Pressing her forehead to the black iron bars mounted across the bottom, she gazed out at the deserted side street, feeling as if she were already locked in a cell. Even the air in here tasted stale, and, remembering Kirk's horror stories about Central American prisons, she had the hideous premonition that she might be breathing it for the next fifty years or so. It wasn't that she didn't believe Zach when he said he'd find a way out; she did...at least she believed that he would try. But common sense told her he had a better chance of rowing a canoe through a hurricane than he did of talking or fighting his way out of this one, especially after they'd been caught red-handed. And no one else who could possibly help even knew they were here.

Resolutely Liz lifted her chin and blinked back the tears hovering behind her lashes. She had to think positively or she would go crazy in this place. Of course they would get out of here. As soon as Kirk returned home alone, her father would send someone to look for her . . . if he hadn't already dispatched a search party when they failed to return on schedule. True, before leaving she had warned him not to interfere in any way, foolishly believing she could rely on Kirk for protection. But a lifetime of experience told Liz that her father would only heed that warning up to a point. In his own way, Thomas Joseph Fitzgerald was every bit as headstrong and ruthless as Zach McCabe. If he thought his youngest daughter was in danger, he would turn this country inside out to find her. A small, tentative smile tugged at the corners of Liz's mouth. Just maybe, if she could convince the authorities here that her father had the power and temperament to do exactly that, she could speed things along a little.

The policeman finally completed his call and demanded her passport, looking none too pleased when Liz explained she'd lost it. He looked even less happy when he commanded her to empty her pockets and she replied that they already were empty. When he reached impatiently for a pen and asked her name, Liz took a deep breath and plunged into her hastily rehearsed speech.

"My name is Elizabeth Randolph," she began in an impressively firm and steady tone, considering how her knees were shaking and her palms were sweating. "And regardless of how it appears, I was not willingly involved in any attempt to break the laws of your country. I don't expect you to take my word for that, but I do expect to be allowed to contact the embassy in Guatemala City and explain what's happened. My father, Thomas Fitzgerald, is a close personal friend of the United States ambassador to your country."

"Impossible," he countered without looking up from the paper on which he was still laboriously attempting to record her name.

"Why is it impossible?"

"Prisoners are not allowed to make phone calls."

"Of course," Liz responded, "but I'm sure you have the authority to make such a call . . . Capitán."

Liz had no idea of his rank, but she suspected it was far enough below captain for him to be flattered by her intentional mistake. When he glanced up in surprise, she gazed at him with such a mixture of awe and humility his chest puffed out even further. If it was possible for a man to swagger while sitting down, he was doing it.

"True, it is within my powers," he said boastfully, then rapped his pen on the desk with a frown. "But I cannot bother the ambassador every time we arrest an *americano* who claims to be a personal friend of his."

Liz nodded understandingly. "Of course not. I'm sure a man does not reach such a position of importance unless he is very cautious . . . and also a very good judge of character. Otherwise you could make a serious diplomatic mistake. For example, if I am who I say I am and you refuse to make that call for me, the consequences could be most unpleasant." As Liz had expected, he appeared singularly unfazed by her vague threat of official repercussions. Which left her only one avenue to pursue. "On the other hand, if you were to help me, I can promise you that my father would be extremely generous with his thanks."

352

His eyes sparked the same way they had at the sight of Zach's money, confirming that he understood exactly what she was getting at. Liz held her breath as he scratched his stomach and regarded her appraisingly. She fought the urge to plead with him not to be misled by her appearance, praying that his greed would blind him to anything but the possibility of making a profit from her misfortune.

Finally he lifted his pencil and looked back at the paper before him. "Spell for me your father's name," he ordered.

Liz quickly complied. She had hoped he would make the call right then and there and wanted to scream with frustration when his fellow officer chose that moment to reappear. Immediately the man sitting behind the desk ordered him to take her away.

Liz panicked. "But you . . . please . . ."

He halted her sputtering with an impatient look. "I will see what can be done," he snapped, adding in a chilling voice, "I only hope, señora, that you are telling me the truth. Otherwise, for *you* the consequences will be most unpleasant."

It took nearly six hours for help to arrive. Liz realized that was an amazingly short time considering the number of long-distance calls which had probably been necessary and the fact that this was, after all, a national holiday. But when you're locked in a barely lit cell reeking of urine and sweat, six hours seems like an eternity. Unbelievably, though, she had actually started to doze off on the filthy mattress tossed in one corner of the tiny cell when the rattle of keys jolted her awake.

"Señora Randolph?" inquired a small, dapper-looking man standing just outside the open cell door. He was dressed in a dark suit and accompanied by the same officer who had locked her up.

Liz nodded cautiously. She had been hoping to see a friendly American face.

"I am Carlos Peralta," the man told her. "An attorney from Puerto Barrios. I have been asked by your embassy to help you. They have already arranged with my government for your release, and I have cleared matters with the police here." With an awkward smile he handed her a large shopping bag. "I am no expert on women's clothing, but I hope this will be sufficient for now. I also have money for you, wired by your father, and tickets for a flight leaving the country first thing in the morning."

The tears Liz had been holding back for hours came in a sudden flood, making it difficult for her to absorb everything he was saying to her. At the mention of money, however, she wiped her eyes with the back of her hand and tried to speak.

"I . . . I sort of promised the man at the desk out there . . ." She broke off, slanting an uneasy glance at the young officer who was standing there listening to every word.

Señor Peralta nodded. "It has all been taken care of," he assured her.

"You mean I'm . . ."

"Free to go?" he supplied, smiling. "Yes, that is precisely what I mean. You will return now with me. . . . I have made reservations for you at the finest hotel in Puerto Barrios. In the morning a commuter flight will deliver you to Guatemala City, and from there, home. You see? Everything has been arranged."

Liz shook her head, once more in control of her emotions. "Not quite everything, Señor Peralta. I appreciate all the trouble you've gone to on my behalf, but there is someone else involved here . . . the man arrested along with me."

"Señor McCabe," he said, his voice suddenly harsh. "You need no longer fear him, señora. Your fiancé, Señor Kirk Allaire, has contacted your embassy also and informed them of your kidnapping and treatment at the hands of this man. You can be sure he will be dealt with most severely for his crimes."

She could well imagine what Kirk had told them. "No . . . he's wrong," she cried. "You don't understand. . . . Zach saved my life."

Liz's mind was reeling, making her explanation of an already complicated situation even more confusing. Señor Peralta and the officer by his side listened with matching expressions of bewilderment until she finally ended with an impassioned plea for him to see that Zach was released along with her.

The young attorney shook his head, his expression bleak and discouraging. "That is out of the question, señora. I'm afraid his situation is very different from your own."

"How is it different?" she demanded. "He's an American citizen, isn't he? Surely the ambassador . . ."

She broke off with a sharp intake of breath, remembering the precarious nature of Zach's status with the U.S. government. Would any official effort be made to help him? And if it were, if she could somehow convince her father to intercede on his behalf and bring him home, would Zach thank her? Or blame her?

When Señor Peralta touched her lightly on the shoulder, Liz looked up at him with eyes that were darkly troubled.

"Señora Randolph," he said quietly, "I must ask that you now change quickly into the clothes I brought so that we may be on our way. The sooner you are away from here, the sooner we can put your father's mind to rest about your safety. Once you are back home," he added soothingly, "things will seem clearer. Then, if you still wish to help Señor McCabe, you may do so through diplomatic channels."

Liz nodded woodenly. "Right. Diplomatic channels." The realization that she had no other option wove a chilly path along her spine.

Señor Peralta waited in the reception area while she was led to a small bathroom to change into the nondescript navy-blue cotton skirt and flowered blouse he'd provided. Before putting them on, she washed up as best she could in the tiny, rust-stained sink and made hurried use of the comb and brush she found in the bottom of the shopping bag. There was also a pair of black vinyl pumps in there which fit as reasonably well as the clothes did, and a matching purse already containing the money from her father.

When she finished dressing, she disposed of the clothes she'd been wearing in the trash basket in the corner, taking a second to transfer the key from her sneakers to her purse before tossing the old shoes in as well. She didn't even bother to glance in the mirror on her way out. She was too preoccupied with the thought that if she walked out of there without Zach now she might never see him again. Only the expressions of surprise and approval on the faces of the two policemen and Señor Peralta when she walked into the room told her how close to miraculous the transformation in her appearance had been.

It wasn't until she was climbing into the car Señor Peralta had waiting outside the door of the police station that Liz actually reached her decision. Hesitating with one foot still on the cracked sidewalk, her eyes were irresistibly drawn to the second-floor windows of the jail. She couldn't see anything behind the sinister-looking black bars. She didn't need to. The knowledge that the man she loved was locked up there was like a fire in her veins. Feeding the flames was the fear that he might well remain there until hell froze over unless she did something about it.

Liz brought her teeth together with a determined little click. Screw diplomatic channels. There was no way she was leaving here without Zach.

The plan, such as it was, formed in her mind as she went along so that she was always only a half step away from not knowing what to do next. Remembering the way he had looked at her when she walked into the reception area all clean and spit-shined, Liz found it easy to charm Señor Peralta into delaying their return to Puerto Barrios long enough to take her to dinner. It was easier still to lose him in the crowd of exuberant festivalgoers who jammed the village's main street. The twinge of guilt she felt over tricking him after he'd gone out of his way to help her was nothing compared to what she felt for Zach.

Once she was sure she'd ditched him, Liz calmed down enough to notice the curious looks she was drawing as she wove her way along the lantern-lit street. Nervously she realized that it wasn't going to be hard for the police to track the only blonde *norteamericana* in the whole village of Livingston, and she took time to dart into the next small shop she passed. When she reemerged, dressed in a white cotton peasant dress adorned with native embroidery, a red scarf hiding her pale hair, she blended easily with the crowd of laughing, dancing natives.

She expected the next crucial step in her plan to be considerably more difficult than the first, but she only had to venture into two waterfront bars before she spotted Jade sitting at a back corner table with a few of the other men. Making her way across the dark, smoke-filled room toward him, Liz barely heard the titters and suggestive mutterings of the strangers she passed. She was too intent on seeing if Rodil was among the familiar faces gathered around the table. When she finally saw him, tipped back in his chair, clutching a shot glass of tequila, she broke into a relieved grin. Maybe her luck was finally changing. For Zach's sake, she hoped so.

''Holy shit,'' Jade cried when he glanced up from his beer and saw her standing next to him. The expressions of the others reflected similar surprise. ''What the... We thought those assholes—pardon my French, but we thought they had you and Zach locked up.''

"They did. But it's a long story," Liz told him. "Mind if I sit down?"

Jade sprang up to drag a chair from the next table, quickly gathering her in a tight hug before he allowed her to sit down. Once she was seated, Liz gave them a shorthand version of everything that had happened since she and Zach landed in the pasture outside Livingston.

"I warned him," Jade declared when she finished, throwing his hands up in exasperation. "I warned him that the damn chopper would attract too much damn attention."

"I'm not convinced the chopper was our downfall," Liz revealed. "Señor Peralta told me that Kirk had been in touch with the embassy in Guatemala City about Zach. Who knows who else he might have talked with, or what he might have told them?"

Jade stared at her with a sad expression of disbelief. "No. You cannot seriously think he would try to screw Zach like that. After the man saved his life? Not to mention turning in his own fiancée in the process."

"Ex-fiancée," corrected Liz. She didn't have to think long about the rest of his question. "Yes. I definitely think Kirk is capable of doing anything for revenge."

"Son of a bitch," Jade muttered. That brought a brief, agreeable silence to the small group. Then he lifted his head with a quizzical look at Liz. "How did you know where to find us anyway?"

"I didn't," she admitted. "For all I knew those two policemen went back to the boat and arrested the rest of you as you showed up. But I remembered hearing Zach warn you to check things out carefully, and I figured that if you didn't see us anywhere around when you arrived, you might get suspicious and back off.''

"Actually, I did see you when I arrived," Jade interjected. "I saw you climbing into the back of that police jeep. That's when I hightailed it back to warn the others. We hid the truck and jeeps outside of town, and then a few of us came back to see what we could find out."

She swept the table with a wryly affectionate grin. "I'm glad you did, because I also figured that if you were anywhere around, you'd be in a joint like this."

Grinning, Jade lifted his bottle in a salute. "Zach's right; you're one smart lady."

"You might not think so after I ask what I'm about to ask you." Liz hesitated, feeling suddenly nervous under their collective wary gaze. "It's sort of a plan really . . . to rescue Zach." She began rattling on more quickly as their brows lifted in unison. "I know it's crazy . . . a hundred-to-one long shot, if that. And a million things can go wrong right up front. For one thing, we'll need to contact someone inside that jail. Someone we can trust or bribe or blackmail or something, into helping us."

To her surprise Rodil put down his glass and spoke for the first time. "That may not be a problem. My brother-in-law, he is a guard here at the jail. And he owes me a favor."

"Oh, thank God," Liz breathed, gathering courage. "That's wonderful. Do you really think he'll help us?"

"Only for a price," Rodil answered with a sly grin.

Liz placed her purse on the table. "I don't have much cash on me, but . . ." She broke off, her eyes widening with sudden insight. "Of course, we still have all the stuff in those crates. That's as good as cash."

"Better," Rodil pronounced solemnly. "My brother-in-law will surely help us now."

"Do you think it will be all right with Zach if we use it to pay him?" she asked, looking at Jade.

"Who cares?" he shot back. "It's all right with you and me. We'll worry about Zach later."

Her forehead creased as she remembered the reason he and Zach had risked all this in the first place. "But what about your..."

"We'll worry about that later too," he interrupted firmly. "Now let's hear this hundred-to-one-shot plan of yours."

"All right." She paused, running her tongue over lips that were suddenly desert-dry and searching for words that would put her ridiculous, foolhardy idea in the best possible light. Finally she sought Rodil's eyes across the small table and began.

"I'm especially glad you're here," she said directly to him, "because the success of this thing will depend as much on your help as on your brother-in-law's...maybe even more. That is, if you're willing."

There were a few seconds of silence when Liz was sure her plan was going to disintegrate even before being put into motion. Then Rodil's face crinkled in a smile.

"You helped me once," he said. "I'll help you now."

Exhaling a pent-up breath, Liz withdrew the helicopter key from her purse and placed it in the center of the table. "Here's what I want you to do."

*　　*　　*

Zach's cell was an eight-foot-square box with a bucket intended for use as a toilet in one corner and a flea-ridden mattress in the other. The only window was a one-by-two-foot rectangle high on the outside wall, and through it Zach watched the azure sky gradually turn as black as his thoughts.

Most of the time since he'd been locked in here he'd sat in the same spot and asked himself the same question over and over. How the hell was he going to keep his promise to Liz to get her out of here? The answer was simple: he couldn't. He'd known even when he said it that he was more likely to be elected pope than to short-circuit Guatemala's infamous system of justice, but he couldn't stop himself. At that moment he would have said or done anything to pierce the look of terror he saw in her eyes.

For a while after he was brought to his cell, he'd even nursed the selfish hope that some of the others might end up in there along with them, thinking that would at least even the odds a bit. But as the day slipped away, he'd concluded that Jade must have been alert and canny enough to prevent that from happening. By now they had probably done the only thing they could do with the *Cindy Ann* under surveillance—divided the spoils and scattered. And Zach couldn't feel anything but glad, even if it did mean he was on his own trying to save himself and Liz from spending the rest of their lives in this stinkhole.

The hell of it was that he knew her best hope was also her worst. He could always tell them the truth, that she was an innocent American tourist whom he'd kidnapped and that she had nothing at all to do with the smuggling. And he would tell them that in a flash if he knew for sure it would help her. But even if they believed him, there was a real possibility that one of these slimy guards would decide that kidnapping a rich American, especially one already so conveniently trapped, wasn't such a bad idea.

The only way to be sure that didn't happen, the only thing he could possibly do to help her now, was to see that someone in authority knew that she was here, preferably someone from the American embassy, but even a trustworthy local official would do ... if such an animal existed, Zach mused bitterly. Until then Liz's position here was worse than vulnerable; it was extremely dangerous. Just the thought of her being spirited out of here in the middle of the night made every muscle in his body throb with impotent rage. Lunging to his feet, he stalked across the cell and slammed knuckles that had already been pounded raw against the cinder-block wall.

A soft chuckle sounded from the corridor outside his cell. "That makes you feel better, señor?"

The only light in the vicinity came from an overhead fixture about fifteen feet away, but Zach could see enough to tell that this wasn't the same guard who'd brought him here and then delivered his supper a few hours later. This man was shorter and older, and he didn't have the same glinty eyes as the other one. When the first guard had turned those eyes on Liz downstairs today, Zach had had to shove his hands into his pockets to keep from breaking his neck.

"The only thing that will make me feel better is getting out of here," he replied stiffly.

At that, the guard released another chuckle, this one ominously cynical, but he took the edge off it by ambling closer to offer a cigarette through the bars. Zach stood where he was, knowing how such acts of kindness were often expected to be repaid in prison.

This time the guard laughed outright. "Go on, take it," he urged. "It is a holiday and I'm feeling generous."

Shrugging, Zach stepped close enough to take the cigarette, bending his head forward so the other man could light it. As he filled his lungs with smoke and held it, he eyed his benefactor curiously, finally deciding to see exactly how generous he was feeling.

"As long as the holiday has put you in such a good mood," he ventured, "perhaps you'd like to do me a little favor."

"Perhaps," the guard countered, turning so he was facing the stairs, his back toward Zach as they continued their little discussion. "It would, of course, depend on the favor."

"Nothing too difficult," Zach assured him. "My woman is downstairs. All I want you to do is check on her for me and give her a message."

"What sort of message?"

"I want you to tell her to keep her chin up and . . ." He licked his lips and added in a hoarse whisper, "And that I love her." He took another deep drag on the cigarette, the smoke wafting between his lips as he spoke. "Then I want you to help me get a message to the American embassy to let them know that she's here."

The guard made a disparaging sound. "That is your idea of nothing too difficult? To contact the embassy, you must go through my commanding officer."

"That's to contact them *officially*," Zach responded.

"There's nothing to stop you from placing a quick phone call on your own time."

"What would make me take such a risk, señor?"

He was going to do it. Zach grinned in the darkness and reached into the small, flat change slot concealed behind his pants pocket.

"I'll bet this would make you do it," he drawled, holding Liz's engagement ring close enough to the bars for the man outside to see without being able to reach it.

Zach knew he was taking a gamble, a big one. As long as he was locked in here, there was nothing he could do to force the guard to keep his part of the deal once he'd accepted the bribe. But under the circumstances it was the only way he knew of to help Liz. Besides, it was fitting that that bastard Kirk should foot the bill for her shot at freedom.

The guard turned to examine the ring more closely. As his hand protruded through the bars, Zach tightened his grip on the diamond-studded gold band and asked, "Do we have a deal?"

"The ring to check on your woman and give a message to her?" the other man responded hesitantly.

"And to get the message to the American embassy...that's the most important part."

The guard's lips curled in a slow smile. "Consider it done, amigo."

"It better be," Zach warned in a softly menacing tone. "I won't be locked in here forever...amigo." He relinquished the ring and watched it disappear into the pocket of the guard's khaki uniform.

"And I expect you to check on her for me right away," he

added emphatically as the guard took a few steps away from the cell and halted. His grin had taken on a sly glimmer that made Zach very uneasy.

"There is no need to check, señor. I can tell you all you wish to know right now. The American woman is gone. She was freed hours ago by a messenger from your embassy in Guatemala City. So you see, it is as I said . . . already done."

"How?" he demanded, his tone harsh. "How did they know she was even here?"

The guard shrugged. "That I do not know. Only that the order for her release came from the office of President Cerezo himself. Your woman's father, this Señor Thomas Fitzgerald, he must be a big man in your country."

Zach's eyes narrowed as he turned the name over in his mind, the family name that Liz had never actually mentioned and that he'd never actually pressed to hear. Fitzgerald. He might read *Time* magazine six months late, but he did occasionally read it, and the name Fitzgerald was as familiar to him as Rockefeller or Du Pont. Christ, she wasn't just rich. She was close to being fucking U.S. royalty.

He didn't even notice the guard shake his head at the crazy-eyed American and walk away. It was as if all the feeling had been crushed out of him except for an icy core of self-loathing. God, he was a fool. All day he'd sat here frantic with worry, envisioning Liz locked in a cell with God knows what form of lowlife, berating himself for letting it happen. And all the time she was long gone, sprung by her rich daddy and gone home, leaving him here to rot.

It filled him with a bitter sense of déjà vu. He felt used and disillusioned, as if he were twenty-one years old and being slapped in the face by Amanda Bellingham all over again. She'd had a rich daddy to get her off the hook too, when she tired of the game they were playing. Knowing exactly who Liz was, and how stinking rich, sure put a different light on her brave decision to risk coming here with him in the first place. Why the hell shouldn't she risk it? Knowing as she must have that at the crook of her little finger her father would send ambassadors, and probably even Marines if necessary, to her rescue.

In a small, rational corner of his brain, Zach knew Liz had only done what any sane person would have under the circumstances. She'd have been crazy to sit around here waiting for him to rescue her. But that didn't lessen the pain of knowing that when push came to shove, she hadn't trusted him . . . or needed him. He walked across the cell and threw himself belly down on the thin mattress, his face pressed against the stained blue-and-white cover.

It was just as well it had ended this way, he told himself. Learning about her family was a potent reminder of the wall that had always existed between them, and always would. He'd been out of his mind ever to think there was any way around it. But it still left him feeling as if there was a raw hole inside him, one that he probed again and again until sleep finally claimed his aching body. Even then his dreams were haunted by a woman with flashing green eyes and a filmy white dress that swirled around her legs as she ran ahead of him through a grassy meadow, always just one step out of reach.

He awoke to the rattle of keys, feeling as if he'd been stomped on by an elephant wearing combat boots. Wincing, he levered his chest off the mattress and looked to see who was swinging open his cell door. He scowled, recognizing the young guard who'd dumped him in here yesterday.

"What the hell do you want?" Zach demanded sleepily. "It's not even light out yet."

"*Por favor, señor* . . . follow me. And quickly."

Zach dropped his head back to the mattress and closed his eyes. "Go to hell."

The unmistakable jab of a gun in the small of his back brought him quickly to his feet.

"What the . . ."

"Quickly," the guard repeated. "Out there."

Zach ambled in the direction he indicated, ignoring his uncomfortable prodding with the gun. "Hell of a time for breakfast," he muttered. "And whatever happened to room service around . . ."

His grousing halted abruptly as the guard yanked him to a stop at the far end of the hall and pulled open a door to the outside. He shoved Zach through it ahead of him. Fastened to the wall just outside was a narrow metal ladder leading to the roof, which the guard was now gesturing for him to climb. Zach hesitated, taking a good long look at the spastic way he was waving his gun around. The guy seemed real antsy and Zach bet he knew why. It wasn't uncommon for prisoners in Central America to be shot in the back while attempting to "escape." Zach had an uncomfortable feeling that, like it or not, he was about to make just such an attempt.

"Quickly . . . up," the guard ordered, glancing around as if he were the one about to be shot in the back.

Slowly Zach climbed the ladder, racking his suddenly wide-awake brain for a way out of this. Even before he set foot on the roof, he'd concluded that there wasn't one. He was alone and unarmed. But at least he was going to force this sucker to look him in the eye when he squeezed the trigger.

It was as he was turning to confront him that he heard it. Low and distant but as familiar to Zach as the sound of his own name. Squinting his eyes, he saw it in the distance, cresting one of the low hills that framed the small village. It was a helicopter. His helicopter. He glanced around to see the guard staring up at it too, a nervous sort of grin twitching at his lips. Still, Zach was afraid to let the pieces fall into place the way they obviously wanted to. Maybe, he cautioned himself, maybe the police had seized the chopper along with the boat and were simply moving it to another location. But as he watched it swing around in the pink-gray sky and cut a path straight to where he was standing, he knew it was no policeman at the controls.

Rodil. He grinned up at the sky. And no doubt with Jade masterminding the whole operation. Adrenaline started pumping through him as he jogged to the center of the roof, waving both hands high in the air. He gave a quick look over his shoulder as what sounded like shots filtered up from somewhere below. Then the whir of the propeller overhead drowned out everything else as Rodil brought the big bird in to hover about fifteen feet above his head. The door opened and Jade's beautiful, grinning face appeared. An even more welcome sight was the submachine gun cradled in his arms as he hung from a rope anchored somewhere inside the helicopter. Zach didn't look back to see what Jade was spraying with bullets, but he felt someone spraying back, coming close enough to shave flesh from him as he lunged for the nearest landing skid and clambered aboard.

As soon as Jade had followed him in, yanking the door shut behind him, Rodil jerked the chopper into a steep climb, bringing it around hard at the same time until they were safely out of reach of the guards still shooting and stumbling over each other on the roof below. Then the metal walls of the chopper vibrated with a chorus of exultant whoops.

Liz clung to an overhead strap at the rear of the chopper, smiling and crying as Zach threw back his head and bellowed with sheer joy. She watched him grab Jade and hug him. Then he grabbed Carlos and Santiago and as much of Rodil as he could reach and hugged them too. Finally he turned, and Liz wanted to weep even harder at the look of amazement on his face when he caught sight of her. It told her that he'd thought exactly what she'd been afraid he would think, that she had deserted him.

Then a smile lifted the corners of his weary mouth and he started weaving his way slowly toward her. It almost sounded as if he was muttering something about being stupid and stubborn, but Liz couldn't be sure if he was talking about her or himself. And she didn't really care. His eyes were telling her all she would ever need to know. They were dark and shimmering with the love he hadn't put into words...yet. He didn't stop until he was so close to her that Liz could count every beloved black whisker on his jaw.

"Do you know you could have gotten yourself killed pulling a foolish stunt like this?" he demanded, his deep voice as stirring to her senses as a caress. "And that you're crazy?" He shook his head and reached for her. "And that I love you? Oh, God, Liz, I love you."

Swept by a wave of relief and happiness almost too pure to bear, Liz let go of the overhead strap and surrendered to his crushing embrace, knowing Zach was strong and steady enough to support her. Always.

EPILOGUE

The Federal Courthouse in downtown Boston was an old building, with all the creaks and drafts and clanging radiators common to the species. It wasn't a particularly comfortable place to while away a cold December afternoon. But that's exactly what Liz was doing. For over an hour she had been sitting on the scarred wooden windowsill outside Judge Kiley's office, waiting for Zach to emerge. Only then would she know what her husband was going to be doing for the next twelve months.

That was the length of time Zach had agreed to work at something "of benefit to the general community." In exchange, all charges stemming from the incident with the munitions train had been officially dropped and he'd been given a suspended sentence for the criminal act of evading the draft. He could have avoided even that if he had been amenable to letting her father pull a few strings, which he definitely and vocally had not been.

Liz was rapidly growing accustomed to watching the two most headstrong men she knew square off in an ongoing battle which, to the amazement of her entire family, was surprisingly equal and increasingly friendly. Thomas Fitzgerald hadn't liked hearing his new son-in-law politely contradict his announcement that he would handle everything. But, as Liz had told an indignant Zach afterward, at least his glare had been one of grudging respect rather than open contempt.

That was a giant step of an improvement from his attitude that day almost three months ago when she had phoned him from Zach's house in Las Margaritas, Mexico, and told him she was getting married. No, of course not to Kirk, she had stunned him by explaining, but to the man who Kirk kept insisting to anyone who would listen had kidnapped and brainwashed her.

And as she was temporarily without her checkbook, she had continued—oblivious to the fact that back in Boston her father was frantically signaling his secretary to have the call traced—could he please send a check for one hundred thousand dollars to a Mr. Russell Jadach in Key West, Florida. She had, she announced, decided to invest in Jade's Charter Services and needed immediate funds to ransom its only vessel, the *Cindy Ann*, from the government of Guatemala. A wise investment it had turned out to be too, despite her father's contention that no real fisherman would be caught dead wearing a braid.

Ceasing her impatient finger tapping on the windowsill, Liz reached for her handbag and rummaged through it for the letter that had arrived that morning postmarked Norfolk, Virginia. That's where Jade and Cindy and their three children had relocated. A "put your feet up and make yourself to home kind of town," in Jade's words. She smiled affectionately as she read his unique description of how happy they all were in their new home. When, he wanted to know, were she and Zach going to grace them with a visit?

Good question. Liz slipped the letter back into her bag and checked her watch with an impatient sigh. One hour and seventeen minutes. How long was it going to take Judge Kiley to decide if he approved of Zach's proposal?

Initially Zach had been stoically resigned to accepting whatever form of community service he was assigned. But during a visit home last month, he had decided that he might as well do something he was good at ... such as teaching others to fly. Seeing how quickly his brother, Dan, picked it up, and how much he enjoyed the soaring feeling of freedom, was all the impetus Zach had needed to start drawing up a rough plan for a training program involving disabled vets here in Massachusetts.

She slid anxiously to her feet as the door of the judge's office opened and Zach stepped into the wide, deserted hallway. He looked strong and lean and every bit as sexy in a conservative dark suit as he did in black denims and a T-shirt. But his face, damn him, still never revealed a thing unless he wanted it to.

"Well?" she prodded as he approached in that lazy, ambling stride of his.

"Well, what?"

"Stop. I've been sitting out here between the radiator and the window, freezing and suffocating, for"—she checked her watch—"one hour and twenty-two minutes. And I want to know what Judge Kiley said about your idea. Now, McCabe," she ordered with a stab at sounding fierce.

"He said," he told her, grinning and looping his arms loosely around her neck, "that he thinks it's brilliant."

Liz clapped her hands together in excitement. "See? That's exactly what I told you."

"Oh, it was you who told me that it was brilliant," Zach countered with mock surprise. "Then it must have been Kiley who said it was a fine idea and that I can start immediately."

"Immediately?" Liz sighed. "I was sort of enjoying this extended honeymoon of ours."

"Sweetheart, one month is what you call extended, two months is stretching it a little, and three months is stretching it a lot." His fingers curled around the back of her neck, squeezing in that seductive, possessive way of his that always made her stomach flutter with anticipation. "However, I did tell the judge that I thought the first week of January sounded like a good time to make a new start. That gives us almost two more weeks to stretch it."

"Mmmm." Her hips bumped his as she went up on her toes to kiss his mouth. "And stretching it is one of my very favorite things."

"Wanton," Zach rasped against her parted lips before quieting her with a kiss that was too deep and too long for a public place, even a deserted public place.

"I think," Liz murmured a bit breathlessly when he

finally lifted his head, "that we should forget about Christmas shopping and go straight home."

Zach grinned. "My thoughts exactly. You know," he continued, reaching for her hand as they walked toward the wide staircase leading to the main entrance, "I've been thinking I might stick with this thing even after the year is up, maybe open a flight school offering a variety of special programs. What do you think?"

A familiar warmth spread through Liz. She knew Zach's question wasn't simply rhetorical, that he really cared what she thought about each small detail of his life and that he was intensely interested in everything that touched her life as well.

"I think it sounds exciting," she told him honestly. "What sort of special programs did you have in mind?"

"Well, I'd like to stick with this one for the disabled, maybe even expand on it. Then maybe I'd offer special introductory classes for people who might have never considered flying as a hobby . . . housewives, kids."

Liz eyed him speculatively. "You really think you have enough patience to teach kids, McCabe?"

"That's where you come in," he replied, stopping as they reached the bottom step, his expression suddenly solemn. "How do you feel about supplying me with a test subject . . . maybe two?"

Liz found it hard to draw a decent breath. "You mean a baby?"

He snapped his fingers. "That's the word I was groping for . . . a baby. Want to make a baby with me, Mrs. McCabe?"

It was the one thing they hadn't talked about during these

glorious, intense honeymoon weeks. At one time not too long ago, Liz would have recoiled from the mere suggestion of having another child, so determined was she never again to open herself to the pain she'd felt after Jeremy's death. But now, with Zach's strong hands holding hers, his dark, loving eyes assuring her that whatever she decided was all right with him, Liz knew she was ready.

"Now that," she told him with a smile, "is a brilliant idea. Let's go home, Zach."

Laughing, Zach lifted her off the floor in a tight hug, leaving one arm curled around her waist when he put her back down.

"Yes," he said, reaching for the brass door handle, "let's go home."

As he swung the courthouse door wide, Liz noticed that it had started to snow while they were inside, and they stepped together into a world that was white and fresh and sparkling with possibilities.